PENGUIN BOOKS

QUEEN KAT, CARMEL & ST. JUDE GET A LIFE

Maureen McCarthy grew up the ninth of ten children on a farm near Yea in Victoria. After working for a while as an art teacher, Maureen became a full-time scriptwriter and author. So far she has written thirteen books, many of which have been highly acclaimed.

Maureen lives in Melbourne with her husband and three children.

By the same author

In Between
Ganglands
Cross My Heart
Chain of Hearts
Flash Jack
When You Wake and Find Me Gone

MAUREEN McCARTHY

Queen Kat, Carmel & St Jude get a life

PENGUIN BOOKS

Penguin Books

Published by the Penguin Group
Penguin Books Australia Ltd
250 Camberwell Road,
Camberwell, Victoria 3124, Australia
Penguin Books Ltd
80 Strand, London WC2R 0RL, England
Penguin Putnam Inc.
375 Hudson Street, New York, New York 10014, USA
Penguin Books, a division of Pearson Canada
10 Alcorn Avenue, Toronto, Ontario, Canada M4V 3B2
Penguin Books (N.Z.) Ltd
Cnr Rosedale and Airborne Roads, Albany, Auckland, New Zealand
Penguin Books (South Africa) (Pty) Ltd
24 Sturdee Avenue, Rosebank, Johannesburg 2196, South Africa
Penguin Books India (P) Ltd
11, Community Centre, Panchsheel Park, New Delhi 110 017, India

First published by Penguin Books Australia, 1995
Penguin edition published, 1997
This edition published, 1999

14 13 12 11 10 9
Copyright © Trout Films, 1995

The moral right of the author has been asserted

All rights reserved. Without limiting the rights under copyright
reserved above, no part of this publication may be reproduced,
stored in or introduced into a retrieval system, or transmitted,
in any form or by any means (electronic, mechanical, photocopying,
recording or otherwise), without the prior written permission
of both the copyright owner and the above publisher of this book.

Photographs by Skip Watkins
Cover: Elissa Elliot as Katerina; Alicia Gardiner as Carmel and Ingrid Ruz as Jude
from the TV mini-series 'Queen Kat, Carmel & St. Jude', produced by Trout Films in
association with the Australian Broadcasting Corporation.

Designed by Glenn Thomas, Penguin Design Studio

Typeset in Caslon 11/14pt by Midland Typesetters, Maryborough, Victoria
Printed and bound in Australia by McPherson's Printing Group, Maryborough, Victoria

National Library of Australia
Cataloguing-in-Publication data:

McCarthy, Maureen, 1953– .
 Queen Kat, Carmel and St Jude get a life.

 ISBN 0 14 028124 X.

 I. Title.

A823.3

The quotation on page 252 is reprinted with permission from
Gray's Anatomy, © 1974 Running Press Book Publishers, Philadelphia.

Every effort has been made to trace the original source of copyright
material contained in this book. The publishers would be pleased to
hear from copyright holders of any errors or omissions.

www.penguin.com.au

This one is for Joe. Because he asked.

Acknowledgements

I would like to warmly thank the following people for their help during the writing of this novel: Juan and Nellie Torres, Alex Varga, Louise Young Harrington and Colin Mclaren.

My sincere gratitude also to Erica Irving from Penguin Books for her hard work and enthusiasm throughout the process of creating this work and to Chris Warner for his support and encouragement.

I heard, read and watched many accounts of the coup in Chile and the events leading up to it. Two books I would especially like to acknowledge are: *Victor Jara – An Unfinished Song* by Joan Jara (Jonathan Cape, London, 1983) and *Audacity to Believe* by Sheila Cassidy (Fount Paperbacks, London, 1978).

Contents

Manella – December	1
Carmel	39
Jude	159
Katerina	317
Manella – October	425

Manella – December

1

'Katerina, you have a choice. University college or a room with your sister. That's final!'

'Well, I won't live with her!'

'Then it's college.'

'Daddy, I've had six years of boarding school. I'm *eighteen* for God's sake!'

'Then it's a room with Louise.'

Katerina took one slim, finely manicured hand out from under the vase she'd been about to fill with her mother's flowers – a lovely smelly heap of white and lilac roses – and deliberately let it slide from her grip. The vase, an antique, made of opaque Waterford crystal which had originally belonged to her grandmother, smashed onto the parquetry floor and sprayed dramatically into a thousand tiny pieces of blue. There was a restrained gasp from her mother and an angry snort from her father. Shocked, the three of them stared mutely at the blue-speckled floor.

It was the last straw for Dr Albert Armstrong. He turned his back to his daughter and snapped the lid of his briefcase down.

'You clumsy girl!'

'It was an accident,' Katerina said defensively. Her father grunted, as though he didn't believe her but had better things to think about.

He stepped towards his wife and kissed her brusquely on the cheek.

'I'll be home at the usual time, dear.'

'Yes, dear.'

He then turned to Katerina, who was still staring at the tiny pieces of glass spread over the floor.

'Try to be a help to your mother today, please, Katerina. Don't be worrying her about ... anything.'

He didn't wait for her to reply, but strode out the door, closing it stiffly behind him. Katerina looked up, following his retreating shape through the beautiful red and green lead-light door leading out into the hall, and wondered why she'd dropped the vase. After all, although she'd given this accommodation business her best shot, she hadn't seriously expected to win. She *was* only eighteen and the main round had been won before the results had come out. That one she'd really insisted on. She wouldn't, simply *couldn't*, live in a university college. Thankfully, they'd conceded on that one. Just the thought of more institutional food, of lectures and meals with groups of hearty, giggling girls with bad skin, who talked loudly, dressed carelessly ... and all their drippy, splotchy-faced boyfriends. Katerina had had enough of that kind of living to last a lifetime.

Although it would be another month before she would receive confirmation of a place in Law at Melbourne University, her excellent results assured her that there had never been any doubt. She'd won dux of her prestigious girls' school, plus the French prize and the maths prize.

As she turned regretfully to the broken vase she was reminded of the bitter fight she'd had with her best friend Claire only three months before the end of term.

'You think it's okay to just step on people, don't you, Katerina?'

'*What?*' Katerina had been shocked. 'Claire, I simply don't want that dreary girl to come!' That it had been over such a trivial matter made it doubly hard to understand. Claire had suggested inviting some boring girl, whose father had recently carked it, to join them for a day down at Portsea. The girl was a shy, plain, moping type who couldn't even play tennis. She would poison their one free day for sure. How was Katerina to know that her friend would build this disagreement into a raging row?

'You would never consider what she might be going through, would you?'

'What do you mean? What do we owe her?' But Claire refused to explain herself any further.

'Get a life, Katerina!' she'd yelled over her shoulder before storming off. 'Just piss off why don't you and get a bloody life!'

'Why don't *you?*' Katerina had called lamely after her, feeling suddenly sick with remorse and incomprehension. What had she done? It was like now in front of this broken vase. *Why did I do this?* Claire had been her best friend. They'd laughed together, plotted their futures, told secrets. But in spite of mutual apologies when Claire arrived back at school that evening, their closeness had ended with that horrible argument. Of course there was the rest of the crowd, Kara in particular, who'd stepped in to fill the gap. But losing Claire's friendship hurt more than Katerina was prepared to admit.

So she would live with her big sister Louise for a year. Never mind. Louise would be in fifth-year Medicine next year. Long hours working in the hospitals, as well as being stuck away every night with her books. With a bit of luck they wouldn't see each other from one week to the next.

'My dear ... It's spoiling everything, you being like this. Your results were so brilliant. Daddy and I are both so proud. I just wish you wouldn't argue so much.'

Katerina looked up, a little surprised at her mother's voice. She'd forgotten about her even being there. And here she was in the watery-green silk dress that matched her eyes, a slightly surprised, harassed look lining her face. Katerina wondered for perhaps the twentieth time that week what she would have to do to make her *really* mad. Her mother especially valued that blue vase ... she knew it. It *was* a beautiful thing. Katerina was ashamed she'd broken it. Yet her mother had simply stood watching, as usual. Watching while her husband and daughter slugged it out. Contained and serene as ever. Why didn't that woman ever *do* anything?

'I'm sorry, Mum. About the vase, too. It was ... careless of me.'

Her mother nodded and sighed again.

'Well, I do ... we both ... want you to try to accept the situation.'

Katerina knew her mother was a nice person. A lovely person. Everyone who'd ever met her said so. She was good-looking, refined, warm when she wanted to be, and kind to just about everyone she met. She never seemed to get angry, hardly ever complained. The perfect country surgeon's wife. Katerina tried to remember all the good points about her mother at the same time as imagining walking over and slapping her nicely preserved face very hard on both cheeks. She couldn't help it. It wasn't so much that her mother agreed with everything her father said. It was the *way* she agreed. So damned ... demure. You never got the impression she thought *anything* apart from what he told her to think. Or had any ideas apart from his. Katerina walked into the pantry and looked around for the dustpan and brush.

'Darling, you did remember that the Crossways are coming for dinner tonight?'

Katerina swallowed her desire to let out a shriek in the small dark room neatly lined with tins and bottles of fruit and packets of dried food. Instead she pushed her head around the door and gave her mother a curt nod. The Crossways were her parents' best friends. Her father had studied Medicine at university with Neil Crossway eons ago, and the family lived in Yassfield, a small town about twenty kilometres from the Armstrongs. The two men were the district's most senior doctors, they shared work in the same hospital and often rang each other to confer about patients. The Crossways' only son

Anton had finished his fourth year of Law the year before and was now doing his articles with a city firm. Katerina knew that this visit had been arranged on her behalf, that her mother and father thought it a good idea to reacquaint their daughter with Anton so she would know someone when she first went to the city. Someone *nice* who, in turn, would introduce her to other *nice* people.

Having located the dustpan and brush, she walked over to the shattered vase and knelt down. The damn thing had spread its tiny pieces into the furthest reaches of the kitchen.

'Do I *have* to be here?' she grumbled, knowing that she did.

'Oh darling, of course you do.' Her mother sounded genuinely hurt. 'Anton is coming. We thought it might be nice for you to know someone in the city when you arrive.'

Katerina began sweeping.

'Mum. Half my year at school will be there ... I'll know heaps.'

'I know, darling. But Anton will know the ropes. And he's someone from home, too.'

Katerina knew her mother really meant *someone like us*. Someone from the right kind of family, with plenty of money and the right social connections. Her mother felt a barely contained horror at the thought of either of her children mixing with people who weren't the *right* sort.

The Crossways were loaded. Not only was old Neil a top-earning doctor, but he'd inherited his father's family farm as well: about three thousand hectares of lush Victorian cattle-grazing country. He employed a manager, of course, who lived on the property and looked after it all, as well as locals for seasonal work. Katerina hadn't seen Anton for about three years, but remembered him as nice enough; a bit shy and rather good-looking. Katerina smiled to herself as she remembered his diffident tone when she'd asked him a few years ago what he did for fun at uni. He'd only been eighteen then and fairly gauche. He was probably breaking hearts all over the city by this stage. But so what? Whatever he was doing didn't interest her in the least. There was no way she intended seeking out the sons of old family friends for contacts when she hit town. That sort of thing was for people who didn't know who they were, who had no confidence in themselves, no plans. She would be perfectly capable on her own.

Katerina swept up most of the glass. There was no point looking too carefully under the table or moving anything. Maria would come later and she actually seemed to like doing the household tasks she was paid to do.

'Okay. Okay. I'll be here,' Katerina sighed, as she moved over to look out of the kitchen window onto the patio and lush backyard. Her family home was a rambling, beautifully restored Edwardian house set on the highest hill above the main street of the busy country town of Manella. The many big trees sheltered the garden from any neighbouring houses or roads. Except for the birds, all was quiet. The garden sloped slightly down to the back fence, which was lined with enormous liquidambars and maples, all green and yellow shade now, rustling in the foul north wind.

Katerina could see the old rope hanging down from what used to be *her* branch on her favourite tree in the corner. The hours she and Louise used to put in down there, hiding from each other in their separate trees, swinging on the rope, pretending they were world-class gymnasts or female Tarzans. A perfect childhood. Until the day her elder sister – her hero, best friend and constant companion – had been wrenched away from her. Well, that's how it had felt anyway. Sent off to boarding school at fourteen, when Katerina had been only ten. That first year of being the only child in the big house was the worst time Katerina could remember. Waking up every morning with Louise gone was like being cut each day in the same spot. Life, which until then had been wonderful, full of jokes, excitement and interesting plans with Louise, became simply a matter of filling in time until Lou-Lou could come back. It was a much worse feeling than her own first year at boarding school, because by then she'd learnt to rely on herself and not to care.

Of course her sister had come home for weekends and holidays, but things were never the same between them. The truth was that Louise hadn't missed her little sister much at all. This was obvious the first weekend she came home, and it had been a bitter pill for the ten-year-old Katerina to swallow. Her sister had made new friends, had new ways of looking at things. She wasn't interested in the old games any more.

Katerina sighed again when she noticed the leaves from the sugar gum swirling around in the swimming pool. Her father had asked her to clean it out yesterday, but she'd forgotten. The high sun shone down onto the iridescent blue water, making a stinging brightness so different from the muted, easy tones of the surrounding trees. She would have a swim later, but not before that wind had subsided.

'Don't be upset, dear,' her mother said, mistaking her sombre musing for further sulking about the housing issue. Surprised by the concerned voice, Katerina turned around to face her mother with a dazzling smile.

'I'm not, Mum, really.' Katerina took her arm. The relief on her mother's face made her feel slightly queasy. Katerina vowed for the millionth time never to get herself into her mother's situation. *Never. Never will I be dependent on other people for how I feel about myself. About anything. I will never be at someone else's mercy.*

'Don't worry, Mum. It'll be fine.'

Her mother pulled her briefly against the cool green silk of her breast and whispered into her hair.

'You sure?'

'Of course.'

Katerina was really just a younger version of her mother. They shared the same lightly tanned, creamy skin, the fair curly hair, and the green eyes. Both were slender and straight with well-proportioned figures and dainty hands and feet. The older woman, almost fifty now, was entering middle age gracefully, the tiny crow's-feet around her eyes and the slight greying of her hair adding to her charm and dignified beauty. Katerina had the same grace and charm about her body, but her face, although very similar to her mother's, was livelier. They were both beautiful. Katerina felt a sudden rush, an almost physical burst of gratitude towards the woman standing in front of her. There had been other attractive girls at her school, but they were, in the main, dark-haired, sultry types or brassy, cheap-looking blondes. Cute, perhaps, in a way. But the kind of looks that ultimately faded into mere prettiness. None of them, she knew, quite matched herself.

'Mum, that green really suits you,' Katerina said softly, pulling away from her mother's embrace, but still holding her hand.

Mrs Armstrong gave a slight smile, then lowered her eyes.

'I'm worried about you being in the city,' she said. 'You will take notice of your big sister, won't you? Let her show you the ropes, and ...'

'Oh Mum! I'll be fine!' Katerina said impatiently. 'Lou and I haven't been ... done things together for years!'

'You're my baby. And I am worried.'

'What could possibly happen?'

'Darling, you're so headstrong. You could get into all sorts of trouble ...'

'I'm *not* headstrong!' Katerina laughed.

'If anything happens you will talk it over with Lou, won't you? Or, better still, ring us?'

'Like what?' Katerina teased. 'Do you think I'm going to get pregnant or something?'

'Katerina! Don't be ridiculous.'

'Well, what?'

'Look, darling, sometimes I think you've had things a bit

easy. Not your fault of course, but ... well, life won't always be neat. Out in the big world it isn't a matter of just passing exams, you know ... coming top in everything. Those things are marvellous, of course. But you won't always be able to have your own way ...'

Katerina's green eyes narrowed.

'I *don't* always have my own way!'

'Of course not,' her mother said. 'Oh dear, I don't know quite what I'm trying to say!' She brought both hands up to her face. Katerina was suddenly interested. Her mother rarely spoke like this. It was interesting to watch her floundering, struggling for words.

'Things ... can get tough,' her mother went on from behind her hands. 'I just don't want to see you get hurt ...' Katerina nodded, but her mother had turned away, frowning unhappily as though she'd really meant to say something else.

'So you think I'll mess everything up because I've had it easy?'

'Oh no, darling ... I'm sure you won't mess anything up ... I ...'

'Well, what?'

Her mother shrugged, then her vulnerable expression slowly slipped back into the more usual, on-top-of-everything smile.

'I think you should go and clean that pool as your father asked you to do yesterday,' she said at last.

'Okay, but I thought I'd wait till it gets a bit cooler.'

'Very well,' her mother said, turning away, 'as long as you don't forget.'

'I won't, Mum. Promise.'

Going to university and getting her Arts/Law degree with honours would only be the first step on a very long road. Katerina had no clear idea of what she wanted to do, only that she certainly didn't want to stop there – simply being a lawyer. Her sister Louise's idea of coming back to their hometown after she'd finished her specialist degree and gradually taking over her ageing father's practice filled Katerina with an angry impatience. Why would anyone want to live in Manella when there was ... well, the rest of the world, for a start?

'Oh well, this will have to do,' her mother said, trying to be cheerful as she pulled a plain glass vase out from under the sink.

'What day does Louise get back from France next week, Mum?'

'Friday, darling. It would be nice if we all went out to meet her.'

Katerina mumbled her assent, knowing that she would, when the time came, be able to think of some excuse not to go.

'So there will just be her and me in the house?'

Her mother frowned disapprovingly as she arranged the flowers.

'Yes. Philippa's gone to live with ... some boy. Silly girl.'

Katerina ignored her mother's moral undertones as her mind clicked into action.

'Do you know if Lou has anyone in mind for the third room?'

'No. In her last letter she said she'd have to find someone when she got back. It won't be too hard. It's a lovely house.'

'What if I could find someone first ... you think she'd mind?'

Mrs Armstrong set the vase of roses in the middle of the table and turned to look at her daughter.

'As long as it was someone suitable, dear ... I can't see why not. After all, it's Daddy's house. He bought it for both you girls. If you can find a suitable friend, I can't think that Louise would mind.'

Katerina was feeling happier by the minute. This was a good idea. By the time bossy old Lou came back from Europe, she'd have someone decent installed in the third bedroom, instead of having to put up with one of her elder sister's awful friends.

She'd ring around some of the girls from last year and see if anyone, like her, wasn't going to live in a college. Katerina ran upstairs in a distinctly happier frame of mind than she'd been in for weeks.

2

Carmel could feel it all slipping away from her: university, a career in music, the future she'd spent many a dreamy afternoon imagining. Within just a few weeks it had slid off into a hole, like a great haul of earth being pushed by one of those huge machines; moving steadily, heavy with its own crazy momentum. First there'd been the fewer than impressive exam results. She'd been half expecting them, but to hold the paper in her own hands and see the awful computerised letters for herself was something else. Four simple passes and two fails. She had excelled at nothing. Seeing that was like feeling something sharp sinking right between her ribs and making her blood pump with a hot sense of helplessness. *This will not be enough to get in anywhere.* But she'd managed to hang on to hope right through the Christmas and New Year celebrations. Maybe this year there would be fewer people applying for music courses. Maybe there'd been some kind of mistake. Surely something would happen to right the situation. But there had been no mistake. These were her marks. The conservatorium had been her first choice and she'd known as soon as she got her results that it would be impossible. Against all reason she pinned her hopes on the College of the Arts. Everyone said that the course there was good. They taught piano and singing and gave concerts – she wasn't exactly sure about much else. All she knew was that she had to be away from Manella and studying music, somewhere. Things would open up for her. They had to. All her teachers said they would.

Then Auntie Mona had written to say that Uncle Peter had had a heart attack, that their daughter Paula was coming home from overseas to help nurse him. It would be impossible now for them to have Carmel in their home for her first year of study because there wouldn't be room. Mona was her father's sister and she had generously offered to board Carmel for nothing in return for a bit of housework. Until Uncle Peter fell ill. So now there was nowhere cheap for her to stay anyway.

Then January had arrived and the places had come out. Not only had she missed out on the College of the Arts, but also on her next three choices. What was being offered was her fifth option, the last thing she'd scribbled down before handing the piece of paper back to Sister Bernadette when they'd filled in the forms. An obscure teacher's course. Kids with disabilities or something. She'd whacked it down because there was room for five courses and she'd joked to the girl beside her that if she was ever reduced to it she'd slit her throat. They'd both laughed. Everyone knew there were no jobs for teachers. Everyone also knew that Carmel McCaffrey belonged in a music school somewhere. That by some crazy twist of fate, in spite of her being the only girl in that huge, bizarre family of boys, with the eccentric parents, that lived out on the hillbilly farm that no one in the town had stepped foot on for years, the big, awkward girl was talented. Her singing was mainly confined to the school choir and ten o'clock Mass each Sunday. But then there were the other social events: weddings, funerals, Christmas, and Anzac Day at the old people's home. Most of the locals had heard her sing at least once, and had been stunned by the depth and richness of her voice. If they hadn't heard her voice then they'd heard about it and planned to be there next time. Shame that she was so overweight and shy; the way she blushed and bumbled around when people complimented her made them wonder if she'd ever get it together enough to do something with her talent.

'There are no jobs for teachers,' her mother had snapped, 'and where do you think you're gunna live while you're doing this useless course?' Both her parents were unimpressed with

Carmel's vague, badly articulated pleas about needing to get away from Manella – even if only to do the teaching course that she had no desire to do. Carmel could see that her mother was getting some kind of perverse pleasure out of her predicament and this made the pain worse. She had always flustered easily, but this deep sense of panic was something else. She could see herself, an enormous captured insect, or a fat spider, her legs and arms flailing around uselessly, the pin sticking right through the centre of her heart. Each minute that went past and the more she kicked, the tighter she stuck to the backboard of Manella.

'But, Mum, you ... you don't want me here.'

'What do you mean, girl?' Her mother was ironing a pile of men's shirts. Every time she shifted a garment around, the iron was slapped down with a sharp thud on the end of the board.

'Well, I cost so much to feed and keep ...' Carmel's voice trailed off. Her parents were always complaining about how much it cost to feed and clothe them all, so it was the only thing she could think to say that might work. But she could see by her mother's face that it was hopeless.

'You'd cost a damn sight more to keep in the city!'

It was oddly satisfying for Nance McCaffrey to know that all the talk about her daughter being talented had come to nothing. She didn't understand music herself. Didn't even like it. The girl must have got it from Nev's mother. She remembered that old cow playing piano sometimes in between whingeing about her arthritis. Any fool could see that a career in music wasn't a realistic path for a country kid from a farming family to follow. Now she'd been proved right. Nev and she were basic people; they worked hard with their hands for not much return. Everything was a struggle. What reason had she to think that it would be any different for her daughter? Those teachers ought to have their heads read, giving kids all these bloody fancy ideas! The McCaffreys had just enough land to make a decent living when the rain came at the right time and the prices were reasonable. But now, with the drought and the loss of overseas markets, it was just plain impossible. Who ever heard of making a living out of something like music? That dreamy lump of a girl of hers would be better off going by bus to the local college in the next big town and learning how to use one of those new-fangled computers. That at least would lead to a job; perhaps in the bank or a nice clean office somewhere.

Mrs McCaffery herself hardly ever went to town these days. The bread was delivered every second day with the mail. They killed their own meat, kept a few scraggy chooks, grew pumpkins, and bought spuds from their neighbour. Anyway, what would she want to be going to town for?

Of course, like most gruff people Mrs McCaffrey had another, deeper layer under her tough, brittle, no-nonsense surface. A small corner of her tired heart grieved for her daughter as she watched the girl blunder around in her disappointment. This part of Nance McCaffrey wanted the best for Carmel, to see her happy and settled, even fulfilled. But the softer, kinder side so often got lost beneath the hardness of everyday life. Whole weeks passed where it lay dormant, waiting for the spring, for some change in the family's circumstances, to wake it. Sometimes in the dead of night, lying next to Nev, she woke shivering with shame at the harsh way she'd stepped on one or other of her kids' feelings, the needless hurt she'd caused to their fledgeling senses of themselves by her snapping and complaining. Even the young boys, harmless and playful as a couple of clumsy puppies, felt the heat of her tongue most days. At such times, she wondered if she'd lost the person she once was altogether, and longed for something to happen that would bring it back to life.

Then Vince arrived, out of the blue. Carmel was inside at the sink finishing off the lunch dishes. The men – her father and brothers, seventeen-year-old Anthony, fifteen-year-old Bernie, and thirteen-year-old Gavan – had gone back up to the shed to finish the crutching. She was staring out of the back window watching the younger boys, eight-year-old twins Joe and Shane, playing in the dried-up, dusty yard. A few chooks were scratching around and a couple of the sheepdogs were sitting panting in the shade of the mulberry tree when the bike suddenly appeared. It roared up the dirt track, around the house and stopped suddenly halfway between the shed and the house. Carmel stopped breathing and waited. The figure on the bike sat there, taking his time and staring around. Suddenly he tipped off the helmet and got off the bike. Carmel gasped. It *was* him! The tall, strongly built leather-clad figure of her brother was slowly walking on down to the house.

'Mum!' she yelled. 'It's Vince! Vincent is home!' Her mother came running into the kitchen.

'No,' she said flatly, but her face was loose with expectation.

'Yes, Mum. Look!'

Mrs McCaffrey was short and slightly built compared to her daughter. She peered through the window at her eldest son letting himself in through the back gate.

'Well, I wonder what he wants,' she sniffed.

'Mum, please,' begged Carmel, laying one hand on her mother's thin, freckled arm, 'can't we just welcome him and ...'

'Welcome him!' her mother snorted, pulling her arm away. 'Not a letter in six months and before that those piddly little postcards. He doesn't deserve anything from us. He thinks he can ...' But Carmel had run for the door. She didn't care at that moment what her mother was going to say. Even the idea of her own dismal future, which had been blocking her vision for the last two days, faded away. It meant nothing. Vincent was home.

'Vince!' she shouted, bounding along the path to greet him. He stopped, dropped the helmet, and held out both arms, smiling.

'G'day, Carma, girl! How ya going?'

'Okay, okay,' she said. They locked arms around each other and began slowly to spin around where they stood. He smelt wonderful, just as she remembered, of oil and grass and cigarettes.

'Hey, you smoking again?'

'Nah. Why?' When they pulled away Vince looked back to the house. His mother was standing watching at the back door.

'Everything still the same?' he said, turning back to Carmel with a laugh.

'Yes,' she answered softly, trying not to cry, trying to keep the desperation out of her voice. 'Everything is still the same.'

That night they all sat around the table, together for the first time in nearly two years. Her mother and father, the six boys, and herself, everyone soaking up the wonderful Vincent. He told stories about being up north in Cape York, how hot it was and how hard the work was in outback Queensland and New South Wales killing pigs. He'd got himself a couple of dogs and a gun, but he'd left them all with a mate in Albury. He was going back soon. His teeth, when he threw his head back to laugh, shone. His hair, a wavy, coppery brown like Carmel's, and his eyes gleamed with youth and purpose. At twenty-three, he'd grown up, become more controlled. Carmel could see both her parents struggling with the difference. Vincent seemed to understand their need to punish him after such a long absence, but it wasn't worrying him at all. Carmel pushed the peas onto her fork and smiled to herself as she watched him choose not to take offence at their brusque questions, their terse dismissal of his opinions about this or that. And the way he looked up in quiet appreciation when his mother gave him the choicest piece of meat.

'What are you gawking at?' Mrs McCaffrey snapped, breaking in on her daughter's happiness in that quick and deadly way she had.

'Nothing,' Carmel flinched, wondering suddenly how she could possibly go on living in this house when Vince had gone again. The bleak days stretched endlessly before her. In one flash she saw the meals that had to be prepared, saw herself coming home from some dreary computer course to chop pumpkin, break up Joe and Shane's fights, and deal with her short-tempered mother. She would have to sneak away for a few minutes to the old piano out in the back room. The resentment, now that she didn't have exams to work for, would build up and get harder and stronger. And her mother would win in the end. There was nothing surer.

Their father talked more in the first half hour of that meal than he had to any of them for about a year. Vince's homecoming was the catalyst. It was as though Nev McCaffrey had just discovered that his own tongue could be used for something other than a terse explanation, an order or a complaint. Joe and Shane sat and stared at everyone, goggle-eyed with excitement as the older ones, mainly Vince and his father, talked about dogs and horse-racing. And about boxing. Vince had had three fights up in Brisbane and had won two of them. He was considering taking up training seriously.

'Ah, that's a bloody mug's game!' their father growled.

'Good money, but ... ' Vince replied with a careless grin at Carmel.

'If ya win, boy, if ya win! Most people don't.'

At eight years old, Joe and Shane could only wonder at the tension that welled up every few minutes and swam in dark circular currents around the table. All they knew for sure was that their eldest brother was home, that he had brought news of different places, and that their parents had sparked up somehow.

Finally Carmel's future came up.

'How did you go, sis?' Vince asked nonchalantly. Carmel looked away, feeling a flush of unhappiness beginning on her neck.

'Not good enough,' her mother said drily.

'What does that mean?' Vince asked. Carmel couldn't speak,

but she noted the steel entering his grey eyes. She hadn't spoken to anyone about her poor results. No one had rung from school to ask her how she'd gone. That made her feel even more left out and afraid. No one wanted to talk to her. She'd let them all down. Now the whole business was going to be brought out like dirty underwear for her brother to see. He'd always been so encouraging, telling her that she could do anything, and she hadn't been able to deliver the goods.

'She didn't get into the course at the university,' her mother went on.

'Can't see the point of anything else,' her father said. Carmel turned and stared from one to the other in open-mouthed fury. Vince sensed the quickening of her temper, caught her eye and winked. He seemed to be saying, trust me, keep cool. Carmel shut her mouth, sat back and tried to do both.

'Did you get in anywhere?' he asked mildly, smiling up at his mother as she unceremoniously plonked the home-made lemon pudding in the middle of the table. God! Carmel thought. He's become a charmer! Then she remembered that he'd always had that in him. It was just that in the past his quick temper had got the better of the charm. Joe and Shane looked at each other and grinned. Pudding! What a treat.

'Yes,' Carmel mumbled, scraping up the last of her meal.

'So what course did you make?'

'A teaching one.'

'Do you want to do it?'

'Well ... no, but ... I think, I ... yes,' she ended defiantly, glancing first at her father and then at her mother. 'But I haven't anywhere to live. And we can't afford it ... ' The tears that she thought she'd had under control the day before rushed into her eyes. The family sitting around her began to swim in front of her. She knew all her brothers were staring curiously at her. Feminine displays of emotion in the home were rare indeed. But she was so miserable she didn't care.

'Well, of course you've got to go,' Vincent said matter-of-factly. His parents stopped eating, their mouths settling into identical grimaces. The convivial atmosphere moved up a notch, nearer to some vague danger-zone. Suddenly no one was looking at anyone else. At opposite ends of the table the parents, sour at being caught off guard, sought each other's eyes before turning back to their meals.

'Oh, and I suppose Mr Moneybags will pay for her board, will he?' The sarcasm of her tone surprised everyone, even her husband. Nance was usually just dry and to the point in her complaints or remarks. She rarely descended to real nastiness. Carmel saw her brother take in a sharp breath before he spoke.

'Well, yeah,' Vincent said. 'That's exactly what I was going to say, Mum. Until she gets on her feet, maybe gets a part-time job, I'm prepared to help her out.'

'Well, of all the bloody useless things to spend your money on ... ' she expostulated.

'Haven't you heard there are no jobs for teachers ... ?'

'I don't want her in the city by herself!'

The protests flew around the room. One after another like sodden lumps of clothing – from father to son, from mother to father, and back again. Vince sat there as cool and composed as a prince. Carmel could feel bubbles of elation growing like white foamy soapsuds inside her. They were protesting about the plan, pointing out all the reasons why it didn't make sense, but in spite of all that, she could tell that they'd accepted Vince's offer. She'd be able to go for a year anyway. Within the two hours he'd been home Vince had assumed power. It was as though they didn't have the fight in them to defy him.

Vince promised to find a place for her to live when he went back to town and said he would pay the rent for the first six months. He assured his parents it would be somewhere safe; maybe some boarding-house or college for students. He'd look into it all as soon as he went back to collect his gun and dogs. There was nothing for them to worry about. She'd get a small government allowance, and he'd set her up somewhere till she could find a part-time job.

'How is she going to get a part-time job?'

'Look around. Ask people,' he replied mildly. 'Just like everyone else.'

'She's never worked in her life!'

'I don't like the idea of her working in the city.'

'Everyone does it,' he replied, as though it were the simplest thing in the world.

A few hours later the family was sitting quietly in the kitchen. For the first time in probably five years the television had been forgotten.

'You don't look too well, Mum,' Vince said casually as he dried the knives and forks and put them away. The whole family stopped, Carmel included, and looked at the prematurely ageing woman sitting by the stove, darning socks. She looked up in surprise. Nance McCaffrey was fifty-three and no one had commented on the way she looked for easily ten years. Carmel and Anthony were surprised too. Mum was Mum. She never changed. She never looked different except when she went to town. Then she'd exchange her tattered work dress for a less tattered clean one, put a couple of strokes of plain red on her mouth and that was it. If it was winter she'd put on the rather well cut, but worn, red coat her sister had given her about six years before. That was all.

'I'm all right, son,' she sighed. Carmel looked at her brother for a sign. What was he up to? But Vince's face was full of genuine concern.

'You look crook to me.'

'Ah, go on with ya!' Mrs McCaffrey went on with her darning, but she was pleased with his attention in her own way. They could all see that. 'I'm all right.'

'When was the last time you went to a doctor?'

She actually gave a short laugh and everyone smiled. They all knew that it was a matter of pride for their mother that she never went to the doctor. The last time had been when the twins were born.

'Well, I'm taking you into town tomorrow,' said Vince, 'we'll ring up in the morning for an appointment.'

Mrs McCaffrey's eyes began to twinkle. The kids couldn't believe it. Their mother was laughing! She put down her darning and settled both her thin hands over her belly.

'And who says so?' she said, the laugh twitching around the sides of her mouth and lighting up her eyes.

'Me,' he replied shortly.

'And why would I go to the doctor when there is nothing wrong with me?' Vince shrugged and looked her squarely back in the eye.

'You need some kind of ... I dunno ... a tonic,' he replied. 'You're too bloody pale and thin.'

'It's called hard work,' their mother chortled. Joe and Shane edged in a little nearer to her. It was so rare for them to see her relaxed and lighthearted. They nestled near her knees and she actually stretched out both arms and patted their heads with her red, knobbly hands.

'Even so,' Vince replied confidently, 'we're gunna get ya checked out.'

'Is that so?'

'Yep. I'll take her in the truck, Dad. Hey?'

Their father, who was sitting at the table pretending to consider the racing pages, was in fact listening intently.

'Anyone that can get her to the quack deserves what he gets,' was all he said.

Vince not only got his mother to the doctor the next day, but also managed to tie up Carmel's housing arrangements at the same time. They got home from Manella at about five. As Mrs McCaffrey had expected, the doctor had found nothing wrong with her that 'a bit of a break' and 'a little rest-up' wouldn't fix. She'd sniffed dismissively when she'd left the surgery, muttering that it's all very well for a doctor to talk about resting, but he wasn't going to be the one that would step in and do her work if she wasn't there to do it, was he? But the outing had done her good, nevertheless. She had been buoyed up to be in town with her handsome eldest son, and had stopped to talk to a few old acquaintances. Shown off a bit. Already there was a bit of colour in her cheeks and a new spryness to her step.

They'd come inside and Carmel was putting on the kettle when Vince dropped the bombshell.

'Found you a place to stay next year, Carm.'

'What?' Carmel spun around.

'Yeah,' he went on blithely, 'got talking to Dr Armstrong's wife while I was waiting for Mum. Bit of good luck. Daughter needs another flatmate for the little house they've got in Fitzroy. The eldest sister changed plans at the last moment. She's putting off coming back from overseas for six months, won't be back till July. I said you'd take a room till then ... ' Carmel gulped.

'You don't mean ... ' she spluttered in horror. 'Not *Katerina Armstrong*!'

'Yeah,' he went on, puzzled by her expression, 'that real pretty one with the blonde hair.' Carmel sat down, her mouth dry.

'Do you know her or what?' he asked, still puzzled. Carmel looked at her mother, who could only shake her head. She knew instinctively that Carmel would have reservations.

'I told Vince he should speak to you first,' she said wearily. Carmel was still sitting so Mrs McCaffrey got up to make the tea herself. 'Said that you mightn't feel comfortable with the girl ... '

'But I can't ... ' Carmel wailed. 'She's, oh God, I don't know ... she's ... '

'What?' Vince snapped impatiently. 'What is she?'

'She's so beautiful and brilliant and she's a complete snob and ... everyone around town absolutely hates her, and ...'

'Has she ever done anything to you?' he asked.

'She wouldn't even *speak* to me,' Carmel burst out passionately. 'She wouldn't even know I existed!'

'Why not?' Vince asked, meeting her eyes. Carmel sighed and looked away. The thing she most loved about her brother was that social hierarchies meant nothing to him. Even when he was living in Manella he never judged himself or anyone else by what clothes they wore or what money they had or what airs and graces they gave themselves. His handsome looks and ability to work hard won him admiration from many different quarters. She didn't know how to tell him what it was like for her without risking him thinking less of her. Vince pulled his chair up.

'Listen, Carm,' he said quietly, 'her mother told me that her daughter needed someone in the house. She's your age. They don't want her living alone. I said we were looking for somewhere for you. She rang through to her daughter back at the house and she okayed it. Apparently she was let down by one of her own friends. It's too late now for her to organise anything else. They both remembered you ... they'd both heard you sing.'

'But she's on a *different planet* from me ...' Carmel blundered.

'How do you mean?'

'Socially ... I mean, she went to that ... that boarding school and she's ...'

'Bah!' Vince banged his hand down on the table, 'stuff all that shit! What's all that to you? There's a nice little room in a house near the uni you'll be going to. Won't cost too much ... very reasonable. Listen, give me a *real* reason and I'll call them and cancel it now.'

Carmel could think of a million reasons, but not a single one that would make sense to Vince.

3

Jude's mother Cynthia was at a meditation workshop when her daughter's results came. She'd been buoyed up all week about meeting some new spiritual healer from America and had simply got up, had breakfast, kissed Jude's frowning forehead and disappeared out the door, forgetting altogether that this day was going to be a big one in her daughter's life. Not that Jude expected anything else. All the New Age stuff that Cynthia had begun talking about lately only made Jude clam up with irritation. *Getting in touch with inner feelings, listening to the child inside, learning to love your faults . . .* Oh spare me! Jude didn't want to be anywhere near her mother when she went on with that crap. It had been Cynthia who had brought Jude up believing that this kind of pseudo-religious psychobabble was, like patriotism and consumerism, for the weak-minded; for people who couldn't think or work out things for themselves. 'Open your eyes, Jude,' the slim, fair-skinned, red-haired Cynthia used to say to her sturdy, small, dark-haired daughter, 'and see and understand for yourself how terrible and how beautiful things *really* are in this world.' Jude had obediently opened her eyes and seen that there was much that was beautiful, and much to be afraid of, too. Now this same woman was talking about finding '*my centre*' and 'being on the side of *The Light*'.

What light? More to the point, what was Jude meant to do about it all?

So Jude was alone behind the counter of Manella's Artistic and Creative Supplies store in the centre of town when Ernie Ridge pulled his bike up on the footpath outside, rummaged through his ordered pile of mail, and pushed the door open. The bell on the door gave an irritating little ring that set Jude's nerves jangling even further.

'Hello love. Mum not here?' Ernie was always easy and friendly. And for him today was just any old day.

'No ... she's gone ... for most of the day.'

Her mother had left, telling Jude in her new airy way simply to 'close up shop' whenever she felt like it. Over the last few months Cynthia had been gradually letting the business slide. Bills were not being paid on time and new stock was not arriving. Long-term customers would come to pick up items that weren't there. The place needed a thorough dusting and a coat of paint. Over the last few months, as she'd concentrated on her study, Jude had become very good at not thinking about the consequences of closing the business down. Surely her mother would get back on track soon, get it all into order again. Jude really didn't want to think of what might happen if she didn't.

Amazingly, and much to the astonishment of the hard-nosed locals, who'd warned Cynthia that she'd never make a go of it, the unlikely business – basic art supplies coupled with health and herbal remedies – had boomed for a number of years. Passing trade, mainly tourists on their way to somewhere else, had stopped and bought the packs of tarot cards, the sketching pads and thick colourful pastels and paints, the small knick-knacks, the 'down to earth' packaged soap, the painted china eggcups, the magic crystals hanging from leather thonging, and all kinds of healing oils and perfumes. When Jude saw similar stores in the city she always felt proud. Their shop was superior in every way; her mother had a sure eye for the choicest lines of this kind of merchandise. Initially Cynthia had packaged a lot of the stuff herself in attractive old bottles and hand-printed paper. She also wrote the simple, homely instructions pasted to the side. Often Jude helped her. *If used correctly this merchandise should ease some of the stress of everyday life.* Jude was constantly amazed by the range of people who bought such things. Men in business suits and rich women fitted out in snow gear would sometimes buy up a whole line of a particular herbal remedy. The bottles of 'Gran's General Tonic for Happy and Healthy Children' always went quickly during the winter months. Cynthia would often sigh when the last customer had gone for the day, flop down on the shop's polished wood floor, and stick her feet up on the counter. 'Some people think they can *buy* peace and happiness, Jude,' she'd say softly. 'Sometimes it takes a whole lifetime to realise that they can't.'

Grudgingly, and only after a number of years, the locals began to accept the quiet woman with the red hair, and her sweet-looking, brown-eyed little daughter. Cynthia earned their respect, if not their total acceptance, with her sense of purpose. She'd unwittingly confided to one local busybody back in the early days that she was going to make the business work if it killed her. Unbeknown to Cynthia that comment spread around the town like wildfire, and she immediately went up about twenty notches in everyone's estimation. So within about six years she was an accepted, if not popular, person around town. Part of the townspeople's reluctance to accept her was that they found it very hard to believe that Jude was in fact her daughter. Almost all the locals were from Celtic or Anglo stock. Cynthia was tall and fair-skinned, with bright blue eyes – rather like themselves in fact – while her daughter was short, with almond-shaped brown eyes and hair so black and wiry that in certain lights it was almost blue. But in the end there was nothing for it but to believe the woman's story about the dead South American husband.

Jude stood by the cash register counting change for the bank and looked blankly at the pile of letters in Ernie's hand. Her thick hair was tied back into a rough ponytail. She was eighteen, but she could have passed for someone two or three years younger or oddly enough two or three years older. Her face often changed from innocent and childlike to mature and knowing within a few moments. She felt her mouth go dry as she tried to move her eyes away from the letters. *Please make him go quickly. I just won't be able to stand it if he starts talking about it all.*

'So, big day, hey?' He was grinning like a good-natured labrador, looking at her and holding the letters playfully, making out he wasn't going to let her have them.

'Yes.' She held out her hand without meeting his eyes.

Everybody in the town loved Ernie Ridge. His heavy-featured, good-natured face was sunburnt and he had a stripe of white cream on his nose. There was no way she could be rude to him. He handed her the letters then leant against the counter, watching her.

'How come you didn't get the post office to hold your mail so you could have picked it up earlier like everyone else?'

Jude shrugged, and felt her fingers go cold as she flipped through the letters until she came to the right one, a slim envelope with her computerised details on the front. A stab of panic hit her. How would a computer be able to get it right? A computer would never know how hard she'd worked or how much she wanted ... *needed* ... the right marks. In this innocuous envelope was her future. Whatever was in here would decide whether or not she'd be able to leave this town, go to the city to study and achieve things she'd always dreamed of achieving. Until recently her mother had wanted a good education for her as much as she'd wanted it for herself. Jude had grown up hearing how important it was that she have her own career, that she learn to think and to reason; that her father, a well-educated man, had come from a poor Chilean family who'd had to stuggle desperately to allow him to enter university. But as Cynthia had become more involved with her New Age interests she'd become less enthusiastic about Jude going away to the city. She'd made veiled hints a couple of months before that perhaps Jude should wait a while before going on to university. That she should think of possibilities other than Medicine. Maybe she could hang around Manella for a couple of years and *just relax*. Only the week before Cynthia had said she wouldn't mind in the least if Jude *didn't* do well; that an education wasn't everything. Jude had run from the room, hands over her ears, refusing to listen. The idea of hanging out in Manella for 'a couple of years' horrified her. Yet she knew that it would take money to set her up in the city. Maybe that's what her mother was trying to tell her: that they didn't have it. Then a wild dry fury would overtake her. She'd bang her fists into the wall and kick her toes against the iron bedstead until they hurt.

Jude turned her back on Ernie Ridge and opened the envelope. Her hands were trembling as she pulled out the slip of paper. Once more she had a deep feeling of panic. How could a computer possibly . . . ? There they were in front of her. Sitting neatly alongside her five subjects.

A whole row of A pluses! And then the overall score. Close enough to perfect. Was it possible? She looked away to the window – two people were outside staring in at the display – and then back again. Was this real? An 'A' beside each of her subjects! A plus beside the five of them. And the total score! Jude's stomach gave an almighty lurch. She thought she'd done well, but this was almost too wonderful to believe! She turned to Ernie Ridge, her eyes shining with sudden tears.

'How did you go, love?' His voice teetered warmly on the edge of concern. He was waiting for a sign from her. Suddenly Jude was so glad he was there with her; so glad that she wasn't alone.

'Good, Ernie,' she said coming out from behind the counter towards him, holding out the piece of paper for him to read. 'Really good!'

Ernie's eyes widened as he took in the score, then he held out both arms and she fell into them, laughing and crying at the same time. After giving her a quick, tight squeeze, Ernie held her by the shoulders at arm's length.

'Of course you did!' he boomed. 'Our little Jude! The cleverest girl at the secondary college, hey? Everyone knew you'd do well!'

'But I didn't know ... I ...'

'Well we all did!' He let her go, picked up his mailbag and grinned. 'Good effort, girl! Can I tell everyone?'

'Sure. Thanks, Ernie.'

'Good. I'll be off now. You go and tell your mother. She'll be tickled pink!'

Jude watched him go. The bell tinkled at the door and the lumbering noisy figure disappeared. She stood still, her heart pounding, and listened to the last high notes of his monotonous whistle. Then she was alone again. She folded the piece of paper carefully, put it in a safe place at the back of the cash register, and resumed counting the money for the bank. There really wasn't that much else to do, except wait until her mother got home, and she had no idea when that would be.

There was no one else in Jude's life. No one close anyway. They'd been a unit, Jude and Cynthia, since Jude was two. That was the year when the generals had ordered the killing of her father in Chile. He'd disappeared, along with a lot of others, when the Allende government had been crushed by the military dictatorship in 1973, but had surfaced again for a little while – long enough to set up house with the tall, good-looking, red-haired Australian he'd fallen in love with one night at a political meeting. And to father Jude. They'd had two years together, the three of them, before Carlos was captured again one night. Months later they'd found his body, riddled with bullet wounds, lying with half a dozen others on a bridge over the Mapocho River just out of Santiago. Cynthia had been tipped off anonymously. The next day she had gathered up her tiny, dark-skinned, Spanish-speaking daughter, taken all their meagre savings out of the bank, bribed twenty people for a plot of dirt in the Santiago cemetery, organised the burial, and then, with only one case of possessions, had flown back to Australia.

The shots that had killed her husband had also just as surely shot to pieces Cynthia's sense that there were bigger things than herself and her immediate family worth fighting for. She would go back to her parents for a while, then get some kind of work. Carlos had died. She would make sure his daughter survived.

Of course Jude couldn't remember any of that. All she knew was that she and her mother were as close as could be. They were like the two hands of a clock. One was the hour, the other the minute. Off in different directions a lot of the time, but joined together at the centre, where it mattered.

Hardly anyone ever trespassed into their lives. Cynthia had her business to run, her daughter to bring up, and of course her memories to contend with. And as the years passed it was as though Cynthia's memories had merged to become Jude's as well. Jude felt sure she could remember her father, during the last chaotic year before the coup, standing up on a box outside the factory gates and addressing a small group of workers who had refused to strike. He'd spoken loudly and bravely, even when the long, narrow barrels of the surrounding tanks had pointed straight at him. She could hear the deep resonance of the Spanish words as they flew out defiantly to the worn, anxious crowd of workers.

'Courage, friends! Remember this day belongs to you . . . !'

The march he'd led through the streets of Santiago was another event she could 'remember', even though, logically, she couldn't even have been born. But it was so real to her that she secretly felt her mother was wrong, that she *must* have been there. How could someone else's simple words conjure up such vivid colours and noise? In bed at night she could slot herself back there at will, feel herself on her father's shoulders, being carried along the streets of that big sprawling dirty city, dipping and soaring above the bursting crowd. Rows of people, their arms joined, followed him in a public protest in support of the democratically elected government under threat, and against the right-wing forces that were creating the strikes and chaos – right up to the *Palacio de la Moneda* in the centre of the city. She could smell the excitement all around her and feel the quickening fear as swarms of armed and battle-dressed soldiers suddenly appeared at every corner, their faces blocked with perspex shields. The people had raised their fists and voices. The shouting was so loud that after a time it was almost like no noise at all. Out of the corner of her eye she could see the uniformed men edging closer, their guns being lowered, cocked, readied ...

She could conjure up the smell of her father too. See his blood running into the gutter of the concrete courtyard of the old prison where he'd been shot in the bright, hot sunlight. And hear his last words to his wife before he was taken away for the last time. 'I love you. Look after our baby ... Fight for justice ... '

And she could recall the way he had laughed and sung and bent forward over the table to enjoy his food. Her mother spoke often about that laugh. But Jude knew she'd remember it even if her mother hadn't said a word. She truly believed that she could remember him.

By the time Cynthia got home, Jude was already in bed trying to concentrate on her book. She quickly turned out her light and waited, her heart pounding as she listened to Cynthia moving quietly around the kitchen. More than anything she wanted her mother to come in and check that she was all right. *I'm not all right, I'm not all right!* was the cry in her heart. A cry she didn't understand herself. If she wanted her mother to come in, why had she turned out the light? The aching need for comfort bubbled over and became a throbbing, painful anger. She imagined herself bursting into her English teacher's house.

'I can't go to university. My recently demented mother doesn't approve.' Worse than not being able to go, and having to hang out in Manella forever, would be to feel everyone's pity.

'Jude, are you awake?' came Cynthia's low whisper. Jude hesitated. The roar of her imagining rushed to a stop at the sound of her mother's gentle voice. It still held such power. For years they'd slept together in the same bed. That voice had lulled her off to sleep with all kinds of stories and songs and little poems in Spanish and English. Part of her desperately wanted not to answer, but she couldn't resist.

'Yes ... I'm awake.'

'Can I come in?'

'What for?'

'To see how you are?'

'Okay ... I'm all right.'

The older woman slipped silently into the room without turning on the light and sat on the bed. Jude watched her profile warily. The face, with its long straight nose, mouth and pointed chin, was silhouetted against the light from the moon outside. She knew the shape of her mother's face better than her own. The anger sank away, replaced by a terrible ache. Her mother was sitting right next to her, yet it was as though a deep, dangerous chasm was running right there between them. She longed to jump over to the other side, but was suddenly aware of some kind of risk.

'My results came,' she said, wanting to hurt Cynthia for her lack of interest. Her mother drew her breath in sharply.

'And ... ?'

'I did well ... very well. A's for everything.'

'Oh, Jude! Really? That's ... wonderful!' Her mother sounded genuinely delighted. She leaned forward and put her bony hands on Jude's shoulders, then she kissed her daughter warmly on both cheeks. In spite of her inner hostility, Jude felt some of the ache subside.

'You're just like your father, you know,' Cynthia whispered

down into her face. 'Clever in the way he was ... ' Jude turned towards the window and summoned up her courage. She would know soon. Why not now? She took a deep breath.

'So, can I go? I mean, can I go to university?' Her voice was thin with panic.

'Of course you'll go to university!' Cynthia replied quickly, surprised. Jude's head jerked back around to face her.

'But you said ... you wanted me to ... stay here and ... '

'But you don't want to do that, do you?'

'No ... but what about ... ?'

Her mother was sounding normal for once. She wasn't off with the fairies or looking away as though she had more important things to think about. Jude felt the sobs of relief rising within her, but she managed to contain them. She wanted to be absolutely sure about it all.

'The money ... and everything?' she whispered. Cynthia gripped her daughter's shoulders more tightly.

'Don't worry about the money, Tot,' she answered, using the old, half-forgotten pet name. 'You must go to university. We'll find the money.'

'You mean it?'

'Of course I mean it! Your father would have wanted it.' When Cynthia bent down again to reassure her daughter the cheek she kissed was wet with tears.

'Jude,' she said anxiously, 'what is it?'

'Nothing.'

'Did you really think I wouldn't be able to find the money for you to go?'

'I didn't think you *wanted* me to go.'

Cynthia buried her face in her daughter's neck where it met the shoulder. Jude breathed in the soapy smell of her mother's skin and wished the moment would go on and on. When she felt her mother might be going to pull away she pushed back the sheets, lifted up her arms and wrapped them around Cynthia's back.

'Well, of course I don't want you to go, Jude!' Her mother was tearful now. 'You know that! I'm going to miss you terribly.'

That night Jude had the best sleep she'd had in weeks. She woke wondering if she'd imagined the last six months. Perhaps nothing had changed at all. Maybe that gradually widening, shifting space between her mother and herself was all in her head. But when she went out to the kitchen there was a pile of leaflets on the table along with a big notepad filled with her mother's large, scrawling, green-inked handwriting. Jude picked up the notepad and flipped through it. The pages were filled with half-sentences and small quotes: *Where would any of us be without forgiveness? What does it mean to be alive?* Oh God! Jude groaned. There were asterisks, exclamation marks and circles around some of the words. And short comments that had been added with a thicker texta in another colour.

Why can't I understand this! This is too hard! ... But how do I put this into practice? Cynthia's comments to herself. Dates for further sessions were noted too. Some of the headings were underlined.

My gifts. How can I use them to best advantage?
Working through to spiritual enlightenment.
Coming out the other side of sorrow and guilt.

Jude read on and the familar chill of incomprehension began. *What is happening to my mother?* Only six months ago Cynthia would have joined her in a few derisive sniggers about this kind of stuff. She remembered her mother's scorn only last Christmas when they'd watched some actress on television pontificating about how important her *inner wellbeing* was. How they'd groaned together, and laughed.

'*The Hollywood answer to the world's problems: concentrate on yourself,*' her mother had scoffed.

Betrayed. That's how Jude felt. She sighed as she felt the anger simmering away in the pit of her gut. If Cynthia insisted on getting into all this New Age crap, she could at least keep it away from Jude.

'The shared areas of this house will remain crap free,' Jude hissed under her breath before picking up all the papers from the table, pushing them roughly into a plastic bag, and making her way through the lounge and into the hallway. She hesitated for a moment outside her mother's open bedroom door before hurling the bag inside. She didn't wait to watch half of the papers spill out onto the hand-woven Mexican rug, but slammed the door, ran back out to the kitchen, grabbed her bag and stormed out of the house. *I am Jude Torres . . . Carlos's daughter. The daughter of a revolutionary doctor who died fighting for justice. Seventeen years on, and there are still fresh flowers on his grave. I owe it to him to keep faith. I won't give in . . .*

'Jude, where are you going?'

Jude heard her mother's anxious voice as she unlocked the front gate, but she didn't stop.

'I'm just going out,' she called over her shoulder. 'See if I can find somewhere to live. Be back soon.'

Carmel

1

What I remember most about that first day was the crushing sense of doom that filled me when the car pulled into the kerb. It was not a new feeling. Since my exam results it had been with me constantly. It was just that on this day, at this hour, the feeling was stronger than ever. We'd driven around for about forty minutes, lost in the unfamiliar city streets, and we were both hot and sweaty. The vinyl seats were roasting me alive – the backs of my thighs were wet and I could see that Dad's shirt, carefully ironed that morning, was damp. A sour smell was exuding from him. From both of us.

Now that it was imminent, a part of me hoped we'd never find the street or the house. Then we could just give up and go home.

Then, suddenly, the street sign came to life. Quickly after that the small row of six white terraces, small and pretty with ironwork along the front, very close to the street. It wasn't just apprehension that rose inside me. It was fear.

'It'll be one of these,' Dad muttered, slowing the car right down. 'Now what was that number?'

'Forty-five,' I said, looking out the window.

'Well, this is it.' My father sighed. He'd done his duty. That morning I'd heard them arguing. He hadn't wanted to come. He had too much work to do. Couldn't they put me on the train or something?

'Well, how else is the poor wretch going to get her things down there?' my mother had shouted. A poor wretch. They didn't believe I should be doing this course and neither did I.

Vince had gone up north again. With him had gone my absolute belief that I should leave Manella. In fact I was beginning to think that my parents were right. I should be living at home and doing a computer course. I watched Dad slowly get out of the car and open the boot. He wasn't going to muck around, that much was obvious. He was going to pull out my things and leave as soon as he was able. I tried to quell the sickening rush of fear inside my stomach as I opened my door and got out.

'So, you've arrived?'

We were bending over the suitcases and hadn't seen the door open in the house nearest to us. There she was, this magnificent blonde creature, whom I'd only ever seen in the distance in Manella, standing outside the front door smiling at us coldly. I was so aware of how we looked, my father and myself, red-faced with the heat, wilted and sweating. I felt her eyes sweep over me, just once. I flushed with shame, knowing now that the new light-blue denim skirt I'd been so happy with in Manella was ridiculous. And the white blouse with the embroidery around the collar was just as stupid and old-fashioned. She had on tight jeans cut off at the knee, and a low-cut sloppy turquoise T-shirt that matched her eyes. The short sleeves were rolled up to her shoulders and her sandals were of a bronze-coloured leather. There was the sweetest little gold chain around one of her ankles. I would have killed for ankles like that, and for that little gold chain.

'Yes, we're here,' I stammered. A wave of annoyance flitted across the girl's face. She was put out. She must have been on her way to somewhere important. She gave off that impatient, bored air that said she had far more important things to do than to stand talking to us. She turned around and pushed the door open for us. Instead of walking in, to my horror, Dad put both cases down and held out his hand.

'Well, you must be Dr Armstrong's daughter,' he said shyly. She hesitated long enough to make him feel he'd done the wrong thing, then took his hand limply in her own for a few seconds, looking past him out onto the street.

'Yes. That's right. Katerina. Pleased to meet you,' was her clipped reply. Poor old Dad, I found myself thinking as I saw the rush of confusion sweep across his face. He was way out of his depth.

'Look, I'm due somewhere ... but do come in. I'll show you your room,' she went on lightly. 'The other girl arrived last night, but she's out somewhere.' The other girl? I hadn't known there would be anyone else. Now there were two of them and one of me. Dad and I followed her into the dark, cool hallway. By the time our eyes had adjusted, Katerina was already striding down the narrow corridor.

'I'm afraid you've got the last room,' she called. 'It's smaller than the others and it's near the kitchen.' Then she turned back to me and fluttered her lashes mockingly. 'I hope you're a good sleeper.'

I nodded, and she flung the door open, stepping aside for me to enter. The room was lovely. Well, plain and small, I suppose, but lovely to me. Light streamed in through one long, wood-framed window. It was painted in pristine white and had an old fireplace surrounded by dark wood and a heavy mantelpiece. There was another long window on the opposite wall that looked out onto a red brick fence, a single bed in the corner, unmade with a couple of blankets folded on the end, and a cupboard and small wooden dressing-table. Everything about the room was much nicer than what I had at home.

'Pretty basic. You'll want to bring your own stuff, I'm sure,' she said.

'No. It's fine,' I mumbled back. A look of bewilderment suddenly suffused Dad's face. Now that it was time for him to leave he was having second thoughts.

'So how are Mum and Dad?' he asked Katerina. It was as though he couldn't quite believe that anyone could be so snooty and aloof.

'Just fine,' she snapped tossing her head without looking at him. I cringed.

'He did a little op for me last year, you know,' Dad went on, smiling blindly, 'had a mole out that looked a bit dangerous.'

I turned away, unable to bear it. It's bad enough when my parents behave in their usual embarrassing, small-town way. It's a lot worse seeing them flounder. Dad had no idea how to deal with this little snob. Nor did I, of course, but at least I knew to shut up.

The cases were dumped on the floor.

'Can I see the kitchen?' I asked desperately. 'Dad might want a drink or something before he goes.'

'Of course,' her mouth twisted into a cold little laugh, 'this way.' We all edged our way out of the room and into the hallway and she led the way through a large lounge room covered with horrible purple carpet. It was simply furnished with an old leather lounge suite, a piano, a stereo and a couple of small tables. Then we were in the kitchen.

'Someone said you didn't get into the course you wanted,' she said off-handedly as she poured a glass of cold water and held it out to Dad. 'Music, wasn't it?'

'Yes. Music. Er, no ... I didn't get in.'

'Hard luck,' she said, looking at me shrewdly. I turned away.

'Yeah.'

We waited, listening to Dad gulp down the water. Then she took it from him with a small smile and refilled it, once again quite pleasantly.

'I guess we'll talk about everything tonight,' she said, turning to me again. 'We'll have a house-meeting. You know, talk about money, cooking, food, shopping and ... anything else.' I nodded. 'Judith will be back then,' she added.

'Yes. Sure,' I said, not being clear what she was talking about. 'Er, who's Judith?'

'You don't know Judith!' she frowned incredulously. I shook

my head, bewildered. How could I know who she meant?

'I'm sorry, I should have told you,' she said quickly, 'Judith ... er, actually maybe her name is Jude. That's what everyone calls her, I think. She's from Manella. Dark hair ... you know. You must know her. Her mother runs that little art shop in the main street.'

'Oh!' I said in surprise. 'Yes, I know who you mean.' The short, bright-eyed girl who went to the secondary college. Everyone knew she was born in some foreign country, and that her father was dead, and that her mother was good-looking and owned that funny shop in the middle of town. That was about all I knew about her. That and the fact she was known to be a bit strange, sort of an odd-ball, a clever wordy type. So I was going to be living with her too. Another stranger.

There was no house-meeting that night. Katerina left for wherever she was going fairly soon after Dad had gone. And the other girl didn't come home at all. I didn't mind it much at first. At least I could breathe easy. There was no one to see how uncomfortable I felt. I took the opportunity to snoop around a bit. The front room I guessed would be Katerina's. I very gently turned the round knob, took one swift peep through the door, and quickly closed it again. The room was full of lovely things. Mirrors and lace curtains and pastel paintings on the wall. The bed was huge, wrought iron with a white cotton lace cover. There were about six little floral-and-lace-covered cushions bunched around at the top, just like in those magazine pictures of home furnishings. It was any girl's fantasy room. I stepped away guiltily and wandered back down the hallway and around the rest of the house. The other bedroom was as bare as my own, except that the bed was made up and a few cases and boxes were stacked up against the wall. There were two big posters on the wall, of older men I didn't recognise. That made me feel a little better. Then I walked out the back to the small concrete yard, which housed an old disused laundry on the left. The fence was high and consisted of old slabs of corrugated iron. I peered through a crack and saw a cobbled laneway and other back gates.

When I turned to the house I was surprised to see that there were wooden steps leading up to another room at the rear of the house. For a few moments I wasn't game to investigate, but once up there on the little landing I was glad. I could see out over the fence into the other surrounding backyards. The door was locked, but I saw in through the window. It was a long, oblong room. There was a narrow bed, a dressing-table, and all kinds of rocks and stones and pieces of clay, moulded and shaped. I wished suddenly that I could live in this room, that it could be mine. That I could stay out the back here out of everyone's way and never have to deal with that little blonde princess. And Judith ... Jude. To think I'd now be living with two people I'd been too shy to speak to at home!

I descended the stairs slowly, trying to ignore the gnawing panic. Why had I come? Why had I been so desperate to leave Manella? At least there I was someone. I had a family of sorts. And I had my music. The singing. I knew I would not fit in here at all.

After a while the panic gave way to a sense of eeriness. To be so suddenly alone in this house I didn't know. Everything I saw and smelt was unfamiliar. Although there were all kinds of sounds from the street outside, the quietness of the house was overpowering.

There was nothing else to do after a while but sit in the kitchen on one of the cane chairs, rest my elbows on the small wooden table, and watch the sun through the window as it slowly sank. I got out the map Vince had made me. He'd worked out my route to uni. I went over it as a way to calm myself. The next morning I had to walk straight out my front door, turn right, then up to the nearest big road, which would be Lygon Street. There I would catch the tram. It would take me around a sharp corner and all the way to university. I would know I was almost there when I saw a big red brick building on my right. I would get used to it all in a couple of days. There was nothing to worry about at all, Vince had said. I would get used to everything.

At first I ignored the piano altogether. Deliberately. Kept getting up from my chair and looking out the window and making myself cups of tea, using the same tea-bag three times. There was a radio on top of the fridge, but I couldn't get it to work. Then I tiptoed into the lounge room, nervous as a cat, as though I expected someone to be waiting there to pounce on me. It was quite gloomy, but I didn't think to put on the light. I opened the piano lid and very gently sat down and felt for the keys. Some chords first. Ah ... the thing was in tune and it had quite a good tone. I wondered who it belonged to. Did she play? Would she mind me using it? F sharp, C, and then some minor chords. They vibrated through my fingers and up into my arms, making me feel better. Slowly I began to play: the sweetest little piece I'd learnt for my exam. I hadn't played it since that day and it had been my favourite. I loved the lilting melody that ran through it like a scampering animal – a bush rat or possum – stopping here and there to twitch its nose and then hop off again. And the way the sadness running underneath it was introduced so tentatively: almost nothing at first, it slowly built like a gathering storm, stronger and stronger, until by the end of the piece it had completely taken over ...

I kept playing. One piece after another as the light in the room faded away. I couldn't find any music to read so I played every single piece I could remember, everything from the most complicated pieces I'd learnt for my exams over the years to bush songs that I'd played for the old people at the Manella nursing home: 'Click Go the Shears' and Irish reels that went on and on.

At one stage I thought I heard the lock opening and the

front door bang. I jumped up, put down the piano lid quickly and moved away, feeling ridiculous to be so furtive, but unable to help myself. For some odd reason I didn't want to be caught playing. But the door didn't open, no one appeared. I ventured up the darkening hallway to the front door to investigate. It was only a tin can on the front step. Someone must have thrown it there. I picked it up and stood looking out into the grey street. The line of palm trees planted in the nature strip caught my attention. Funny that I hadn't noticed them when we'd arrived. I stepped out onto the footpath and looked up and down. Everything had become muted in the fading light and whoever had thrown the can onto our tiny verandah had disappeared. Lights were being turned on in the houses opposite. The odd car glided up and down the grey concrete and I could see a few people coming and going from the houses, some getting into cars, others walking about the streets. The palm trees, dotted at even intervals, were rustling slightly with nesting birds. They stood out high and dark and strong against the deepening sky and they gave me heart. Surely they didn't belong there! Palm trees belong to tropical islands and boats and smiling, dark-skinned people ... They're right out of place amid all this grey concrete. Like me. And yet they are surviving.

Back inside. The purple carpet looked rich and heavy in the last rays of yellow light trickling in from the west window. I went back to the piano and played a Chopin prelude. Its playfulness brought the twins into my head. I could almost hear them as I ran my fingers over the keys, shouting and laughing and running around. I played on and for a while it was as though I was out in the back room at our old piano, the smell of dry grass and the distinctive sweet smell of the huge peppermint gum just outside wafting in through the flywire, while the boys were mucking around on the steps leading up into the room. I kept moving my hands over the keys, trying to ignore the dam that was getting ready to burst inside me. With a sudden intense physical rush I looked up from the keys, longing with everything that was in me to see those drooping heavy bunches of gum leaves swaying at my window and to hear the excited squabbling voices of my brothers as they teased each other. If I kept playing, I thought, then the feeling would gradually have to fade away. My hands went on moving over the keys, through the bars of music like clockwork. It was as though my hands were disconnected from the rest of me.

I must have cried myself right out because I remember patting my eyes with a third soggy hanky, feeling quite exhausted and numb. After a while I became aware that I was very hungry too. Ravenous. When I looked in the fridge there was nothing to eat and for the first time in my life I wasn't sure what to do about it. I realised with a small shock that I wouldn't have felt right about eating anything from the fridge anyway. She hadn't suggested that I make myself at home and eat her food. I had some money. I should go out and see if I could find a shop open. Alone? At night? The thought terrified me. I picked up my bag and made for the door. But what if I got lost? What if I couldn't find my way back in the dark? I suddenly remembered the box of things Mum had packed for me. Eggs and chops and some packets of biscuits, cheese and fruit, a whole pumpkin that she'd grown herself. Only that morning I'd watched her packing the box with dismay. How embarrassed I was going to feel arriving with a whole lot of food from the country! I hadn't known what to say to make her stop. There were jars of preserved fruit and even a lemonade bottle full of fresh milk from the cow Dad had milked that morning. A wave of gratitude flooded me as I made my way into my room, picked up the box, and heaved it into the kitchen.

I unpacked it nervously. There were pots and pans under the sink and cups and plates up on the high shelves. Would it be okay to put these things alongside what was already here? I actually felt desperately like eating something substantial.

Something like chops and eggs with perhaps some fried potatoes and tomatoes on the side, but I didn't dare. The kitchen would fill up with the smell of cooking. And what if that girl came back and found me feeding my face at the table? I was so conscious of being overweight. She'd probably find the sight of me eating really disgusting. She would be one of those people who never thought about food. She would just nibble bits and pieces as she moved through her exciting life. So instead of cooking something I pulled out a packet of dry biscuits and cut slices from the lump of cheese Mum had provided, then smothered all that in home-made chutney and washed it down with still more cups of tea. It was nearly ten and quite dark outside. By this stage, with my hunger at least partially satisfied, I had no idea what else I could do except sit at the table and stare at the things in front of me.

How many times at home had I longed for peace and solitude? How could I have known that it would be so terrible? Every time I moved I heard myself, the scuffing of my own shoes on the floor. I heard the dry biscuits crunching up in my mouth and the sound of my cup being moved and placed on the table. It was like being in a prison. And how slowly the time went. I looked up at the electric clock above the sink and saw that it was ten-thirty. I waited ages before I looked again. In fact I got up, cleared the table, washed my few dishes, and packed away some more food before looking again. Only ten minutes had gone by! I'd never liked TV much, but I suddenly longed to be able to switch one on. To fill up all the empty space of that little house with noise and movement and colour. What if neither of them ever came back?

By eleven anxiety was gnawing away at my insides. In the end I had to make myself get up, sneak into my room, and get my toothbrush. Then I rushed to the bathroom and shut myself in. My blood was racing and my breathing had gone short as I leant back against the door, trying to calm myself. Was I afraid of an intruder? Or of the others getting home and finding me so obviously ill at ease and out of place? But I couldn't pinpoint my fear to anything specific.

The bathroom was a small, sparkling place all done out in white and blue tiles with deep-blue borders around the skirting boards, window frames, and mirror. What would they say if they saw the bathroom at home? The grime around the basin and bath and the worn squares of lino on the floor, the bundles of stinking wet towels and the smell of boys, their sweat and hair, the foul odour of their socks that were piled up everywhere. This bathroom was so pristine and *girly*. I bent over the basin and began to scrub my teeth, feeling as clumsy as an elephant. After finishing that I rushed through the kitchen to my room and made up the bed. Then I quickly shut the cupboard door, switched off the light and pulled off my clothes. I put on the stiff new nightie my mother had bought for me, pulled back the bedclothes, and got in. I lay on my back panting a little, as rigid as a corpse, hands folded across my chest, listening to the small, unfamiliar sounds in all that silence, hating the hardness of the bed, wondering how I could possibly go on living. I tried to pray.

Dear God help me, help me. Help me cope with all this. Let me go home. Make me confident like that girl. Make her not hate me. Make me lose weight ... please make me lose weight! Let something awful happen to her so she could see what a nice person I am. No! That's terrible. Let something happen to me. So I can go home ...

I thought that I'd be awake all night, that there was no way I'd be able to get to sleep in this terrible bed. But I did. I think I went to sleep quite quickly.

2

When I woke it was morning. I lay in bed grateful for the wall between myself and whoever was moving around out there. I'd forgotten to shut one of the blinds the night before and so could see the sky outside, grey and overcast. It would be autumn soon, my favourite season. I snuggled down into the bed refusing to let my mind register where I was, instead letting it flit over the bright leaves that fell from the liquidambars and maples in the main street of Manella; the way the green underneath would push up through all the long, brown summer grass in the paddocks out on our farm. Spring and autumn were the best seasons. I loved seeing everything changing slowly before my eyes. A short sharp knock at the door broke into my rambling thoughts.

'Yes?' I said timidly, pulling the sheets up to my chin, dreading that anyone, much less the perfect Katerina, should see me in bed.

'It's me, Katerina. Do you want a cup of tea?'

'Er ... no,' I threw the blankets back and put my feet on the floor, 'thank you, but I'll be up ... I'm getting up ... '

'Okay.' The footsteps disappeared back into the kitchen again. The smell of burnt toast seeped into my nostrils. Did I dare walk out through the kitchen in my old cotton housecoat? No. It would be better to be dressed when I saw that girl again. The denim skirt I'd worn the day before would do. I rummaged through my things and found the wide blue T-shirt that might help hide some of my size, then collected some underwear and a towel. Trying to steady my nerves I let myself out of the bedroom and opened the door into the kitchen.

There were two of them there. Katerina, her hair piled up on top of her head in a messy ponytail, was dressed more or less as the day before, in cut-off jeans and this time a short, flimsy purple T-shirt that showed off her figure. She was standing by the toaster trying to bang something out of it and looking very irate. The other girl was sitting at the table, reading the paper, in a worn pink-checked dressing-gown, a cup of tea in front of her, her long, dark hair half covering her face. They both looked up when I entered the room.

'Oh, hello,' Katerina said, sounding really annoyed as she banged the toaster. 'How did you sleep?'

'Hi ... okay ... ' I replied, 'er, have you burnt the toast?'

Katerina sniffed dismissively, pulled the plug out and began poking a fork into the toaster. I turned nervously to speak to the other girl and found that I was being stared at.

'I'm Carmel,' I said, trying to smile, feeling the hot flush beginning on my neck.

'Yes, I know,' the dark girl replied nodding seriously. 'You sing. I've heard you. I'm Jude. Good to see you.' She paused, then looked away, as though she didn't quite know what to say next. *Should I leave now? Have my shower?*

'You want a cup of something?' Jude asked, waving at the pot in the middle of the table. I hesitated. Perhaps this was my cue to sit down. That might be the polite thing to do.

'I'm ... no. I'm ... er, just off to the shower,' I stammered, 'perhaps in a minute ... ' I turned away and walked towards the bathroom door.

'What time do you start today?' Katerina called out sharply. I almost jumped, but turned back and saw them both staring at me, waiting for my reply.

'How ... how do you mean?'

'At your college or uni or wherever it is you're going?' Katerina snapped.

'Er ... ten I think,' I mumbled.

'So after you've showered you'll have time to have a talk to arrange things then?' she asked.

'Yes, I suppose so ...' I heard my voice, soft, far away from myself.

'Good. I've got a set of keys for you. We'll have to talk about locking up and all those kinds of boring things.'

'Yes.'

They continued to stare at me. I suppose they were waiting for me to go. But the oddest thing was happening. I'd caught the sound of next door's radio up loud. Beethoven. A string quartet. Which one? The loveliness of it took me out of myself for a few moments. I'd known that piece so well only a couple of years ago and hadn't heard it for ages. It was amazing how music stayed inside you like that, and then when you heard it again years later you just knew it, something inside just sat up and reached out to meet it.

'Are you *okay*?' Katerina asked loudly. I started, but managed to switch back again. Both of them were watching me with blankly curious faces.

'Sorry ... I was ...' I didn't want to explain. Neither of them had even heard it. That made standing there, probably with a dumb faraway look on my face, seem all the more ridiculous. Blindly I turned away and pushed at the bathroom door.

'I'm sorry you didn't get into your course ... the one you wanted ...' The voice came after me. I turned around. It was the dark one, watching me from where she sat at the table. The deep brown eyes looked straight into my own. I felt my lip tremble slightly but didn't have a clue what to reply, so I simply nodded.

'It's rotten the way that happens sometimes with exams,' the exotic girl went on conversationally. 'Did you get nervous and mess up?'

I gulped and nodded again. Jude got up and went over to the cupboard for a plate to indicate that she had nothing more to say. In relief I went into the bathroom and shut the door.

The water pressure was fierce. I stepped into the warm steam, gasping as the hard, hot spray hit my face and shoulders. At home the showers were lukewarm and feeble, and the shower recess was usually greasy with dirt. This was blissful. Home. I would be helping to get breakfast at this time. There would be noise and arguments. Not those two looking at me as though I were a strange species. I soaped myself thoroughly and tried to think of all the reasons why I'd come to the city.

With a jolt I remembered that there might be limited hot water, and the dark girl obviously hadn't showered yet. I reluctantly turned off the taps, stepped out of the shower recess, and stared at myself in the long, foggy mirror on the back of the door, slowly rubbing myself dry. My big creamy-white body stood before me, full and shapely with splotches of pink from the warmth of the shower. The heaviness of my breasts and shoulders, belly and legs made me want to cry out in despair. There were no long mirrors at home so I'd rarely even seen myself unclothed like this. It was the sheer bigness that struck me. This body, this *place* I'd been forced to inhabit all my life was so far from the accepted ideal of beauty that I knew I would never in a million years measure up.

I heard the radio go on in the kitchen. The news. There had been a fire overnight in some outer suburb. Three people had died. I tried to care as I moved in closer so that only my head and shoulders were in view. These parts I could handle. I hardly dared admit, even to myself, that my face and neck were pretty. I'm fair-skinned with a smattering of light freckles over the bridge of my nose. There are definite cheekbones and a rather pointy chin. My eyes stare back at me, large, and clear grey-brown with long lashes. My nose is rather long, but straight. I pull a handful of hair up at the back, letting my neck show, and the small curls spring around my face. I consider my hair to be my one plainly positive feature. It falls to my shoulders, loosely curled and coppery-brown.

When I emerged from the bathroom dressed in my skirt and

T-shirt, a gust of steam poured out behind me into the kitchen. Katerina looked up from where she was writing a list at the table and frowned.

'Didn't you turn on the fan?'

'What?' I was immediately flustered.

'There's a fan there next to the light switch ... '

'Oh ... I'm sorry.' I turned back and shut the door to the bathroom properly. To my dismay the steam then wafted up from under the door.

'Try to remember, if you can, otherwise the rooms will be filled with mildew,' Katerina went on, still frowning as she ticked things off on her list. I nodded and wondered where I should sit. Was the meeting to be here or in the lounge room? There didn't seem to be enough chairs in the kitchen and Katerina had spread a lot of papers out over the table.

Jude sauntered in from the other door, dressed now in tight jeans and a boy's white shirt. Her hair, brushed and shiny, was hanging in dark waves to her shoulders pulled back from her face with a thick rounded clasp that fitted snugly to her head. She was carrying a canvas bag full of textbooks and eating an apple. She looked so fit and easy, so *together*, that a stab of pure envy sliced through me before I'd had time to ward it off.

'So, we all ready then?' Jude smiled at me, squeezing onto the chair between the wall and table. 'Pull up a chair why don't you?' I nodded and began to drag the rather rickety cane chair from the corner to the table. Trying to affect the same kind of easy nonchalance that I'd just seen Jude display, I sat down too quickly and heavily. The chair wobbled. There was an awful sound of splitting wood. Then a crunch as the chair crumbled, and finally collapsed outright beneath me. I fell heavily in an ungainly heap on the kitchen floor.

'Oh I ... I'm sorry,' I gasped, trying to get up. One leg was caught painfully beneath me. The others were staring down at me with open mouths. Then Katerina gave a shrill giggle and covered her mouth. My skirt had flown up over my fat knees, showing part of my plain white underpants. There was a nasty scrape at the back of my knee where a piece of broken chair-leg had stuck into me. Within a few seconds my shock gave way to intense embarrassment. I could feel the heat begin to creep up my neck into my face. It was too awful.

'Oh shit! Are you okay?' Jude asked, trying to cover her amusement by standing up and grabbing my elbow. I pulled away and brushed down my skirt. Almost blind with humiliation, I could nevertheless see that the other two were on the verge of bursting into laughter. Inside I raged as I acted concerned about the chair.

'Who does this belong to? I'm sorry ... I should have known ... ' I was staring at the broken pieces on the floor. *I hate them both. If only I weren't here. If I could just leave ... walk out now!* Biting my lip I picked up a couple of the pieces and tried hopelessly to fit them back onto the chair, all the while trying not to cry. To be laughed at was bad enough, but to break down and cry in front of these two would be much worse.

'Don't worry about it,' Katerina said, getting up grandly, 'I should have thrown it out ages ago.' *So why didn't you ... you horrible little bitch?*

'No I ... I shouldn't have sat on it. I didn't think ... '

'You *are* rather large, aren't you?' said Katerina, going over to a cupboard and pulling out a packet of Band-Aids. I stared after her in astonishment. Then I was filled with a powerful urge to punch her.

'Here, take these and I'll find some antiseptic.'

'I'm all right ... really, it's nothing.'

'It looks a bit painful,' said Jude. All trace of amusement was gone from her expression as she held out a damp face-washer. A thin dribble of blood was heading towards my ankle. I dabbed at it and took the Band-Aid from Katerina, fitting it over the scrape.

'You'll probably have a bruise there by tonight,' Jude added kindly.

'It doesn't matter.'

'You sure you feel all right?' Katerina asked as she carted in a strong chair from the lounge room and settled it at the table next to me. I nodded, hating their solicitous questions more than their laughter.

'I'm fine.'

'Well, if you're sure,' said Katerina, settling herself down at the table, 'I think we should get on with this because we've all got to get going.' To my relief neither of them referred to the chair again.

'This is my father's house,' Katerina began, smiling at us both primly. 'He's given me the responsibility of making sure it's looked after ... so each of us has to remember to lock up if we are the only one home ... okay?'

I nodded and Jude grunted her assent.

'Now I don't know about you two, but I won't be in every night to make dinner,' she went on, 'so what shall we do about buying things? Shall we have a kitty?' She looked at me and I started a little and looked back blankly. *A kitty? Have I heard wrong? What have cats got to do with making food every night?*

Katerina seemed to sense my bewilderment. 'A kitty,' she said with a condescending smile, 'is a pool of money, which we each contribute to every week, and which is used to buy things so we can all use them. I suggest some small amount, just for coffee, tea, milk, fruit and breakfast things, because I won't be in most nights ... '

'Sounds a good idea,' I mumbled, looking away and trying not to let my face heat up all over again.

'Yeah,' Jude added, 'that's all right by me.'

I looked up. Jude's voice was low and interesting and she was tapping her fingers on the table as though she was bored. She looks shrewd, I thought, sort of knowing in some way. *I wonder what she's thinking.*

So it was decided. We would have a kitty and we'd share the cooking when we were in. And they decided many other things too, like how we'd pay our bills, what kind of food we'd buy. They discussed what time they liked to eat, sleep and shower. I tried to join in, to have an opinion so I wouldn't appear utterly stupid. But I couldn't bring myself to care about any of it. What was the difference betwen *real* coffee and instant? I had only ever had instant at home, which was apparently a *no-no*. But the other two seemed quite passionate about this so I decided to keep quiet. When they agreed that they'd ask people not to smoke in the house, I felt vaguely disappointed. I'd been half-intending to take up cigarettes. Apparently everyone got used to the horrible taste after a while, and I'd heard girls at home say it made them lose weight. But after hearing their strong opinions I didn't dare tell them mine.

When Katerina became coy about overnight visitors, their showers and whether they would be welcome at breakfast, my mouth literally fell open before I could stop it. This girl had surely just stepped out of a magazine! Jude also seemed a little taken aback by Katerina's easy allusion to lovers and boyfriends. I guessed that she mightn't have had much experience in that area either.

At last the meeting was over. Katerina had noted down all the decisions and promised to write up some of the more obvious things (like when the garbage went out) and pin it on the notice-board in the kitchen that night. With that she was out, running up the hallway to collect her things and be off for her first lecture. Jude and I were left looking at each other.

'Don't be too intimidated,' Jude said, smiling at me, 'she obviously thinks she's the boss, but we'll put her right about that ... hey?'

'Yes, I suppose ...' I was almost sick with relief at Jude's joking tone.

'So what was the convent like?' Jude asked.

'Well, all right, I suppose ...' I said softly. 'You were at the secondary college weren't you?'

'Yeah. Boy was I was glad to leave.'

'Were you?' I was slightly surprised by her strong, impatient tone.

'Of course. Why? Weren't you?'

'What?'

'Glad to leave? The convent would have been awful, wouldn't it?'

'Oh, yes, I guess so. Well ... in a way I was glad, but ...' My voice trailed off. I looked away from the steady gaze of the dark-eyed girl sitting opposite me and wondered how I could explain that I'd been sorry to leave; that I'd loved school. Most of my teachers had been wonderful. Only a few old nuns were left, but they'd singled me out because of my music. I'd been invited into their private parlour to play on their shiny grand piano any time I felt like it. Compared to home, school was blissful. How could I explain that although I'd been too dreamy and lazy to make a good student, I'd loved the place?

3

I managed, without any major hiccups, to find the right building. The tram ride was enjoyable, but once I'd got inside the funny, rundown red-brick building the sense of doom resurfaced. There were people everywhere. Young people, my own age mostly, chattering, giggling, lining up in queues and studying handbooks and bits of paper. Older people, I supposed they were the teachers or lecturers, sat at tables marking off names and handing out more bits of paper. Everyone seemed to have something to smile about.

'Please pay fees over at that counter...'

'Sorry, but Developmental Psychology is a second-year subject.'

They all looked so sure about what they were doing. I stood for a while watching, having no idea what was expected of me. Eventually I tacked myself onto the end of a queue and waited to have my name ticked off. The woman peered up at me through enormous round glasses and handed me a couple of bits of paper.

'Carmel McCaffrey. Here's your subject list. Now, do you know what to do next?'

'Er... no.'

'Well,' said the woman, trying not to sound as bored as she looked, 'get yourself registered over there, then choose your subjects and join the end of that queue...'

'Thank you,' I said.

I went and stood where she had pointed and stared at the lists of compulsory and elective subjects. Titles like Cognitive Development and Psychology for the Disabled Child made my hands go cold with panic. How could I possibly choose? I went over and joined the enquiries queue. The bearded man sitting at the desk looked nice. Perhaps he'd be able to explain. As I waited my turn I tried to work out some sensible questions. I even started writing a few words down next to the subjects to remind me of what I must find out. Slowly the queue inched forward. I couldn't help staring around. Everyone else seemed to know each other. The place was buzzing with chatter and high-pitched laughter. The two girls in front of me were talking excitedly of what they'd done the night before. I glanced down at the old watch Mum had given me. I'd been waiting in the queue for over twenty minutes.

At last it was my turn. The bearded man stood up and smiled. I thought he was going to introduce himself formally, but he was pushing his chair in.

'I'm terribly sorry,' he said, smiling through gleaming white teeth, 'but I'm going to have to disappear for a few moments and make an important phone call. I'll be as quick as I can.'

'Okay,' I said stupidly, 'that's all right.'

It made no sense, but his going made me feel desperate. I stood at the desk. Two people who'd joined the queue behind me groaned impatiently and wandered off together. I was the only one left waiting. That was when I began to feel very strange. The noise in the room seemed to have risen to a deafening pitch. I felt my body beginning to teeter where I was standing. I'd never fainted in my life, but at that moment it was all I could do not to fall over. All around me people were yelling out, screaming, laughing and hugging each other. Groups of them with arms interlocked, some grinning maniacally, passed by on their way in and out of the huge room. I caught snippets of their conversations, none of which made any sense.

'I'll catch you later in A block!'

'Ten minutes.'

'Did you get into Psych 1?'

'Wanna have lunch?'

Disconnected words ebbed and flowed around me as I waited for the man to come back. He would take care of me. I clung to this idea like a drowning person clinging to a life-raft. He would tell me what everything meant. He might even sense that I shouldn't be doing this course at all and work out a way of getting me into a more suitable one. He looked so kind and friendly. Everything would be okay when he got back.

But he didn't come back. I kept waiting, telling myself to count to ten, to fifty. More minutes rolled by. The crowd was gradually thinning out. Around me other students were walking off in groups, their business finished. I looked at my watch and decided to give him five more minutes. By then he'd surely be back and I wouldn't have to stand there any more feeling like such a geek.

In the end I gave up. There seemed only to be some teachers left, sitting at their tables chatting to each other – not noticing me – and a few groups of dawdling students. My cheeks were flaming as I sidled over to a chair by the wall. I pulled a pen out of my bag and filled in the elective-subjects list any old how. Then I hurried over to one of the desks and handed over my bits of paper.

'What do I do now?' I asked, trying to keep the anxiety out of my voice. The woman didn't answer. She didn't even look at me as she took the sheets of paper – and studied them. It was about a minute before she looked up.

'That all seems fine,' she smiled. 'Now what was it you wanted to know?' So she'd heard my question, but hadn't bothered answering until she was ready. Humiliation and anger burned inside me. I loathed her well-cut orange dress, her styled hair, her stupid, expensive, too-big earrings and her bland smile. But at the same time I felt completely, chillingly intimidated by everything about her.

'What do I do now?' I said again. The smile disappeared, replaced by a slightly amused frown.

'Well, now,' she said in a maddeningly gentle voice. She might have been addressing an imbecile. 'That depends on what you *want* to do ... I suggest you buy some lunch in the cafe over there,' she pointed to the door leading out, 'then go down to the lawn outside. I believe there is a rock band playing ... the third- and fourth-year students have arranged it as part of today.' I stared at her and she stared back.

'I see ... ' I said slowly, 'a band ... '

'It's all on the sheet that you got in the mail,' she said, just the tiniest bit reproachfully, 'and at four o'clock there'll be wine and cheese for the first years ... '

'Oh, I see. Yes,' I stammered, glancing down at the bundle of sheets in my hands, 'thank you.' I wanted to smash her face with both fists, break her jaw with one almighty blow the way I'd seen it done in cartoons. I turned quickly and began to walk out.

'Just turn left out those big doors,' she said, 'you'll find the cafe.'

'Yes. Thank you.'

'You're welcome!' she called after me. 'Enjoy it all, won't you!'

I rushed out through the glass doors, down a stairwell, and out into the fresh air. The sound of loud, grating guitars hit me. I'd ended up outside the back of the building, so I headed blindly up the nearest small lane towards the noise. I hurried around the corner of the building and stopped. There was a large square courtyard in front of me, crowded with young people, some sitting, others lying on the grass, listening to the band that was playing on the makeshift wooden stage in front of them. My first instinct was to flee. The music was so loud and tuneless and the members of the band looked so bored – four of them standing in a dull line, eyes closed and playing with a kind of remote, passionless fever, as though they were asleep. In some kind of trance anyway. Two of them, the guitarist and the drummer, were so pale they looked sick. But no one else seemed to notice.

I made myself stay. I bought a bottle of soft drink from a nearby stall and walked towards the crowd. There was no room to sit at the edges so, very self-consciously, I made my way tentatively into the middle. It was hard to find a spot, but eventually I managed to locate a patch of grass. There were two groups near me. One was a very excited bunch of heavily made-up girls who took no notice of me. The other was a mixed group. One of the boys smiled briefly as he made room for me to sit down. But he turned straight back to his friends again. Over the next two hours I tried to smile and look friendly, as a prelude to making some kind of conversation. But it was as though I wasn't there. There was no response. No one spoke to me at all. After about half an hour I wanted to leave, but I'd used up all my courage walking into the middle of that crowd. I had none left to edge my way back out again. So I sat there, uncomfortable, hating the music and myself, but not daring to move.

Finally the band finished. There was some desultory applause and the four thin, pale men jumped down from the stage and began packing up. Suddenly they were animated and looked like they couldn't wait to get away. A message over the loudspeaker asked all the first years to head up to the first floor of the red-brick building for wine and cheese. I rose with the people around me, allowing myself to be carried along. But at the doorway something in me baulked. My feet had decided, rather than me. The last few hours had made my mind go numb. I turned around at the big glass door and pushed back through the crowd the way I'd come, vaguely aware of a couple of annoyed faces looking back at me. Relief spread through me as I came out into a very busy street shaded with some lovely big peppercorn trees. I had no idea where I was, so I walked up to the nearest intersection and approached an older lady who was waiting for the lights to change so she could cross.

'Excuse me, could you tell me where Swanston Street is?' I asked. She smiled in a tired way.

'It's this street here, love,' she said, pointing to the intersecting road. 'Which part of it do you want?' I hesitated for a moment, forgetting everything.

'I want to catch the tram,' I said.

'Ah! Into the city or out?'

'Out,' I said quickly, 'I want to go back to Fitzroy.'

She walked with me to the edge of the road and pointed up the block to a tramstop.

'Up there. That tram will take you up Lygon Street.'

'Thanks,' I smiled weakly. 'Sorry to trouble you.'

'Not to worry, love.'

I walked up to the tramstop and waited. It was a perfect day: warm, sunny and blue. I felt numb, hardly even alive. I just wanted to get back to my own room in that little house and dive under the blankets.

But I didn't get a chance. To be alone, I mean. I let myself into the house thinking that the others wouldn't be there. It was only five o'clock and I'd heard Katerina say that she had a seven o'clock tutorial and wouldn't be back until late. Jude, I figured, would be out too. I walked down the passage through the lounge room on my way to the bathroom.

'Hello,' said a low voice.

I turned in surprise. Jude was sitting at the little table in almost the same position as that morning. I must have jumped a little at the sound of her voice because she smiled apologetically.

'Sorry. I gave you a fright.'

'Er ... no. I wasn't expecting ... ' I said. 'Hello.'

'You had a good day?' I gave what I thought was a noncommittal half-smile and shrugged.

'It was ... okay.'

'You don't look as though it was okay,' she countered cheerfully. I gulped, more embarrassed than ever, and without thinking covered my mouth with one hand. *Why do I have to be that obvious?*

'I had a complete bummer too,' she went on. I stared, thinking I'd heard wrong. She looked so absolutely *right* sitting there in her tight blue jeans – the very picture of an attractive first-year student, talented, smart and spunky. Nothing in a million years would ever go wrong with her, I was sure of it.

'Did you?' I asked, not knowing what else to say. She smiled ruefully and pulled out a chair.

'Wanna sit down?'

I moved across to the chair and hesitated. If I sat down I might be stuck there, and I was afraid I'd have nothing to talk to her about. And the humiliation of breaking the chair that morning was still with me. I didn't think I'd be able to handle her referring to it.

'First off, I got lost,' she said, scowling. 'I've been there a week already and I still messed up where the lecture room was. So I missed my first anatomy lecture. Then when I got to the next one I couldn't understand anything the lecturer was saying ... '

'What course are you doing?' I broke in.

'Medicine,' she replied, 'but I dunno ... '

'What? I mean what don't you know?'

'I think I might be doing the wrong course,' she said, then started to laugh. 'Oh, hell, Carmel. I'm *sure* I'm doing the right course! But it seems as though it's going to be pretty boring. Learning stuff off by heart ... '

'Well, you've only had a few days,' I ventured, feeling myself relax a little. 'Maybe you'll get to like it. Is there a lot of maths and ... adding up and figures?'

'No!' She gave a short hoot of laughter. 'And I love maths!' She picked up her canvas bag and slammed it theatrically on the table. 'There's just a whole lot of rote learning. No ideas or differences. No interpretations. I mean, I don't know why I'm surprised. It's not as though there could be any question about what a particular bone is called or what drug might treat some disease. I mean, I'll be able to do it with my eyes closed, but, you know, it's weighing on me. Six years of swotting up information!' She slumped down into her chair and groaned, her face hidden by her hands. 'Why? Why did my father have to be a doctor?' She dropped her hands and grinned. 'Why do I have to be the dork who wants to follow in his footsteps?'

I sat down on the chair. I was enjoying her theatrics and the way she looked, too, her flashing dark eyes, olive skin, and deep, funny voice. There wasn't an inch of self-consciousness about her. And for once I wasn't aware of myself at all either. I was enjoying just being there after the terrible uptight day I'd spent not talking to anyone.

'Is that why you're doing it? Because your father was a doctor?'

'Yeah,' she sighed, and rubbed her eyes. 'But not here. He was trained in London,' she said proudly. 'He was a specialist in obstetrics. But he went back to Chile. And worked in the poorest hospitals ...'

'Why?' I asked. She gave me an odd look and smiled.

'Why what?'

'Why did he go back to Chile and work in the poorest hospitals?'

She shrugged and stretched, and I thought with a sinking heart that I'd probably put her off by asking a dumb question.

'A bit mad, I suppose,' she said after a while, as though she didn't want to pursue the topic, 'like me.'

'You're not mad,' I protested, wanting to cheer her. 'You just didn't know what it'd be like ... and you'll get used to it.'

She looked up at me with a small smile, groaned and nodded. 'Yep, I guess you're right, Carmel.'

'Besides,' I butted in recklessly, 'you're not the only one. I know I'm going to absolutely hate my course too!'

Jude looked up in surprise.

'Yeah?'

'Yeah,' I said. She flopped back into her chair and slapped

both hands down on her knees. Her eyes were dancing. I started to laugh too. It was such a relief just to tell someone.

'Oh great!' she chortled. 'Two of us, hey?'

'Yep.'

'What happened to you?'

I shrugged, feeling myself clam up. I was not ready to expose myself further.

'Hard to explain ... '

'Try,' she said, 'go on.'

There was nothing for it but to plunge in.

'I haven't spoken to a single person all day, except to say sorry and thank you!'

Jude broke out into a fresh snort of laughter. 'Me too! Me too!' she spluttered. 'Isn't it revolting? My course is full of all these private-school kids and they all know each other!' I looked at her in wonder.

'But why wouldn't they ... ?' I gasped without thinking, my eyes flicking over her decidedly normal and attractive figure.

'Why what?' she asked.

'Well, I mean ... why wouldn't they talk to *you*?'

'Same reason they ignored you, I suppose,' she shrugged. 'They don't know you so ... '

'But you're so ... so attractive ... ' I said.

All trace of her laugh disappeared. She cupped her chin in her hand and rested both elbows on the table, taking her time. I shifted in my seat, hot with embarrassment. I hadn't wanted the conversation to get onto this level at all.

'So are you,' she said quietly.

I shrugged miserably.

'Besides,' she went on, the teasing tone returning to her voice, 'I was asking them for money and they hate that!'

'For money?' I said, bewildered.

'Yeah. I was trying to sell badges. I only got rid of three! In a whole afternoon. Two of them I had to give away!'

'Badges?'

'I'm in Amnesty.'

'When did you join?'

'Oh, I've been in it for years. But on my first day there last week I joined SAF as well.'

'On your first day?' I repeated in awe. 'What does SAF mean?'

'Students against Fascism,' she said. 'It's a group that supports democracy in countries all over the world. I'm especially interested in South America, but there are political systems all over the world that deny people their basic human rights ... '

'I see ... '

'I was born in Chile ... ' she went on, 'so I have a special interest.'

I nodded, pretending I understood the connection. But I only had a very vague idea where Chile was. I knew nothing of its current political situation, or of its history for that matter.

'This year they're going to have a special emphasis on South American countries,' she said. 'We're trying to raise money for someone to go over there.'

'What for? I mean ... what to do?' I asked.

'Bring back more information about all the gaoled students and dissidents, and about the situation of the disappeared ... '

I nodded, pretending I understood what she meant. The words she was using had only the faintest meaning for me. Democracy, dissidents, politics; they were words I'd heard every now and again at school. It hadn't occurred to me until then that someone my own age would actually know how to use them.

'Anyway,' she went on with a grin, 'in the morning I didn't understand the lecturer, I got lost, I had no one to eat lunch with, and then in the afternoon I only managed to sell one badge. A complete disaster! I was meant to go to this social function for all the first-year Med students. But I cleared before it was over. I couldn't stand another minute in the place!'

'That's exactly what I did,' I said smiling.

We chatted on a bit about different things.

'You know, Carmel,' she said, leaning forward and touching my arm warmly at one stage, 'I liked you as soon as I saw you up close this morning ... ' That caught me completely unawares. I looked away, quite tongue-tied. 'I think we'll be fine here, don't you?'

'Here?' I repeated, not trusting myself to acknowledge what she was really saying.

'Yeah,' she went on blithely, 'I think we'll get on. Don't you?' I nodded and felt the heat rising in my face, but didn't care. I was suddenly so happy I couldn't have spoken even if I had thought of anything to say.

'I think it will be good,' I said, amazed to realise that I was speaking the truth. I *did* right at that moment think it would be good. Within the space of approximately fifteen minutes I'd changed my mind completely about everything. Suddenly the whole future seemed possible. I looked up and she was smiling at me.

'If we can manage to deal with Queen Katerina,' she added impishly, 'we'll be able to manage anything! How come we've never really met before?' she asked. 'In Manella, I mean. I'd never met you.'

I shrugged. 'Do you think we will manage her?' I said shyly, more for something to say than anything else.

'Of course!' she replied with gusto. 'She's all front. You wait! I know how to deal with her type.'

At around six o'clock Jude suggested we walk down to a nearby pizza restaurant and bring ourselves back something for tea. I shrugged and pretended to consider the idea. But inside I could hardly believe it was happening to me. I felt as though I was in a movie as I walked along the warm concrete street holding the square white box with my dinner inside. *So this is what it feels like*, I kept thinking. To have a friend! All through secondary school I'd got on all right with people. I mean I wasn't shunned or ostracised. But I only ever had one person to be with on a constant, one-to-one basis. Jenny Owens was a small, thin girl with long plaits and bad skin. But ours wasn't a talking relationship. We were the two gifted music students and we simply hung around together in between our lessons and practice. We talked music, what we'd heard, what we liked and, sometimes, vaguely what our plans were. We both expected to be studying music in one way or another, but even that we didn't talk about much. She was from a poor town family – her father was an invalid and her mother worked as a cleaner in the local hospital – but she never wanted to talk about her family, so we didn't. I heard that she did well in her exams and won her place to study music at the conservatorium. I tried to be glad for her, because I knew she deserved it. But deep down I was jealous. When I heard of her results I burst into tears. Somehow they made my own seem so much worse. But I made myself write her a note to wish her luck. We hadn't seen each other since school ended.

'Do you think you'll get homesick?' Jude asked me.

I nodded, shamefaced, hoping she wouldn't despise me for it, but unable to lie. After only an hour I'd at least had the brains to realise that there was something there in Jude that demanded the truth.

'Last night ... I wished I was home,' I said flatly, 'that I'd never come ... '

'But did you ... you know?' Her hands flew all over the place while she talked. 'Did you cry and *really* wish you were back there in old Manella?'

'Yes, I cried ... and really wished ... it.'

She frowned thoughtfully, as though she was thinking about what I'd said and found it very interesting.

'I didn't,' she said after a while. 'I was glad to get away.' Her tone caught me. Although there were a million things I could have said, wanted to ask, I kept quiet. I sensed a sadness in her, and it held me back.

'I missed my younger brothers actually,' I burst out, suddenly needing to talk, 'and Mum and Dad and ... the tree outside the back room.' I couldn't stop, in spite of feeling foolish. 'I just love trees ... and grass ... especially in autumn when the green underneath is just coming up through ... I walk sometimes for hours through the grass by myself ... singing, down to our creek. There's a little bridge that my grandfather made. Dad was only four and he remembers helping him ... he held the nails while my grandfather hammered them in ... '

I stopped suddenly and looked at her. She was smiling, making me feel it was perfectly all right to go on in this dumb way.

'I would have given anything for even one brother,' she said wistfully before I had a chance to apologise for blabbing on.

'What about now?'

'Well, I'd still like one ... '

'They're not at all what they're cracked up to be,' I said, 'I get really sick of mine. They're so bloody dirty and lazy ... I think of my brothers and I think of piles of dirty socks and washing up ... ' Jude gave one of her snorts of laughter.

'What's so funny?'

'The way you come out with stuff like that!'

'Stuff like what?'

'Country talk. You talk like a country person ... *not what they're cracked up to be* ... I love that!'

'Well, I'm a country girl,' I said somewhat defensively.

'So am I,' she said quickly, 'but it must be different actually living out on the farm. Has your Dad always been a farmer?'

'Yeah. And his father and his father, too. All the men in my family are farmers.'

'What about that hunky brother of yours?' she smiled. 'What's he do?'

I was proud that she knew about Vince.

'He works in the bush, too. Just not around home. But one

day he might come back. Everyone's hoping for that ... '

'You mean your mum and dad are hoping?'

I nodded. 'And me too.'

'Is there just you and your mum?' I asked tentatively. She gave a deep sigh.

'Yeah. There's just me and Mum.'

'You must get on,' I ventured. 'You must be close.'

'Yeah. We are. Pretty close ... '

We were home again by this stage. She didn't seem to want to talk any more about her mother so I let it drop. When we walked in, Katerina was there. She smiled at us as we passed her in the hall and went on with her phone conversation. I hoped that we weren't going to have to share our pizza with her, then immediately felt ashamed. Typical, I admonished myself. I was such a greedy pig. I was hardly even conscious of it any more, I just thought like a guts. I pulled out three plates, and knives and forks, thinking that it was no wonder I was so fat.

4

The days went by in a haze. I attended lectures, sitting by myself most of the time, on the edge of the crowd. I took the notes, the assignment sheets, and told myself I would read them carefully when I got back to the house. But I hardly ever did. Each day I got up and told myself that this would be the day when I would ask questions and find out what I needed to know. This would be the day when doing the course would suddenly make sense to me. But I couldn't somehow. I went every day for three weeks before it finally hit me that no one was actually going to notice if I stayed away.

My fellow students bored me senseless and, at the same time, scared the hell out of me. I would sit with a group of them sometimes in the university cafe, and I would try to listen and participate in their conversations, but my mind would wander. Everything they said sounded inane. I would find myself staring at someone's hands or watching the way their hair curled. I would wonder about them. What kind of families did they come from? What did they look like when they were asleep? I was nervous all the time when I was sitting with the others, drinking coffee and trying to be part of their breezy conversations. I developed the rather startling condition of nervous diarrhoea. Nearly every day it happened at least once. I'd be tagging along with a group, perhaps to have a coffee between lectures, and it would hit me, my breath would shorten and I'd feel an urgent, terrifying need to go to the toilet.

There was a young man in my group named Paul. He was tall, well-muscled and brown, and had a smart, sassy way about him and a quick tongue. He seemed to be everyone's favourite. Sometimes I would watch him and a kind of longing would build up inside me. If only he would notice me, I used to think, even just a little bit. If only he would say hello or have a joke with me the way he seemed to with everyone else. He almost always had something friendly or funny to say to everyone, but he never spoke to me. He would look past me when we met in the corridor or lecture theatre, as though I didn't exist.

I suppose, thinking back, it was around the time that he made it plain that he *had* noticed me that I started to pull out of the course. There were twenty in my tutorial group and about ten of us were sitting in the cafe after a two-hour morning class. I was feeling better than usual. The psychology lecturer had asked my opinion on something and I'd managed a halfway decent reply. There were two very pretty girls in the group, Kerri and Elizabeth, who'd been to the same school and were always together. They were both nice girls, in an ordinary kind of way. The both lived at home with their parents and had all the feminine trappings: stylish clothes, make-up, and high-pitched giggles, especially for the boys' jokes. But they went out of their way to be friendly to everyone. This day they brought their coffees over to the table where I was sitting and sat down on either side of me. I was trying, without success, to enjoy my coffee without sugar, and was aware of a happy little buzz inside me because I'd been able to answer the lecturer in front of all those people.

'You did well today,' Kerri said to me cheerfully, 'I wouldn't have known what to say if he'd asked me.' She was exaggerating and we both knew it. Even so, I appreciated her friendliness. Just at that moment there was a lull in the general conversation and the rest of the group at the table turned to look at us.

'Yeah. Well done, Carmel,' called Leon from the other end. 'How come you knew what to say?' He was a skinny, friendly boy, one of Paul's closest buddies. I blushed.

'I guess I'm just brainy,' I joked, trying to imitate the droll, bored tones of some of the ones in the group who got the laughs. No one exactly laughed at my reply, but there were a few smiles that made me think my answer hadn't been a complete disaster.

'Well, you'd have to have something going for you.' It was Paul's voice cutting in, low and deadly from the other end of the table. Everyone heard. I was so stunned I could hardly believe I'd heard right. I looked up at him, but he was staring impatiently at the group of girls who'd just come through the doors and were lining up waiting to be served. The others sitting around the table were stunned too. I saw Kerri and Elizabeth shoot anxious looks across me to each other. No one seemed to know what to say. My cheeks burned as I lifted the coffee cup again to my mouth. If only someone would say something! I didn't want their sympathy, I just wanted to be ignored. In spite of myself, tears of humiliation were beginning to form in my eyes. *Why do you have to be so nasty?* I wanted to yell. *Why? What have I ever done to you?*

Leon tried to relieve the situation by making light of it. 'Did you get out of bed on the wrong side today or something?' he asked Paul, giving him a playful poke in the ribs. But Paul simply sat there, his eyes now downcast, glowering. A bolt of anxiety shot straight through my misery as I watched his face twitch a couple of times and then set into a tight frown. He was either going to apologise or say something worse.

'Those exercise videos are *everywhere*,' he said finally, flinging the words into the air, not looking at me or anyone else as he got up. I stared down at myself, my blue rumpled T-shirt and thick legs encased in the new dark jeans I'd bought to disguise my size. The big sweaty feet in the ugly brown sandals.

'There's no need for anyone to be fat these days,' he went on. 'Sorry, but I can't help it. I find fat people disgusting.' He slung the last line at us loudly before disappearing through the glass doors. I don't think I breathed, in or out, for about a minute. I was in shock rather than pain, although I knew that would come later. It was as though I'd been hit with a hard fist between the ribs.

In their own way every one of the people who remained at the table with me tried to be kind. Kerri and Elizabeth moved closer.

'Don't take any notice,' Kerri whispered, 'he can be a pig.'

'He's a complete dickhead!' Elizabeth said, quite loudly. There was a general murmur of agreement. I felt a few tears spill over and down my burning cheeks.

A blonde girl named Sharon, usually cool and offhand with me, squeezed my fingers as she passed over a few tissues.

'He's a moron,' she said confidently. 'I should know, I went through school with him. He was a moron in Year 7 too!' We all laughed at that, even me, through my tears. A couple of the boys who'd been sitting with Paul down the other end got up and collected their bags.

'Well, I've got a lecture now,' said one.

'Yeah. Me too.'

But on their way out each of them touched my shoulder in either a quick pat or a squeeze of support.

'He's a dickhead,' Leon murmured, leaning down for a couple of seconds, 'don't worry about it.'

'Yeah. You're all right, Carmel,' said another, 'don't let him get to you.' Their kindness reminded me so much of my brothers that I was overcome with an incredibly strong pang of homesickness. My brothers' names were on the tip of my tougue. I wanted to shout them out and sob. I wanted all these people to know about Vince; that I had a handsome brother who loved me. But I nodded to them all and tried to smile as I got up slowly and collected my bag.

'I've got to go to the toilet before History,' I said, with as much dignity as I could summon up, 'see you all then.'

'Yeah, see you, Carmel!'

'Good on ya, Carmel,' one of the boys called after me encouragingly. 'We'll see you there, hey?'

But I didn't make it to History that afternoon, or the next day. In fact I didn't come back to uni until the following week. And by then it was too late. I'd discovered the hypnotic pleasures of public transport; trams in particular were my downfall. I would get on to my morning tram for uni, telling myself severely that this day I must get out at the right stop. But at the last moment somehow I couldn't move. I would find myself still sitting there. The conductor would pull the cord, and the cumbersome thing would be rolling forward again. Then a rush of pure unadulterated elation would bolt through me. *I am free for one more day.* Once that stop was passed I never thought about going back, until the end of the day when I'd arrive home exhausted from my travels and alarmed that I'd missed another day of my course. But that moment on the tram was euphoric. Once the indecision was over I would find myself smiling and looking forward like an eager child to my day in the city.

It was exhilarating just to hop down and become one among the bustling crowd. So many different people! Old shambling people with walking-sticks, stern, spry policemen, weary shoppers, harried office-workers, and gangs of bored skinheads that I hardly dared look at. I loved it all. I would get off at the Swanston and Bourke streets intersection, aware of the varied, odd-shaped bodies moving off in separate directions around me. I'd wander off in any direction, maybe following someone for a little way if I liked their shoes, then switching to someone else who had a pretty baby in a pram. For the first hour or two it was blissful. Like being a little kid let out of a dull, dark old schoolroom with a crabby teacher for an unexpected half-day holiday in the sun. Off I'd go, prowling through the ground floors of the big stores, David Jones and Myer, Daimaru and Georges, my eyes feasting on all the lovely things: the pretty packages of hosiery and stationery, the fancy French make-up and perfumes, the fabulous bargain tables filled with shiny shoes and jewellery. A lot of people hate the music in those places. But I loved its bland breezy nothingness, which demanded nothing of me. I'd find myself whistling and humming the tunes under my breath, gradually lulling myself into a relaxed state of weightlessness. Like floating in water. I never thought of anything while I was checking out those stores, except how nice something looked or felt. After wandering through the ground floor I would either head up the escalator to the ladies' fashions or lingerie, or come out into one of the back streets.

By around midday my craving for food would be intense. Eating was the best part of the day. After I'd eaten, my mood would steadily decline until it was time for me to catch the tram home again. But the half hour during which I would wander around, smelling all the lovely, greasy, spicy smells from the cafes and restaurants, trying to decide what food I would buy that day, was wonderful. Chinese spring rolls one day and maybe a hot Lebanese felafel the next. Things I'd hardly heard of at home. I would eat as I walked along, my fingers tearing off a piece of hot salty fish, seasoned bread or spicy meat, loving the fact that I was indulging myself in the anonymous crowd. No one here knew me and I didn't have to feel self-conscious or guilty about eating. I was just one more fat person in the street. There were a lot of us about.

Gradually I dared to start trying things on and I suppose that's when everything took a turn for the worse. Most of the really expensive clothing didn't come in my size, but the cheaper labels did, and when I finally decided to brave the lady waiting with her little plastic numbers at the door leading into the fitting rooms, a rather strange addiction began. Strange because I couldn't work out why I was doing it. It hardly ever brought me any pleasure to see myself in the clothes. Most of them I certainly couldn't afford, but more importantly the small bright rooms were merciless in the way they showed me to myself. All the imperfections seemed to magnify under the harsh fluorescent light. I would take perhaps five or six garments into the cubicle and begin the painful business of taking off my own clothes and trying them all on. During the process I would catch glimpses of the unsightly rolls of fat around my midriff, my plump arms and heavy thighs, and a sense of desperation would overcome me. Perhaps this next shirt or dress or skirt might make me look different? Occasionally it would. And if it wasn't too expensive I would walk away with the item wrapped in a bag under my arm feeling excited, but alarmed too, at the money I'd spent. Vince had put a lump sum in the bank for me. It was six months' rent plus an extra few hundred. Nearly two thousand of his hard-earned dollars. There really wasn't the money there to spend on clothes.

Very occasionally I would venture into one of the smaller boutiques, always making sure there was at least one other person browsing. I was terrified of the women in charge of those places. Even when I could see that they were clearly old and plain, they somehow always seemed perfect. And they had eyes like hawks.

'May I help you, dear?' with a faint sneer, the eyes flicking up over my size and cheap, unfashionable clothes. They seemed to be able to tell that I was an impostor; somehow they *knew* how I was frittering away my days and wasting my brother's money.

Every now and again I thought I saw one of the people in my group from college and a flash of panic would jolt through me.

I didn't tell Jude about skipping my lectures. Whenever she asked how things were going I just made out everything was fine. Most nights we'd have a couple of hours together making dinner and eating our meal before she'd excuse herself and go into her room to study. She must have assumed that I had heaps of work to do too, and I never bothered to enlighten her. Sometimes she wouldn't come home until very late, and on those nights I'd find myself wandering around the house feeling desperate and lonely. I never said anything about these times to her, though. I was determinded not to come across as a complete loser. And it was easy to evade her questions about the people and activities I was part of. I was able to make up a few things that seemed to ring true. I thought that if she knew about the *real me*, the person who had no friends, or interests, or future to speak of, then she wouldn't want to be friends with me any more. I was too shy to question her about her life at university. But I found myself praying that it wouldn't become so enticing that she'd forget to come home.

It was the skirt in David Jones that launched me into my shoplifting phase, although I didn't end up stealing that particular skirt. It was made of pure woven cotton, a tiny black and red flower print that was cut on the cross. It fitted me perfectly and flattered my figure. It also cost over three hundred dollars. I knew from the start that there was no way I could afford to pay for it, and because all the expensive items in this part of the store were fitted with electronic devices, I knew that there was no easy way to steal it either. Had there been a way, I would have. It shocked me at first to realise that. Knowing I could steal separated me from my life back in Manella, the life I'd had with my simple, old-fashioned, boring family. This new idea of myself rattled and unnerved me, but excited me too. Part of me wanted to see how far I could go. The longing to make myself into something different from them made it possible to suspend the simple moral code I'd been brought up to follow.

So I began to steal small items like lipsticks and cheap blouses, packets of stockings and perfume. The odd thing was that I was always too nervous and guilty to pick the right item. If it was lipstick I'd get the wrong colour; with socks and stockings I'd get the wrong size. I was not a casual or brazen thief. My heart would pound like mad as I headed for the doorway, and I never quite had the courage to check properly, and make sure I got the size, colour and style that I really wanted. It was more than greed. The tingling sense of dread that would fill me when I walked into a store, knowing I was there to steal something. The rush of relief when I managed to control my fear – sometimes I was unable to do this and would leave 'empty-handed'. Then my heart's crazy thumping panic as I walked back out the door. The stolen item always seemed to be burning a hole in my bag or pocket. With every step I half-expected to feel a firm pull on my arm.

'Excuse me, Miss. We have reason to believe ... '

I'd walk on up the street, one block and then two, far enough to know I was safe, then a wave of elation would pulsate through me. I had pushed fate and won again. It was the danger, I suppose, that hooked me in.

The phase went on for about three weeks and it stopped as abruptly as it had begun. I'd gone into the ground floor of Myer, planning to steal a silk scarf to tie around my hair in the way I'd noticed was fashionable. I was already sweating slightly, fingering the colourful scarves, trying this time to pick the right one, when suddenly there was a commotion behind me. People stepped back, staring. Two policemen were escorting a tearful girl around my age through the store towards the manager's office.

'Shoplifting,' murmured one of the shop assistants behind the counter, by way of explanation to the people waiting to be served. A woman standing next to me nodded and pursed her lips disapprovingly. I watched the young policemen's expressions, so bored and contemptuous, and I was horribly fascinated. *That could be me!* The trio disappeared behind a door and I walked out of the store knowing I'd never risk it again.

Although I wasn't tempted to steal again, the shops started to lose their appeal. I found myself going further out on the tram; sometimes to South Yarra or South Melbourne. One day I went right down to Port Melbourne, where the ships from all around the world docked. There were big, ugly, rusty-red ships from China and the Middle East. There were bales of wool being loaded into the huge hold of a Russian ship. I was excited to think that some of that wool may have come from home. I walked up and down the docks watching the sailors, intimidated by their blatant stares and the occasional wolf-whistle and crude invitation to 'come aboard', but unable to curb my deep curiosity. The ships had caught my imagination. All was surely not lost, I would think. There would be a niche for someone like me somewhere in the world. I fantasised about stowing myself aboard and waking up the next morning in another country.

Then I found the more arty, bohemian end of the city. Up over Victoria Street to Nicholson and Brunswick streets. It was here I 'discovered' the cafe society I'd only heard vaguely about. I would look longingly through glass doors and windows at the groups of young people inside. At the girls mostly. They fascinated me. They were all thin and seemed at first to be dressed identically too; in black, tight pants or short skirts, and skimpy, sombre silk blouses. Most were beautiful, with white faces, blood-red lips and close-cropped hair. And they all seemed to know what they were doing. *What do they do?* From morning to late afternoon the cafes were packed with them. The men were often just as handsome as the girls, hair tied back into ponytails, wearing worn jeans and old vests over uni-roned shirts. Did they study or work or just ... exist to look so wonderful?

Once I dared to open the door of one of those places. I'd spied an empty wooden table in one corner and suddenly feeling brave I ventured in. The door had closed behind me, so I knew I couldn't turn back without feeling worse. I hurried to the little table and sat down, aware that a few pairs of eyes had followed me. I picked up the menu and breathed in, loving the musty smells around me: cigarettes and coffee and garlic and oil. Mint too, and other herbs, sweet and tangy.

Almost immediately a tall young man of about twenty came over to me and smiled. He had a short, grubby-white piece of material tied around his jeans as an apron, which was the only thing that let me know he was a waiter.

'What can I get you?' He was a plain boy, with uneven teeth and bad skin. But his gentle voice and friendly, brisk manner made my terror subside a little.

'I'll just have coffee, thanks,' I said, feeling a deep flush begin on my neck.

'Of course,' he said, 'what kind?' My mind immediately went blank. Floundering, I opened my mouth hoping something would simply arrive on my tongue.

'What kinds are there ...?' I whispered, deeply ashamed. The heat in my face began to pulsate.

He looked away to make out he hadn't seen.

'Cappuccino, long black, flat white ... anything you like,' he said, giving me a friendly smile. His hands were large and knobbly; not at all like the hands of the boys at college. They were strong and practical like a country boy's. It was on the tip of my tongue to ask him where he was from, but I didn't dare.

'Oh, cappuccino!' I exclaimed in relief, a little too loudly, and he nodded and we both smiled at each other.

'Won't be a minute.' He picked the menu out of my hands and I watched him dance off between the tables towards the counter like some kind of long-legged, agile animal. I relaxed a little, sat back and looked around. There was one other man by himself reading a book, but everyone else seemed to be with someone. Small groups of three or four at each table. I watched the way they lolled around, laughing occasionally, talking in low voices. The general buzz of talk was cheering. New people arrived, others left, palms were smacked together, cheeks kissed, hellos and goodbyes abounded. There was a wonderful refined easiness in the way they sat and moved and spoke and walked. It was as though they all belonged to a secret club. I sat and simply absorbed this exotic and wonderful world and wished with all my heart that I could belong to it.

Underneath the chatter I could hear music playing. Suddenly the volume rose and I recognised the aria. *That's Puccini. From* Turandot. *But what's it called?* I strained towards the nearest speaker, forgetting where I was as the music washed through me. When it finished there was a crackling sound and then nothing. I ordered more coffee, but was too shy to ask the waiter to put the tape on again.

As I sat there drinking my coffee, the few operas that I'd been introduced to by my music teachers over the years began to gnaw around the edges of my imaginings. *La Bohème. The Marriage of Figaro. Carmen.* The old favourites. Tales of lust and misery, high passion and despair. A song from *Tosca* swung into my mind with a kind of blazing force that skittled everything else away. I was suddenly humming inside! The cafe was making me remember, helping to galvanise my love for that music. It had been sleeping now for weeks. I hadn't played the piano since my first night in the Fitzroy house. With a jolt I thought, *I have almost forgotten about music.* I became conscious of my head sitting squarely on my shoulders, my heart beating in my chest, and my toes, all ten of them, twitching in the sweaty grime of my old, worn sandals. I remembered what it was like to sing. Vividly. To open my mouth and push out the notes; make them soar and dip and swing out into the air. And remembering that set up a longing in me.

I walked out of the restaurant full of a strange melancholy, longing to be part of everything I wasn't. While I'd been inside the sky had clouded over and the light had faded dramatically. The nippy breeze brought up goosebumps on my bare arms and so, shivering a little and clutching myself, I lowered my head and made for the tram stop. Having neither umbrella nor proper shoes, I wanted to be home before it began raining. It must have been after six o'clock because the shops were beginning to light up and fresh crowds were roaming around the bars and restaurants looking for somewhere to eat.

About three metres from the tram stop I stopped suddenly and turned around. Music was pulsating out from the side street I'd just passed. Loud, brash and inviting. Ignoring my sore feet, I walked quickly back to the side street and towards the back garden of an old pub. There were perhaps fifteen tables set outside on the lawn around a small stage, and masses of people were sitting there, in the half-light, some on the grass, drinking, smoking and talking, lolling back and listening to the band. There was a strong brass section, with a trumpet and clarinet and I think even a horn, plus drums, keyboards and guitar. But my eyes were on the singer. Only a girl, really. Well, perhaps in her mid-twenties. She was wearing a fitted black dress and her hair was flung back; when she twisted around I could see it almost reached her waist. Her voice was okay, but she was singing in an awkward way that I couldn't identify. At that stage my entire musical knowledge could be slotted under either classical or church music, folk or bush ballads. And, of course, the rock music that I'd heard on the radio and television. I listened to the uneven rhythms and strange, changing tempo. Initially I thought they were incompetent, but I couldn't tear myself away. I stood just inside the fence and drank it all in. There was something ... Of course I'd read about jazz, but I don't think I'd actually heard it being played. It was hypnotic – and nerve-racking. Where was the melody line? And the rhythm? The girl seemed to be singing up and down a couple of octaves, but I couldn't really follow it.

I stayed for perhaps an hour, leaning against the wall, the sound growing on me by the minute. The darkness deepened. A couple of simple spotlights were hooked up over the stage, and the many cigarette tips glowed brightly. Every time the girl did something different with her voice I was mentally testing it out on myself; what I knew my own voice could do. *I could do that*, I thought as I listened to her, *only I could do it better . . . I'd just stop at that high point and then I'd trickle down the scale . . . Ah, that was nice . . .* One minute she was deep and soulful, and the next she was tripping around the notes like a kid on roller-skates. I watched the people ebb and flow around the bar and tables, as the music went on over their conversations. Before I knew it the whole thing was over. Disappointed I watched them organise the packing up, feeling oddly let down. I was just getting the hang of it and it had to finish.

A sudden burst of curiosity had me walking closer to the band members as they packed up. I wanted to know who they were and more about the music they were playing. I took a deep breath and sidled over to one of the musicians.

'That was good,' I said, 'I enjoyed it.' He looked up with a smile. I was surprised to see he wasn't a young man at all. Up close I could see that his hair was thinning out. A gold front tooth flashed and there were wrinkles around his light-blue eyes.

'Glad you liked it,' he said.

'Is it . . . er, is it jazz?' I asked, then immediately felt stupid. I needed to know, but it sounded so dumb. Like I was a hick who knew nothing. But he didn't seem to think it an odd question at all. He shrugged and rested a sneakered foot on one of the speakers, then bent over and retied the lace.

'Yeah. Mainly jazz. Bit of blues.' Then he looked lazily up at the metal-grey sky. 'Hey, it didn't rain on us!' I looked up and felt a shot of adrenalin zip through me.

'I play too,' I said shyly, 'and sing.' He looked at me and this time smiled in a very friendly way.

'Do you?'

'Yeah.' Once again I felt like an idiot, but I didn't seem able to stop myself. 'I've learnt for years . . . '

'So what do you play?' he asked.

'Piano. And I, er, sing a bit.'

He nodded thoughtfully and opened his mouth to say something else, but the girl singer was tapping his elbow. He turned around.

'See you tomorrow then, Alan,' she said with a smile that completely cut me out.

'Yeah, see ya, mate.' She waved and was gone. He watched her leave for a few moments and then turned back to me.

'Now what were you saying?' he said. But by this stage my bumbling self had come back. I gulped, aware of the heat climbing up my neck.

'I play piano,' I whispered, beginning to edge away, 'and sing.' He took a step towards me.

'Well good!' he laughed in a genuine, warm way. 'Where do you work?'

'How do you mean?' I was wishing like mad I'd never started the conversation. What in the name of God did I think I was doing just going up to a strange man and telling him I played piano?

'I mean, do you have a job playing or singing anywhere?' he explained kindly.

'Er, no,' I mumbled and took a couple more steps away. 'Anyway thanks again. I enjoyed it . . . ' I gave him a stupid little wave, a smile of apology, then turned and began to walk off.

'Hey, hang on!' he called. I turned back to find him digging in his pocket for something. I waited, aware that my breath had become short. What did he want? Perhaps I should just run . . . He held out a small white card for me to take. I walked back and took it with a gulp, not meeting his eye.

'That's our name and everything,' he said, 'we're playing at the Prince Patrick next Saturday night, if you want to come. Bring some friends.'

'Well, thank you,' I said, taking the card. The word 'Fandangle' in red ink was at the top, then the names of six musicians and their instruments, and a contact phone number.

'I could maybe introduce you to a few people,' he went on. 'They might know of singing or keyboard work going ... ' I looked up at him questioningly.

'Er, thanks, but I, er ... wasn't really looking for ... '

'I thought you might have been interested in some work,' he grinned and it suddenly occurred to me that he found my nervousness interesting. 'It depends on whether you're any good, I suppose.'

I smiled, embarrassed, but said nothing.

'*Are* you any good?' he grinned again.

I took a breath and looked away. What could I say? I didn't know if I was really pleased that he was taking the time to be nice to me or acutely anxious. Probably both. But knowing that didn't make it any easier. I shrugged.

'Yes. I'm good,' I said. At least I *think* that's what I said. Something like that just came out from somewhere. He moved closer, stood right in front of me in fact, so I had to look him in the eyes. He was skinny and old and I could smell the sweat through his tatty black T-shirt.

'Hey,' he said softly, 'that's not good enough, girl. You gotta look me right in the eye and say it like this.' He took a deep breath and growled loudly, *'Of course I'm good, ya fuckwit!'*

I jumped. Then he laughed and I laughed too. He turned around to finish his packing, and I walked back out onto the street.

I was buoyed up when I got home that evening, strangely excited about everything. It wasn't as though I was actually planning to go to that pub the following Saturday. I mean, I didn't even know where it was, and I hadn't ever been inside a pub in my life. The very idea of playing in a band – any kind of band – was ... well, it was just too far-fetched even to think about. The truth was that all my vague yearnings for a career in music had no context at all. I was dismayed to realise that I had only one clear image in my head. Me, dressed in some voluminous evening gown in perhaps red or black silk, one that would hide my size anyway, sitting at a shiny grand piano in an enormous concert hall, playing ... *playing what?* Well, I supposed I'd be playing some beautiful piece by Bach or Mozart. There would be the audience, huge, well-dressed and appreciative, clapping at the end of each piece and calling for more. I don't think I'd ever been to such a concert myself, although I'd seen and enjoyed them on TV. On the tram journey home I thought back to the conversation I'd had with the musician. His eyes had been glassy blue and very clear. The wrinkles around them were smile lines, really. He had not been condescending. He had taken me seriously. I felt good about having dared to speak to him.

5

We had a brilliant time the following night, Jude and me. One that cemented us as real friends. By this stage we were both getting on all right with Katerina. The three of us were polite to each other. Quite friendly even. But Katerina was always on her way out, or coming home late looking exhausted. It made it hard to get to know her. The truth was she intimidated me and I was always glad when she was out. And although Jude often joked wryly about making a date to see Katerina so she could hear about her amazing social life, I could tell at times that her presence tended to constrain Jude, too.

I'd been in the city most of the day, feeling increasingly bored and frustrated, but on impulse I'd bought a CD. Katerina had installed a really good hi-fi system in our first week in the house, but I hardly ever listened to anything because I hated her choice in music. She had heaps of CDs, but they were all that middle-of-the-road stuff: Billy Joel, Whitney Houston, Rick Price, Madonna. That kind of music leaves me cold. I would rather listen to a grunge band like Pearl Jam or REM, or even some heavy-metal bands, than the bland, over-produced stuff she obviously went for. That morning I'd decided that, even though I couldn't really afford it, I would start my own music collection. I walked into the lounge room and looked at Jude, who was sitting quietly by the window reading a book.

'You mind if I put something on?' I said a little tentatively. We'd never talked seriously about music. She might hate opera. She looked up and grinned from where she was on the couch.

'What ya got?'

'Dame Kiri ... in concert,' I said, a little defensively, 'er, it was cheap.'

'Great! Whack it on!'

I slipped the CD on then lay on my back on the floor and closed my eyes. Neither of us spoke until we'd heard the whole thing through. It was outrageous stuff. Completely over the top. So rich and full and complete that within a minute I was overwhelmed, transported. My head had swung right away from my own life and into the heavy dramatic world of the music. When it ended I still lay there, almost breathless, forgetting Jude was even in the room, feeling as though I was in an enormous, warm, delightfully fragrant bubble-bath. I was slipping and sliding around in all those soaring crescendos and spellbinding arias. I was aching with it. The notes were still vibrating around that little room well after the silence had descended; beating at me through the pores of my skin. This is *Life*, I kept thinking, Life with a capital L. This is what it's all about. Nothing else matters.

'Here, have a drink.' Her voice startled me. I sat up, shook my head a little, and took the cup of tea Jude was offering me.

'That was great,' she said.

'Yeah,' I sighed.

'You should be doing that,' she said simply.

'What?'

'Singing.'

'Yeah.'

'So, why don't you sing something now?'

'What, here?' I said in surprise. 'But I'd be such a let-down after that ... '

'I know that, Carmel!' she grinned. 'After Kiri we both know you'll sound like a howling dog, but ... I'd still like to hear you.'

I laughed and got up and went to the piano. I *did* feel like singing. And what's more I suddenly knew I didn't have to carry on with a whole lot of apologies with Jude. So I was out of practice. Big deal! I ran my fingers through a few scales, up and down the piano, then launched into a French love song that was popular at weddings. My voice was a bit croaky at first, but after a few lines it warmed up. I remembered the last time I'd sung in Manella – I think it was at the old people's home. How when I'd started there'd been some noise in the room; shuffles and a few whispered conversations. As I went on the silence had deepened until everyone was listening. That was always a wonderful feeling, hearing the silence suddenly shift downwards another notch, into a deeper concentration. When that song ended I started on a rather difficult piece by Schubert that I'd learnt last year. Halfway through it I thought, *Ah stuff it!* I wasn't playing it very well and anyway this wasn't the time. There was so much to play. A few old folk classics tumbled forward into my mind. 'The Night They Drove Old Dixie Down'. I opened my mouth and let the words come rolling out. A couple of verses from a bush ballad, then Roy Orbison. 'The Great Pretender' and the Beatles. 'Let It Be' was one of my favourites. After the first couple of lines, Jude began to harmonise with me. Her voice was thin, but strong, and she sang the harmony well.

'Let it be, let it be, let it be, let it be. Whisper words of wisdom . . .'

We caught each other's eye every now and again as we sang, pleased at how we sounded. On and on we went, getting livelier and more confident with each new song. When I couldn't think of anything else I started on a ponderous old hymn that was a favourite of mine, 'Nearer my God to Thee', and was surprised when she was able to join in on that too.

'I didn't think you'd know that,' I said when we'd finished.

'I know a lot of hymns,' she said, then added shyly, 'Want to hear this one in Spanish?'

'Sure.' I knew by the change in her expression that she was letting me into a private side of herself. She ran off quickly to her room and came back with a guitar.

'This one is about the pain of the world ... ' she said sombrely. 'It's a kind of prayer asking for understanding of the pain of the world.' I nodded. She giggled as she tuned the instrument. 'There are a lot of Spanish songs about the pain of the world!'

'So get on with it!'

It was a fantastic song. The first Spanish song I'd really listened to. Its sad rhythm complemented the despair and longing of the lyrics in the subtlest way. It put me into a place I'd never been before. It was something like being in a big church at night with candles alight all around me. It made me yearn to be there; yearn for the sense of being born again that I always experienced on Easter Sunday when I got to sing all those songs of rebirth. Jude had only translated a few lines, but they were enough. I could feel the rest.

We went on, taking it in turns. She taught me a few bits and pieces of Spanish songs and I taught her some other songs too.

'Have you ever had a boyfriend?' Jude asked suddenly. I was back lying on the floor, gingerly taking a few sips from the glass of wine she'd poured for me, listening to her picking the guitar. I'd hardly ever tasted wine before and I couldn't decide if I liked it or not. By this stage the night had come down and there were a few messy plates between us, covered with the remains of our meal: fresh bread and cheese, chopped tomatoes and ham.

'No,' I said, 'and I can't imagine I ever will.'

'*What?*'

I turned to look at her and shrugged. She'd been sitting up against the couch on the floor, but she suddenly set the guitar down and sat up straight as though something had bitten her.

'Why do you say that?' she demanded reproachfully.

'I just can't ... ' I repeated, annoyed. Did she want me to spell it out?

'But *why?*' she asked. I looked at her and couldn't help smiling. She was genuinely bewildered. Had she honestly not noticed my size-eighteen figure, my continual blushing, my awkwardness, my absolute inability to do anything much, to get anything right? Even the fact that the first recording I buy in my entire life is of an *opera* star in her fifties! I mean what kind of eighteen-year-old girl does that? I couldn't even put a sentence together if I was nervous. Then I remembered that I'd never told her about skipping my classes, or about my furtive addiction to the city. I'd kept quiet about so much.

'Well ... ' I began, wondering how I might put it without sounding sorry for myself, 'I mean, what sort of guy would look at someone as *fat* as me, for a start?' She took a sharp breath in and then threw her head back and closed her eyes as though she was thinking hard about something. I got up and changed the CD, wishing that the conversation hadn't taken this turn. *The Flutes of the Andes* began to play and I sat back to listen, fascinated by the sound. I hadn't heard anything like it before and I wondered how they combined that deeply rhythmic, sensual feel with the airiness of the flutes.

'And don't tell me I could go on a diet,' I added, sitting forward, 'I've tried so many diets. From the time I was ten. They never last. I haven't got the willpower ... I can't stick at them.'

'I wouldn't dream of telling you to go on a diet!' Jude retorted sharply over the music, 'I think you're ... *really sexy!*' My mouth fell open in surprise and I began to laugh. 'And I think there would be a lot of guys around who'd find you really attractive, too,' she went on.

'You're serious?'

'Deadly.'

She obviously had no idea what it was like. Paul's comments suddenly flew back at me. 'Sorry, but ... I find fat people disgusting.' There was a stab of fresh pain as I remembered that day, the way he'd said it in front of all those people. But really he was only one person, and not a very important one either. Just the latest in a line of people throughout my whole life who thought they could say all kinds of things, take all kinds of liberties with me, because I was fat. All the names I'd been called through primary school – fatso, brickhouse, slug and ten-ton tessie, just to mention a few – that was only the beginning. Through most of high school there were dismissive, cruel and sometimes, even I had to admit, really humorous puns, jokes and comments made about my size. I would get advice about diets from women I hardly knew in shops, at sports meetings, then more advice from well-meaning teachers about tactics and strategies I could use to lose weight. Then there was all the stuff I didn't quite hear, said under the breath, the sly smiles and sniggers that weren't exactly meant for me, but that I heard anyway. You pick up a sixth sense for insults when you're fat. So much of it came from boys too. And people think that only girls are bitchy!

'I mean it, Carmel ...'

'Yeah, Jude,' I shouted stupidly, suddenly wanting to cry. 'Sure! And pigs might fly, and ...'

'I'm serious!' she cut in, sitting up and looking at me with those intense brown eyes. 'I think you're very beautiful! Your hair, your face ... Your body is big. But I think all your curves are beautiful. You're like one of those women in those old paintings. Go and look in the art gallery sometime!' She sounded almost angry. 'Look in the art books. At the paintings from centuries ago. They're just like you!'

The flutes played in the air between us like lovely chimes on a windy, sad day.

'Well, thanks,' I managed to mutter after a while, then turned away trying to concentrate on the music, 'but I can't really see it myself.'

'Well, start looking,' she snapped. I turned to her, surprised by her sharp tone.

'You gotta start thinking about how beautiful and talented

you are, Carmel,' she said quickly. 'Do you want a refill?' I held out my glass.

'You see,' she said with a quick grin, 'I'm planning for us – for both of us – to have a good time this year!' I smiled and sipped my wine and tapped my foot down in time with the music to indicate I didn't want to talk any more.

'*And* you know about love, too,' she said, 'I know you do.' At first I thought I'd heard wrong. I knew nothing about love. I had never even had a boyfriend. I had never been on a date, or felt that any guy had ever found me attractive.

'What do you mean?' I asked.

'You've got . . . a lot of love in you,' she said slowly, staring into her glass. I couldn't tell whether she was uncomfortable now or not. 'I have, too,' she went on, still frowning and looking down. 'That's why I can recognise it in you.'

In the early hours of the next morning, when I was beginning to feel sleepy, but we were still singing and there were still more things to talk about, I dragged them all out – those words she'd said – and went over them again. And the more I thought about what she'd said, the more I was aware of this . . . this little *something* starting to kick itself alive inside my chest. It felt like a tough little worm, a flower that didn't need much sunlight, a hard spike with a diamond point, pushing through all those layers of concrete that were packed so neatly and heavily over my heart. That night I became aware that I had a new life springing up under all that stone. The *inside* of me wanted to get out!

Jude played different tracks from a few CDs, then we'd choose one to learn. She'd pick the tunes out on her guitar and I'd do what I could with them on the piano. All the while she was explaining what the words meant and how they should be phrased. I just loved it.

There were so many firsts for me that night. It was the first time I'd stayed up until morning. The first time I'd had wine. It was the first time I'd heard that South American music;

those plaintive love songs and crying guitars; the songs about struggle and pain, about rivers and mountains and heroes; that mad gypsy sound of flutes and pipes and drums. The first time I was not too self-conscious to dance. That night we both *had* to dance. Round and round the lounge room and up and down the hallway. Laughing and singing and shouting out. And it was the first time someone had told me I was beautiful. And the odd thing about *that* was that it felt like I'd known it all along.

I woke up around midday that day, gloriously dizzy and trying to work out why I'd had such a good time. If you wanted to get objective then it didn't amount to that much. Just a couple of tipsy girls, eating, laughing, talking and dancing, and the music of course; the playing and the listening. But it was more than that. Sometimes your life just changes and you don't know why. A kind of shift happens and it doesn't seem to have that much to do with whether you want it to happen or not. When I look back I know that night with Jude was somehow the end of one part and the beginning of something new.

I knew it at the time, too. I was standing by the window watching the watery daybreak start edging into my room. We'd said goodnight and joked about how ratshit we'd look when we'd see each other next.

'I hope the Queen won't come home! She always looks so bloody perfect. Even if she's been out all night.'

'I know,' I groaned.

'My eyes will be hanging out like golf balls.'

'I get these *bags* under mine,' I laughed. It was true. If I didn't get enough sleep I looked like I was about forty-nine the next day.

'So what.'

'Yeah, so what.'

'We'll both still look bloody fanstastic!'

'Right,' I laughed as I pushed my door open, 'night then, Jude!'

'Yeah. *Good morning*, Carmel!'

I went over to the window and pulled the blind down and felt the half-darkness close in around me. A bit of light was still coming in around the edges of the blind and I turned to watch this lovely square of pink colour flickering on the wall near the foot of my bed. I stretched my hand onto it, my five long, white fingers, and I remember thinking, *Well, that's over, eighteen years, three months and fifteen days. From now on it will be different.*

I wasn't even that excited. I just knew.

I slept naked that night for the first time in my life. I threw off every bit of clothing and slipped my big curvy body between those cool cotton sheets. It was the only way I could think of to mark the event. I went to sleep deciding I'd go to the art gallery the very next day and stare at the paintings of women who had bodies like mine. And I felt really good about it and glad to be where I was. Very glad to be alive.

6

It was almost Easter. Mum had written a long letter and sent me the fare home. She said that they were all looking forward to seeing me and would be there to meet the train. I wanted desperately to go. I was longing to see the house, the twins; I wanted to see the paddocks and climb the old stone wall into the overgrown orchard and lie under my quince tree. It was a physical longing for the place as much as for my family. But a big part of me was dreading it too. I was terrified of getting sucked back into that world. Would I continue to lie about my course? Even if I didn't tell them now, they'd know within a couple of months. My money was running out. Each day I planned to look for work, but I allowed anything that came up to divert me from making the all-important first phone calls. If I came clean with them I knew there would be a showdown and the upshot would be that I'd never get back to the city. So I was pulled between a longing to go home and a terror of doing so.

And then Katerina came up with an invitation that would change my life in a most remarkable way.

It was a Sunday afternoon. Illapu, my favourite of the South American bands Jude had introduced me to, were playing loudly in the lounge room and Jude and I were singing along as we made crumpets with honey and laughed about the old Italian man next door. He'd come in earlier that day with a gift of a bucket of apricots from his tree, but had used the event to regale us with his view on what was wrong with the world. In the end we'd virtually had to push him out the door.

Katerina bounded in excitedly. It was the first time we'd seen her in a couple of days.

'Hello, you two!'

'Oh hi,' I said, 'you want a crumpet?' She shook her head.

'No thanks, I'm actually not stopping ...' She began opening kitchen cupboards, pulling things out and rummaging wildly through plates and dusty dishes at the back, searching for something. Jude watched her for a while and then turned around to me with a raised eyebrow.

'So what are you looking for?' she finally asked. Katerina mumbled something, but she obviously didn't want to explain. She let out a loud sigh of relief when she came across a small notepad.

'Gotcha! Oh great!'

The relief on her face was almost tangible. I was standing up at this stage, over near the sink, putting fresh boiling water in the teapot, so I could see that what she had was a doctor's prescription pad. The white cover and yellow border at the top of the front page when she opened it were unmistakable.

'Have you got someone waiting outside?' I asked, trying again to be friendly.

'Yes,' she said, 'he's a guy I've been seeing a bit of,' then she looked down at us both with a coy smile.

'You both must meet him sometime,' she added.

We nodded politely. I saw a twinge around Jude's mouth as she took a bite of her crumpet and knew she'd make a joke about it as soon as Katerina left.

'Oh God. The boyfriend, no less! I can hardly wait.'

Katerina was about to run out, but hesitated. I looked up at her by the door and had a momentary feeling that I was actually *inside* her wavering state of mind. I realised with a short rush of surprise that she didn't want to go. We probably seemed relaxed and ordinary in a way that she was not. Judging by the flush on her cheeks and her bright manner, the guy she was with was probably anything but ordinary. It might feel strange to come home and see that the people you live with have a life there in the house, quite apart from you. She suddenly put down her bag and fetched a cup from the top shelf.

'I might have a little cup of tea,' she said in a small-girl voice.

'Sure,' said Jude pushing the teapot towards her, 'go ahead. Don't you want to invite him in?'

'No. It will do him good to wait,' Katerina giggled, and sat down.

'So where are you off too?' Jude asked simply. It startled me. It was a kind of unspoken rule that we never asked Katerina anything about who she mixed with or where she went. She was always heading out, dressed up or down, looking fabulous either way, but always in a hurry to be somewhere else. This day she was wearing some beautifully cut baggy white bermuda pants, with a fitted stretch-cotton navy T-shirt on top. Her dainty feet were encased in white sandals. She looked like she'd stepped straight out of a magazine, as usual.

'Sailing actually,' she said. 'My friend has a yacht and he wants to get some time in before the race ... '

'What race?'

'Oh, I don't know, there's some big yacht race next month. He'll be competing in it.'

For some reason neither of us could think of anything to say to that. It had been totally easy before she'd come in. My conversation with Jude had been dipping in and out of serious subjects, bizarre jokes and recipes for pickles. I tried not to let Katerina's arrival change the mood, but of course it did.

'So, Katerina,' I said, feigning a nonchalance I didn't feel with her, 'know any recipes for pickles?' I suppose I was proud of my friendship with Jude and I wanted to show her something of it so she wouldn't have quite as much reason to dismiss me.

'Well, no, I don't,' she replied pleasantly. 'But my Gran is a great jam-maker. I used to love helping her. She had a mulberry tree. I'd climb up it with a little saucepan and pick them. She'd stand underneath and tell me the ones I was missing!'

Jude and I smiled and waited for her to continue. But the small personal admission must have rattled her because her face suddenly closed over. She looked at her watch, then jumped up, downing the rest of her tea in a gulp.

'I'd better go,' she said, picking up her bag again. 'Look, er ... I'm giving a party at Easter. It's next week, you know. Would you both like to come? We're holding it on the Sunday night.'

'What? Here?' said Jude in surprise.

'Heavens no!' Katerina smiled. 'In Manella, at my parents' house.' Jude took a hurried sip of tea, and I got up to turn off the dripping tap. I was glad that Katerina was looking at Jude and that Jude was nodding thoughtfully as she considered the invitation, because I had fallen into my usual kind of nervous confusion.

The Armstrongs were known for their expensive and stylish entertaining. *The squire is giving another party for his kids* would be the wry comment from the butcher or the postman. None of the ordinary people around town were ever invited.

I could see that the full import of the invitation was unsettling Jude, too. She was no fool; I could see her trying to work out what to do. She and her mother were also not part of the set who would normally be invited.

'What do you reckon, Carmel?' Jude said, turning to me. 'Will you be going home at Easter?' I pretended to consider this, the heat rising up my neck. We both knew that I was going home.

'Yeah. I think so,' I ended up saying brightly.

'So you'll come?' Katerina was looking at us from the door, her face devoid of expression, except perhaps mild amusement. I had a flash that she might be laughing at us behind those beautiful eyes. As if either of us would ever refuse, her calm controlled smile might have been saying. Just for a moment I fantasised about doing just that.

So sorry, but I have something else on that night.

But I knew I would never say it. The temptation was too strong. I had grown up in that town, after all. I wanted to get a look inside that house. I wanted to see if all the rumours were true; that the rooms were huge and high and wood-panelled, that there was an enormous patio outside covered in wisteria, that the front formal room opened up into the family lounge, which in turn opened up into a third sitting-room. And that this huge space was about the size of two ordinary houses. In spite of knowing I was a complete disaster socially – I'd only been to a few parties and hated them unreservedly – I knew I would go. I would probably suffer all night. My face would flush, my clothes would be ridiculous, I'd look fat and out of place among a whole lot of confident, beautiful people. Even so, curiosity was already flaming in me. As was my pride. What will my family think when I tell them I'm going to *that* house for a party?

'Well, I'd love to come,' I said quietly. Katerina's smile brightened as she turned to Jude.

'I'll be there, too,' Jude said. 'Er, what kind of party is it? Do we wear our glad rags or what?'

'Oh sure!' Katerina laughed. 'Wear all your glad rags if you like. Or none if you don't like!'

We laughed. She gave us a cheerful wave and was gone.

Jude and I didn't talk about the invitation. But I think she was pondering it too. I don't think either of us could quite work out how we felt about it. I know I was excited and troubled at the same time.

'Feel like a walk?' I said. It was a nice day and I had been looking forward to exploring; to walking down past the university to the city proper and then on to the botanic gardens.

'I'd love one,' Jude said, screwing up her nose wistfully, 'but I've got too much study to do.'

'Okay.'

I took off on my own, a little depressed. Jude was a terrific friend, but her answer had highlighted the differences between us. She studied hard as well as taking an interest in everything around her. She had long-term plans as well as short-term interests. I was simply treading water. I could see no clear path ahead of me, except the one I dreaded most and tried not to think about: back to Manella, in disgrace.

7

There didn't seem to be anyone at home when I let myself in the Tuesday before Easter. I took a deep breath and bounded down the hall. Jude might be out the back putting clothes on the line or something. I wanted to tell her what I'd seen at the art gallery. I stopped dead in the kitchen. There was a large, official-looking yellow envelope propped up on the kitchen table with my name in neat type across the front. My hands trembled as I picked it up and saw the university's insignia printed in one top corner. My stomach gave a sudden terrible lurch.

The craziest thoughts went through my mind as I tentatively picked it up and opened it with a knife. I was going to be disgraced. They would tell my parents for sure. I couldn't, I *wouldn't*, go back to Manella. Anger burst inside me as I began to read.

Dear Ms McCaffrey,

It has come to our attention that you have not been attending classes and that your work requirements have not been met. Could you please contact this office to explain the situation at the earliest opportunity. Trained counsellors are available if you are having any personal difficulties ...

Personal difficulties! Tears sprang into my eyes. What did that mean? It would probably only apply when someone close to you had died, or you'd been in a serious car accident, or something like that. Just feeling awful wouldn't constitute 'personal difficulties', would it? Nor would feeling fat and awkward and utterly hopeless most of the time. I slumped miserably onto a chair and sobbed, not knowing what to do. Strange that over the last few weeks I'd often felt sharp pangs of homesickness, yet I desperately didn't want to *have* to go home. Whenever I'd had vague feelings that perhaps I'd better come clean, tell everyone that the course had been a mistake, that I'd better go home, one of Mum's letters would arrive just in time. Terse little notes about the weather and the twins' school reports and the chooks that had been taken by a fox the night before. She'd usually end on something like the price of lambs ... and that she hoped I was working hard. And I'd think, *Oh God, no, no. I just can't!*

The weeks had been sliding by and the money was running out. Vince had written to me with a few contacts to follow up about part-time jobs, but I hadn't done anything about it. The thought of working terrified me even more than going back to class. How would I be able to give change in a shop? I was hopeless at arithmetic. I would never be able to pull a beer or make milkshakes. My parents were right. I'd never worked before. I was too vague and clumsy. Tears poured from my eyes. There was nothing for it. I would have to go home.

Jude found me blubbering at the kitchen table. She'd been out the back, clearing through all the rubbish in the little shed at the bottom of the yard, and had come in to find the dustpan and brush. She had a scarf around her head and was dusty, hot and bothered.

'Carmel! What's up?'

I looked up. I suppose my eyes were red raw. I knew my face would be blotched. I didn't care. She sat down next to me and waited. It didn't take me long to spill out the whole sorry story, because she didn't interrupt or even act surprised. I told her everything. Missing my classes, the addiction to trying on clothes, the shoplifting, the food I used to gorge myself on, my sneaking belief that I would never be able to find a place for myself in this world. She smiled every now and again, but on the whole she just looked thoughtful until I finished talking.

'So what can we do?' she said after we'd spent a few moments in dreary silence. I can't tell you what it was like hearing her say *we*. It made me feel better at once. But I was ashamed that I'd more or less lied to her for weeks.

'Sorry about not being straight with you, Jude,' I said. 'I mean, this will probably sound crazy, but I kept thinking I'd go back to uni. Telling myself every day that I'd go back tomorrow. But the time has sort of flown by and ... '

She shrugged off my apology with a smile.

'That doesn't matter, Carmel. What matters is what will happen next.'

'Well, I guess I'll have to go home and ... '

'No way!' she said. 'I won't allow it.'

'But Jude, my money is running out. I've been a complete ... ' She held up her hand like a traffic cop.

'They'll cut off my student allowance, for sure,' I sniffed.

'You have to get a job, that's all,' she said, 'a job that will give you enough to live on ... '

'But I can't go on lying to my parents and my brother ... and ... '

'Why not?' she grinned. 'Just for a bit longer you can, until you find your feet.'

'My feet?' I said bitterly, lifting one of my large sweaty ones onto the table, 'my feet are the bloody easiest part of me to find.' She laughed and slapped my leg, and I put it down.

'Did you go to the gallery?' she asked.

'Yeah.'

'Did you see the Bonnard and the Renoir?'

'Yes.'

'What did you think?'

'I loved seeing them,' I sighed.

'See, I told you,' she teased. 'Listen, there's a cafe where all the Chileans hang out. I heard the owner say that he'd be needing someone for a while. His wife has gone overseas. Want to come down and see if we can get you a job there?'

'Doing what?'

'Waitressing, I dunno,' she shrugged. 'I know the guy who owns it. He might have a few ideas'.

'But I'm not, you know, Chilean. And I can't speak Spanish.'

'That won't matter,' she said.

'I haven't had any experience,' I said. 'I mean waitressing.'

She shrugged as though that wouldn't matter either and smiled. 'And look, when you get a job, how about helping me in your spare time instead of hanging out in Myer?'

'Help you?' I said puzzled. 'Sure. But what with?'

'I'm coordinator of the protest. There's an amazing amount of work to do and those lazy bastards have put me in charge.'

'What protest?'

'Didn't I tell you? The Chilean president is coming here in June. We're going to make sure that he gets to know that we don't approve of what's going on over there.'

I nodded. Jude had talked a lot about Chile over recent weeks. I was starting to find it interesting. She'd given me a few books and a couple of pamphlets, and I'd surprised myself by reading them all. Many people had died in the seventies. When the military coup happened in 1973, thousands had been rounded up and incarcerated in the city's huge football stadium. Some were held without being charged for months, her father among them. Many were tortured, others killed. Most had simply been students and teachers, ordinary people who happened not to agree with the military takeover. But very few of the former torturers and corrupt police of the old regime had been tried or gaoled for what they'd done. In fact, many of them were still in positions of power. There were small pressure groups around the world trying to bring them to justice. Jude, of course, saw herself as part of it because her father had been one of the people who'd died. The present government was trying to forget about the promises it had made to bring these people to justice. It wanted to forget all about the people who'd died and disappeared during that time.

'I'll help in any way I can,' I said tentatively. Jude held out her hand and I slapped it with my own.

'So, how do you go about organising a ... er, a protest?' I asked, really interested. 'Who invited the president here anyway?'

Jude shrugged. 'Oh, the Australian government. It's a trade thing. I'm going to use the back shed out there to store stuff. This guy Joe will be around later with a computer. I told him to come through the back gate. We're going to set up a desk out there, with a computer and printer ... '

'But what about your study?' I asked. 'Are you going to go on with your own course?' I was afraid that there might be two of us, two drop-outs in the house at the same time. It seemed much worse than one.

'Of course I am,' she grinned, 'but come on. Let's get down to Juan's and see if we can get you a job!' At that moment we heard a key turn in the front door.

'That will be Katerina,' I said.

'Listen, Carmel,' Jude leant forward and lowered her voice, 'don't say anything to Katerina about me using the back room, eh?'

'But won't she see?'

'She never goes out there. What she doesn't know won't hurt her.'

'Okay,' I agreed, 'I won't say a word.'

Katerina bustled into the room, loaded up with shopping.

'Hi there!' she smiled at us and dumped her packages onto the table. 'Isn't it hot? I'm completely wrecked!' As usual, she looked anything but wrecked. In fact she looked breathtaking, in spite of the few beads of sweat on her forehead and the smudge of grime along her chin. Her hair was pulled away from her face with a bright blue headband and she was wearing a lovely little straight dress in the same colour. It stopped about four inches above her knees, showing off her golden-brown legs to perfection.

'You been shopping?' I asked.

'Yes.' Katerina took a couple of deep gulps from the glass of cold water she'd poured herself and turned to us. 'Look, I'm making a special meal tonight. I'm having a ... er, a guest,' she said. 'You'd both be very welcome to stay. Actually I meant to ask you yesterday.' I hesitated and looked at Jude.

'Maybe you'd like us to be out ... out of the way, I mean.' Jude said quickly. The same idea had occurred to me. 'Feel free to say so. We don't mind, do we, Carmel? We were going out anyway to ... '

'Of course,' I said, thinking that I'd rather have tea out with Jude anyway.

'No, no!' Katerina said, shaking her curls emphatically. 'That's not what I meant at all. I'd really *love* you both to be here. It's a guy I've been seeing a bit of lately. I thought we could have a dinner party ... all of us together. I haven't seen much of you two since you moved in ... ' She was giving off these imploring little vibes that confused me. 'Were you really both planning to be out?' she asked.

'Not really,' I looked at Jude for confirmation. Jude looked at her watch.

'What time are you planning to eat?' she asked Katerina.

'About eight.'

'Well, we'll be back by then,' Jude said. 'Come on, Carmel. Let's get down to the cafe.' She turned back to Katerina apologetically. 'Sorry about not being here to help cook.'

'That's fine,' Katerina said. 'I'm better on my own anyway. I'll see you back here at eight. And be hungry!'

'We'll probably be back before then,' Jude said. 'We'll want to change for ... for *the man*.' Jude pulled a wicked face. 'Whacko!' she yelled, clicking her fingers and rotating her hips, 'I can't wait to meet him!' Katerina grinned at Jude's teasing tone. I smiled too. At that moment Katerina was just an ordinary girl, like us. Beautiful, but ordinary. Funny that most of the time I didn't think of her like that though. Her incredible looks, her braininess, and the cool, superior air she had about her made me feel wary most of the time.

'Okay. Then you can both set the table.'

'It's a deal,' Jude grinned, and waved goodbye. I picked up my bag and followed her out of the house.

'It'll be interesting to meet whoever he is,' Jude said gleefully. We were on the bus to Collingwood and I was beginning to feel sick. Buses always make me queasy, but it wasn't just the bus. I felt jumpy inside. I'd never been for a job interview before. I wanted to ask Jude how I should behave, but was too churned up about it. I felt sure she was being unrealistic, that there would be no chance I'd get any kind of job.

'For sure he'll be good-looking,' Jude babbled on, 'but there'll be something else about him. He'll be rich, if I know her.' She turned to me questioningly. 'It's interesting to speculate on the kind of guy that'd be attracted to her ... '

'Oh Jude!' I said impatiently, staring out the window at the people hurrying along the footpath, all of whom would have jobs already and neat, interesting lives. 'Any man would be attracted to Katerina ... '

'Not necessarily,' Jude said thoughtfully, biting her nails. 'Sure they'd all want to get into her pants, but I get the feeling this one is different.' I was getting used to the casual way Jude would drop in crude little phrases like that. Still, I was glad she was looking at the window because sometimes, much to my embarrassment, it still made me blush a bit.

'Maybe he's one of those,' I said, trying to sound offhand and cool. Jude looked around at me with interest.

'What do you mean?'

'I mean one of the ones who wants to ... er,' I could feel the heat rising in my face, 'get into her pants.' Jude watched me stumble over the words and grinned.

'God, you're a treat, Carmel!' she teased, digging me in the ribs. 'Practise saying it, come on!' I laughed and shook my head.

My mother's term for anyone who used coarse language was 'guttermouth'. I was about to regale Jude with that side of my upbringing when she suddenly stood up.

'Come on. This is it.'

Inside, the long narrow Smith Street cafe was plain, except for a brightly painted mural along the left-hand wall. I wanted to stop and examine it. I'd never seen such a long painting. It was full of simple, finely painted figures of birds and people, buildings and animals, held together by a meandering road that widened and narrowed, rose and fell, as the story progressed through the depth of the room. *What did that eagle symbolise? Why did that little group of people look so cowed and frightened?* But Jude was motioning for me to follow her up through the sparsely populated tables towards a man who was standing behind the kitchen area with his back to us.

'Hi Juan. It's me,' she called cheerfully. The man turned around, but I couldn't see his face because my eyes were still adjusting to the dim light. The place, although clean, smelt of coffee and stale cigarettes. The walls were white, the tables were bare laminex, and the floor was covered in chipped brown tiles.

'This is my friend Carmel, Juan. Isn't she just gorgeous?' The thin, tall, swarthy-skinned man came out from behind the coffee machine, smiled, and held out his hand. He was dressed neatly in dark trousers and a white shirt, and the flecks of grey through his hair and moustache made him seem handsome and impossibly distinguished. Like a professor of some very esoteric subject. *Arabic poetry*, I thought wildly as I took his hand and tried to smile. Jude's words were still rattling around my brain. I felt like running, or curling up in a corner. *Isn't she gorgeous.* Jude had given me no warning she was going to introduce me like that. The smile on my mouth turned rigid as the man's dark, intense eyes bore down into my own. So dark and liquid, so utterly ... mysterious. I had to look away or I would have been drawn right into them.

'Pleased to meet you, Carmella,' he said in a thick accent.

'Yes. You too,' I managed to mutter. Then he stepped away and looked me up and down in the direct, matter-of-fact way someone might check over a dog or a fridge before they bought it. I had on a new straight red skirt that came down to mid-calf, my old sandals, and my long black loose T-shirt. I knew my hair did look nice, I'd washed it that morning and the curls were springy and soft. I'd also put on some glossy lipstick and a little eye make-up. He seemed to be taking it all in.

'Yes,' he said with a laugh, 'she is gorgeous.' My hand flew to my mouth and my face immediately flushed. I didn't know if I was going to laugh or cry. God, I'd never been so embarrassed, or pleased, in my life. He'd said it as though he really meant it. As though it were obvious.

'I've got no experience or anything ...' I stammered, forgetting that the man hadn't the faintest idea why he was being introduced to me. 'I mean, I've never worked and I'm not sure that I could do ... this job, and I ...' Jude stepped in before I could do any further damage. She grabbed one of my arms and held it out for him to look at.

'Juan,' she said, smiling. Then they both stared down at the whiteness of the inside of my arm. 'Perfect, isn't it?' I had no idea what was going on, only that I felt intensely embarrassed. They were examining me like I was a piece of fancy porcelain.

'Lovely,' the man said, and then he ran one deep brown finger along it, from the inside of my elbow to my wrist. I pulled away sharply, as if I'd been electrocuted.

'Jude,' I hissed, 'come on. I don't want to ...' I'd had enough. This was getting creepy.

'It's okay,' she said mildly, then looked at the man again. 'Carmel needs a job, Juan,' she said firmly. The man shrugged.

'Okay,' was all he said, and then he smiled at me and shrugged. 'You've got one.' I just stood there like a prize geek, not understanding anything and looking from one to the other. Jude gave me a nudge.

'See, you've got a job,' she said with a broad smile.

'But ...' I stammered. 'I mean ... what do I do? I mean when do I start?'

'You can make coffee, sweep the floor ...' Juan said, as if what I'd actually do was unimportant, 'serve the food. When would you like to start?'

'But I can't make coffee!' I wailed, almost in tears. Suddenly a suspicion hit me. Maybe they were both making fun of me. It was hideous, too cruel to contemplate. Jude, my friend, was ridiculing me in front of this stranger! I stood there trying to summon up the courage to run. No one just walked into a cafe and got a job like this! Employers were meant to ask all kinds of questions. Everyone said jobs were incredibly hard to get. I took a panicky glance at Jude's face. She seemed quite relaxed as she felt around in her bag and pulled out a pen. She had her practical, let's-get-down-to-business look on. I suddenly remembered that she'd warned me in the bus.

'Juan is a bit strange, but don't let him put you off. He's okay.'

'How much do I get paid an hour?' I asked, surprising myself almost as much as both of them. Jude gave me a warm, congratulatory grin. I smiled back tentatively, feeling as if I'd just passed some test. Juan shrugged and looked at Jude.

'Well, what do you pay *him*?' Jude asked impatiently, pointing at a short plump man who was bringing coffees over to a table of men. It was at that point I realised that everyone in the cafe, everyone except Jude and me, was male. I shifted a little uneasily.

'What kind of, er ... cafe is this?' I cut in, trying to keep the suspicion out of my voice. But they'd both seen me staring around apprehensively at all the men and laughed.

'It's a sad place, Carmella,' Juan said, smiling in a slow, wistful way, 'wouldn't you say so, Jude?' Jude nodded.

'And it's a happy place, too,' he added as a kind of afterthought, staring out of the grimy window.

Jeeze. The guy is a nutter! I thought. *I gotta get out of here!* But I also sensed that he was telling the truth. At least his version of it.

'Juan, Carmel wants to know what she'll be paid,' Jude snapped, 'it's very important!'

'Twelve ... fifteen?' he shrugged, as though that was the last thing he'd give even a moment's consideration to. Jude looked at me questioningly. As if it were up to me! I opened my mouth, but nothing came out.

'Let's say twelve an hour for the first couple of weeks,' she said. 'Is that all right by you, Carmel?' I nodded, thinking that as soon as I got out of this place I'd tell her that there was no way I'd work here.

'And then when you've learnt the ropes,' she went on blithely, 'say after a couple of weeks, raise it to fifteen. Does that seem fair?' She was looking at Juan now. He smiled at her warmly and made a gesture with his hands that said it was all right.

'Good,' Jude said, 'now come over here and I'll teach you to make coffee.' I followed her behind the counter and watched her turn on the machine and twist the knobs. A familiar rope of panic began to coil up inside me. There was no way I'd be able to do this. I was sure of it.

'See, here's the coffee. You just fill this little thing and screw it in there. Make sure you have two cups beneath. Have a go. That's right. And this is the milk for the cappuccinos and flat whites. You probably won't have to make many of them, still you'd better know how.' She stepped out of the way suddenly.

'Come on. You do it now from the start.' I did what I was told and within about ten minutes I'd learnt how to make all the different kinds of coffee. Such a simple thing, and I'd thought it was beyond me.

After that we decided on the hours I'd work. Juan said he'd like me to start on the early-morning shift until his wife got back. After that I could work in the evenings if I wanted. A lot of his customers were shift workers who came in to get a meal and meet some friends before they went home to sleep. Could I be there at seven? I gulped and nodded. It would mean getting up at six, considering the half-hour bus ride.

'Sure. Until when?'

'Say midday or one. Business eases off in the afternoon, then gets strong again in the late afternoon and evening.'

'Okay. When do I start?'

The same sad smile, the intense eyes.

'When do you want to start?'

'A week after Easter. The Monday?'

He took my hand and shook it as if I was really doing him a favour.

'See you Monday, Señorita.'

'Yeah, see you then,' I said uneasily, pulling my hand away.

'So, what do you reckon?' Jude was grinning at me like the cat who'd just eaten the cream. 'It's great, isn't it?' I nodded warily. We'd rushed out of the cafe and were waiting for our bus home.

'I don't know, Jude ...'

'You'll be fine.'

'You think so?'

'Of course.'

'He's a weird man.'

'I know.'

'How do you know him so well?'

'He was a friend of my father's.'
'What? Back in Chile?'
'Yeah. He was with my father in prison.'
'Oh God, Jude!' It hit me like a wet sheet in the wind, smacking against my face and blinding me momentarily. And now the bus was coming. I mean, I'd known all along, like everyone else in Manella, that her father was dead. But knowing something and really *knowing* it were two different things. I hadn't *thought* about it at all.

'Shit, I'm really sorry, Jude,' I swore easily, for probably the first time in my life.

'What about? Come on! Here's the bus.'

We scrambled on, showed our tickets to the surly driver, and found ourselves a seat.

'Jude, I'm ... sorry about your father being dead and ... everything!' I burst out.

She smiled at me. The bus lurched off. To steady herself she clasped the seat in front with both her small brown hands. I watched them grip hard then ease up as the ride became steadier.

'I know,' she said, after a while.

'What?'

'I know you're sorry. About my father being dead.' I nodded and we were silent. Then she began to speak, very softly and carefully. Each word sort of took me downwards onto a deeper, different plane. It was like music.

'They tortured that man, same as they did to my father. They strung them both up for six hours at a time, sometimes longer, day after day for weeks. They wanted information, names of people they worked with in the resistance. They hung them from their wrists. Until their sinews broke and their muscles tore ... sometimes they'd wet them all over and then use electric cattle prods on their sensitive parts ... ' Her voice choked as she dropped her head between her two outstretched arms. 'Then they'd beat the soles of their feet,' she continued, her voice muffled. 'They couldn't walk or even stand up because their feet were so swollen and bloody ... but the next day they would do it again.'

When she stopped talking I looked up and I wondered if I was still breathing.

'How do you know?' I whispered.

'They let my father out after one time. He'd spent six months in one of their gaols. He told my mother everything ... '

'Have you talked about it with ... with that man too?'

'Yes.'

'Did he know your father well?'

'They were friends at university.'

'Does your mother know about him being here?'

'No.'

'Are you ... are you going to tell her ... about him?'

'I don't know.'

It was after eight by the time we opened the door of our little house. We stood in the hallway and breathed in. The smell of cooking coming from the kitchen was wonderful.

'Roast pork!' Jude whispered, crinkling up her nose. 'What do you reckon?'

'Nah,' I said, taking a deep whiff, 'it's some kind of chicken or beef.'

'There's a big difference between a hen and a cow, you idiot!' Jude growled. With that we both collapsed against the walls in spasms of nervous giggling.

After we had laughed ourselves out we walked down into the kitchen, grimacing at each other when we saw that the table in the lounge room had already been laid. Not only were we late, we hadn't fulfilled our part of the deal. Were we going to get into trouble with the headmistress?

'Hello, you two,' Katerina called, welcoming us with one of her wide, gushing smiles.

We walked into the kitchen to find her hauling a couple of roast birds out of the oven. Plates were already laid out on the kitchen table. Katerina had a little frilly apron on over a stunning blackbeaded dress that was split up the back, sheer black stockings, and high heels.

'I'd like you to meet Glen Simons,' she said with a proud smile. We both turned in surprise to see the man sitting down at the end of the table. He looked up, olive-skinned, good-looking, clutching a glass in one hand and a bowl of cherries in the other, and at least fifty years old.

'Glen, these are my housemates. Jude and Carmel.'

He waved the hand that was holding the wine by way of greeting, but didn't smile. He was incredibly good-looking, probably the most handsome *old* man I'd ever seen – on screen or off. *But he's old enough to be her father. Easily. Grandfather?* There was silver in his hair and deep wrinkles around his glass-cold blue eyes.

'Hello, Glen!' we chorused.

'Hello, girls,' he said in a deeply bored voice, as if he thought we were mildly amusing, 'nice to meet you.' But his eyes were already on something else by the time he'd finished the sentence. I took one glance at Jude and I could see that she had been similarly stunned. The silver-streaked hair, the ice-blue eyes, and the slight sagginess around the fashionable stubble on his chin. He wore a cream silk shirt and navy linen pants with slip-on leather shoes. His skin was tanned and ... Wow! It flashed through my mind that if those two ever got together they would make a pretty amazing kid.

'So, what is it you're cooking?' I asked, for something to say.

'Duck with orange,' Katerina smiled, 'but there's home-made pâté and iced Mexican soup first, so why don't you both just go in and sit down?'

'Are you sure we can't help?' we protested. She waved us away.

'No, everything is under control. Take Glen into the lounge room and seat yourselves at the table.' We both edged towards the door, thinking that he'd get up and follow. But he didn't look as if he planned to go anywhere. After the diversion of being introduced to us, his eyes had moved back to Katerina. Jude and I stood by the doorway and watched him ogling her as she moved around the kitchen. But she gave no indication that she was aware of it.

'I got a job,' I said lamely. 'In a cafe.' Katerina looked up from where she was dishing up the soup.

'That's great, Carmel,' she said in a kind of uninterested voice. Glen gave no indication that he'd heard. He was still staring at her, eating her up with his eyes. Katerina turned her back on him and lifted both her arms up to get a bowl from the top shelf. The movement made her dress rise up her legs. I watched him watching that.

'So, Glen,' Jude said sharply, 'what do you do?'

'I'm in business,' he said dismissively. The lustful look in his eyes was fascinating. He'd hardly taken them off Katerina to answer. The guy was almost licking his lips!

'Oh yeah?' Jude said. 'What kind of business?'

'The rag trade,' he replied, without enthusiasm. 'I have a company in South Melbourne. We supply a lot of piece work for the fashion labels.' He was still watching Katerina.

'We ... ?'

He turned then and smiled condescendingly at Jude.

'Well, I don't do it myself,' he said. 'I employ a lot of people to do the work.'

'Women?' Jude said. Glen frowned.

'Yes, mainly women,' he said. Jude nodded thoughtfully.

'You got a problem with that?' he asked sarcastically.

'Migrant women?' she said, ignoring his tone, running her fingernail along the table and making a horrible scaping sound.

'Yes. Migrant women.'

'Migrant women who can't speak English, eh?'

'They're glad of the work,' he replied shortly and stood up. 'Bathroom in here?' pushing on the door.

'Yes,' Jude answered coolly. He walked through and shut the door. End of conversation. Jude was still frowning. I gave her a nudge and we went through to the lounge room and sat down at the table.

'He's a creep,' she said. We were sitting opposite each other and the door to the kitchen was open.

'Ssssh,' I said urgently, 'he'll hear!'

'I don't care,' she shrugged, picking up a piece of crusty bread from the plate and smothering it with butter, 'hope he does.'

The dinner progressed woodenly. I tried to open up the conversation a couple of times, but no one followed through. Katerina and I did most of the talking, and it was stiff and constrained with the other two just sitting there, more or less silent, as they listened to us blabber on about nothing.

'So, a job, Carmel? When do you start?'

'Next Monday morning at seven o'clock.'

'You'll be tired when you get home with such an early start.'

'I guess so.'

Glen made it obvious that he wasn't in the least interested in either Jude or me, or in anything that was being said. Even at the table, while we were eating, his eyes hardly left Katerina. When she reached out for a piece of bread he stopped her hand with his own and sort of stroked it, making her meet his eye over their touching hands. And when she handed him his plate of duck and fancy sauce he let her put it down in front of him and then grabbed her waist from behind and tried to make her sit on his knee! Yuck! I looked down at my plate not daring to catch Jude's eye. It was nauseating, just watching him waiting to pounce at the first opportunity. Jude sat glowering down at her end of the table for most of the meal. Her abrupt answers to any questions that were put to her were verging on rude. After a while I couldn't understand anything that was going on. All I did know was that I felt uncomfortable and bored. Katerina had gone to so much trouble. And I was baffled. Why had she wanted us there? I'd never even had a halfway decent conversation with her since moving into the house. But I couldn't help feeling sorry for her. No one could possibly call this dinner pleasant, in spite of the fancy food.

By the end of the first course I saw that Katerina was starting to look strained and decided I'd had enough. I was about to hop up and collect the plates and then excuse myself by doing the dishes. But it was exactly at that moment that Jude spoke.

'So, how many women have you got working for you, Glen?' she asked in this amazingly loud, aggressive voice. My mouth fell open and I began to squirm in my chair. I saw that he had also been taken by surprise.

'Depends on what's on,' he shrugged. 'Sometimes two hundred. Sometimes three.'

'Where is the factory?' Jude asked, her voice saturated with a meaning that I didn't get. I looked over at Katerina, who was looking at Jude with hurt surprise. Glen leant over and took Katerina's hand, as if he was protecting her from the crass, loud-mouthed Jude.

'Well, my office, as I think I said before, is in South Melbourne,' he said coldly, 'but most of the work is done out.' He turned to Katerina with a small, tense smile.

'You mean piece work?' Jude said.

'Yes. That's right.'

'So you don't pay for any of the overheads, right? Electricity. Not to mention sick leave or holidays? What's the name of your company?'

'Clothes-that-go.'

Katerina was beginning to look uncomfortable. The frown on her face was becoming more strained by the second. Jude suddenly got up and stormed out into the kitchen. I looked at the other two, but they were obviously determined to let pass whatever Jude was on about.

Glen picked up the bottle of wine and poured some into my glass.

'What are you studying, er ... my dear?' he said in his patronising way. Hell. I saw red. I was livid. This creep was just playing games. I hadn't been good enough to talk to before, but now, for some reason, probably to do with Jude's questions, he'd decided he'd better at least be civil to one of us.

'I don't study at all,' I said sharply. Katerina gave a little jump as though I'd bitten her.

'What do you mean, Carmel?' she said. 'You're doing a teaching course at Melbourne, aren't you?'

'No,' I said bluntly. 'I've finished with that.'

'Since when?'

'Since about three weeks into term.'

'So, what are you going to do?' she asked with a forced smile.

'I just told you,' I answered coldly. 'I told you both out there that I've got a job in a cafe!'

'Oh!' she said. 'I thought you meant that you'd be doing it in between lectures or after them or ... whatever ... ' As far as I was concerned all that showed was that she was basically uninterested in anything to do with my life. I got up, picked up a couple of plates from the table, and went out to the kitchen. I wanted to get away from both of them. I wished with all my heart that it was just Jude and me in the house. We would have got along together just fine. This creepy old bore and Katerina were making me feel sick. I realised that I would never want to be Katerina if it meant having to mince around for someone like him!

Jude was waiting for me in the kitchen. She pulled me into the bathroom, shut the door and cornered me with those blazing brown eyes. My legs felt weak. I desperately wanted to go to the toilet and I couldn't stop giggling.

'He's married,' she snapped.

'Oh, Jude, how do you know?' I burst out.

'I saw pictures of his kids in his wallet. Three. A boy of about twelve and two younger girls.'

'So?' It was no surprise to me. Someone that age was sure to be married.

'What do you mean, so?'

'So, it's none of our business,' I said sternly.

She stopped at that, closing her eyes for a few brief moments.

'It *is* our business. I think we should sabotage it,' she said.

'Please go out, Jude,' I sighed. 'I've just got to go to the toilet.' At the door she stopped and turned to me, her back very straight and both arms at her sides.

'We must sabotage it. We should align ourselves with the wife and kids who are waiting for him at home.'

'Jude! Get a grip on yourself!' But I couldn't stop giggling. She looked as if she was preparing for war standing to attention like that. But when the door was shut and I was sitting on the toilet a shiver of apprehension went though me.

'Besides, I *know* him,' she whispered venomously into the keyhole.

'What do you mean?'

'Well, not *personally*, but I recognise the company name. He employs a lot of South Americans and Vietnamese people. The ones that can't speak English. Women that can't get work anywhere else. Pays them nothing. Makes me sick to see that big car out there ...'

'What car?'

'I went and checked it out. It's a bloody brand-new silver Jag!'

'Jude,' I whispered back, 'he is none of our business. I don't want to get into any kind of *thing* with Katerina.' Jude gave a furious impatient snort.

'It doesn't matter!' I went on. 'I've got no inclination to delve into her private life. Besides, what's the point?' On the other side of the door Jude was quiet. I could almost hear the cogs of her brain turning over, brooding and churning.

When I flushed the toilet and opened the door she met me with this look of absolute determination as she stepped into the bathroom with me.

'Listen,' I said as calmly as I could, washing my hands, 'it's her business.'

'No,' she replied angrily, 'it's ours. We have to be in solidarity with those workers!'

'But what can we do?' I sighed. 'They're probably in there smooching all over the floor by now ... '

'We could pour water over them,' she hissed.

'What?'

To my relief I saw a grin beginning at the corners of her mouth.

'Boiling water!' she said loudly. 'That'd sort them out.' I began to get the giggles again. My legs became weak. I sank back against the bath and tried to stop, but I just couldn't. It was built-up tension, I suppose, and nervousness. The idea of crossing Katerina sent shivers up my cowardly spine.

'Or we could go out and put a few nice, deep scratches in his Jag ... ' She was semi-serious again.

'Oh Jude,' I spluttered. 'We can't ... we can't do anything!'

'You go in and keep them occupied,' she said, 'and I'll ring his wife.'

'You don't even know his number,' I groaned.

'I've got his number.' She pulled a scrap of paper from her pocket and brandished it under my nose.

'How ... did you get that?' I asked. But before I'd even finished the sentence I caught sight of the navy linen coat lying across the chair he'd been sitting on.

'God!' I said. 'Have you been rifling through his pockets?'

'So?' she said defensively.

'Jude,' I took her arm, 'his wife might be horrible! We don't know ... anything about him.'

'Wives are never horrible in these situations,' she countered stubbornly. We were both quiet for a few moments. I made the mistake of thinking that I'd managed to make her see sense, that I'd calmed her down. But she suddenly leapt away from where we were both standing, her eyes blazing, and, before I could stop her, dashed into the lounge room.

'So, where does your wife think you are now, dickhead?' I heard her yell. I groaned and shut my eyes. The door between the two rooms suddenly slammed shut. There was a burst of yelling. The man's voice and Jude's too. Somewhere among it all I could make out Katerina's as well, high-pitched and frantic, coming in over the others every now and again.

'Would you please leave this room ... now!'

'Not until he leaves this house!'

But I didn't hear exactly what transpired. I didn't want to. I think I covered both ears with my hands and slipped backwards into the bathroom and closed the door. I was trembling. Jude had gone too far.

I heard the door from the lounge to the kitchen open and then slam again. Someone was out in the kitchen flouncing around, banging things. I opened the door tentatively. As I expected it was Jude. She slumped down into a chair and crossed her feet on the kitchen table, something I hadn't seen anyone do in that house before. I looked at her and then over at the kettle that she'd set to boil on the stove.

'Where's Katerina?' I said nervously.

'Saying goodbye to old lover-boy, I suppose,' Jude said. But I could see from the colour in her cheeks and the flashing in her eyes that she was gearing up for round two. The idea that we'd somehow driven him from the house appalled me.

'Shit, Jude, has he really gone?'

'Yep,' she said with a small victorious grin. She picked up a couple of soup spoons and began playing a tune on the table-top, beating out a loud rap rhythm.

'Gone, gone, gone,' she breathed in time with her tune, 'thank the Lord!'

'Ah, shut up, Jude!' I said loudly. I was actually wringing my hands as I stood there. She looked up at me in surprise.

'What's eating you? We got ... '

'Nothing is eating me,' I snapped, 'it's just that ... '

'What?'

'I hope Katerina has left with him ... for the night,' I said, lowering my voice. 'I don't want to get embroiled in a real fight with her, Jude! I mean, she might kick us out ... ' My heart gave a dive. I could hear swift, clipped footsteps coming down the hallway towards us. I gulped as the door opened and Katerina came in. She stood in the doorway. Magnificent. Her face was dazzling, lit from within with the pure flame of anger. I took one glance and had to look away. It was like staring down into the coals of a very hot fire. Feigning nonchalance, Jude picked up her spoons again and began drumming them loudly on the table.

'So what was that all about?' Katerina spat out in her high, cold, top-private-school voice. I looked back at her. Why was she fixing those incredible green eyes on me? I hadn't told her boyfriend to leave. I took a panicky look at Jude, who had suddenly stopped drumming. She was now glowering down at the table. A bolt of fear hit my stomach then broke into a thousand pieces, fluttering around my guts. Both of them were so strong. Something terrible might happen.

'Katerina,' I gulped, making myself look right at her. 'I'm so sorry! I think Jude is, too ... '

'I'm not sorry at all!' Jude yelled, looking up from where she was sitting, her bare feet crossed on the table.

'Would you mind getting your feet off that table!' Katerina hissed, walking right into the room. A pause. I could see Katerina was stunned not to be obeyed immediately, but the feet didn't move. Not one inch. I waited on the sidelines, my heart in my mouth.

'That obnoxious, exploitative, rich old pathetic jerk is

married,' she said calmly. Katerina gave a small snort. Her hands were clenching and unclenching, as if any minute she was going to strike out with a punch or a slap.

'So what?' she fumed. 'What's that to you?'

Jude shrugged and said nothing.

'How dare you insult a friend of mine in *my* house ... ' Katerina went on. 'I invite you to dinner and you behave like a cretin, a hick idiot, sitting down the end of the table and ... *glowering* into your soup! I was so embarrassed, so ... '

'So you should be embarrassed!' Jude cut in. 'You should be *ashamed*. That creep has got a wife and kids. You're the hick, the fool. He's using you ... the way he uses those poor old ducks who do the piece work for him! Do you think he gives them a fair deal? No way! They're all desperate so he gives them about fifty cents an hour. What he's doing is against the law! Did you know he's being scrutinised by the labour department?'

Katerina reeled a little. Jude spoke so confidently. I had no way of telling if she was speaking the truth or not. Nor did Katerina, but that didn't deter her from making her feelings obvious.

'I don't care what you think about any of that,' she was almost screaming, 'think what you like! Your petty moral concerns don't interest me at all. Do ... you ... understand? The fact is, this is *my* house!'

'No it's not!' Jude shouted, jumping up suddenly and heaving the chair into the table noisily. Katerina took a step backwards, taken by surprise. Then they became like a couple of wild dogs circling each other. Both sure of themselves, each looking for the other's weak point, a crack in the other's armour.

Now Jude was on the attack again.

'You manipulative little snob! It's your parents' house! Your father and your mother are my landlords! *Not you!* So get off your friggin' high horse about that! Until I get kicked out by them, it's my house – and Carmel's house – as much as it is yours! We pay rent in case you've forgotten.'

'I only have to ring them and they'll agree,' Katerina flew back with an icy smile.

'So *do it*, you little prig! Ring them now!' Jude's arm flew up, pointing to the phone on the wall. Katerina didn't move.

'Actually they're away at the moment,' she said.

'*Actually they're away at the moment!*' Jude mimicked, as if she thought Katerina was making it up. 'Just remember that we've got to have one month's notice, *in writing*! Or we'll take them to the tenants' union!'

This took the wind out of Katerina's sails. She obviously had no idea whether what Jude was saying was true or not. She wasn't used to these kinds of arguments. I could tell by the way her hands were shaking. But nor was she used to being contradicted or shouted at by anyone. Much less by people she considered her inferiors.

'That's not the point,' Katerina said at last. 'What gives you the right to interfere like this? He is ... my friend ... '

'He's using you,' Jude sneered mercilessly, 'don't you realise that? And he's got kids and everything ... '

'For your information I've been seeing Glen for some time now,' Katerina said. It was her strongest bow, that ability to hold herself absolutely erect, to turn up the corners of her mouth and narrow her eyes; combined with her beauty, it gave her an air of superiority that seemed to exude from her every pore. It was hard not to be taken in by it. 'We're very close. And, also for your information,' she took a deep breath, stepped towards Jude and lowered her voice, 'yes, I know he's married and that he has young children. I also happen to know that these are the nineteen-nineties. A fact that seems to have passed you two by ... ' Her eyes swept around to me for an instant and then refocused on Jude. I gulped, completely dumbfounded. Even if I'd known what to say, the cold sureness of her was astounding.

'You're just a slut to him,' Jude countered, 'because you're young and good-looking ... '

Katerina winced at the word 'slut'. I could tell that she had never in a million years thought of herself as even within a mile's radius of such a word. It *was* a horrible word. I wished Jude would stop. Katerina would have us both kicked out for sure. And that would probably mean back to Manella for me. My heart did a ghastly nose-dive and crashed on the bottom of my stomach. Manella would mean having to face up to my parents and to Vince. *Oh, God, no!* I realised then that I had been excited about having a job to go to the next week. I panicked as I watched them, buoyed up with fury and indignation, each waiting for the other to speak.

'Why do *you* care?' Katerina asked. The anger was still simmering, but she was slightly calmer now and I could see she was genuinely curious.

'I'm on the side of the underdog,' Jude said simply. 'My mother told me what it's like having to bring up a kid on her own ... '

'But I have no intention of taking him away from her ... or from them. I have no intention of *marrying* him!' Katerina shook her head and half smiled at the thought. 'In fact, I couldn't think of anything worse. You really do have a very simplistic view of things ... '

'But it's still wrong,' Jude said doggedly. 'How do you think she feels?'

'*Who?*'

'His wife, of course.'

'Why should I care what ... ?' Katerina's sentence petered out, but as we stared at her beautiful face we both understood her meaning. She must have seen this because she immediately tried to cover up. She managed a funny grimace of exasperation that told me she was actually flummoxed, by Jude especially.

'She hasn't anything to do with me,' she said softly. 'Can't you see that? Nor do any of the women who sew for him ... What has any of it got to do with me? I really don't understand you ... '

At that point I wanted to leave the room. I couldn't see the point of talking about anything. She had never had to consider anyone else because for her life was just fine. She took whoever and whatever came along. Anything she wanted was hers for the taking. And she had been adored, pampered and praised while she did it.

'So start,' Jude growled slowly, her deep brown eyes boring into Katerina's. 'Start thinking of how it might feel to have him off screwing some little tart two or three nights a week. Start thinking what it might be like to work all day and half the night over a bloody machine and only make twenty-five bucks for it. Start *thinking*, Katerina. You don't want to be a complete fuckwit all your life, do you?'

Katerina gasped, her face moving through a quick series of expressions: shock, fury, and a kind of bewilderment. Then she shrugged again and I could see her trying to summon that deadly mocking smile onto her face. But it came up wrong, not half as sure or arrogant as before. I actually felt sorry for her. She suddenly trembled, all over, like a cat shaking off a few drops of water.

'So what do *you* think, Carmel?' she said, turning her shocked, brilliant eyes on me. She had nothing to say so she was daring me, it seemed, to think for even a minute that I could be anything more than what she'd pigeon-holed me as: a frumpy, uninteresting fat country girl, easily intimidated. Someone who knew nothing. I opened my mouth and began to stammer. I wanted out. *Finito!* I knew there was something else going on underneath their words, but I had only a vague idea what it was. Something was going on between those two, something about territory and power, which had nothing to do with me. They were working out who was the top dog. I was on the outside looking in.

Then I remembered how I'd felt getting into bed after being up all night singing and talking with Jude. Had that been just a flash-in-the-pan feeling or had it meant something? I *desperately* wanted to be something else than what she had in mind for me. Jude was wrong. She'd gone off half-cocked. She had no business holding Katerina to account like this. But I knew where Jude was coming from. Too bad about being kicked out of the house, too bad about Manella, too bad about all this unpleasantness. Too bad about everything.

'I'm with Jude,' I said, looking her straight in the eyes, my voice sounding much more savage and assured than I had intended, 'all the way. He's a creep and what you're doing stinks... and what is more, I refuse to consider this *your* house.'

Instead of bursting into a vitriolic diatribe or fixing me with that cold stare, Katerina simply looked away.

'Well, it looks like I've got myself holed up with a couple of members from the moral squad,' she said, still not really looking at either of us. 'I just wish I'd been warned before you moved in...'

'Ah, well...' Jude mumbled noncommittally, pulling a piece of duck off one of the plates and stuffing it into her mouth, 'that's the way it goes. This duck is really good.' I stared at Jude. She was calmly chewing duck. No. She was sitting down, pulling a clean plate towards her and scraping bits and pieces onto it. Then she began picking the food up with her fingers and eating it with gusto. I looked over to Katerina and saw that her expression had suddenly relaxed a little too.

'Do you think so?' she asked in an intense, low voice.

'Oh yes!' Jude nodded enthusiastically. 'The sauce is really tasty. I've never had it like that before.'

'I love cooking,' Katerina said. 'It was a recipe that my grandmother used to make at Christmas. Duck orange...' she stopped suddenly, embarrassed at herself.

'It *was* great,' I lied. I couldn't even remember what it had tasted like. The kettle had been boiling unnoticed for a few minutes. We both watched Katerina move to turn it off.

'Do you feel like a cup of coffee?' she asked tentatively. We both nodded. I tried to catch Jude's eye, but she was still eating, wiping up some of the sauce with bits of crusty bread and stuffing them into her mouth. Katerina put the steaming cups in front of us, and sat down to nibble some of the leftover duck herself. She smiled at me. The first genuine smile I'd ever had from her.

'So it's a truce, then, is it?' she asked simply. I nodded and tried not to seem as nervous as I felt. I picked up my coffee.

'Sure,' I said, 'I'm happy with that.'

'Good,' said Jude as though everything was now settled.

'Are you both still coming Easter Sunday?' Katerina asked. We looked up. 'To the party ... at home?'

'Oh,' Jude sounded fazed, 'the party.'

'Do you remember, I asked you, before ...' All trace of superiority was gone. 'It's just that I have to let them know ... numbers and everything.'

'Do you *want* us to come?' I burst out, 'I mean ... er, you might rather we didn't ...?'

'Of course I do,' she said. 'Er ... Glen won't be there. He's going overseas.' Jude burst into a roar of delighted laughter.

'Well, good! I'm definitely coming!' she said. Still laughing, she picked up a nearby tea-towel, wiped the grease off her hands and mouth, lolled back in her chair and sighed good-humouredly. 'What about you, Carmel?'

'I wouldn't miss it for the world.' I raised my cup. There were smiles all around as the others clinked their cups with mine.

'To the party!'

'Yeah. To the party!'

I took a sip and almost heard my mother's nagging voice. Who's going to take you? How will you get home? What do you want to be hanging around those toffs for? But I was eighteen. I'd been invited to a party. Why shouldn't I go?

8

It rained all Good Friday. All through the Stations of the Cross there was ominous rolling thunder and the sound of rain like driving nails hitting the slate roof of Manella's Sacred Heart Church. I was upstairs at the back playing the organ, so I could spy on the congregation without them seeing much of me. I loved watching the younger kids shiver and nudge each other with each new clap of thunder. I knew that for some of them in that darkening atmosphere, John's long, involving account of Christ's passion would take on the same dramatic impact that it had for me at their age.

The last stark picture of the three crosses on the bare hill was with me as I settled my fingers onto the keys for the final hymn. It felt as if some of the pain and thirst and suffering was in my own hands as I began to play.

After the service the members of the congregation began to run for their cars in the sloshing mud. But three girls I'd been to school with the year before approached me tentatively as I was leaving the church.

'So, how are things?' Mary-Lou Bishop asked slyly, swinging her long straight hair back over her shoulder, her narrow eyes flicking over my red skirt and old coat. I remembered Mary-Lou trying to remember my name for some swimming carnival at the beginning of the previous year.

'You know!' she'd yelled impatiently to her friends, 'that ... that fat dag with curly reddish hair who plays piano!'

'Pretty good,' I said, dipping my hand into the holy-water font and blessing myself so I'd be able to get away quickly. 'What about you?'

'Good . . .' they answered, as though they weren't at all sure. They obviously knew about me being invited to the Armstrongs'. The puzzled envy was written all over their faces. I hadn't even been worth saying hello to before. Now I had become interesting. What a turn-up.

'Do you really share a house with Katerina Armstrong?' one of them asked.

'Yes,' I said, not meeting their eyes, a sort of rootless anger swelling within me.

'How did you . . . I mean, how did that happen? I didn't think you knew her,' Mary-Lou bumbled on. She could see that I wanted to go. That I was edging away. They were all waiting for me to speak. They wanted to sink their teeth into the details of how such a social nobody could possibly be living with the likes of Katerina.

'Oh, well,' I said blithely, 'I know her.' I left before I could say another word. But I couldn't help a little smile as I turned and waved goodbye then followed my parents to the car.

By Sunday the weather had more or less cleared, although there had been some intermittent rain and strong winds in the early afternoon. Jude and I arrived at the party together in Cynthia's old battered Toyota. The invitation had been for seven, so at five to seven we were winding our way up the narrow road to the big house on the hill. The atmosphere after all the rain had become warm and still. Cynthia stopped the car and we prepared to get out. In the half-light, the bits of the house we could see through the surrounding hedge and large overhanging trees looked like a castle. I'd never been this close to it before.

'How do we get in?' I mumbled.

'There,' Jude pointed to a small white gate in the middle of the hedge.

'Have a great time, you two!' Cynthia said gaily. 'I'll come for you when you ring.'

'Okay, Mum. Thanks.'

I smiled at Cynthia and thought disloyally how wonderful it would be to have a mother who was so beautiful ... and modern. My own mother had simply sniffed when I'd told her about the party, and told me I had nothing to wear and she wasn't about to buy me anything as useless as an evening frock. When I'd said that I was happy to go in my red skirt and T-shirt she'd sniffed again and said that I'd disgrace them all by doing that. Only two months before I would have given in. I would have thought, *Of course she's right. I can't go because I don't have the right clothes.* But I stayed firm. I wasn't expecting to be glamorous and beautiful like everyone else. I knew I wouldn't fit in. But the red skirt teamed with the long black T-shirt was an outfit I felt vaguely comfortable in. I would wear it. At home I'd washed and ironed it carefully then folded it and put it in the back seat of the car. Dad had agreed to drop me in town at Jude's at about three in the afternoon. I could tell both my parents had deep reservations about me going to the Armstrong party, but I refused to draw them out of their silences; their uneasy glances and frowns.

We both got out. I tried to quell my nervousness by smoothing the creases out of my red skirt and picking imaginary bits of fluff from the lovely beaded top Cynthia had loaned me. She leant across and wound down the window.

'Carmel,' she called, 'come here.' I walked back to the car.

'You look terrific!' she whispered. 'Get in there now and enjoy yourself.'

'Thanks,' I said, and remembered the spurt of joy I'd felt when I'd checked myself in Jude's mirror before leaving. That feeling had disappeared now. Now I was out in the world about to meet strangers. They would size up my fat, blushing awkwardness with cold, amused, unforgiving eyes. The way they always did. They would not pass over it like Cynthia and Jude.

I'd been euphoric for most of the afternoon. Cynthia's large room at the front of the house was jam-packed with all kinds of stuff, and she'd invited us in to hunt for anything we could find that took our fancy. Belts and silk scarves, fancy Mexican pins for our hair, and shoes for all occasions. Much of the clothing was old and tattered. Everything I picked up had something exceptional about it, though: the cut or the line, a bit of lace here or lovely edging somewhere else. I enjoyed just looking at it all, touching and examining everything. I loved listening to their prattle – half in Spanish – about everything. I'd never whiled away time on something as frivolous as clothing with my own mother. She was always too busy and anyway she hated that kind of thing. I had thought I hated it too, but this afternoon with Jude and Cynthia I realised I loved it.

Cynthia had two large old trunks, and an enormous heavy cupboard, all full-to-bursting with different bits and pieces. The three of us pulled the stuff on, wrapped it around each other, and pranced around like show ponies. I didn't even feel self-conscious when I told them that I would wear my simple everyday outfit. But when, towards the end of the afternoon, Cynthia dragged out an evening top that she thought might interest me, I suddenly clammed up with shyness. Even before I tried it on I knew I loved it.

It was a black, finely knitted, clinging thing with a narrow band of tiny bright pink and red beading around the wide neckline. It was long and loose with three-quarter-length sleeves, and had a stylish night-time feel to it, despite being quite simple. And it went beautifully with my red skirt. As soon as I put it on I felt it had been sent to me by someone who knew exactly how I wanted to look. I felt dressed up, but comfortable and unfussy. Part of the joy of it was that it had been so unexpected. They'd just fished it up from the bottom of one of the trunks. It had belonged to one of Cynthia's aunts, and out of the blue it had turned up, as if it had been waiting for me.

As soon as I put it on Cynthia went quiet. She walked

around me slowly as if I was a prize pekingese in a show, studying me seriously.

'What do you think?' I asked, hoping like mad that I was right in thinking it looked good. It fitted closely around my breasts and shoulders and hung loose to my hips in the most flattering way.

'Oh, it's perfect,' she said, 'absolutely perfect.' Jude came in from the other room and clapped her hands in glee.

'Fantastic!' she glowed. 'You look stunning.' Cynthia dived into her handbag and pulled out a deep-red lipstick.

'No!' I said, edging away. Enough was enough. I didn't even want to try it. 'It's too strong and bright. I only ever wear clear gloss ... ' But she insisted, making me stand there and open my mouth, drawing it on me herself. With the lipstick on, my face took on a totally different look. I stared at myself in disbelief. I looked brazen, as though I knew exactly who I was and what I wanted.

Over the next couple of hours, in between cups of tea and jokes, the two of them proceeded to do up my eyes and roll my hair up into a soft bun secured with one of Cynthia's tortoise-shell clips.

'I can't look like this,' I said into Cynthia's bedroom mirror, excited by the transformation, but scared witless too.

'Yes you can!' Jude and Cynthia yelled together and then fell about me, laughing with delight. 'You can! You can!'

'You look really *vampy*!' Cynthia sighed, popping the lipstick into my little bag and patting it so that I'd notice. 'Now remember,' she said seriously, 'at odd moments during the party you are to go out to the bathroom and replenish this. This colour really suits you.'

We waved as Cynthia turned the car around and disappeared.

'Well, here we go,' Jude said, as we reached the gate. Jude at that moment exactly fitted my vision of a gypsy. She had chosen an old black silk dress of her mother's; a tight, skimpy bodice with a wide, full skirt embroidered in red and silver flowers that came down almost to her ankles. A red leather belt clinched her waist and her small feet were in shiny, red, very high-heeled shoes. Silver bangles clattered on both her wrists and her hair, pulled back from her face with a silver clasp, fell in dark curls down her back. She looked very exotic and very wild. We opened the gate and stepped into the large garden. A steep row of steps flanked by rose bushes led up through the rolling lawns to the house. It sat there shimmering in the half-light. So substantial, and yet pretty too, with its iron-lace-worked verandah. We could see some people standing about on the lawn and verandah, and heard the faint buzz of talk and the tinkle of glass and laughter.

'We should have come in around the back,' I whispered. Jude nodded and we both began to climb the stairs. Our car had been the only one down the front when we'd arrived, but we hadn't known to take the dirt track around the right of the house. Now I understood it would have led us to where all the other cars were probably parked. I cursed our stupidity. We were going to look foolish walking up these steps, coming into the party this way. The thick smell of the roses on each side of the narrow stone stairs wafted towards me, making me reel. I loved roses and these were particularly lovely, heavy white and various delicate shades of lilac, but the lushness of the smell made me feel like puking. The sweeping lawns were dotted with small beds of lavender, pansies and violets. It was as perfect as ... as perfect as Katerina.

My stomach suddenly did its usual dive and I was busting to go to the toilet.

'Jude! I've gotta go to the toilet!' I hissed.

We were steadily getting nearer to the small group of perhaps a dozen people standing outside. I could see now that two big glass doors leading into the lighted room were open. The room seemed to be full of people. The hum of chatter was punctuated by an occasional little scream of excitement.

'Oh, I haven't seen you for *ages*!'

'How was LA? I heard you ... '

Underneath all that I could hear the sound of instruments tuning up. I felt ill.

'Can't you hang on?' she whispered.

'Not really.'

'Okay, come on.' Her pretty, dark face set into a determined grimace. I felt hopelessly ashamed, conscious of what a drag it must be for Jude to have someone like me tagging along making all these embarrassing demands.

We had reached the house now and were only two steps away from the guests outside, who'd turned to peer at us around the wisteria-covered verandah posts. The girls, with their gleaming hair, thin strapless dresses and tanned skins, edged forward to get a better look. They threw their heads back to giggle.

'Did they *really* walk up all those stairs?'

'You saw it, Caitlin.'

'Oh, gosh, they must be fit!' More titters and then a loud guffaw as a young man's glass smashed onto the stone floor. For a moment they turned their attention away from us.

The young men were standing uneasily beside the girls trying to affect a supercilious slightly amused air. But they weren't convincing. At this early time in the night they were definitely waiting for the girls to call the shots and that somehow made them seem childish and fake in comparison.

I knew these people. I'd known them all my life. I'd never actually *met* them, but they were the stuff of my nightmares. I desperately wanted to run. What if there was no toilet nearby? Perhaps the thing that I feared most would happen. Here, of all places! I could feel my face beginning to heat up as their eyes bore down on us again, a slightly questioning look on every face.

'So, who are you both?' a tall dark girl dressed in a tight silver dress and long black gloves asked lightly, her friendly stance belied by the hard glint in her narrowed eyes. I hesitated, about to blurt out an explanation. Anything to stop them looking at us. But Jude beat me to it.

'I'm not sure,' she countered calmly. 'Who are you?' A faint ripple of nervous laughter fanned out behind the girl. I gulped. *Oh Jude, Jude! Shit, don't do this to me. Not here. Not now.* There were a few muttered comments. The girl's eyes had narrowed further. I wanted to scream and break free. What if I couldn't hold ... it back? What if ... I ... ? More stifled giggles. Someone was sweeping up the glass.

'Well, it's good to see you all!' Jude said with a laugh, leaning forward to nod at each face in the tight little group as if she knew them all very well. No one said anything, but they fixed us with those blank half-smiles that said they were *almost* ready to give us the benefit of the doubt because Jude had called their bluff so nicely. Jude grabbed my arm, pulled me up onto the verandah and swept me around, then we both hurried off along the verandah.

'Phew!' she said with a grin. 'That was close. Now to find you a toilet!' The verandah was tiled in a lovely intricate design. Some of the tiles had come loose and I kept tripping, almost falling over in the high heels.

'Oh God, Jude,' I moaned. 'I need to go! I wish we'd never come.'

'Come on. Around the back,' she replied calmly. 'And we'll ask someone.'

But to my great relief, when we turned the next corner we came across an outhouse lavatory hidden under a huge sweet-smelling jasmine bush. It must have been there for the gardener's use. Although we could hear the party noises no one was around this side of the house so only Jude saw my anxious rush towards it. She waited for me under a nearby tree.

'Thank you God,' I prayed with a rush of gratitude. 'For this lavatory, for this wonderful top and for Jude ... '

I found a little garden tap nearby and washed my hands.

Without another word we walked straight towards the bright lights and the music. We stepped into the formal lobby and were met by Katerina, who unsurprisingly looked fantastic in a simple, long, dark-blue velvet dress that showed off her arms and shoulders. What's more she seemed genuinely pleased to see us and proudly introduced us to her parents.

'Dad. My housemates, Carmel McCaffrey and Jude Torres.'

'Oh yes, of course! So glad you could both come.' The father was polite, but distant, as though he would rather have been somewhere else. But her mother was warm and genuinely charming.

'I'm so pleased the house worked out the way it did,' she enthused, linking arms with us briefly, 'two lovely local girls!' We were both smiling uneasily, but she didn't seem to notice. 'Now how are you all managing with the cooking and housework?' she asked seriously. 'I hope Katerina is doing her fair share.'

Jude and I looked at each other, then both caught Katerina's eye. Who was going to break the news that so far nothing much apart from the occasional wash-up was ever done? Thankfully, Katerina's mother was called away to meet someone else so we were off the hook. Katerina smiled at us as if we were old and very special friends, and led us down the long wide hallway to the formal ballroom at the front of the house.

'I'm so glad you gals could make it,' she said warmly, as though she'd been half-expecting us not to turn up.

The ballroom was packed, well, crowded anyway, but not unpleasantly so. It was a long high room, papered in some fancy embossed stuff. There were mirrors all around and three sets of lovely glass doors leading out onto the verandah and lawn gardens outside. The muted light from the chandeliers above played over the crowd. There were couples dancing in the middle of the floor, and clusters of perfectly dressed girls around the edges who were sort of dancing together and sort of standing about laughing nervously. I stood mesmerised for a few moments.

Then someone handed me a flute of pale yellow champagne from a silver tray. I took a deep sip and turned to Jude and Katerina. It suddenly hit me how wonderful everything was. The beautiful room. All the bright, pretty people. The way they shone, twice, first in the flesh and again in the mirrors on the wall. How absolutely brilliant it all was.

'Wow!' I said with real feeling. Katerina and Jude both burst out laughing in agreement.

'Yeah,' echoed Jude, 'Wow! Wow! WOW!'

Katerina glowed with pleasure. When she looked at us I had a strong sense that she'd been waiting for this moment; waiting to show us her lovely house and the fantastic party, and it made me wonder. There was so much about her that mystified me. *Why did she need us to be there?* It was on the tip of my tongue to ask her to explain herself. *What's with old Glen?* I wanted to ask. *Where does he fit into the picture? And what do you really think of Jude? And how about me?* Thank goodness I didn't get the chance. An older lady dressed like a maid in black with a small white apron tapped Katerina's shoulder.

'Your mother says to come back out. More people have arrived.'

'Okay, Mrs Gardiner, coming.' She gave us an apologetic smile and stepped back into the hallway.

'Come on,' Jude said with a grin, 'let's go up here and see if we can find anyone to dance with us.' I followed her to the front of the room, where the music was coming from. It pounded out, bright and breezy, but old-fashioned in a way, renditions of light pop songs. The kind of thing I normally hated, but in this context it was all right. I wondered if it would get more interesting as the night progressed. I peered over the heads and made out the four musicians dressed in formal dinner suits standing on a makeshift stage. There was a double-bass, keyboard, guitar and drums.

Jude and I danced, first with each other then a bit later with a couple of young men who'd been dancing with two other girls who wanted to sit down in the middle of the set. Jude collared the guys before they had a chance to follow the girls over to the side of the room.

'Hey, you want to keep dancing with us?' she asked cheekily, pulling the jacket sleeve of one of the boys. He was tall and well-built with a clean-cut smile.

'Sure,' he said, smiling at her directness. When he saw me he pulled his friend back. 'Andrew,' he joked, 'the lady here wants a partner. I'm Peter,' he said confidently, 'and this is Andrew.' The other guy turned back and smiled politely. Although he was dark he had the same well-washed, clean-cut directness about him.

The next number had already started. We smiled at each other and began to move.

To my surprise I found I could dance as well as anyone. Better than most of the guys in the room actually. I felt very self-conscious at first, but it was a big crowd and no one was watching so I gradually relaxed. The four of us pranced and jerked around each other, smiling and exchanging names and bits and pieces of information between numbers, as if it was the most natural thing in the world. I could hardly believe that I was behaving in such a normal way.

The two boys were friends and were both studying at an agricultural college. Neither of them said anything even remotely interesting, but they both had an attractive steadiness about them nevertheless. And they were touchingly polite. I realised later that it was to do with the fact that they were farm boys; they lived on adjoining properties north-west of the town. I recognised that steadiness like an old familiar friend. It came when you were sure about your place in the world, what you'd be doing in ten, twenty, even fifty years' time.

When the bracket was over we walked towards the glass doors. I thought they were going to drop us, but they had only moved forward to get us drinks from a tray. They held out chairs for us and the four of us sat down. Then we proceeded to talk in a stilted, offhand way. But I was managing all right. I wasn't overly self-conscious. In fact I was enjoying just being there; watching all the pretty girls, listening to the chattering and the music all around me. Jude kept our little table lively enough by teasing the boys mercilessly. They were dressed almost identically in moleskin pants, elastic-sided boots, beautifully cut check shirts and ties.

'I bet you guys rang each other to check that you would be wearing the same clothes, right?' They had the grace to grin.

'So which one has the shares in the moleskin factory?'

At one stage Andrew mildly declared that the country was 'ruined' because it was being run by socialists. I was wary until I saw that Jude had no intention of being outraged.

'You really reckon that?' was all she said, in an easy, friendly way. They both nodded sagely.

'People just don't expect to have to work any more,' Andrew said, po-faced. Jude laughed as though the statement was hilarious, then she gave him a dig in the ribs.

'I bet you've never even been for a job yourself,' she teased.

'Well ...' he laughed sheepishly. Jude was bringing out his better side, egging him on to lighten up.

'Come on, admit it,' she grinned.

'We're too busy working,' Colin cut in. 'At harvesting time we get up at four. We work until eight at night.'

'Yeah, but how long does harvesting take?'

'About three or four weeks ... but then there's the ...'

'I bet the rest of the time you're lying in bed until about ten!' she said. Both of them were laughing, enjoying the ribbing.

'So what about you, smartie,' Peter said, leaning forward towards Jude. I could tell he was really interested in her. She looked so attractive and sparky sitting there with her exotic dress and dark skin. 'Where do you come from?'

'What do you mean?' Jude was all mock outrage. 'Manella, of course!'

'Well you look like a ... a migrant,' Peter continued gamely.

'Chile,' Jude said sticking her chin out. 'So what ya gunna do about it?'

'Chile is okay,' Andrew said. 'They buy our wheat. So you must be okay.'

'Okay?' Jude laughed and punched him lightly on the arm. 'I'm much better than okay, mate. I'm bloody ... fantastic!'

'May we join you?' It was Katerina and she was pulling a reluctant young man by the hand.

'This is an old friend, Anton Crossway,' Katerina said, smiling at us and pulling up chairs. 'This is Carmel and Jude, whom I live with, and I think you guys know each other.' Peter and Andrew both nodded, and held out their hands to shake Anton's. Jude and I nodded, but he only met our eyes for a second before looking away.

They settled themselves and Jude, Katerina, Peter and Andrew began to talk. I tried not to stare at Anton, but I couldn't help it. It was impossible. Unlike everyone else at the party, he was dressed plainly: blue jeans that didn't even look clean and an unironed black cotton shirt with two buttons missing. He was of medium height and slender, with wide shoulders and a finely chiselled face. It wasn't handsome in the ordinary sense; it was too uneven. A long, not-quite-straight nose that kind of squared off at the end, a thin mouth that kept moving around at the edges, and straight uncombed fair hair pulled back roughly into a ponytail. But there was something interesting about him. He had three or four moles on his face and neck, but apart from these his skin was unblemished and golden-brown; the sort of skin that hasn't been tanned in the sun, but is naturally that colour. He sat next to Katerina staring at his hands most of the time, sometimes sitting on them, only occasionally looking around the room. I tried to work out if he was self-conscious or bored.

'So, Anton, how long are you home for?' Andrew asked politely. Anton looked up to answer. And that's when I saw his eyes properly. Although they weren't big they startled me. They were bright, and sort of lively, sitting in his face like two small bits of ocean. Blue water shored by dark lashes. He shrugged simply. Again I couldn't work out if he was being superior or just shy.

'Just a few days, I think.'

'You like getting home?' This time it was Peter. I could tell that Anton wasn't one of them. The other two were wary of him, treating him with caution.

'Oh, yeah. Sure. I like getting out with the horses and ... the air ... you know.'

His voice trailed away. There was the faintest trace of a lisp that seemed almost childish. But the edgy impatience of his body movements was very adult. Very male. He looked fit and muscular enough to jump out of his own skin at any moment. Was he uninterested in the company or simply uncomfortable in this dressy social scene?

'Last year of your course, isn't it?' Andrew asked.

'Nah, I've finished now,' Anton smiled, 'I'm doing my articles.'

'Decided if you're going to come home?'

'Nope. Not really ... '

I looked down to remove the temptation to stare at him and I saw his feet. Thongs! Cheap white rubber thongs. I jerked my head up for another look at him. This time I caught his eye and we both turned swiftly away. To wear thongs to a party like this? You would have to be very indifferent to everyone, or stupid, or very poor, or absolutely non-caring. Or so supremely confident in who you are that you think you can wear anything you want. I wondered which category he fell into as I felt the terrible flush creeping up my neck. Damn it. I shifted myself around in my chair and pretended to stare at the band. My heart was beginning to race and my palms had gone sweaty.

'How is it going?' Katerina nudged me in a friendly way. 'Having a good time?'

'It's just great, Katerina,' I said. 'It's a terrific party. A lovely party. I love dancing.'

'So how about another dance, girls?'

Peter held out his hand to Jude. I turned and was thankful to see Andrew expecting to dance with me. Profoundly relieved and profoundly disappointed. If we had been left together at the table, maybe Anton would have spoken to me, asked me to dance. I got up with the others and tried to take myself in hand.

I threw myself into the dancing, enjoying it while trying to throw off the introspectiveness that was threatening to open up on me like a rain cloud. I found myself caught up in a circle of eight dancers all doing a sort of group rock-and-roll. Changing partners and whizzing people left and right. It was simple enough and I found I could manage. There was a lot of laughing and bumbling around. No one seemed to care if I didn't get to my spot on time. It came to an end and I caught sight of Anton standing by the wall, looking on, one thonged foot resting nonchalantly on the wall, hands in his pockets. Like he was waiting for a bus on a city street.

We went back to dancing with our partners in a more subdued way for the next slow number. Andrew took my slightly sweaty hand into his and put one arm lightly around my back. We managed in a shuffling sort of way to dance quite well. I couldn't help thinking that if I hadn't been introduced to Anton, if I wasn't constantly taking little glimpses of him over Andrew's shoulder, I would have been enjoying this whole thing immensely. I had never danced like this before. This was proper, grown-up dancing. Here I was, fat Carmel, being held by this reasonable-looking, rather nice young man and being whisked around the floor. And I was managing. I was keeping in step. I wasn't falling over or saying anything particularly stupid. I didn't even want to go to the toilet. If only my mother could be here to see me.

But my eyes kept wandering to the figure in the black shirt standing by the wall.

I was dancing around the room, talking politely to my partner, laughing at Jude's little jokes and grimaces as she flew past, and at the same time keeping close watch on Anton whenever I got the chance. At different times I saw groups of people approaching him. Crazy panic would rise in me. Was he going to walk off with them? Disappear? *Which girl would he choose to dance with?* But they would only stay for a while and he'd be on his own again. I began, ever so slowly, to edge my partner nearer to him. I was filled with a sick curiosity. I wanted to be nearby when he was whisked away by some girl.

My fleeting glances could now pick up a lot from his face. He looked oddly out of it, as though he didn't quite know what to do with himself. I stiffened. A group of three lovely-looking girls approached him and my heart hit my mouth. I watched him smile and nod, respond to their flirting. One of them was stunning. She was supermodel thin, and had masses of black curly hair bunched up on her head, half of it falling luxuriantly down her back. Her white dress was backless; well, almost, just a couple of narrow sequined straps holding it onto her deeply tanned shoulders. Her eyes were flashing and she was laughing as she slipped one of her slender arms around his waist. She was pretending to carry him off. He was laughing and trying to resist. *He will be coming onto the floor any minute to dance with that gorgeous creature. And I don't think I will be able to stand it!*

It was totally unnerving. I turned my back and refused to watch any more. The number finished and we all clapped. We stood on one side of the dancing crowd, in a foursome, puffing from the exertion and smiling at each other.

'Queen Kat's *old friend* is a bit of a hunk, hey?' Jude said gaily, loud enough for the other two to hear. A protective shield clunked into place around my chest, like a steel roller-door slamming down.

'Yes,' I said, feeling my face heat up. But Jude's eyes were already darting around, looking for something else to talk about.

'That guy will inherit Yassfield,' Peter laughed drily, 'and he walks around as if he hasn't got two bucks to rub together ... ' The trace of anger under his words only heightened my curiosity.

'Oh,' I said, as carelessly as I was able. Everyone knew that Yassfield was the biggest property this side of the ranges.

'He's the only son,' Peter explained. 'Katerina's father and his father are best friends. Have been since university.'

'Oh,' I said again.

'What does he do?' Jude asked. 'Apart from being the son of a wealthy landowner?'

'He's just finished Law at uni,' Andrew replied. 'He took a year off to travel last year.' He sneered his way through the last sentence as if there was something slightly suspect in such an activity. I nodded, trying to act as though none of it meant anything to me. I watched my left hand fiddling around with the bottom of that lovely top of Cynthia's, and saw that it was trembling.

We all began to dance again, but it wasn't long before my resistance gave out. I turned around expecting to see that he'd gone; the blank, empty space by the wall where he'd been. But no, there he was, still standing by the wall. A reckless bubble of relief broke inside me. I was in a clinch with Andrew. It was a slow number and we were dancing like old professionals now. One hand resting on his arm, my face staring over his shoulder. We were shuffling around one little section of the floor, barely moving. Suddenly Anton looked up and met my eyes. I took in a sharp breath. A deep, strong pull that came from somewhere deep inside held my eyes steadfast, looking at him. I didn't turn away. We stared at each other, across a sea of bobbing heads, for perhaps five seconds. Straight into each other's eyes. Very seriously. Then he smiled.

He smiled and it was the most exquisite, simple, totally genuine smile I'd ever seen. His head sort of jerked back and he exuded this ... warmth and pleasure, something like the way a baby might smile when its mother came back into the room after an hour of missing her. He raised one hand to his head and scratched as though he couldn't believe it either. As if he was absolutely, totally delighted with me. I smiled back. That took perhaps another three seconds. After which I think I turned away.

'Hey, let's get a drink,' said Andrew.

'Okay,' I answered.

We all walked over to one of the big glass doors. Tables were set up outside on the verandah for the supper. I bent and considered the tiny baked asparagus pastries, the plate of curried prawns and wild rice, the marinated chicken on skewers, the smoked salmon pâté and crackers. I lifted something delicious to my mouth and ate but didn't taste it. A glass was pressed into my hand. I drank, but I didn't taste that either. My heart was hammering in my chest. That smile was the best thing that had ever happened to me. I felt as daring as a sky-diver might feel having just come down after completing a difficult and dangerous drop. I couldn't believe that I'd been so brave.

We ate and talked and danced some more. I was no longer on the lookout for Anton. I no longer needed to know where he was. I knew he would be somewhere, and I knew that when the time came, certainly before the end of the night, we would speak to each other.

'What are you smiling at?' said Jude, leaning towards me at one stage. We were sitting in a group of about a dozen out on the lawn at a small table. I looked at her and sighed, but I couldn't speak. She laughed, delighted, and waited. My face must have told her that something good was happening. I opened my mouth to speak, but nothing came out. I shrugged helplessly.

'I'll speak to you later, girl!' she hissed, before turning away to comment on something Andrew had said.

Gradually the elation ebbed away. The night moved along at its own pace. Suddenly someone said it was midnight, and that it was time for the speeches and toasts. Although I hadn't set eyes on Anton since we'd smiled at each other, I wasn't worried. A huge ball was rolling forward and I had been caught up by it. I stood dreamily with everyone else, laughing in the right places, clapping and joining in. Inside I was operating in a completely different sphere. So when my name was called out over one of the loudspeakers I was completely unprepared.

'Carmel McCaffrey! Is Carmel McCaffrey here?'

'Yes. Here . . . '

'How about a song, Carmel?'

I started awkwardly, almost losing my balance in the high heels I wasn't used to. Jerked awake from my dreamy, spaced-out state of mind. I looked around with astonishment to see that people were gradually edging away, still looking at me with smiles on their faces. They began to clap in unison.

'A song, Carmel. A song!'

My God! I looked around in alarm for somewhere to hide, something to duck behind, some way for this to finish. Who had started it? Was someone trying to play a rotten joke? Everyone was looking and smiling. Where was Jude? Only a minute ago she'd been standing right next to me and now she was nowhere to be seen. A passageway was being created, from me and heading right through to the band on the stage.

I stood, in shock I suppose, certainly feeling myself on the edge of a giant precipice. *All these nice people want me to jump!*

I must have teetered there for a few seconds, feeling that there was no way I could sing. I was rigid with fear. I wanted to explain nicely that they had the wrong person. That I really had only ever sung in church or for old people in nursing homes.

Then I saw Jude's face peering down at me from near the stage. She was smiling at me, beckoning me with her arm. I breathed out furiously and began to walk through the crowd to the stage. This was over the top! She hadn't asked me. Hadn't even suggested this. Now she'd got me into this crazy situation. I was nearly crying by the time I reached her. I wanted to slap her face. The domineering, bossy little ... wog! I could have killed her.

She pretended not to notice my anger.

'Why don't you sing ... ?'

'Why don't *you*?' I retorted in a low hiss. 'Jude, how could you? I don't want to sing. You're wrecking everything!' My face was burning, but for once I didn't care. I was beyond it. My outrage was cut off by a squeeze on the arm. I turned abruptly and looked into the eyes of someone I vaguely recognised. It was one of the musicians dressed in his dinner suit, but his eyes were a sort of glassy blue with lots of friendly wrinkles around them.

'Don't blame her, Carmel,' he said indicating Jude, 'it was me. I recognised you.'

'Who are you?' I whispered.

'Alan,' he said simply. 'Last time you saw me I was playing keyboard in that Fitzroy pub. You didn't turn up that Saturday night, so I thought ... well, Jude here said you were terrific ... '

'But this isn't your band,' I said incredulously, 'you had a girl singer and you were playing jazz ... '

'So what?' he laughed. 'I move in and out of different bands. Actually that girl singer is heading overseas next week and we're looking for a replacement. Come on, show us what you can do.' I gulped. Behind us the people were still clapping. I looked from Alan to Jude then straightened my shoulders.

'I don't think that's possible,' I said.

'How about ... "One Perfect Day"?' Jude suggested. 'She sings that really well.'

'Nah.' Alan's face wrinkled up. 'This is a pretty straight

crowd. Give 'em a pleaser like "The Rose" or something.'

'I don't know that!' I exclaimed angrily.

'Well, what about that other Bette Midler tune? You know, that corny thing, "The Wind Beneath My Wings".'

I wavered then and looked at Jude. We'd learnt that one together back in town during one of our evenings of playing and singing. I actually liked that song a lot. I didn't like it being described as corny. Okay, it wasn't the best song ever written, and it *was* a bit corny, but there was something I liked about it. Jude pinched my elbow reassuringly.

'You sing that well. Go on.'

'Jude, I can't sing *here* ... ' I said.

Alan shrugged and went over to the piano.

'I'll play through the first four lines, okay ... give you the timing? Then you go for it, okay?'

'But I ... ' I held up my hand to stop him.

'Come on,' he whispered hoarsely. 'A crowd of country hicks. You can do it. What does it matter?' He grinned. 'Come on, I'm serious. I wanna see what you can do.'

I suppose that must have done the trick. I gave a faint nod, and stepped up onto the stage.

The clapping stopped and the room suddenly fell quiet. I stood alone by the piano, which had mysteriously been shifted forward. I turned to face the audience, saw them standing below me, so dressed up and made up, so expensive and frightening, looking up with expectant faces.

'Come on. They're just a pack of country hicks. Let's see what you can do ... '

Alan ran through the first bars of the tune.

I couldn't believe that within a few moments I would be opening my mouth and singing in front of all these people. But another part of me was picking up on the pacing and getting ready to come in. His playing was good, strong and slow and delicate. I turned to him and he gave me a nod. I opened my mouth and sang.

At first my voice was thin and tentative, but with each line I gained strength and confidence. By the end I was singing with passion, letting my voice feel out the words, through the notes, letting certain phrases hang in the air for a fraction longer than essential, giving weight and complexity to the ideas behind the lyrics. I fell back on what I'd been taught – to concentrate on what I was singing, and to believe in what I was singing.

'You are the wind beneath my wings ... '

At the end the sea of people below me broke into loud applause. I could see Katerina standing next to her parents, and the three of them clapping warmly.

'More! More!'

I shook my head, bowed, and stepped down from the stage, elated and wiped out. I looked down and saw that my hands were shaking violently. There was no way I was going to sing anything else. People rushed forward to tell me how much they'd enjoyed it. People I hadn't met at all during the night; surprise and delight on every face.

'Where did you learn to sing?'

'You ought to get a recording contract ... '

'You're as good as anyone ... '

Then Peter and Andrew with their funny little formal comments of praise. Their pleasure in the surprise I'd given them. Even the beautiful girl in the white dress who'd passed me in the toilet only ten minutes before without so much as a nod in my direction.

'That was *so* good,' she purred, giving my upper arm a squeeze. I smiled shyly, amazed to see the envy in her eyes. And her so beautiful. I moved through the crowd accepting kisses and congratulatory comments. But it was only when I saw in front of me the black shirt with the two buttons missing that I realised what I'd been unconsciously looking for all along. From the moment I had finished the song and come down from the stage I'd been waiting for this. Now I could slow down. Everything was all right. He'd been here, he'd heard me sing.

'Carmel,' he said and held out his hand. I reached out with my own, excited and pleased, but I couldn't speak. I could do nothing but wait for him to release my hand. Slowly he let my hand go. We were about the same height standing there, only inches apart. Perhaps I was a fraction taller. Anyway, I could stare straight into his face, into the ocean eyes that were smiling at me in that warm, hesitant way.

'You're wonderful,' he said simply and I could feel his breath on my face. The crowd had thinned out around us. I was no longer the centre of attention. I nodded, but still couldn't say anything. He laughed, delighted with my response, which he obviously took to be agreement. Ah. If only he knew. I laughed too and decided that I would let him think that. Parts of me could wait. Let him think I thought I was wonderful. Why not?

Suddenly the band started up again. Some jerky, old-fashioned number. People appeared from an adjoining room; about ten older couples hit the dance floor with great aplomb. The younger crowd could only watch. It was some kind of complicated foxtrot and they didn't know the steps. The oldies were very good. Crowds of young people stood by the sides and watched in reluctant admiration.

'I can't do that,' Anton said, taking my hand, 'can you?'

'No,' I managed to whisper.

'Will we dance anyway?'

'Yes,' I replied, as though in a dream. 'Let's dance anyway.'

Jude

1

I wake with the early light. It is the morning after the party and I can hear Carmel's deep even breaths. She is lying on her back in the makeshift bed my mother had set up opposite me. A shaft of watery light has broken through the tear in the old blind and the breeze from the open window makes it flutter around the room occasionally, as if someone is outside with a tiny torch looking into the room. I turn on my side and gradually make out the features of her face: the calm brow, straight nose, innocent mouth. I think of her singing the night before. In front of all those people; how nervous she was and how angry with me for arranging it. Then, how wonderful she'd been as she felt her gift slowly rise within her – like a bird taking off – from her legs to her stomach, chest and throat – the way she'd calmed down and let herself fly. It was something. Really something to see and hear her do that.

It had to be done. I'd seen the looks passing between them. That smile. She had to be pushed forward against her will for him to understand how wonderful she was. My body curls into a ball of delight as I lie in bed and remember watching them dance. She is in love in a way I will never be. Already she looks different. Even asleep she looks different.

I am happy for her, but anxious, too. Who knows what pain is in store for her?

At home I always wake early. I love to watch everything come to life as the light gently seeps into the room. There is the old wooden cupboard in the corner that used to frighten me when I was younger. The scratched white-painted dresser. The bookcase. All my books and posters. Last year's school texts piled on top of the desk, dusty and forgotten. The Mexican peasant's hat pinned to the wall. A black-and-white photo of my father shaking Allende's hand after the election in 1970 – the same one as I have in my room in Melbourne. My father is in profile, but Allende's smile is full of warmth. Above Carmel's bed I can just make out Pablo Neruda's words, framed in cheap wood: a gift from my father to my mother on their wedding day. The words are scrawled in black-ink copperplate, written carefully but inexpertly. They are surrounded by pressed flower petals. Faded now. I remember my mother laughing when I'd asked about it, telling me that she could never in her wildest dreams imagine my father arranging *flower petals*! But he'd told her that on the day before their wedding he had gone out and picked the flowers and made the whole thing for her. I have grown up with those words. They are as familiar to me as my own toe-nails. They were seared into my brain with the flaming-hot branding-iron of death, before I could talk.

And you will ask: Why doesn't his poetry speak of dreams and leaves
  and great volcanoes of his native land?
Come and see the blood in the streets.
Come and see the blood in the streets.
Come and see the blood in the streets.

The first time they had taken him away, he'd been on his way to work at the hospital. A green Fiat had pulled up alongside him and four well-dressed men in suits and sunglasses had got out and surrounded him with hardly a word. They bundled him into the car and sped off. His wrists were tied and he was blindfolded. When he'd asked where they were taking him one of them hit him in the face with the butt of a rifle, breaking his nose and dislodging two teeth; the sudden rush of blood from his nose and mouth soaked the front of his shirt. Then he was hit again. This time about the face and neck, still with no words of explanation. After a trip of over an hour he was pushed out of the car and made to walk up a rather long flight of beautiful marble steps towards an ornate wooden door. He told my mother that his blindfold had dislodged a little from the blows in the car, and although he didn't dare raise his head to look about he was able to see that they'd led him onto the porch of a big white house – the kind owned by the very rich, aristocratic families up in the hills around the city. There was a wonderful smell of flowers: roses, honeysuckle and jasmine. Through the blindfold he could see a vast expanse of bright purple bougainvillea growing in two lovely porcelain *jardinières* around a row of pillars. Except for the faint buzz of bees all was quiet as they waited for the door to open. My father was aware of the drips of blood from his broken nose splattering onto the white marble of the doorstep and was on the point of asking for a handkerchief to stem the flow. But then the door opened and he was led inside.

It is easy for me now, over twenty years later, to imagine it, to watch the blood dripping from his face into his hands onto the white marble. My father was held in that first place for over a month. My mother said he came out of there a different man. Quieter, older, more loving and more steadfast. He went straight back to work in the poor areas, even after this first dire warning. Did the blood form small crimson pools in the tiny pits and crevices of the marble, around where he stood waiting for that door to open? I wonder who hosed it down when he was taken inside. Or was it left to dry there, to get dark and sticky with flies? There was a time when I could talk quite naturally to my mother about such things. About the time, two years later, when she and her friend managed to talk the soldiers into letting her take the body and arrange a private burial. About her fear that he would end up in an unmarked grave along with so many of the other disappeared. About how they had fought and bribed and cursed their way into the general cemetery in Santiago and buried him properly. She is less inclined now, more cagey, less interested. Perhaps that is natural. Perhaps it is the only way for her.

Sometimes I think that I see everything. Understand everything. When I was ten I remember my mother laughing and telling someone: 'Jude's ten going on thirty-five!' I only half-understood then. Now that I'm nineteen I know exactly what she meant. Now it feels as if I'm going on seventy-five.

A friend wrote last year to say that there are always fresh flowers on his grave. Still. After all this time. All through the years of oppression since the coup in 1973, someone has been brave enough to go and put flowers on my father's grave. Maybe it's one of the children he saved back then. My mother tells me that there were always calls in the night. Or perhaps it is one of the mothers or one of the babies now a grown man or woman.

'*Por favor*, doctor!' The anxious voice calling, the face barely lit by the streetlight. 'My child . . . my husband . . . my mother. I have no money . . . ' And my father rubbing the sleep from his eyes, already dressed, grabbing his bag and rushing off into the night with some woman bundled up in various layers of rags against the cold, often with one or two children in tow. Solemn children with eyes so much older than their years. I wonder what her reaction will be when I tell her about Juan.

Carmel is beginning to stir. She stretches languidly into half-consciousness then settles back into her dreams, unaware that I am watching her closely, enjoying the faint smile on her mouth, the pulse on her white neck, all the tiny signs of her new life.

There are clues at a first meeting that often do not surface again for a long time, so I try to remember what I saw in Anton's face when we were first introduced. Gentleness. Yes. And a certain genuine artlessness too. Was there an arrogance as well? A kind of refined male carelessness that is easy to hide, but could turn into something deadly for anyone who decides to love him? He is only a boy. I must remember that.

An oddly handsome, interesting, intelligent rich young man. In spite of the careless way he was dressed, his wealth and breeding were obvious as soon as I saw him. Does he know he is cute? I think so although I couldn't be sure. I get anxious just thinking about the power this stranger will have over my friend's life. Part of me wants to get up right now and ring him. 'Listen, Anton,' I want to say. 'Carmel's sense of herself and what is possible is only just beginning to bloom. You mess her around and I swear you'll have me to mess around with too! Just remember that, buddy.' But I stay where I am. It is the part of myself I have to watch; the tendency to get too bossy and intervene in situations in which I don't belong. My best traits are also my worst ones. I have noticed that it is often the case in other people too. For someone who has never had a child I am very maternal: I love protectively and generously. I am over-indulgent with love. There is nothing I wouldn't do for certain people. Carmel is one of them. I am my father's daughter after all.

She must be allowed to make her own mistakes or in the end she will hate me. I know that much. Thank God.

There were a couple of low knocks on the door. I knew it would be my mother with breakfast. I could smell the toast.

'Are you awake?' Her voice was soft, barely audible.

'Yes,' I called, only just loud enough for her to hear. 'Come in, Mum.'

The door slowly slid open and Mum and I began to laugh silently as she came over with the tray. She set it on the small table between us and bent down to pour steaming tea into two cups. The laughing was half nerves, fear really, of the way we had grown apart. Carmel and I had both been subdued in the car driving home from the party last night. Mum had asked questions, but we'd answered only vaguely. I had been too tired and Carmel had been too overwhelmed and excited. My mother was hoping for more details this morning.

'I don't think Carmel's awake yet,' she whispered, disappointed.

'Yes I am,' came a sleepy murmur from the other bed. Mum and I looked over at her rumpled shape shifting around in the bed and laughed again.

'Do you want to go back to sleep?' Mum asked gently. But Carmel was already sitting up and rubbing her eyes.

'No. I'm awake.'

Mum went over to the window and pulled the blind. We all stared at each other in the bright morning, blinking and smiling.

'Tea, Carmel?'

'Thank you.'

It was a shock to see my mother through Carmel's eyes. How beautiful she still was, standing there by my bed wearing her tatty green silk dressing-gown, pulled in at the waist with an old elastic belt. The silk hung around her hips and legs in elegant folds, giving only so much away. She might have been a movie star from the forties. Her natural grace and style were astounding. How my father must have been fascinated with her feminine hands and light body, the wiry fair hair. Everything. I suddenly wondered why she had never taken a lover since his death. What a waste, I found myself thinking, knowing how cruel and uncooperative I would have been if she'd even thought to do such a thing. Once when I was about twelve I'd heard someone tell her she should get married again.

'Jude's father was the best there was,' she'd said. 'After being married to him I don't think I could live with anyone else.' Of course that had pleased me. It was what I wanted to hear. I don't think the subject had been broached since then.

After she'd served us, Mum poured out a cup of tea for herself.

'Now,' she said, 'tell me all about it. What happened? I

know something happened by the way you were both behaving last night!' I looked across at Carmel and we both burst out laughing.

'You begin, Carmel,' I ordered. 'After all, you were the star of the show!'

'Well, somehow... I can hardly believe this. I *sang*!' Carmel declared. She shivered then and looked across at me in disbelief. 'Jude, did I dream that or was it real?'

'It was real, you idiot,' I snapped back happily. 'Come on, tell Mum about it...'

Carmel explained simply how she'd sung. How nervous she'd been and how well she had been received. Mum was thrilled. At one stage she moved over and gave Carmel a quick hug.

'Aren't you wonderful! See how silly you were to be nervous?'

Carmel's eyes were shining as she went on to describe the dancing, the girls' dresses, the brilliant mirrored room. She didn't mention Anton, and although it was on the tip of my tongue to spill out all the details about him to Mum, I managed to restrain myself. I could tell that it was all too new for Carmel, too precious and unresolved, still too hard for her even to believe. I decided to keep my mouth shut until she was ready.

'Enough about all the others' dresses. Did you feel lovely yourselves? Because you both looked perfect when you left here. Carmel, I hope you remembered to replenish the lipstick!'

We laughed and chatted on into the morning, taking it in turns to get up for further supplies of toast and tea.

Suddenly it was midday. Carmel jumped up from the table when she saw the time.

'Dad will be here to pick me up in an hour,' she said, and hurriedly began to gather her things together. 'I'd better not keep him waiting.'

'Give him a ring, why don't you? I'll take you home,' Mum said quickly.

'Oh no, Cynthia ... I don't think.'

'Why ever not?' Mum had picked up the phone and handed it to Carmel.

'Come on. So you don't have to hurry.' I could see that Carmel was uncomfortable with the idea, but she relented at our insistence.

'Er, Mum ... it's me, Carmel,' she said into the phone. 'Tell Dad not to worry about picking me up. They're going to drive me out. Yeah. That's okay. Bye.'

It was still quite dry out there, in spite of it being April, though there was a faint tinge of green coming up through the long brown grass. I was about to turn to Carmel and remind her of the day she told me that was what she liked best about living in the country: the green autumn shoots coming up through the dead grass. But when I turned around to her in the back seat her face was set, strained. She didn't look like she wanted to be reminded of anything, so I shut up. We turned in from the main road and began to travel up a windy dirt track, over a rattling wooden bridge, and up and around a few rises. Heavy gum trees stood clumped together in groups by the track, leaning towards each other like friends talking; the strong sweet eucalypt smell was overpowering. We passed a few gates that led into farms; often only the roofs were visible behind leafy gardens. All was quiet and tranquil. I pictured Carmel as the solitary little girl she would have been, growing up among all those brothers amid this beauty.

'This one,' she said suddenly. Mum braked and we turned in between two faded white fence posts and across a cattlepit, then began to ascend a small hill towards a house set squarely at the top. I loved it immediately. The scene before us was like something out of a book of fairytales. The house was old and made of timber. It seemed to have no formal design at all.

Just a higgledy mess of rooms all sticking out from one another. A partially collapsed verandah ran from one uneven end of the structure to the other. At the back of the house was a tall windmill and the dome shape of an underground tank. As we got nearer, I saw that the weatherboards were peeling badly. The whole place seemed to be an integral part of the surrounding dry hills, almost like a large gnarled tree root that had been there forever – its unique shape making its own unique sense. I took a quick look at Mum as she pulled the car up in front of the lopsided picket fence and saw that she was similarly entranced. I almost turned around to Carmel to ask if we could come in, but something stopped me. I knew she'd make some excuse and we'd have to leave without seeing it all.

'Well, thanks a lot you two. Cynthia, thanks . . . ' Carmel said quickly before jumping out and turning to smile. But Mum beat her to it. Before she got a chance to leave, Mum had hopped out of the car.

'I might just say hello to your mother,' Mum said lightly. I got out too.

'Oh . . . er.' Carmel looked at us uncomfortably. 'I don't know if she's home.'

'There's someone there,' Mum said gaily, pointing to the figure of a thin woman taking clothes off a line of wire that hung between two dead trees at the side of the house. Carmel shrugged resignedly and the three of us walked towards the rusted old back gate.

'Hi, Mum,' Carmel called in a careful, thin voice. The woman, her arms full of sheets and towels, had stopped what she was doing and was already squinting at us as we walked through the gate into the dusty yard.

'Oh, it's you,' she said drily. Her face was like the house, wind-worn and bare. But her eyes were full of shrewd watchfulness. I sussed her out as a clever woman. Thin, worn-out and clever, I thought to myself. I also sensed she was daring us to come any further without an invitation. That thought must have hit Mum at the same time as me. We both stopped on the path, halfway between the gate and the back door, and waited. I turned away from the woman's quizzical look to stare at the back verandah. There were men's boots by the back door, wheat bags and shovels and a pile of used fruit tins with the labels still on. A few geraniums were trying to grow in a couple of cut-in-half rusted forty-four-gallon drums by the back step. Somehow they, more than anything else, gave a desolate tone to the place.

'I'm Cynthia,' my mother began. 'Jude's mother ...'

'Yes,' the woman said quickly. 'Well, thanks for bringing her back.' Her dress was worn and grubby and her straight grey hair was cut as short as a man's.

'That's no trouble at all,' Mum said with a warm smile. That smile usually won strangers over. I watched her flounder a little when Carmel's mother's hard expression didn't change. Mum opened her mouth and then closed it again.

'It's nice for the girls to share the house in Melbourne, isn't it?' she managed lamely after a couple of uncomfortable moments. The woman turned away. For a moment I thought she was going to ignore us altogether, but she was only bending down to put the pile of washing into the basket.

'Would you like a cup of tea?' she said flatly, not looking directly at us, as though somehow resigned to the inevitable. I looked over at Carmel, who was standing by the back door. I knew she didn't want us to come in so I reluctantly nudged Mum to suggest we should leave. But Mum obviously had other ideas.

'Oh, that would be lovely!' she said enthusiastically. 'If it isn't too much trouble.'

'Well, no,' the woman said in a slightly more friendly tone and, picking up the basket of washing, began to walk towards the door. 'I was going to have a cup myself anyway.' She stopped just before we walked into the house. 'I'm Nancy by the way. Nance McCaffrey.'

'Nancy,' Mum said, taking the thin rough hand into her own. 'Pleased to meet you.'

'Call me Nance.'

'Okay,' said Mum, and meekly followed her inside.

The kitchen was large and full of so many things. The huge table in the middle of the room was covered in a horrible plastic tartan tablecloth. Down one end sat a disconnected microwave oven still in its box, and down the other end were half a dozen gutted rabbits. Their dead grey eyes made me shudder. In the middle of the table sat an ice-cream container filled with lemons. Every bench was cluttered with things; practical useful things like tins of golden syrup and peaches, nails, balls of green twine, packets of matches and cartridges, a pocket-knife, cheque books, a set of screwdrivers and nails. There were piles of boxing magazines on top of a large packing box and a calendar advertising local businesses pinned to the wall. Farm management statistics were written in pencil on the doorway into the next room: *24 ewes @ $63.90. 15 head of cattle. 13 calves* etc. In the far corner there were two shotguns and a kid's cricket bat, in the other a pile of saucepans with no lids, three of them filled with dirt-encrusted fresh eggs. It was all clean though. The worn lino had recently been washed and there were no dirty dishes hanging around. Nance swiftly slung the rabbits off the table and into the enamel sink, then wiped the blood off the table with a pink cloth.

'Take a seat,' she ordered. 'I'll make the tea.' The big kettle on the old black wood stove was already whistling. Mum and I sat at the table. Carmel, her eyes downcast, walked over to the dresser and began to get out cups and saucers.

'So, how did the party go?' Nance asked sharply, turning to her daughter with a frown. Carmel was taking great care to wipe the cups and put them with the right saucers and so didn't answer immediately.

'It was okay,' she shrugged.

Something about the way she answered perturbed me. So subdued and sad. So *crushed*. I understood with a jolt why Carmel found things so hard, why her belief in herself was so minuscule. *This is where she comes from.* I had a sudden gut feeling that no one around here would be allowed to get enthusiastic about anything for a long while. I liked the rough house and poor farm. None of that was standing in her way. It was this sharp, practical woman in front of us, with her tough no-nonsense approach to everything, that was stifling Carmel. I just knew that in my bones. I also knew – I know this will seem too crazy – but I also knew that there would be a fight for Carmel one day. Between this woman and me. It would be a bitter fight and I wasn't at all sure who'd win.

'It was really good,' I piped up, unable to keep my mouth shut any longer. Mrs McCaffrey turned to me, as if she'd only just noticed I was there.

'Did you get anyone to dance with you?' she asked suspiciously. The way she said it! Like it wasn't at all probable that either of us would have anyone to dance with. It took my breath away for a couple of moments. I wanted to scream.

'Of course,' I said, 'we both danced all night.'

'That true, Carmel?' her mother snapped.

'Well, yes ... ' Carmel looked up unhappily, only holding her mother's look for a brief moment. 'We both enjoyed ourselves ... ' She ventured the last part tentatively. She didn't expect her mother to believe her. I could feel I was going to say something very stupid even before I said it. I did try to calm myself. I knew it wasn't my place to interfere with this woman's way of doing things, especially in her own house. But that attitude made me see red.

'Carmel was dancing all night,' I said loudly, looking straight at her mother, 'then the most attractive man in the whole place fell in love with her ... '

'*Jude* ...!' Carmel groaned. I looked over at her defiantly, but her eyes were downcast and a terrible pink blush was beginning to suffuse her neck and face.

'And who was that?' Mrs McCaffrey asked with a grim, sarcastic smile as she pulled some biscuits out of a tin, set them on a plate, and sat down. 'Who *fell in love* with Carmel?' Her voice was dripping irony as if it was the most stupid phrase she'd ever heard.

'Anton Crossway,' I muttered savagely. Now that I'd made the mistake of going up this path I wasn't about to pike out before I'd finished. A sudden burst of pure unadulterated hatred for this woman began to pulse through me. I wouldn't let her have the satisfaction, even if Carmel never spoke to me again. Mrs McCaffrey sniffed and frowned. The rest of us were silent as we gingerly sipped our tea. Mum took one of the offered biscuits with a little smile, as much to relieve the tension as anything.

'Thanks, I'd love one ...'

'You mean the Crossways from Yassfield?' Mrs McCaffrey asked. I looked swiftly at Carmel, but she was hunkered down in her chair, not meeting anyone's eyes, sipping her tea as if her life depended on it.

'Yeah,' I said, 'that *rich* family with all the property.' Then, much to my dismay, I began to babble.

'Anton's twenty-two and has finished his Law course. He's doing his articles with a city firm. He's very charming and very good-looking. Apparently he's undecided about what he'll be doing next year, once he's admitted to practice. He might come back to the family property or stay in town ...'

'But that's a bit ... ' Mrs McCaffrey cut in disbelievingly. 'What in God's name would *he* see in Carmel?' We all stared at her in silence. The words swam around us where we sat.

When they finally registered properly I had to stop myself from jumping up and punching her. Even Mum was outraged. I looked across the table and saw that her mouth had tightened and her eyes were flashing all over the place. A sure sign. But Mum has always been much better at controlling her feelings than I am.

'Carmel looked absolutely wonderful last night ... Nance,' Mum began evenly. 'It's a shame you didn't see her ... well, both of them really, dressed up ... Jude and Carmel both looked wonderful.'

'Because she's beautiful,' I cut in furiously, 'and she's a ... she's a *shithot* singer too!' Mrs McCaffrey started in her chair as if she'd been shot. The word *shit* hung in the air between us like soiled underwear. As soon as I'd said it I realised I was pouring more fuel into the flames. Mrs McCaffrey fixed me with a savage glare of disapproval. I thought for a moment that she was going to tell me to get out of her house, but she remained silent. The whole scene was getting too hot for Carmel. She rose quickly and for some reason began hauling canisters down from the top shelf of the dresser, her face the colour of beetroot.

'It's nothing, Mum,' she whispered. 'He doesn't ... er, *love* me or anything. Jude's exaggerating ... did you want me to clean all of these today?' I knew this was our cue to leave. I desperately didn't want to go yet. I had to talk to Carmel. I wanted to apologise. I also wanted to point out that this woman, her mother, was bloody *poison*. Until she got her life together she must stay away from her. I silently offered up a prayer of thanks for the job we'd organised with Juan.

'Yes, they'll have to be washed out,' her mother replied. Mum and I rose to go. I was surprised to see the look of weariness on Mrs McCaffrey's face. The fight seemed to have gone right out of her as she sat looking at her daughter, holding both arms tightly across her thin chest.

'Well, he'd be quite a catch, Carm,' she said, with a dry little laugh, 'but I'd watch myself if I were you.'

Well, you're not her are you, you stupid old cow! The uncomfortable atmosphere was broken by the shrill ringing of the telephone in the far corner of the kitchen. Carmel took a couple of steps towards it, but her mother waved her back, getting up slowly from her chair.

'I'll get it,' she said with a sigh. 'It'll only be Jim Slavin wanting to know if we've got the rams.' She turned to Mum and me politely before picking up the receiver.

'Won't be a minute. Then I'll see you out.' We nodded and stood waiting for her to finish.

'Hello. Yes? Oh ... ' Her face gave nothing away as she turned to Carmel.

'It's for you, Carmel,' she muttered. 'Hurry, will you. Jim will be calling soon.'

Carmel gulped and hurried over.

'Yes. Carmel speaking. Oh yes. Oh yes. Hello!' I watched and knew it must be him because her face was suddenly glowing with a kind of nervous delight. I looked at Mum and we both winked and smiled at exactly the same time. Mrs McCaffrey was studying us sourly, as if it was somehow our fault that her daughter was behaving in such an outrageous way. The three of us eavesdropped. We couldn't help it.

'Yes,' Carmel kept saying breathlessly. 'Yes, yes.' Then, 'No, no. I'm sorry I don't think I can ... ' I began to get worried until I heard her tone pick up again.

'Yes. That will be all right. Good. Thank you. Goodbye.' She put the receiver down and turned around. Her face was blazing with ... well, with happiness. She was looking right at me and she wasn't trying to hide it at all.

'Jude,' she began breathlessly. 'He's asked me out when we get back to Melbourne ... do you think I should? I said yes. Do you think I ... ?'

I loved seeing her so forthrightly happy for a few precious moments in front of this dour woman. I wiped the grin from my face and frowned, very deadpan.

'No,' I answered slowly, tapping my fingers severely on the table. 'I won't allow it.' I turned to her mother. 'Mrs

McCaffrey, rest assured, I won't allow it. Men simply take our minds off the higher concerns, such as our study ... Trust me. I'll get the ... er, young man's number from this wanton girl and ring him straight back ...'

After a couple of odd initial moments of total confusion, they were all laughing, Mum, Carmel and even Mrs McCaffrey. When she finally realised I was joking her face softened and her eyes began to twinkle. The smile took about ten years off her age. It was a pleasure – I think we all felt it – to see her smile. I remember thinking that perhaps underneath she wasn't as bad as I'd first thought.

On the way out to the car Carmel and I moved away a little from the other two, agreeing to meet on the train back to the city the next day.

'See you tomorrow then,' I said, squeezing her arm, 'at four.'

'Yeah,' Carmel sighed. 'Do you think he likes me?'

'No, Carmel. That's why he's taken so long to ring. God, I mean it's a full half day since he's seen you! I'd say he probably despises you.'

'But me!' she said, giggling and shaking her head. 'I mean with all those other beautiful girls ...'

'Ah, all those little bimbos,' I growled. 'Listen, he's obviously a man of taste, you idiot!'

'See you tomorrow then!'

'Yep, tomorrow!'

My mother and I didn't talk much on our way back to Manella. We were both thinking, I guess, about that strange shambling house, and the thin sharp woman who was so different from her daughter. I was hoping like mad it would work out for Carmel.

That night I told Mum about Juan. I hadn't planned to. But we'd got talking about Carmel and Mum had wanted to know about her uni course, how she was doing, and what her plans were. Without too much angst I decided simply to tell her the truth – Mum wasn't someone who'd go blabbing it to anyone.

'But how will she live?' she asked, surprised and worried. 'They'll cut off her student allowance, won't they?' We were sitting in the lounge room sipping cocoa before bed. There'd been a fine tension over everything since I'd got home, something hard to explain. Mum had welcomed me with open arms, made all my favourite foods, and tried to engage me in conversation, but still I felt there was something wrong. Maybe spilling the beans about Carmel was an unconscious way to bring this uneasiness to a head, to get on the level with her.

'She's got a job, starting next week,' I said. Mum's face brightened.

'Oh, that's good. What kind of job?'

'Waitressing.' I ploughed on, hoping that she wouldn't ask any more questions.

'Where?' my mother asked. I looked up and saw that the anxious glint in her eyes had returned as she tried to read my face. All my life I have known my mother well; she has always been like an extension of myself. It was a new, almost frightening, experience to be suddenly aware of her as someone totally different.

'Remember that cafe where a lot of Chileans hang out?' I said carefully.

'I know it,' she snapped. I looked up at her defensively.

'Do they mind that she doesn't speak Spanish?' Mum eventually asked.

'No. But I'm teaching her anyway. She picks up the songs really easily, so I reckon she'll learn a bit. Enough anyway.'

'Do you go there often?' she asked, trying to sound casual. 'I was hoping that you'd forget all about that ... and mix more ... I was hoping you'd not stay tied up ...'

Her voice dropped away. I saw that she couldn't finish the sentence. She was really upset.

'You were hoping that I'd not stay *tied up* with my father?' I asked drily. I longed to go over to her and hug her tightly.

Tell her I loved her and would never do anything to make her unhappy. A year ago I would have done just that. But this year I sat there heavily, watching her, my stone heart cracking and rubbing itself raw.

'Who runs it now?' she asked quietly.

'Juan Enriquez,' I replied. She jumped up from her chair, then sat down again as if I'd shot her.

'Oh, Jude,' she whispered, tears forming in her eyes, 'oh, darling, please!' I watched two of them roll down her cheeks and still couldn't move.

'You remember him?' I asked stiffly. I had to know. There was so much she hadn't told me.

She nodded. 'Of course I remember him ... '

'So why don't you come down and see him? He'd love to see you, I'm sure. We talk about ... about my father, about Carlos, often. He's told me a lot already. Why don't you come?'

But she was shaking her head, gasping as though in pain.

'Jude, let it go! Please ... ' she emplored softly. I got up, moved away from the table and stood by the sink. Our lunch dishes were still stacked haphazardly over the benches. Mum had cooked us wonderful *completos* for lunch. Carmel and I had had three each. Now the ants were out, already organised into small secret labour lines, methodically carrying off the surplus from the plates. I hated the smell of ants, but I also hated killing them. It seemed criminal somehow to destroy such ingenuity, such sure purposeful work. I let the hot tap run for a while and then filled a cup with steaming water. Then I drowned the ants. I watched fascinated, horrified really, as their ordered little world collapsed. Their bodies flayed wildly as they headed for the plughole. I refilled the cup and finished the job.

'Mum,' I said slowly. 'He was ... my father ... '

'But see how it's ... wrecked my life,' she whispered. I looked up quickly, shocked.

'What do you mean ... wrecked your life?'

'Living in the past,' she said, 'living for memories. Jude, I want you to enjoy life here. Now! Don't live in the past ...'

'I don't live in the past!' I cut in angrily.

'So go out! Meet all different people. Get involved with other things. Have fun. Jude, I came ... I came back from Chile all those years ago so that you could have a life!'

I believed her. I felt for her, too. Maybe I would have done the same thing myself if I'd had a daughter. Gone back to where it was safe and secure.

'Jude, all my friends were over there! My life was there! I've hidden myself in this bloody town for you!' She was speaking loudly now. So that I would understand what she meant. Her hands were working overtime, the way they do when she speaks Spanish. But now she was speaking English. 'I could have had ... I could have married ... again over there. I could have ... Jude, I've done everything I could to give you a chance, haven't I?' I shrugged and she slumped back into her seat.

'I haven't stopped you ...' I muttered uncomfortably.

'No, but Jude there was always your father,' she said. 'He was a wonderful man. Compassionate, loving, totally committed ... but he was killed, Jude. Died, working so hard, so selflessly ... He's gone. He's been dead for nearly twenty years!' I stared at her sullenly.

'*You can't take up his burdens!*' she shouted.

'Why not?'

'This is a different country! The times have changed. Even if you go back to Chile, there isn't the popular feeling for change that surrounded us in the early seventies. Everything's changed ...'

'How do you know?'

'I know! People write ... Jude, it's the truth.'

'So you think my father wasted his life?' I said furiously.

'In the broad scheme of things his life was ... not wasted,' she answered slowly. 'It is important for the world to know ... for people to know that there are brave men and women around who will not be silenced, who will die for what they know to be right, but ... ' She raised her face and looked at me.

'But what?' I whispered. A coldness had crept into my chest, a sort of chill tingling from my throat, all the way down my legs.

'As far as the *small* picture goes,' she continued. 'I mean the effect his death had on us, even on Chile, on the immediate situation there, then, yes, his life was wasted. I think he should have stopped after the coup, after 1973. When they let him out of detention the first time he should have given up and tried to get out of the country ... the way I wanted him to. There were people who would have helped us ... '

I sat very still refusing to let her words settle into my head. I didn't need them. I had no wish to understand things from her point of view. Down that path lay weakness, emptiness, failure. I was filled with an angry indifference that probably showed in my face, but I didn't care. We sat there for some time, not speaking, not even looking at each other.

'I'm organising the protest with Juan,' I said eventually.

'What protest?'

'The Chilean president is coming here in June,' I said, 'and we plan to be everywhere he is. Public halls, hotels, the World Trade Centre ... '

'Who is "we"?' she asked.

'Fifty, sixty people,' I said, 'maybe a hundred in Melbourne.'

'Why, Jude? What do you think you will achieve?'

'Not that much,' I shrugged. 'We just want him to know that *we know*. That people in other parts of the world care. He was elected on the understanding that he would bring some of those bastards to justice and acknowledge the ones who disappeared. We want to keep the pressure on for proper trials ... '

'I know the situation,' she cut in with a dry laugh. 'Everyone knows there will never be proper trials while the army has so much power. What I mean is, why are you involved?'

We went on into the night. We were both so tired, but we couldn't give it up. Most of the time we were talking around each other, coming at the same thing from totally different angles. Whatever it was that was happening she couldn't stop talking. I knew she wanted the best for me. But at the same time I was furious. Unlike my father, she had been a committed communist. He would simply have described himself as a doctor working for change. She used to think there were things worth fighting for. I despised her for not having the strength to hang on the way he had. But I loved her, too, so it was complicated. Most of all I desperately didn't want to be dragged into her way of seeing things.

Eventually we said goodnight. It must have been about three in the morning. She came over to embrace me in the usual way, but I pulled away after a brief kiss.

'What do you see in all that stuff, Mum?' I asked bluntly, pointing at the poster pinned to the wall. It was a colourful abstract design advertising a 'spiritual awakening' conference to be held in Sydney later in the year. The day before I'd been going to tear it up and chuck it in the bin, but I'd thought better of it. After all, Mum had never tried to shove any of those things down my throat and the next day I'd be going back to the city.

'I want peace, Jude,' she said in a small voice, 'some kind of peace. I've seen things I can't forget.'

'*What kind of things?*' I wanted to scream. '*Tell me. Tell me. Tell me. I want to know everything.*'

As I was drifting off to sleep I thought about peace. I don't think it's as important as everyone believes it is. This will sound crazy, but when my mother had been talking about my father having no thought for the danger he was in, of the way he went on fearlessly organising and working, keeping faith with what he believed in – in a way implying that he had brought about his own death – my love for him was renewed in a deep, almost physical way. I was filled with a powerful attraction for that kind of life. It wasn't simply a matter of being proud of him. I realised that I wanted that for myself too.

My father was shot for refusing to stop working towards a just society. His beliefs were simple. He wanted a society in which the poor would have enough food, schools for their children, medicine when they were sick, shoes for the winter. All things that we take for granted in Australia. And in Chile that was enough to get him killed. Some guys of forty die of cirrhosis of the liver from drinking too much, or of cancer from smoking. And many more die of the same self-inflicted things ten or twenty years later. What's the use of having the extra twenty years if you do nothing with them? From the age of about ten, I have felt that I would die young. And that knowledge or hunch has never worried me. In fact, I want to nurture the feeling and make sure that when the time comes I will be giving my life for something worthwhile. That's what's important. I think it would be a privilege to die the way he did, totally in command, having made no compromise, no retreat, no surrender.

Someone in Chile continues to put flowers on my father's grave. That is enough for me. For me that means he is still alive.

When I have finished my medical training I will go back there and carry on the work. I know I won't be alone. In every country there are people who are willing to put themselves on the line. If I end up with a bullet in my head, so be it. Perhaps I will end up alongside him. Together at last. Lying side by side in the Santiago cemetery, looking up at the enormous tree that my mother tells me stretches over at least thirty graves.

I sit all day in lectures and tutes and learn how the human

body works. I also learn from my fellow students about how the world is organised for the benefit of the middle classes and upwards. The whole place, my course especially, is filled with kids from Brighton and Toorak and Doncaster; from private schools all over the state. Most of them are very nice, friendly anyway, fine to pass the time with between lectures and share lunch with in the cafe. I think I am the only one in first-year Medicine who has come from a country state secondary college. This fills me with inordinate pride.

I have made only one real friend within the medical faculty. Declan is twenty-two and in fifth year – the one other student I've met who was educated at a country state school. I met him and his girlfriend Annie at the Amnesty group in my first week. After only half an hour with them over a coffee I felt like I'd known them both all my life. Declan is tall and thin-faced with brown curly hair and a dark serious face. He doesn't talk about himself much. But over the months I've slowly been able to build up a portrait of him. He is one of those freaky types who has had no advantages at all and yet manages to be *naturally* everything he wasn't meant to be. He loves music and plays well, although he's never been formally taught. He is a thinker, even though there were no books in his house and his parents thought anyone who even read the paper was up themselves. According to Annie his family had lived on the verge of poverty for most of his young life; the dominant memory of his childhood a never-ending screaming match between his parents and his older siblings. For some reason that Declan hasn't yet explained to me he has been a committed member of Amnesty since he was fifteen. He writes letters, calls meetings, formulates policy, and badgers politicians and journalists. He is always the first to arrive at meetings and the last to leave.

Annie is a small, pretty blonde woman with a gutsy laugh and a dry salty way of seeing things. She ribs me about my hot Latin temperament, teases me about my inability to be cool. 'Try and curb that passion, Jude!' she drawls, throwing an arm lightly around my shoulders and winking at whoever is nearby. 'Keep your mouth shut, girl, and you might become a proper Aussie one day.' It took me a while to realise that her jokes and prettiness – the blonde hair, blue eyes and sexy figure – disguised a person who in her own way was just as passionate as I was. She and Declan are rarely apart, yet I never feel as if I'm in the way when I'm with them.

I'm almost asleep thinking how much I have enjoyed everything in my last few months in the city. Even when I'm with people in my course who are snobby or boring, I know I'm learning something new. When you feel in your bones that you haven't much time everything becomes interesting. Sweeter. Life is always surprising me.

After about three hours of deep sleep I wake up with a start, sweating. I can't remember anything much about the dream except that I'd been with my father. I had been watching him ride a horse down a very steep ravine. I was afraid that the horse would lose its footing and fall. Although I try desperately I can't remember any more of the dream. I lie in the dark trembling, trying to make myself breathe deeply. As I begin to calm, it dawns on me that my mother really is keeping things from me. Perhaps even Juan, too. Both of them have secrets that they are keeping from me.

2

For the first few weeks after Easter life went on as before. Carmel went to work in the early morning and we'd meet up in the evening: eat, talk and play music together. But when she began the evening shift, life changed for me. Nights were suddenly lonely. I'd never been someone who'd had heaps of friends – in fact I'd privately scorned the whole idea of getting around in a crowd – but I'd been used to company, more or less whenever I'd wanted it. My mother had been there all my life. It surprised me to realise that throughout my school days my mother had probably been not only my best friend, but my only real friend.

Katerina was almost always out. I'd arrive home from uni around six most nights and Carmel would have left for work. So I'd cook myself something and then go into my room to study for a few hours. I still enjoyed university, but it was a hard slog. There was so much to learn. Studying medicine was like working at a full-on job every day right through the term. I knew I had to keep up. There were tests and assessments every couple of weeks, as well as the exams at the end. I knew I was capable of doing well and I really wanted to.

May brought the first dissection class for the year. We'd all been warned and knew we'd have to get used to it because it would make up a major part of the course for the next few years. By this stage I'd made a bit of a reputation for myself; I was blunt and fairly tough compared to many of the other girls. Some of the ex-private-school boys found me a little hard to handle, although I know I amused them too. So I suppose it surprised them as well as me that I found dissection a bit hard to deal with at first.

On the day of the first class, two hundred of us made our way dutifully up the stairs to the third floor, then down a corridor and through a couple of glass doors. We were met by the professor of anatomy, who told us that we were never to enter the room without gowns and gloves. There was some general nervous laughter as we donned these. Already the smell of formalin was strong. Silently we trooped into the huge room. About thirty steel tables were lined up each side under the large windows, with another three sitting in the middle. On each table lay an adult human body covered with a white sheet. A shiver passed through me and I was tempted to run straight out.

'Okay, please break up into groups of six,' the professor said loudly, 'then select a table. Pull off the sheet, fold it and put it on the bench nearest to you. After each session you are to cover the cadaver again. You are to remain in the same group with the same cadaver every week for the next six months...'

We all shuffled forward and quickly did as we were told. In my group the sheet was pulled off by a boy I vaguely recognised; a funny Jewish kid I'd joked with last term. Amos. He made a ghoulish face at me and we both smiled. I looked around the room; no one was retching or fainting, but everyone seemed solemn and some had gone very white. All of us were taking quick, sidelong glances at the dead body in front of us.

I got used to dissection, of course, after some time; the smell and the feel, the look of those dead people that I had to work on, became just something else I had to do in my day. I wasn't the only one who found it difficult at first. Only one of us had even seen a dead body before the classes began. That girl had seen a distant relative all laid out in pretty clothes in a shining wooden coffin. She told us that the body had looked like a wax dummy. These dead bodies we had to work on didn't look like wax dummies. They looked like people. But they were so still, they looked like ... well, like ... *dead people*, which was exactly what they were.

Each Tuesday afternoon I would walk over to the table in my white coat and look down at the face of the one assigned to us – a man in his fifties with white hair and yellow skin. He'd died of a massive heart attack apparently. The professor was going to show us the damaged heart when we'd finished dissecting the legs. The curious side of me was quite looking forward to this. It would be interesting to see in real life what I was learning from all those books. But another side of me was appalled. I didn't want to see his messed-up, sad old heart.

'Hello, mate,' I would say as I picked up my scalpel and began slowly to pull the skin and layers of yellow fat back from around his knee. Of course, we were told nothing about the bodies except the cause of death. But I would wonder what secrets and dreams had died inside the flesh I was cutting up. Were they still there in some way? Just hiding beyond my reach? It was hard to forget that the body I was carefully chopping to pieces had once lived and breathed, laughed and made love. Had he been a bastard to his wife or a loving devoted uncle to someone? Sometimes when these thoughts really took over, when they diverted me from the serious business of learning about the intricate systems of the body, I wondered if I was suited to medicine at all.

Within a couple of months I began going to the cafe with various companions at least a couple of nights a week. Sometimes just with Annie and Declan and Patrick, who lived in their house. Other times I'd go with a group from Amnesty. We'd got to know each other well, so some of us would often want to kick on together after our meetings.

Carmel had settled into life at the cafe with hardly a hitch. After the initial two-week morning shift she worked from six until midnight. By eight every night the place had come alive.

By ten, trade was roaring. Carmel was beginning to learn little snatches of Spanish and this, coupled with her white skin and red hair, helped to make her very popular.

'Hey, boss, why you got a gringo working here?' some of the men would joke.

'Because I love her,' Juan would say, or something equally outrageous. And Carmel would blush profusely and move off to another table, pretending she hadn't heard.

At the cafe I would sometimes meet up with the two or three others who were helping me organise the protest against the Chilean president. They were not students, but workers in their early twenties. The main ones were José, an Argentinian who worked as a cleaner in a public hospital, and Eduardo, a good-looking Chilean who worked as a storeman in a Chinese food-manufacturing plant. They were both very good musicians and much of their talk revolved around their next busking effort. They played down on the St Kilda pier together on the weekends, and were occasionally joined by various other *compañeros* who also loved playing and singing South American music. A very pretty girl named Rosa attached herself to the band, too. She played tambourine and sang a bit, but she wasn't very good. I could tell she was only hanging around because she had designs on Eduardo.

It took me a while to admit that I had some vague designs in that direction myself!

Eduardo had curly black hair and a wry smile and always described himself as the 'general dogsbody' in the factory where he worked. He had to pack boxes, service equipment and keep the floors clean. It was hard for me to imagine him in such a humble role. Down at the cafe at night he was always so sharp and quick and funny. Every time we saw him he told us stories about his work: his chief boss the ditherer, the floor manager who was nervous of all the employees, the women on the production line who were always complaining about their husbands and varicose veins. He made that factory sound like the most interesting place; full of the craziest, most eccentric people that had ever lived.

In the middle of our meal he would regale us with terrible descriptions of what actually went into the dim-sims and Chiko rolls. Dead cats found on the side of the road, rotting cabbages that had fallen off the backs of market trucks. Of course he made it all up. But he was so good at providing all the little details that we couldn't help half-believing him.

'Next time you take a bite think of where that nice spicy flavour comes from!'

'Stop it, Eduardo!'

'Shut up you . . . liar!'

He'd have us all snorting with laughter, pretending to be sick, throwing things at him, telling him we'd hold him down and wire up his jaw to make him shut up.

Eduardo and José were opposites. Where Eduardo was sharp and witty, José was slow-talking and easygoing about everything, a great one for telling long-winded, droll stories about his family back in Argentina. But they were also the best of friends. Eduardo would get angry and passionate very quickly, but José always acted as though there was nothing to worry about and all the time in the world for everything. It was the music, I suppose, that held them together.

Everyone more or less got on. We'd eat there and talk. It was easy to convince the non-Chileans to meet and eat at Juan's cafe because he always gave us a good deal. As many *empanadas* and *completos* as we could eat, for six dollars. I liked looking up from my table of friends to see Carmel bustling around with plates of food and drink, smiling and joking with the customers. She still got nervous sometimes, and blushed and bumbled a bit if she mixed up an order or dropped something. But her confidence was growing. I noticed it more every day. She was laughing more easily and didn't get so flustered if someone called out a joke or tried to tease her. That self-conscious movement of her eyes down to her hands, followed by the deep blush, was becoming rarer by the week. Even simple things like the way she walked and sat down at a table had become somehow different after a few weeks of working. Juan and I often had secret little chats about her. We were like two proud parents, telling each other the latest thing she'd accomplished.

And of course there was Anton, too. Carmel was seeing him every few days I think, but apart from an occasional comment I tried not to pry. I knew something must be going right because of the changes I saw in her.

Nights in the cafe were usually great fun. There were jugs of *sangría* and mineral water on the table and always loud music. If a certain group of Juan's old friends was still there by the end of the night, we'd usually push the tables together, and those nights would always end with us singing songs in Spanish and English. Annie was studying Spanish as part of her Arts course. She had an awful accent and a terrible flat singing voice but somehow that just added to the fun. She was always so bubbly; shouting out things in Spanish that no one could understand and beginning songs in completely the wrong key.

When Carmel had finished clearing the tables and stacking the dishwasher, she'd join us. Sometimes people would dance. Other times I'd help Carmel finish so she could join us earlier.

Various men still came around in their fancy cars to collect Katerina, and occasionally she'd come in just as Carmel and I were heading off to bed at midnight. Sometimes she was with a stunning dark girl, Kara, and they'd make tea and toast and go to Katerina's room to smoke dope. Whenever I passed her room on my way out the front door, that sweet distinctive smell would just about bowl me over. I didn't care, I was just grateful that they didn't stink up the rest of the house with it. I'd never been interested in drugs. People can stick whatever they like down their throats, into their lungs, up their noses, or into their veins. None of it interests me.

'Well, hello, you two!' Kara would purr at Carmel and me, tossing her thick black curls and making them bounce like waves about her thin shapely shoulders. 'How's things?' They made a pretty formidable pair – Katerina and Kara – one fair, the other dark, both tall, fashionably slender and elegant. Neither of them looked or dressed like the ordinary grungy students I mixed with. Occasionally they would stop in the lounge room, lolling in front of the TV, giggling and gossiping. There was an unspoken assumption at such times that neither Carmel nor I would join them. I didn't mind that either. After all, most of the time we had the place to ourselves.

The weeks went past. Winter arrived before any of us even noticed. I was so busy with my university work and political activities – we'd set up a computer, small desk and photocopier in the back shed – that the right moment to tell Katerina about what we were working on never quite presented itself. I knew that it wasn't quite right. After all it was her house too. Perhaps I was gutless. I don't know. Sometimes it would be on the tip of my tongue. *'Oh, by the way, Katerina, I thought I'd better mention that this house is the centre for South American resistance activity in Australia. I know you won't mind. There's a group of us organising a demonstration in July against the Chilean president. Our aim is to keep South American social justice issues alive in the daily press . . .* ' Mail would arrive from similar groups in other capital cities and overseas, and sometimes she'd give me a queer look when she handed me a bundle of letters, but I never quite got around to explaining it all.

Eduardo and José would either let themselves in through the back gate or jump over the fence. I'd often come outside and find them already at work: making posters, answering mail, photocopying letters and stuffing them into envelopes. It was Juan, though, who coordinated everything. He hardly ever came around to the back shed, but he knew what we were doing. We'd fill him in on everything when we went to eat at his cafe.

It took a few months of living in that house for me to get a fix on Katerina. She was a hard one to pinpoint. Friendly and easy one day, very cool and distant the next. But she didn't worry me in the way I know she worried Carmel. I wasn't intimidated. More intrigued. I'd think I knew where she was coming from, then something would happen and my ideas about her would jumble up again.

'You want some tea?' I asked. It was Saturday morning and Carmel had wandered down to the kitchen dressed in black jeans and a sloppy jumper, yawning and bleary-eyed. She nodded and grinned lazily, plonking herself down in the nearest chair. I'd had the little bar heater on for over an hour already so the room was cosy and warm.

'How come you're up so early?' she asked. I shrugged and remembered my dream. Another bad one. This time about being caught in a fire. My father was there as usual. For some reason I'd felt quite safe, but he was trapped at the top of the stairs and I'd been unable to help him. The stairs between us were alight with bright flames. I'd been calling out for him to jump. I'd wanted to catch him and break the fall. But I couldn't make him hear me. The roar of the fire was so loud. I'd woken up sweating and dry-mouthed. I was about to tell Carmel, but she cut in, not really expecting me to answer.

'Make me some toast while you're at it,' she ordered.

'Oh sure!' I said, picking up two bits of bread and chucking them into the toaster. 'And what did your last slave die of?'

'Oh, Jude,' she said. 'You're a saint.'

'I know.'

'Saint Jude,' she said again, laughing. 'That suits, y'know. You *are* a bit of a saint.'

'Get stuffed, Carmel!' I said. The toast popped up and I threw the pieces onto the clean plate in front of her.

'Mmm . . .' she said, looking at the fridge, 'now I wonder where the butter is.' I went to the fridge and got it out.

'My God! Look at this!'

I was over at the stove pouring boiling water into the teapot. Her tone made me turn sharply and spill some over my hand.

'Ouch!' I said, sucking my fingers. 'Shit ... what is it?'

Carmel was staring at a copy of *Australian Vogue* on the table. There was a pile of about half a dozen of them. All the same issue. She held up the front cover. A close-up of a sultry-looking blonde, pouting at the camera.

'So?' I said stupidly. I still didn't twig.

'Recognise her?' I stared harder, shook my head then moved closer.

'God,' I whispered. 'It's ... Katerina!'

'Took you long enough, dumbo,' Carmel teased, flipping the magazine open to the inside cover.

'*We spied Katerina Armstrong at a city nightclub,*' Carmel read, '*and asked if we might have a few pics. She was delighted to oblige. Catch some more of this stylish lady in our fashion centrespread!*'

Sure enough, there she was striding out along St Kilda pier; the caption underneath read '*I really love to dance.*' In the next picture she was playfully ogling a couple of grinning fishermen, as she sucked on a huge slice of watermelon, the juice dripping from her chin. '*I relax simply,*' was the caption. '*Give me fresh air and a friend to be with and I'm happy!*' Then, curled up pretending to be asleep on a large cray basket, '*I'll curl up anywhere! Sleep renews me.*' In each picture she was dressed in a different set of stunning clothes, shorts and culottes, billowing see-through blouses, and tight skimpy tops that showed off her midriff.

'What a wank!' I muttered.

'God!' Carmel sighed deeply. 'I'm sick with jealousy! Just imagine ...'

'Mmm, she does look pretty nice,' I agreed grudgingly. She looked fabulous actually. Not many other models – beautiful as they might be – had that kind of vitality and strength about them.

We heard the front door creak open.

'God, it's her!' Carmel said and, as if we doing something shameful, hurriedly slapped the magazine back into the pile.

'Carmel!' I cried, picking it up again. 'We're allowed to look at it!'

'Oh,' she said sheepishly. 'I suppose so ... ' We both bent over the page as we heard the clipped footsteps coming down the hallway. The door opened and she stepped in.

'Well, hi, you two,' she said.

'Hi,' we said in unison. She noticed the magazine and had the grace to look a little embarrassed.

'Oh, you've found those? Sorry, I didn't mean to leave them lying around to ... '

'Show off?' I smiled, making it obvious I was teasing. Katerina laughed weakly and shook her head.

'I didn't mean to show off ... '

'Pretty nice,' Carmel said. 'How did it happen? I mean how did they ... see you ... pick you?' Katerina smiled coyly, then went over to the sink and began to fill the kettle.

'Oh, you know,' she said airily. 'Friend of a friend. Met at a club. You both like a fresh cup?'

'Are you going to do any more?' Carmel asked.

'What?'

'Have any more pictures taken?'

'Well, I don't know,' Katerina shrugged. 'Modelling is actually incredibly boring ... '

'Really?' Carmel asked sceptically.

Katerina flashed Carmel a condescending smile.

'Yes, really!' she said. 'I find it amazing that anyone could think that it was remotely interesting!'

There was a moment's silence.

'There's no need to be so bloody superior about it,' Carmel said in a small voice. I looked up in surprise, thinking that I hadn't heard right. I mean, she didn't say it angrily, but there was no note of deference or apology either. Katerina's eyes widened in surprise. I almost burst out laughing as I watched her open and shut her mouth a couple of times.

'Well ... I ... I certainly didn't mean to sound superior,' she said in a huffy voice. Carmel shrugged, not looking at her.

'Well, you often do, Katerina,' she said quietly. 'You often manage to sound very superior, whether you mean to or not.'

My God! Carmel was such an odd mix! She was always surprising me. Self-effacing and humble to a fault one minute, and then something would snap and she'd manage to say exactly what was on her mind the next. Katerina was looking decidedly uncomfortable. She put down the cup she was drying and threw the tea-towel over the chair.

'Perhaps I'll skip the tea,' she said. 'I mean, I don't want to spoil the nice atmosphere with my superiority!'

'Why don't you sit down,' I said, 'and cut the bullshit ... '

'And why don't you mind your own business?' she snapped back, both hands resting on the back of the chair. I sat back and we stared at each other across the table.

'I live here. Whatever goes on here is my business,' I said mildly. The shrill ring of the phone broke the impasse. Katerina flew over and answered it.

'Yes, I'll get her ... ' Her face was tight as she turned around to Carmel. 'It's for you.'

I pulled a chair out for Katerina.

'Come on, sit down,' I said as breezily as I could. 'Let's have the tea.' She didn't smile back, but sat down stiffly.

'You doing anything special today?' I asked.

'Yes.' She began to pour the tea. 'Kara and I are going to play tennis with a few other people ... ' I watched as she poured three very even cups of tea. She handed me one and I took a sip.

'That should be good,' I said, with fake sincerity. I can't stand sport of any kind. Carmel put down the receiver and turned around, excitement brimming in her eyes.

'Guess what?' she squealed. Katerina and I waited.

'That was Alan!'

We stared at her blankly.

'You know, Alan the musician!' she said. 'Remember I told you he's getting a blues band together? Wants me to try out as a back-up singer. Oh God, Jude!' She was just about jumping out of her skin with excitement. 'He's a good musician, you know. Says he's got together three other guys who are good and interested. There's another girl, too. Really wants me to come by. I said I would. What do you think?'

'Of course,' I said, wondering why Alan would waste her in a back-up position. She should be out front with that voice. 'So when is it?'

'This afternoon!' she said. 'God, in two hours! I'm terrified!'

'Don't be,' I said, making a face. 'You'll piss it in.'

'I'll have to ring Anton,' Carmel bubbled on, thinking aloud. 'He was going to come around this afternoon.' Katerina's head jerked up suddenly.

'Anton!' she said incredulously. 'Anton Crossway? From Manella?'

Carmel and I turned, both suddenly aware of her sitting there primly sipping her tea. No one spoke for a few moments.

'Yes,' Carmel said. I saw the terrible flush rush to her cheeks and spread down her neck.

'What? Are you ... er, seeing him?' Katerina asked disbelievingly.

'Er ... yes. Didn't you know?'

Katerina shook her head in amazement. I could see that underneath she was disapproving, scathing even, of the whole idea of Carmel going with an old friend of *her* family. But she wasn't going to risk saying so after being pulled up short only minutes before.

'Well, that's nice,' she said feebly, putting her cup down. 'Look, I've got to go. Good luck with the ... er, rehearsal, Carmel. I hope you get a spot or whatever it is you want. And, er ... say hello to Anton for me, will you?'

'Yes, I will. Thanks.'

When we heard the front door slam, Carmel gave a deep groan. 'Oh God! She makes me feel terrible! What are you grinning about, Jude?'

'Carmel,' I replied. 'I think we made another crack in that icy wall.'

'What do you mean?'

'She'll think twice about stepping on your toes again!'

'But did you see how she reacted to me and Anton?'

'So what?'

'She thinks he's my boyfriend!'

'Well, he is, isn't he?' I said quickly, surprised.

'Oh, Jude, I don't know . . . ' Carmel's face was bright pink, 'I think we're just good friends. We both love music and . . . '

'Come on, Carmel,' I teased, 'you're more than just good friends . . . aren't you?'

She got up from the table frowning unhappily, and began stacking up the dishes.

'What should I wear to this thing this afternoon, Jude?' she asked, abruptly changing the subject. 'I don't want to look ridiculous.'

'You won't, Carmel,' I said, longing for her to tell me more about her relationship with Anton, but knowing that I mustn't intrude. 'You always look beautiful.'

She gave a heavy sigh. She had her back to me, staring out the window, filling the sink with water.

As far as I could tell, Carmel was seeing quite a lot of Anton during the afternoons and on the weekends. But I couldn't work out quite what was happening with them. What I did understand after we'd been back from Manella a couple of weeks was that it was the most delicate of relationships; one I didn't feel right about questioning. I had simply thought that within a couple of weeks I'd wake up and find him in the kitchen after having spent the night in Carmel's bed. But not so. They seemed to go out together in an old-fashioned way. Sometimes, if I got out early from my lectures, I'd arrive home in the late afternoon. Carmel and Anton would be there, sitting at different ends of the lounge room eating bread rolls and drinking cups of tea and listening to music. I used to wonder if they'd been to bed together before I got there, but my gut feeling told me that this wasn't the case. There was no real easiness between them, just this nervous kind of tenderness.

After my outburst to her mother I was determined not to intrude. Could they have decided just to be friends? That, I knew, would be terrible for Carmel because she was madly in love with him. Perhaps he was involved with someone else and was holding Carmel at bay until he'd finished it with her? I watched and waited, all ears and eyes, sure that I'd pick up what was happening sooner or later.

Once the three of us went to a party together. There was a big crowd bunched up in a tiny space drinking cask wine and eating lumps of horrible cheese and stale salami. The very loud music made talking impossible. I didn't like those kinds of parties very much. They made me long for my Chilean friends, for the life we had in the cafe, with Juan and the others, where all the ghosts of the dead and disappeared were just as important as those who were physically there. But when the dancing started, and Anton and Carmel took to the floor, my fears about them vanished. They were definitely in love. The way he looked into her eyes and laughed. At one point they kissed lightly. I looked around and saw that everyone in the room had seen that kiss. The handsome young man and the plump girl smiling at each other, oblivious of everyone else. Mesmerising.

When it was over we went home together; the three of us squashed into the front seat of Anton's little Renault. Carmel was sitting in the middle. We talked about nothing much. Anton was very quiet, but not aloof. He joined in every now and again with a short comment or a laugh. As soon as I got inside the door I said goodnight and disappeared into my room, pleased to think that my fears about them were groundless. I lay in bed thinking that if it hadn't happened before, tonight would be the night.

Then I heard footsteps coming back down the hallway, and muttered farewells outside the front door. Damn it! Why was he going? I was filled with an impatience that made sleep impossible. I got up as soon as I heard his car drive off, pretending to get a drink of water. But Carmel didn't appear. She must have gone straight to her room without using the bathroom. I waited a few more minutes, puzzled, then decided to pull back. After all, the relationship wasn't mine.

It must have been some hours later when I woke to find Carmel sitting on my bed shaking me.

'Come on, Jude!' she demanded. 'Wake up! You've had a bad dream. Please. Come on, wake up!' I rubbed my eyes, amazed to find that my face was hot, and wet with tears.

'My God,' I said. 'I didn't know anyone cried in their sleep, did you?'

'Thank God you're awake,' Carmel said and switched on the light. 'You were really shouting out and crying, Jude.' Her worried face peered into my own. 'What were you dreaming about? You were so hard to wake!'

'Why don't you sleep with him?' I asked suddenly, too disoriented to remember my former resolve not to pry.

'What?'

'Anton,' I said. 'Why don't you sleep with him?'

'I want to! I really do,' she said, laughing a little.

'Then why didn't he stay tonight?' I persisted.

'Because ... Oh, Jude, come on! Let's go and get a drink. We'll talk about Anton later. Tell me what you were dreaming about. If you talk about it you won't have to dream it again. That's what they say, anyway.'

Carmel put a cup of hot milky cocoa in front of me. It was nearly four in the morning and the kitchen had warmed up with the radiator on full blast. We'd been quiet for a while, with me just sitting there staring into space, wondering about Carmel and Anton, and about this terrible spate of dreams I'd been having, while she bustled around getting the cups and heating the milk.

'Was it your father again?' she probed gently.

I nodded and began to speak, trying to fit my dream into a context – for myself, as much as for her.

'After 1972, when Allende had been voted in a second time, the right-wing forces in the country couldn't take it. They knew then that they couldn't get the power back democratically, so they decided to pull off the gloves ... '

'How do you mean?' Carmel cut in, frowning. 'Pulled the gloves off? What does that mean?'

'Well, since 1970 there was this deliberate behind-the-scenes policy of destabilisation. They fought really dirty, making up all kinds of lies about Allende, about his government, anything they could think of to bring him down. But none of it worked. The Popular Unity government got in again with an increased majority in 1972. So the right-wing forces decided to get really nasty. With help from the United States of course. Nixon and the CIA ... ' I added bitterly. 'It was deliberate. They couldn't bear for this popular government to work ... '

Carmel nodded. I had no idea if she understood anything I was saying. But I was beyond caring. I somehow needed to say all this stuff; go over the snippets of history I knew. Speak them. Try and understand it all over again.

'They began to orchestrate strikes. Chile is such a long difficult country geographically. Depends absolutely on its transport system – the roads and trains – to get the supplies of food and materials into the cities, towns and out into the countryside. First, the truck drivers went on strike. They were paid by God knows who – the Americans, everyone says – not to work, so of course they didn't. Everything began to grind to a halt. Supplies of basic items became spasmodic. Strikes broke out everywhere. My mother says it was terrible. First there was no meat, then no cloth to make clothes, and then the supply of fruit and vegetables dried up. Then beans, chilli, chocolate. The kerosene that people used for their heating and cooking. You name it ... one by one.

'But the people fought back. They knew what was going on. They knew that the right wing was deliberately creating chaos. So all kinds of people – factory-workers, singers, teachers, doctors, university professors, housewives – joined work units. They knew that everything they'd worked for over the previous few years was being threatened. They became truck drivers and fruit sellers in their spare time. My mother was in charge of a unit of housewives whose job it was to guard the local shops from sabotage. Basic goods like coffee and beans were being bought up in bulk by factions in the army and the right-wing forces, and either sold on the black market for exorbitant prices or stored for when "order" was re-established. Sometimes these supplies were actually thrown away. Into the rivers or into deep pits ... Can you believe that? They destroyed food when people were hungry. One day there would be coffee and beans in a local shop, the next day none. My mother organised women to stand outside the shops to watch for the smuggling of bulk goods; and just by being there they helped stop many of the most blatant abuses by insisting that only locals could buy basic goods from local shops. You see, it was all being organised covertly. The army and the right wing made out that people were mad even to suggest that this was going on. They wanted the people to blame Allende and his government for the shortages ... '

Carmel was staring at me. Her eyes wide, like a child listening to an incredible story.

'Then they began to kill people,' I went on bluntly. 'Not

only radicals or socialists, but their own people, too. A few generals in the army who happened to believe in democracy were murdered. Rumours began to circulate. Fear spread in the streets. Mum said it was sort of like a fog. It came in slowly, low and deadly, like a poisonous cloud. The people who'd voted Allende in kept working, refusing to give up their dream. But the ground was being prepared right in front of their eyes. People knew the coup was coming, but they had no idea it would be so cruel, or so vicious.

'Medical supplies, you know, basic drugs, bandages and equipment, began to disappear from the hospital where my father worked. Replacements never arrived. Everyone knew that they were being stolen, but no one was game to say so. People were too frightened to step out of line. Meanwhile patients in the hospital were dying. Medicines that had been available only the week before became suddenly impossible to get.

'The second time they picked up my father he and another young doctor from the hospital were stealing back a stash of medical supplies that had been stolen only the week before. So, you see, they had a real reason to put him in gaol then. He was caught stealing. The fact that it was for the hospital and had been stolen in the first place didn't matter. My father was one of only half a dozen doctors who had refused to go on strike at this time. He was blacklisted and threatened, even though he was only doing his job. People were dying all over the place for want of the most simple medical procedures. The right-wing forces just wanted their own people back in power, they didn't care what had to happen, so long as that took place. Most of the other doctors, and the staff in the hospital, were too afraid to keep working and they tried to make my father feel afraid, too.'

I stopped, exhausted.

'You don't want to know all this, Carmel,' I whispered. 'I mean, what has it got to do with anything ... I'm sorry ... I keep burdening you with my dreams ... '

'Yes, I do,' she said quickly. 'I want to know.'

'Well, in my dream I was watching my father stealing back the medical supplies, in just the way my mother has described it happening. He and his friend had hired a truck and a driver. They'd found the site and were busy packing the boxes into the van when they were caught. Red-handed.

'At the same time as being able to see my father packing the van, I could also see the *carbiñeros* heading out along the street towards the empty warehouse. It was packed with police, laughing together. They'd been tipped off. Maybe even set the whole operation up. Who knows? They all had ... ' Here my voice cracked. 'They had painted faces. Grotesque masks. It was like a film, Carmel, cutting back and forth between the two. My father trying to steal back the supplies for the hospital and this truck of laughing men with painted faces. I was trying to warn him, but I knew he was doomed. I knew what was going to happen.'

I gasped, shivering as tears filled my eyes. Carmel reached out across the table. I took a couple of deep breaths and tried to calm myself.

'It must all have been such a bitter disappointment when hopes ran so high,' she said.

'But why am I dreaming about this stuff? I don't think about these things during the day. I mean, I know what happened. I don't need to think about it any more.' Carmel opened her mouth to reply, but closed it again without speaking. We both heard the key in the front door and the quick footsteps making their way towards the kitchen.

The door flew open and Katerina, face set in an irate frown, burst in. When she saw us, she gave a small gasp of surprise and quickly rearranged her expression to one of polite curiosity.

'Oh, hello,' she said. When she noticed my splotchy tear-stained cheeks her expression changed again to one of concern.

'What ... what is the matter, Jude?' I suppose we did look a bit odd. Carmel had moved around to my side of the table and her arm was still around my shoulders. I shrugged.

'Oh nothing ...' I said, not really wanting to explain, to her of all people. 'I've been having bad dreams, that's all ...'

'What about?' she asked in quite a kind, neutral voice, putting one elbow on the table and resting her chin in her hand.

'All about my father in ... Chile.'

'Do you remember your father?' she asked.

I nodded, embarrassed. 'My mother tells me that I was only two when he died, so it's almost impossible that I can. But I seem to ... I ... know I can remember him.'

'No,' she said emphatically, as if she knew all about it. 'It's not impossible, some people can remember that far back. What kind of things do you remember?'

'Not a lot. I can remember some events. Like sitting on his shoulders in a protest march ...' My voice petered out. 'Things like that. But my mother said I wasn't even born then, so ...' I shrugged and looked at Carmel.

'God, how fascinating,' Katerina said seriously. I looked up and saw that she genuinely was fascinated. I smiled.

'Yeah,' I said. 'Crazy isn't it?'

'Not crazy, Jude,' she said suddenly. 'Interesting and ... it means you are a person with deep insight.'

I smiled shaking my head a little. 'I ... don't know about that.' *Deep insight?* A laugh rose in my throat. The phrase sounded hilarious coming from Katerina.

The three of us were silent for a while. Quiet night sounds began to invade the room. The low buzz of the fridge, the wind outside. I began to think of my mother. The way she spoke and her white hands. I was aware of a feeling of deep anxiety for her. I realised that I was angry with her, too, but I didn't know why.

Why did the DINA let her go? They killed others, even others with international passports like her. She'd been taken in and questioned for days. But then they'd let her go. What had she told them? Why won't she talk about that time? All through my life she has told me about my father, never about her own experiences. Why does Juan always give me that glazed look when my mother is mentioned?

'What have you been doing?' I asked Katerina suddenly. She flinched slightly.

'Oh, nothing much. You wouldn't want to know. A bit of a bad dream, you could say.' She gave a hard little laugh and Carmel and I looked at her in surprise.

'Why?'

'Oh, just the usual boyfriend trouble,' she shrugged. 'You know, the ones who think they own you?' Carmel and I didn't answer. Her worldliness was disconcerting.

'Is it Glen?' Carmel asked softly. Katerina laughed.

'Oh God, no!' she leant forward conspiratorially. 'You two were dead right about *him*. He's a real creep! And I didn't see it for ages.'

'Told you so!' I joked, wagging my finger at her.

'You did, too,' Katerina laughed.

'We aren't just pretty faces,' I added drily. 'You want advice on your love life, come to us!' Katerina laughed again good-humouredly and I couldn't help thinking that maybe we'd misjudged her all along. At four on this Saturday morning she suddenly seemed like a rather nice person.

'It's this other guy I've met,' she said, looking down at the table, a little embarrassed. 'The one who has the contact with *Vogue*. Jordan. He's a photographer. Wants me to pose for a pin-up calendar.' She giggled. 'You know, one of those tits and bums things?' Our mouths must have fallen open in surprise because she went on hurriedly, 'Sexy, but ... tasteful, you know? Nothing ... too ... well ... not *pornography*, just ... ' She looked up at Carmel, whose face had tightened, distaste plastered all over it.

'Something wrong, Carmel?' Katerina snapped. Carmel shrugged with embarrassment.

'Oh ... no,' she stuttered. 'Just, er ... surprised.' Katerina turned back to me.

'Just raunchy, you know?' she said, somehow wanting my approval.

I nodded.

'When I said I wanted to think about it,' Katerina went on blithely, 'Jordan was furious ... How could I possibly think of turning down this enormous opportunity to be the next Elle Macpherson, blah, blah. And then the guy I'm going with, Conner, got furious because I was even considering doing it. How could you possibly think of taking your clothes off for everyone to see, blah, blah ... So I left the nightclub tonight with both of them huffy ... '

'How old is he?' Carmel asked suddenly in a low voice. Katerina smiled coyly.

'Who, Conner or Jordan?'

'Your ... er, the one you're going out with,' Carmel said. Katerina shrugged noncommittally.

'Oh, about twenty-eight, I think.' She looked up with a quick laugh. 'Oh, Carmel, I can see you don't approve!'

We all laughed, although I knew that she'd made Carmel feel stupid. Carmel got up suddenly, picked the cups off the table and dropped them roughly into the sink.

'I've got to go to bed,' she said gruffly, not looking at us. I watched Katerina's mouth twist into an ironic little smile as she gazed over at Carmel's back.

'Have I shocked you, Carmel?' she asked sweetly. Carmel spun around, her face flushed with anger.

'What?'

'Shocked you? I don't think you approve of my friends or of me doing the calendar, do you?' Katerina went on lightly.

'It's got nothing to do with me,' Carmel said quietly, refusing to meet her eyes. 'I'm going to bed.'

With that she disappeared into the bathroom. Katerina shrugged and yawned.

'I'm tired, too.'

We could hear Carmel brushing her teeth. When she came out she headed straight for the door leading to the bedrooms.

'Goodnight.'

Katerina and I were left looking at each other.

I got up, not wanting to be there alone with her. I'd had enough heart-to-heart talks in the middle of the night. But on my way to the door I impulsively touched her shoulder.

'Listen,' I said. 'Don't let anyone talk you into anything you're not happy with, okay?'

'Right.' She looked back at me seriously before giving a quick tentative smile. 'Thanks, and listen, Jude ... ' I was at the door, but stopped and turned around.

'What?'

She seemed embarrassed suddenly, lost for words.

'Sleep well, okay? No bad dreams.'

'Sure,' I said gamely. 'You too.'

One night the next week I was working late in my room. I had a chemistry test the following day and I wanted to do well.

'Jude, you awake?'

'Come in, Carmeloo,' I said. I looked up from my books. Her thick hair was pulled back into a rough bun and she was dressed in her old flannelette nightie.

She sat slowly on my bed. When she looked up at the black-and-white photo of Allende on my wall she was frowning, studying it for some answer to her innermost questions.

'What's up?' I asked.

'I don't know how to say it.'

'Carmel, tell me?' I said.

'It's about ... ' She stopped.

'Anton?' I ventured. She nodded and gave a deep sigh.
'He's got a nice face,' she said, still staring at the photo.
'Who? Anton?'
'No,' she smiled. 'Allende.'
'Mmmm,' I said unenthusiastically, not wanting her to change the subject.
'He kind of looks like everyone's uncle ... '
'Mmmm,' I repeated.
'Did your father really know him?'
'Yep.'
'Now they're both dead,' she added slowly as if to herself.
'Yep.'
We smiled gingerly at each other. She knew I was on to her stalling tactics. I tried to think of a subtle way to get her talking.
'You want to sleep with him?' I began. Then grimaced. Typical me. No one in their wildest dreams could call that subtle! To my relief she burst out laughing. I smiled. These days Carmel was looking fantastic. She was still big, with plump arms and shoulders, but her skin glowed.
'Trust you!' she said wryly. 'I might have known you'd be on to it.'
'Well, am I right?' I replied with a grin. She became serious suddenly, troubled again.
'Jude, I don't know how to ... '
'How to what?' I asked gently. She shrugged and looked away.
'Carmel, what do you mean?'
'Well, I don't know how to ... ' she repeated miserably, 'do ... *it*, if you know what I mean.'
I stared at her.
'Oh *it*,' I said after a couple of moments, as if *it* explained everything and from now on everything would be very simple. We both burst out laughing. Not so much because we were embarrassed, but because it suddenly seemed absurd to be

talking about *it* like this. Actually I had no idea what to say, so I said the first thing that came into my head.

'Have you ... er, *tried?*' I asked.

'Well, not really ... well, yes, I guess so.' She sighed. I was about to ask if that answer was a yes or a no, but thought it would be better to save my flippancy for another time.

'Does ... er, *he* know how to do it?'

'I don't know!' She wrung her hands. 'I think so!'

'Are you attracted to him?'

'Jude. Of course I am,' she said.

'Sorry,' I replied. 'I know that was a stupid question.'

'It's just that ... '

'What?' I said.

'It's just that I don't know what I should do ... '

'You've kissed him?'

'Yes. But, like, when it gets to a certain level I ... I pull back. I'm afraid.'

'Have you got any protection?' I asked, thinking of the inevitable.

'Well, no ... but that's not what makes me nervous!' I rolled my chair nearer and leant across to touch her hand briefly.

'Get nervous about that,' I said sternly. 'It's *really* important. A girl like you, Carmel. You'd find it very difficult having an abortion.'

'Jude!' She pulled away, shocked at the idea. 'I'd never have an abortion! Ever!'

'So get something!' I snapped back sharply, then felt sorry when she winced. 'Getting pregnant isn't the only disaster that can happen, you know. Sorry, Carm, it's just that ... well ... ' I shrugged. *Damn it. It was important. Herpes. Bloody AIDS. And I couldn't bear the idea of Carmel going through all that abortion crap.*

'Do *you* know what to do?' she asked shyly, looking down at her hands.

I smiled and shrugged.

'Well, yeah ... I suppose so. I suppose I do.' Her question had stumped me, though. I'd never thought about anyone *not knowing*. I mean, it's not something you even *know* about exactly, just something you do if the situation is right. I don't really know where I'd got my own attitude from. She was looking at me steadily now.

'You don't seem all that interested in guys, Jude.'

'Don't I?' I said, surprised. Would I tell her my own sordid sob story? But I didn't want her to feel intimidated because I'd had more experience. I figured I should shut up for a while.

'I've seen guys looking at you in the cafe,' Carmel went on. 'That guy Eduardo. You know, the good-looking one. And Patrick. He likes you, too.'

'Yeah,' I said noncommittally. 'They're nice, both of them, aren't they?'

'Eduardo's really sweet, eh?' she added. 'He likes you a lot. I can tell.'

'Mmmm,' I smiled. 'Maybe ... he does.'

'He plays good guitar, too.'

'Mmmm.'

I turned towards the window, aware of a burst of heat beginning in the pit of my belly and spreading out to my arms and down my legs. I'd managed to forget about all this for months. Now here it was, rearing its dangerous, beautiful head again, making me remember that I was a body, too. That for all my fancy ideas I was still a body, like everyone else, a body with a life of its own, almost apart from my brain, my soul, my mind, with desires and feelings of its own.

For those few moments I was back there in the half-light in that shabby house in Manella rolling around in David's sheets, in David's arms, stroking his wiry curls and kissing his mouth, loving the feel of his hands on the small of my back. All those hot afternoons between four and six, when my mother thought I was at the library or off studying with girlfriends, I'd been there with him; talking, laughing, arguing and making love. Girlfriends! I didn't have girlfriends. Not really. I got on with people, did enough so that they wouldn't hate me or pick on me. But my head was elsewhere. No one in my class was interested in the things I was interested in. Until the end of Year 11 I had no real confidante, except for my mother. Then at the beginning of Year 12 I met David. It was then that I realised I'd been lonely for years. The only problem was that he was the senior politics and history teacher at the school. I was doing sciences, so thankfully I was never in one of his classes. But it was uncomfortable enough. It began as such fun, such a thunderbolt of unbelievable joy, but it quickly became dicey and dangerous for both of us. Ultimately it was a shameful business, especially for him, and I couldn't bear that. Even so, I'm glad it happened.

I had approached him initially, wanting some political background on a newspaper cutting about El Salvador. But it was only an excuse. The week before I'd heard him speaking to a few Year 7 kids about the motorbike he'd had when he was younger. They were all poring over an illustration of a Harley Davidson. I'd watched him bend down and pat one of the kids' heads when the others had all rushed off to class. He'd patted this pale, grubby little malnourished kid, who came from a local impoverished family, and spoken to him in the gentlest way. Little actions sometimes speak more eloquently than a million words. At that moment I somehow knew instinctively who he was. I mean deep down. Those troubled blue eyes and the slow way his mouth moved before it widened into a smile. I watched him for a few days and decided that I'd have to push some kind of meeting. We met alone for the first time in his office after school. It turned out he'd spent three years travelling throughout South America, spoke Spanish, and knew lots that I wanted to learn.

But in the end he put a stop to it. He said it made him feel too bad. He was thirty-one, you see, unmarried but thirty-one, and I was only seventeen. He wanted to be able to take me out. '*What sort of life is it when you have to hide your girlfriend in your bedroom?*' he used to rant. I didn't care. His grotty bedroom was just fine with me. But he was so afraid we'd be caught. In fact, by the time it ended, in spite of all our care and discretion, a couple of people did know or at least were suspicious. When David found that out he freaked. We'd have to stop it, he said, or it would only be a matter of time and we'd both be ruined. '*For God's sake, David, it's not the nineteenth century,*' I'd yell. These things happen! I tried to persuade him not to care. I did love him: his funny clear mind, his blue eyes and curly black hair, the way he'd groan and breathe my name when we were caught up in our passion. I would have been happy to marry him, to be with him forever. But he was convinced that he had somehow debauched me, taken my innocence. I couldn't bear that. '*David, I have never been young and innocent, even when I was young and innocent! In fact I am much older than you in real terms. I know a lot more about life and death. I'm definitely wiser!*' I said that kind of thing to him so many times and it never failed to make him laugh, in spite of himself. He knew in some crazy way that it was true. I had always known what was going on. He knew that. But after eight months, two weeks and four days it was over. And I had to accept it.

I looked at Carmel. With David it had never been a matter of *not being able* to do it. The big problem was stopping. That was where the pain had been for me. I realised with a small shock that I must still be getting over it, because I hadn't considered anyone else, at least not for more than a moment, since I'd hit the city. But I pushed the thought from my mind.

'What are you afraid of?' I asked slowly.

'I don't know!' she sighed. 'But when he begins to touch me ...' She blushed. 'I sort of clam up and get cold and shaky.'

'It will go,' I said, unsure if I was right or not. 'I'm sure it will go ... Do you feel comfortable with him?'

'I love him!'

'I know, but do you feel comfortable with him?' She shrugged miserably.

'I don't know. Jude, what if I'm one of those frigid girls? That's what he might be thinking!'

'No!' I said emphatically. 'He wouldn't be thinking that. You just need more time. And while you're both taking time, promise me you'll go and find out about contraception.' I was stalling, changing the subject from what Carmel really wanted to talk about. But I didn't think it was a good idea just to shoot from the top of my head. I needed to think a bit more about what she'd said, maybe try to find out more from someone who might know.

'Where,' she asked, 'do I go for that kind of thing?'

'That kind of thing,' I mimicked. 'Stop being coy! At uni, the health clinic ... where do you think?'

'I'm not a student, remember.'

'So go to the clinic down the road! God, Carmel,' I yawned. 'Don't be a dud.'

She stood up and we grinned at each other.

'We will resume this conversation at a later date,' I joked, meaning it quite seriously, of course.

'Okay.' She looked a little relieved as she moved to the door and opened it. 'Night, Jude.'

'Night,' I said lightly. 'And don't worry. It'll sort itself out ... I promise you.'

I went to sleep troubled because I didn't understand my friend's problem at all. And I also thought that my telling her not to worry about it was probably worse than useless.

That talk with Carmel stands out in my mind because it seemed to be the closing of a chapter in our little house. After that night life seemed to speed up for both of us. I had a lot of tests to study for at university so I was very busy, and then there was the protest against the Chilean president that Juan,

Eduardo and José and I were coordinating. And Carmel became very busy too. On top of her work at the cafe, she was rehearsing with her new band every afternoon. She was learning a heap of Aretha Franklin, Stevie Wonder, k.d. lang and Paul Kelly songs and when we'd meet in the kitchen on our way to somewhere else she'd sing a few bars loudly and I'd join in.

Carmel was taking a crash course in a style of music that she'd barely heard only the year before and she was loving it. Some of them were great songs, real blues/rock classics, and they suited her voice beautifully.

Carmel would howl mournfully into the empty hallway or shower. I'd open the door and join in or belt out the next line. Then we'd either finish the song together or, depending on how we were feeling, crack up with laughter.

We were as close as ever, but for a few weeks there we saw each other only in passing, or while we were working with the others on the protest.

And then somehow it was already that clear cold night in July. Three hundred of us huddled together, chanting, outside the Melbourne Town Hall. The mood was up, spirits were high. Even though it was drizzling, the crowd was bigger than we had expected. I'd taken two days off university to help Juan coordinate the four days of protest, and it had gone better than we could have imagined. Early in the week we'd got some prominent news coverage. For some reason the reporters and journalists honed in on me. I suppose I provided an 'angle' that ordinary people could quickly grasp. The fact that I'd been born in Chile and that my father had been killed by the junta encouraged them to suggest that I was on some kind of crusade to avenge his death. Not strictly true, but I didn't care. At least we were getting coverage. The interviews nearly always ended with questions about my plans to return to Chile to continue my father's medical work. I was often asked whether I also intended to agitate for political change once I got there. I always smiled at this point, not wanting to give too much away. 'It depends on what I find when I get there.'

It was after one of these interviews that Carmel asked me wistfully whether I definitely planned to work in Chile after I had finished my degree.

But I could only shrug. It had always been my plan, but now that it was closer than it had ever been, it suddenly seemed an impossibly long time away. Such a long way off that there was no point planning for it.

At some of the day venues only fifty or sixty protesters had been able to come along, because of work commitments. But this night, the last night in the Chilean president's Melbourne itinerary, the crowd was terrific. We stood on the corner of Swanston and Collins streets with our placards, alternately singing and chanting. We didn't actually stop the traffic, but we did slow it down. Tired and sometimes annoyed faces peered out at us from the rows of cars. I was filled with appreciation for the ordinary Australian that night. The tolerance with which we were greeted, by people who obviously had no idea what we were on about, was really something, especially considering that we were holding them up on a cold Friday night when they were trying to get home. Many seemed genuinely interested in what we were on about, their hands diving out of their cars to take the leaflets we were distributing. Others were obviously frustrated at being waylaid. They would shrug impatiently and walk or drive on without taking a leaflet or screw it up without reading it. But almost everyone who passed by, either on foot or in their cars, wore an unspoken expression of forbearance on their faces: there was no fury or hatred. They believed we had a right to be where we were. When I think about how intolerant so many countries are, and about how reckless the authorities in Chile were when they felt their own power being threatened, I realise all over again how much Australia means to me. I love this country with a fierceness that I reckon many people who were actually born here might never feel.

The good grace we were receiving from people passing by might have had a lot to do with the music we were playing and singing. Eduardo, José, and about five of their friends were standing out the front of the crowd on a stage of wooden fruit boxes with their guitars, drums, flutes and *charangos*. The sound was loud and buoyant, the rhythms infectious.

We had twenty-five people handing out leaflets, and at least another twenty-five holding up the banners that Juan, Eduardo, Carmel and I had made over many late nights at the back of the cafe and in our back shed.

10 000 killed, Mr President . . . what are you going to do?
After all this time, still no proper trials.
Chileans in Australia will not forget the disappeared.
You promised, Mr President! You promised!

I was arm in arm with Juan and Carmel. We were at the front of the crowd, rocking together in time with the music. Around us were university friends and different odd-bods from the cafe crowd we'd come to know over the previous five months. Inside, in the warmth and splendour of the lovely old Town Hall, the president was being entertained by business-leaders, politicians, trade ambassadors and prominent Chileans living in Melbourne. He was being wined and dined in company with the best this country had to offer so that he'd go back with a warm fuzzy feeling. And why? Maybe so the trade ties would strengthen. So we'd all be richer. I felt so proud to be part of the group outside, the wind and rain whipping our faces, our bodies inside our parkas and windcheaters slowly getting colder, as our feelings grew hotter. We sang and chanted ceaselessly, hoping our voices might drown out some of the laudatory speech-making inside.

Two rows of police surrounded the crowd. Dressed in their plastic raincoats, they were blank-faced and seemed alternately annoyed and bored. I had to keep reminding myself that they were ultimately harmless. Up close, police and soldiers always sent shivers down my spine. I knew that they played a very different role in Australia than in Chile, but I still always found myself wondering just what each one of them might be capable of if ordered by a superior. Then I heard a young one ask the guy next to him what he'd be doing on the weekend and it made me smile. There was nothing to be afraid of. Nothing.

Eduardo smiled and motioned for Carmel and me to join him on the makeshift stage. The other musicians backed away a little, smiling but still playing, as we reluctantly stepped forward.

'I shouldn't be up here,' Carmel hissed. 'I'm not Chilean. I don't even know Spanish!'

'We need your voice,' I smiled, 'and you do know the songs.'

'Half the time I don't even know what I'm singing!'

'You know.' I laughed and she grinned back.

It was true. Carmel had this uncanny knack of being able to pick up tunes and words from different recordings, without actually knowing what the lyrics meant. She could remember them, too. Occasionally she missed the endings of words, or put the wrong emphasis on a phrase, but mostly, when she was singing anyway, she could easily pass as a fluent Spanish speaker.

'Just don't worry, Carmeloo,' I said. 'Shut up, and sing!' So she did. And beautifully, soulfully, as if every word was coming from her heart. I was so proud of her. I sang underneath her rich voice, finding the harmony where I could.

'Let's interrupt their dinner with our song!' Carmel suddenly shouted in English when we'd come to the end of a particularly fiery number. Almost without consultation, Carmel began the Victor Jara song. Slowly, and full of inner strength, she sang 'Herminda de la Victoria', which was written about a real little girl – a baby of two or three who'd been shot by police when her poor peasant family, along with many others, occupied vacant land on the outskirts of Santiago. They'd come looking for work and had built a shanty-town of cardboard houses there because they had nowhere else to live. These shanty-towns were 'cleared' every now and again by the government authorities, and unarmed people were often killed if they didn't immediately comply. During one such 'clearing' the little girl was shot through the heart by a policeman, and the place was called after her from then on.

Herminda de la Victoria died without having fought.
Straight to heaven she went with her chest pierced.
The bullets of the police killed the innocent child.
Mothers and brothers wept among the crowd of people.

Herminda de la Victoria was born in the mud,
Grew like a butterfly on a piece of waste land won over.
We built our community and it has rained three winters.
Herminda, in our hearts we will keep your memory.

I will never forget that moment. The rain had begun in earnest. I looked over at my friend's glowing face, her springy red curls now flat and plastered around her head, then down at the good-humoured crowd, which had begun to sing along with us. I wanted to weep, to reach out to every single one of them. We weren't singing for ourselves. We were singing for all the people in the world without a voice, for the poor and the disappeared. The ones who had been plucked from their homes, offices, hospitals and factories, detained and tortured, maimed and killed because they had the audacity to believe that life might be different. We were singing for their suffering and the suffering of their relatives and friends who must go on without them. Not just in Chile, not just in Latin America, not just in our own time . . . for all of them, everywhere. We were singing for the man who wrote those words: a popular musician who'd had his hands smashed by rifle butts on the first day of the coup in 1973. By the end of the third day he had been shot, his body riddled with bullets. Two days later his wife had found him under a pile of other bleeding bodies in the Santiago morgue.

And in a very real way I was singing for my father. I had never before felt quite as close to him. It was as though his spirit was sitting like an angel at my shoulder. I would turn around every now and again and sort of expect to see him there. When Carmel and I got down I went and stood next to Juan. I looked up at his profile, lit only by flashing streetlights – this man who'd shared so much with my father all those years ago – and was overcome again with a sense of my father's presence; an almost unbearable stab of grief mingled with the flooding wave of joy pulsing right through me.

Inside I was crying: *I am with you ... my father ... I am with you, always!*

It was nearly midnight. The president's limo was gliding off. We couldn't get very near; the rows of police had surrounded him from the building to the car. Someone had put up a black umbrella so he wouldn't get wet. I saw his face though, small and very grave, staring at us from the warmth and protection of his car. Expressionless. A man who'd done his best to bring down a democratically elected leader and was now in power himself. A man who made deals with thieves and thugs and torturers. A man who, although president, had no real authority over the military, which had grown enormously in power and influence over the previous twenty years.

The night had ended, but I felt like I could have gone on singing forever.

'Where shall we go then?' cried Eduardo. Most of the crowd had dispersed. There were just a dozen of us left, soaking wet and ebullient in the damp city street. We were the organisers and, without being able to articulate it, we wanted somewhere to *rage*, somewhere to mull over what we'd achieved, what had happened. There was Juan's place, but his wife hadn't been well since she'd come back from overseas. We stared around at each other. It was impossible to think that we would simply go home to bed.

'Our place!' Carmel said suddenly, looking at me.

'Yeah,' I said immediately. 'Of course. Come to our place. Everyone's welcome!'

'I need something to eat!' Eduardo's father Miguel growled. We all turned to this old, rather quiet man and laughed. He was easy to forget because he seldom spoke, but he was always there, at the cafe among the men yarning with Juan, at all our meetings. It was Miguel who quietly got things done while everyone else was wasting time gossiping. I looked at Carmel.

'Is there food at home?'

'I think so,' she said, in a way that made me think she wasn't sure at all.

'So we'll pick up some stuff on the way,' suggested Eduardo.

'And drink,' the old man said. 'I want wine tonight.'

'We all do, Pop,' Eduardo said, casually slipping one arm around his father's shoulders, and using the other to lift his guitar up onto his head. Crossing one leg jauntily over the other he grinned at the rest of us, 'Like my hat?'

That silly little action made me think, made me *see* Eduardo properly for the first time: the ruddy face, the white straight teeth and dark curly hair, the whole directness of him. His face was prickly. I've always liked the look of men who haven't shaved for a couple of days, as if they've been too busy to worry about such mundane things. I looked into his bright eyes and wanted to reach out and run my fingers from the bottom of his ear to his chin. Instead, I said exactly what I was thinking.

'I think I could love you,' I said quite loudly, looking straight into his eyes.

Everyone heard. They all stopped talking and laughing and looked quietly from me to him. Rain was still spitting down between us. Eduardo gulped in shock. I looked away in extreme embarrassment, praying that the concrete underneath my feet might give way. Why couldn't I ever keep my trap shut? My only excuse this time was that we were all still so high. It had seemed exactly the right moment to tell the truth. Suddenly everyone began to laugh. Eduardo's friends and father began to thump me on the back.

'Good for you, Jude!' old Miguel chuckled.

'Well said, Jude!'

'Watch out, Eduardo!'

But Eduardo had turned away. And when I next caught a glimpse of his face, he wasn't smiling. He was walking on ahead of the rest, his shoulders hunched over and the hand that wasn't holding his guitar pushed deeply and angrily into the pocket of his old coat.

Ten of us squeezed into two small cars. Eduardo made sure he wasn't with me and Carmel. I didn't say much on the way back to our place because I was too mortified by my own crassness. On the way we stopped at a 7-Eleven and bought cheese and bread, milk and sweet biscuits. The others had gone to pick up some wine from a late-night bottle-shop.

Although the outside light was on when we opened the door to the house and trooped down the hallway into the lounge, it seemed that the place was deserted.

'I'm glad Queen Kat's not here,' Carmel whispered to me as we brought in glasses from the kitchen. 'Something tells me she wouldn't approve of a late-night party.' I shrugged. Katerina was the last person I cared about at that moment.

Carmel turned on the heater and went back into the kitchen to put the food onto plates. Everyone pulled off their coats, plonked themselves into chairs, and began talking animatedly in Spanish. Eduardo, still glowering, kept his coat on and huddled by the heater, rubbing his hands, as if his life depended upon not looking at anyone else in the room. Carmel handed around glasses of wine and we all drank to each other's health. No one must have noticed the tension between Eduardo and me, because the mood was buoyant and lighthearted as we discussed the highlights of the past week.

'What about that woman on the ABC asking you if you were a communist?'

'I wish I'd said yes,' I said, grinning.

'What about the crowd tonight, even in the rain?'

José, the joke-teller of the group, could hardly find anyone prepared to listen. Everyone wanted to talk. Except Eduardo and me.

Juan, Miguel, Carmel and I sat in a group a little further away. I longed to get nearer to the heater, but I was too nervous about Eduardo. Our midnight feast was spread out on the small coffee table. What we'd bought was supplemented with whatever Carmel and I could raid from the fridge: more cheese, tomatoes and onions, Polish sausage, Greek cakes, and some sliced green apple. As I warmed up physically, I began to relax. Too bad about what I'd said. For all Eduardo knew, I could have meant it as a joke. Yeah. That's right. It was a joke! Everyone laughed, didn't they? With every sip of wine I felt more confident. Damn it. The protest week had gone splendidly. Nothing was going to spoil tonight!

'You did well on the radio, *chiquilla*,' Miguel said, touching my shoulder. 'How come you're so good with the bloody English?' Everyone laughed. 'My wife saw you on TV,' he went on drily. 'On that *Good Morning Australia* show. She said they couldn't shut you up!'

'I grew up here, Miguel,' I said. 'Have you forgotten?' He nodded slowly, his eyes twinkling, and took another deep gulp of wine.

'I forget a lot, *chiquilla*,' he said. A burst of laughter came from the other group. José stood up, obviously having found an audience for his latest convoluted story. This guy was a teller of tales in the old way. There was usually nothing intrinsically funny in the story itself, only in the way he told it. This time he was talking about what he had heard his mother telling the family budgie when she thought no one could hear. He broke off and turned to me.

'I have to go to the toilet,' he said. 'Where is it?'

'Nooo!' the others howled. 'You've got to finish! Give us the punchline, you wanker!' José laughed and held up his hand.

'*Compañeros*,' he joked. 'I *will* be back!'

'Piker!'

'Dickhead!'

'Straight through the kitchen,' I said, pointing. 'It's in the bathroom.'

I got up to replenish everyone's wine. When I got to Eduardo I noticed his expression had improved a little. He didn't exactly look at me or smile, but there was a faint twist at one end of his mouth when he grunted thanks. Fifty-fifty, I thought. He might be going to forgive me.

Suddenly José was back in the room, his face flat.

'Jude! Carmel! There's someone in your bathroom!'

'What?' we replied in unison.

'A girl,' he went on. 'She doesn't look too well! I think she's ... she's collapsed.'

Carmel and I rushed in. Most of the others followed us. Sure enough, there was someone sprawled over the bathroom floor – Katerina. Her face was as white as a sheet and she was lying against the bath. One of her temples was grazed and her woollen skirt was bunched up around her thighs. Her breath was coming irregularly in deep sudden gasps. Carmel and I looked at each other in shock.

'What do you think ... ?'

'I don't know!' There were no signs of an intruder. The bathroom window was still intact, and nothing had been taken.

'Do you think she's been attacked?' Carmel asked in a small voice. I shrugged and began to feel her body for broken bones. She groaned a bit as my hands went over her legs and torso, her eyes half opening.

'What is ... it?' she said, twisting around to the light and bringing an arm up to her face. 'I don't ... know.'

'Someone call an ambulance,' I ordered. 'Quickly!' A couple of them disappeared back into the kitchen. Eduardo, I noticed, was still standing watching.

'I think we can safely move her,' I said to him shortly. 'Will you help?' He nodded. Katerina was now moving around, groaning and half sitting up.

'Katerina,' I said as firmly as I could. 'You've had some kind of accident. We're going to move you into the lounge room so you'll be more comfortable. Okay?'

She nodded sleepily, but shook her head when Eduardo knelt and put one arm under her knees and the other around her back in order to lift her.

'No. I'm fine. Honestly.' Her voice was stronger now and her eyes seemed more focused. 'Honestly,' she said again with a little laugh, 'I'm okay. Really.' But she couldn't get up by herself. Eduardo and I got on either side of her and lifted. Once she was upright she was able to totter forward out of the room leaning on Eduardo and me for support. We settled her on the most comfortable chair in the lounge room. Carmel draped a shawl around her legs, but Katerina pushed it away.

'No. No. Thanks, but I'm hot!'

'Would you like the heater turned down?' I said.

'Yes,' she whispered, her head lolling back a little, eyes closed. I turned the heater down. José came in from the kitchen.

'The ambulance will be here in five minutes,' he said.

'I'm not going to hospital,' Katerina said. The rest of us turned to each other. I shrugged. I wasn't going to argue. The ambulance officers would know what to do.

'Do you know what happened?' Eduardo ventured. Katerina shook her head and straightened up. I could see her eyes trying to focus on him.

'Who *are* you?' she demanded.

'He's a friend of mine,' I butted in. Katerina looked at the food on the table, and the half-empty glasses of wine, then around at the others who were all watching her.

'I see,' she said coldly. 'Is this a party or something?'

'You could say that,' Carmel said brightly.

'What for?' Katerina's voice had become slurred again.

'We had the protest tonight,' Carmel said.

'A protest?' Katerina looked as if she didn't understand what the word meant. 'What ... what about?'

'Why don't we talk about it when you're well,' Eduardo cut in. There was a loud knock at the door.

'That will be the ambulance,' José said. 'I'll go.' Katerina gave an exasperated sigh.

'There was no need to call an ambulance ...'

José arrived back in the room, but it was not an ambulance officer behind him, it was Anton.

'Katerina's had ... some kind of accident,' Carmel said slowly.

'That's no good,' he said. 'What happened, Kats?'

'I don't remember,' she said.

Anton moved over to Carmel and put an arm around her and they smiled at each other in the sweetest way. I caught a brief, very odd look on Katerina's face as she watched them, as though their closeness was an affront to her in some way.

'Look, if you all don't mind, I think I'll go to my room,' she said tersely. She was now standing by herself, but tottering a little. A couple of the guys moved forward to help her, but she waved them away impatiently.

'Anton. Could you please help me?' Anton moved to her side immediately. *You little racist*, I thought savagely. *You didn't want any of these dark, roughly dressed strangers to touch you, did you?*

'I've been hearing strange things about you, Anton.' Katerina gave a slurred giggle as she put one hand on his shoulder.

'Who from?' he asked casually. We were all watching. She knew we could all hear.

'Mummy and Daddy were talking to *your* mummy and daddy ... ' She was laughing and moving slowly towards the door, leaning on him.

'What about?'

'Well, they're worried ... '

'What about?'

'Not happy about your ... er ... ' Katerina twisted around groggily and shot a light grin at Carmel. 'Er, your ... love life.'

I glanced over at Carmel. Her face was blank, but a flush was already settling into her neck and cheeks.

'Is that so?' Anton's answer was brief and noncommittal. They both disappeared into the hallway.

'Yes,' came her unsteady voice. 'And to think that I didn't know you were seeing each other! It's a bit *strange*, Anton. After all, I live in the same house as Carmel ... and no one told me ... '

'I met Carmel at your party.'

'Huh? So I'm to blame, am I?'

'I think you should be quiet now ... ' he said. Then there was the creak of the bedroom door opening and closing.

'I think she should be quiet, too,' Carmel said vehemently. I laughed delightedly and slapped Carmel's shoulder.

'Yeah,' I said. 'Come on, everyone, let's drink and eat.'

But somehow the buoyancy had gone. It wasn't just the shock of finding Katerina like that. I think it was her cool beauty as much as anything that must have made our visitors uneasy. The younger ones, Eduardo included, finished their drinks and then made to leave. By this stage Juan and Miguel were deep in conversation near the heater. They just waved casually as the others left. At the front door, Eduardo turned to me as though he was going to say something, but he must have thought better of it. He just said a general goodbye and headed straight for the car. Declan and Annie, my friends from Amnesty, hugged me warmly before jumping into the car beside Eduardo. As they drove off the ambulance arrived. I looked at the time. It had been more than fifteen minutes since it had been called.

'Too bad if she'd been dying,' I said drily. Carmel nodded and we showed the two uniformed officers into the house. I knocked on Katerina's door.

'The ambulance is here,' I said, opening the door and ushering the men straight through. I rushed off, catching Carmel's hand on the way and urging her into the kitchen.

'Let them deal with her,' I whispered. 'If she does need to go to hospital, I don't want to be around to listen to her complain about it.

Carmel and I were quiet as we cleaned up the lounge room and brought all the dishes and glasses through to the kitchen. Juan and Miguel's voices were still droning on in Spanish.

'All in all it's been quite a night!' Carmel said, yawning. 'I feel like hitting the sack.'

'You go then,' I said lightly. 'I'll be all right with Katerina, if she wants anything.'

'You sure?' Carmel hesitated, then shrugged sourly. 'I suppose Anton's with her, too ... '

'But you want him tonight, don't you?' I replied, grinning.

'Yeah,' she sighed, and pulled the plug out of the sink. I put the tea-towel down and grabbed hold of her from behind.

'How is all *that* going, Carm?' I said softly, letting her go.

'Well ... ' She smiled.

'Well what?'

'Well, it's getting better, I suppose,' she said slowly.

'You mean you've ... done it?'

'Well, not quite, but ... we're getting there.'

'Will he stay tonight?'

'I hope so. I mean, that was the plan, but with Katerina getting ill ... I don't know.'

'Have you stayed all night together before?'

'Not really.'

'So this might be the big night, eh?'

'Yes,' she whispered, blushing.

There were footsteps and then Anton came into the room.

'She won't go to hospital. Wants me to take her over to her uncle's place in Toorak.' Carmel's face fell, but she nodded.

'Okay.'

'Why?' I snapped angrily. 'If she doesn't want to go to hospital, why doesn't she stay here?' Anton shrugged unhappily.

'Says it's too noisy or something. Her uncle is a doctor.'

'Spoilt bitch.' It was out before I could help myself. I closed my eyes tight.

'I'm sorry,' I said. When I opened my eyes I saw that Anton was laughing silently.

'You're not wrong,' he said, 'but I'll have to do it ... ' He turned to Carmel. 'I think I'll probably have to stay there and make sure she's all right, or I'll hear about it from my parents ... '

'I guess so.'

'Any idea what could have happened?' I asked. He shrugged and shook his head.

'No idea. Seems to have forgotten everything about what she was doing.'

'I think she's on drugs,' Carmel said simply. Anton and I stared at her.

'What?' I said. But I sensed that Carmel was probably right. I was the medical student, and I hadn't even thought about that. We'd learnt a bit about the signs of drug overdose. At least some of them were there. The slurred voice, the dilated pupils.

'But ... Katerina?' I said incredulously. 'I mean ... I can't imagine ... '

'I can't either,' Anton said shortly, looking away. 'Katerina is too sensible for that ... '

'Just a thought ... ' Carmel said, and shrugged.

Anton put both arms around Carmel's waist, and drew her to him, smiling.

'You gotta watch that imagination of yours, girl,' he teased. Carmel laughed.

'How did the protest go?' Anton asked her.

'Oh, terrific,' Carmel said, enthused. 'So many people. And we sang and yelled out for hours, didn't we, Jude?'

'It was great,' I replied.

'So, you're both fully paid-up members of rent-a-crowd now, are you?' he continued, in the same lighthearted tone. I shook my head. A second take. What the shit was he getting at?

'What do you mean?' I heard Carmel say. I'd turned my back on them so they wouldn't see my reaction.

'Nothing, nothing!' he joked. I turned around and saw that Carmel wasn't laughing.

'What? Are you saying I shouldn't have gone?' she asked evenly.

'Not at all,' Anton replied. 'It's a free country. Anyone can do anything they like in this country. Even stop the traffic in the middle of the city on a Friday night.'

'What are you trying to say, Anton?' Carmel asked. She sounded calm, but I could tell she was getting upset.

Anton moved to the door. He didn't look angry or even particularly interested in the conversation.

'I'll have to go and take Katerina. Look ...' He glanced over at me with an apologetic smile. 'Can we have this conversation tomorrow? I'll come over around four. Okay?'

'What did you mean?' Carmel repeated.

'Well,' he sighed impatiently. 'I really don't see why you would go to something like that, Carmel.' He looked at me. 'I mean both of you. What did you think you were going to achieve? That man is the president of a foreign country, whether you like it or not! We have trade agreements with Chile. What kind of impression will a whole lot of ... *singing* protesters give him of this country?' I was staring at him very hard. He must have sensed it because he suddenly turned to me, both hands spread out in a friendly, I-don't-want-to-fight

gesture. So bloody attractive, with his wide shoulders and interesting crooked nose! 'Perhaps, Jude, your situation is a bit different,' he conceded. 'Your father and ... er, everything.'
Oh, Thank you very much, you ruling-class fucker ...!
'And why not Carmel?' I asked. 'Why shouldn't she have been there?'
'Well ... what has it got to do with Carmel? I mean, really!' He was almost laughing, imploring me to understand. 'Chile?' he said, with one of his charming wry shrugs. He leant forward and put a hand on Carmel's shoulder. 'She's never even been there ...'
'So?' I snapped. 'The world shouldn't have protested when the Chinese authorities shot down all those students in Tiananmen Square, because most of us have never been to China? Is that what you're saying?'
'That's different,' he said shortly, the smile disappearing. 'I mean that was so blatant ...'
'It was pretty blatant in Chile, too,' Carmel cut in angrily. 'Ten thousand people died and many more disappeared! A lot of people!'
'Oh sure ... sure ... I mean.'
'What *do* you mean?'
'Well ... if those figures are ... er, correct.' He looked at us both. 'There is some question about that figure, you realise. I mean some pretty eminent people refute it ...'
'There are also *eminent* people who say that six million people were not exterminated in Hitler's death camps,' I said quietly. 'All those Jews and gypsies and communists ... it's really important for some people not to believe that was true ... But it *was* true. It happened.'
'Oh sure, sure. I take your point,' he said uncomfortably. 'I'm not saying *I* refute it, but ...'
'But?'
'Well, I guess I don't see what it's got to do with ... *today*. I mean here in Australia. The military coup happened over

twenty years ago. All very sad and everything, but ... well, a lot of people think that the takeover was for the best ... That Pinochet and his military rule are the best things that ever happened to Chile ... I mean, the economy there is really looking up ... '

The economy there is really looking up ...

I stared into those sparkling, brilliant blue eyes, and felt a deep coldness wash over me.

My mother had told me that ordinary city life had gone on during the terrible purges after the coup. Thousands of people were being detained, taken at night by armed men, sometimes even whole families disappeared. Husbands and wives, friends and relations were sometimes tortured in front of each other so that they'd speak and give more names to the insatiable military machine. But on the surface, people simply went on with their business, pretending that nothing was happening. Many of them were pleased. The military coup had put more goods in the shops, and public transport was running again. Who cared that a democratically elected leader had been brought down by the systematic destabilisation of the military? They went out and bought ice-cream and re-employed their housemaids at half the price. They continued to meet for lunch on Saturdays, as they'd always done.

'*Don't talk to me! I don't know anything,*' a close neighbour had hissed through the crack in her door when my frantic mother had come home to find my father missing and their flat ransacked. Had she seen anything that afternoon? my mother wanted to know. '*Go away! I know nothing.*' As long as it wasn't *her* brother, husband, daughter or teacher, it was easier to pretend that the atrocities weren't happening.

'Well, sure,' I cut in calmly, 'because they benefited! You see, Anton,' I went on reasonably, 'they owned all the land and the industry before. I'm talking about one or two per cent of the population owning ninety per cent of the country's wealth. The military coup meant that situation could return! Millions of peasants on that land, Anton, worked all their lives for virtually nothing. Generation after generation. Lucky if they had enough to eat!' I stopped, aware that I was raving. I actually wanted to walk over to him, grab him by the scruff of the neck and push him hard up against the wall – rub his nose in the truth.

'Well, we have to get on with things here, don't we?' he said. 'I mean, we don't live there.'

I sighed. He obviously wanted to get away, and I was suddenly exhausted. At that moment just getting horizontal seemed to be the one thing worth doing. I looked at Carmel, but she was frowning and staring at her feet.

'I mean, realistically, Carmel,' Anton said quietly. 'You wouldn't have got involved with this if you hadn't been friends with Jude, would you?'

'So?' she shrugged. 'What's that got to do with anything? Don't *you* get influenced by other people?'

She was about to say something else. Her mouth was open, her eyes wide and troubled, and one hand was in mid-air about to make a point. But Anton suddenly strode over to her and picked her up off the ground in a bear hug.

'Shut up!' he said. 'Shut up. Shut up, shut up! I've got to go!' It was like I wasn't in the room. Carmel's flushed face broke open into a surprised laugh. I smiled too, because, although I hated him for doing it, I had to admit it was kind of cute. A really sexy thing to do. He dropped her back to floor level and began kissing her. I watched her white hands tentatively making their way around his broad back. Love was weakening her resolve, I thought darkly. Women are always being shut up with kisses. Perhaps I was jealous. I didn't have anyone to kiss like that. And a deep longing to kiss *someone* overwhelmed me.

Anton left with Katerina, and Carmel had gone to bed when I walked outside with Juan and Miguel. They were still discussing Chilean politics, but I was only half listening. I had begun thinking about Eduardo again, wondering how I might contact him privately, without it looking like I was doing it. The factory he worked in was way down in South Melbourne, so that would be out of the question. Maybe I should wait around longer after our meals in the cafe, try 'bumping' into him on his way home.

'Well, what purpose would it serve to tell her?' Juan hissed in Spanish. I'd fallen behind the two men to examine all the junk in our letter-box.

I knew he meant me. *Tell her what?*

They were both looking at me.

'Bye then, *Señorita*!' Miguel called in a slightly forced jovial voice.

'See you soon,' Juan waved, avoiding my eyes.

'Tell me *what*?' I demanded, coming nearer. I saw their faces in the street light. Old, both of them. Old and serious, not knowing if they should speak.

'Come on, Juan,' I said. 'I'm a big girl. Tell me ... '

Juan shrugged unhappily and looked at Miguel.

'Ah, no,' he said in Spanish. 'I don't think ... '

My curiosity had really flared up now. I moved closer to Juan and put my arm through his.

'What?' I said sternly. They were both silent.

'Tell her, Juan,' the older man said bluntly. 'It's not as if she can do anything ... ' Juan sighed again.

'But it's upsetting, Miguel ... '

'What?' I said more loudly. Juan took both my hands in his own and caressed them lightly.

'You remember that wedding I went to last week,' he said.

'Yeah,' I said. He had joked that the families were from the more well-to-do groups from the other side of town; the ones who gave the balls and the dinner dances and never wanted to hear anything unpleasant about Chile. Juan had not been looking forward to the event at all.

'Well, I met someone there,' Juan continued. 'A man we ... er, a man we knew back in Chile.'

233

'Who was he?'

Juan shrugged again. He looked away, his face suddenly anguished.

'He was in the ... er, military. A commander ... in the DINA.'

'*What?*'

I stepped away. The DINA, the brutal wing of the police force in Chile. They were responsible for most of the arbitrary detentions. It was they who had organised the mass killings and the torture sessions in secret gaols all around the city. They were above the law, or apart from it. The government knew what they were doing, but turned a blind eye. When someone was in the hands of the DINA all their rights stopped. They didn't charge or sentence. They were a law unto themselves.

'In gaol?' I said. 'You *knew* him in gaol?'

'Yes,' Juan went on quietly. 'He was the one your father and I faced when we first arrived. He was one of the top brass ... ' Juan's voice faded away. The reality of what he was telling me made my vision go haywire. The peaceful Melbourne street in front of me, bathed in the golden light from the old-fashioned lamps, started to swim around and around. For the first time in my life I thought I would faint.

'And you met him at a wedding?' I whispered incredulously. '*Here*? In Melbourne?'

'Yes.'

'What did he ... *look* like?' I asked.

'Oh, the same,' Juan said. 'Just older. Heavier. He was ... he *is*, a very handsome man, not much older than me.'

'Did he recognise you?'

'I don't know. We locked eyes a couple of times. And I think ... I think I saw him ask who I was, but I couldn't be sure. I tell you *chiquilla*, after I'd recognised him, I was feeling so strange that I might have imagined anything!'

'Was he the head of it all?' I asked. 'I mean of the gaol?'

'Yes. Well, I think so,' Juan replied. 'Of couse he would have had superiors elsewhere. When I was first interrogated he was firing the questions. There were two other men sitting there, too, although neither of them was present for any of our ... sessions. Remember how I told you that they got me mixed up with someone else?' I nodded. There was a small, strange buzzing sound near us. For a few moments I thought it was happening in my head. But suddenly one of the streetlights popped. We looked up in surprise, the gloom now making it almost impossible to see each other's faces.

The 'sessions' Juan was referring to had involved him being tied naked onto an iron bed, with electrodes attached to his temples, to his nipples, and inserted up his anus. A heavy gag was placed over his mouth. He was given a small hand device, which he was instructed to press when he was prepared to 'talk', and the torture would stop. The gag would be removed, and if what he had to say was not what the men in the room wanted to hear, it would all start again. Juan had merely been a left-sympathiser, not a member of any party, but they'd made the mistake of thinking he was a member of the ultra-left-wing MIR organisation, and wanted him to spill the beans on other party members. Juan had genuinely not known any of the names they threw at him, but his protestations were only met with harsher treatment. When he had realised after a few days that the torture sessions would go on and on, he tried to commit suicide by tying a smuggled leather strap around his neck and attempting to hang himself from the bars on the cell window. It was only pure luck that my father, his fellow prisoner, had found him and saved him. On that same day, a petty army official arrived at the gaol and informed the DINA of Juan's true identity as a *benign*. Not a member of MIR at all. He was freed that day and never saw my father alive again.

'He was the one who let me go eventually, too,' Juan went on. 'He smiled at me as I walked out of the gate, before I got into the truck, apologising for the inconvenience.' Juan gave a shrill laugh that broke through the cold night like a steel spike. 'And he was probably the one who interrogated your father, too. He would have been the one who ordered his death after ... after they'd got everything they could from him.'

'But they ...' My heart was bouncing in my chest. 'They didn't get anything from my father ...'

'No, no,' Juan smiled at me. 'Your father died a true hero ...'

'What does this man do in Australia?' I asked.

'He runs a restaurant,' Juan said. 'Apparently it's a very fine one. He's doing well ... nice wife ... children.'

'Where is it?' I whispered. Juan grabbed me by the shoulders.

'I want you to promise me you'll try to forget all this ...' he said, staring into my face. When I didn't say anything he shook me a little. 'Believe me, there is no purpose in doing anything at all ...' I nodded slowly, thinking hard, making myself stare right back into his face.

'Orlando,' Juan said. 'And of course he's called his restaurant after himself.' Juan laughed and Miguel, who up to this time had simply been watching us, quietly began to laugh, too. My skin felt as though it was shrinking over my body, becoming thick like old, half-rotten orange peel. I had the oddest sensation of not knowing who I was. It was as though I had no name and lived nowhere. I had no sense of where I was standing at that moment. Just this terrifying feeling of being competely alone. But I said nothing, and as I waited my sense of myself gradually came back.

'Do you promise me?' Juan insisted.

'I promise,' I said, and throwing my arms open I hugged Juan, tightly, pulling his thin, ageing, cigarette-smelling body as close as I could to my own. 'You're right,' I said. 'There is nothing I could say to such a man.'

'That's the girl,' he said and kissed my cheek. 'Come on, Miguel, let's get home. It's freezing!'

'I'm ready.'

The two men got into the car and waved sombrely as they drove off into the night.

The next day I woke late in a mad panic. Groggy with tiredness I sat up quickly, sure that something was dreadfully wrong. It took me ages to work out that it was only the shrill sound of the phone ringing. I almost flopped back down under the covers when I realised what it was. Damn it! If I just ignored it, it would be sure to stop. Wouldn't it? I peered out over the blankets and groaned. On it went, screaming out its monotonous note. I pulled a dressing-gown on and stumbled irritably down to the kitchen.

'Hello,' I growled, thinking that if it was someone wanting to do a survey on the household then I'd spit into the phone before I hung up.

'I want to speak to my daughter!' It took a couple of moments for the voice to register. Nance McCaffrey. Carmel's mother.

'She's in bed, Mrs McCaffrey,' I said in my best polite voice. 'She got to bed very late ... '

'I bet she did!'

'Do you want me to wake her?' I asked.

'Yes, I do!' her voice snapped back at me.

'Okay,' I said, a feeling of dread beginning to simmer in my foggy brain. 'I'll go and get her now. If you will just wait ... '

'What do you think you're doing, dragging my daughter onto the streets?' she screeched at me.

'How do you know that?' I said stupidly.

'We saw her on TV! We saw both of you!' she said. *Oh God! The modern age, eh? No bloody secrets from anyone.* I didn't know what to say.

'I don't care what *you* do,' she went on vehemently. 'Your mother has just been around here spouting all that drivel at me! Trying to excuse it.' She sniffed scornfully and I felt hatred rise in my heart, like a poisonous blancmange.

'*You* do what you like, missy!' she went on. 'But I don't want ... we don't want our daughter out on the street with all that ... riff-raff!'

'You're talking about my friends, Mrs McCaffrey. They are good people who would never hurt anyone ... ' The fury in my head was dancing like ribbons of white light. I could hardly see the pale-green wall in front of me. 'I think you should be careful what you say.'

'Hey? What's that you said?' She hadn't heard, so I didn't repeat myself.

'God,' was all I said. Thoughtfully, and to myself really. So the demo had been on TV. I remembered the cameras that had arrived about eleven. I hadn't registered it at the time.

'Everyone in Manella is talking about it!' she went on. 'Everyone is ringing me up, checking that it was my daughter! I just have to ... '

'Do you want me to get Carmel?' I cut.

'Yes.' I was at the point of putting the receiver down when she shouted, 'No! Waiting for her to get to the phone would be just wasting money. Tell her, from me, that her father is on his way. He's coming down there to bring her home!'

'No, he's not,' I said quietly. There was an icy pause.

'I beg your pardon?' Her voice sounded like a long scratch along tin.

'I won't allow it,' I said steadily.

'Who do you think you are?' she said savagely. 'Some little ... tramp from *nowhere*. We've lived in this town all our lives. My husband's grandfather was born in this house! We owe money to no one. You understand? The McCaffreys are people of substance! And we won't be brought down by a little ... '

My God! What is this woman talking about?

'I'm her friend.'

A loud dismissive snort blasted through into my ear, but I stayed there.

'Well, just you tell her this, missy. Tell her that we're on to all her tricks. Her father is just finishing up the milking and he'll be down to get her. You tell her that!' The receiver crashed down in my ear. She'd hung up on me. I *hate* it when people do that. Luckily I didn't have her number at hand, or I would have rung her straight back and sworn at her in the wildest, dirtiest way I knew how.

I was wide awake now and trembling. My feet were freezing. Suddenly the phone began to ring again. This time I picked it up gingerly. What would I say if it was her again? But it was Mum.

'Jude, darling.'

'Mum,' I said hoarsely, immensely relieved. 'Listen, I know.'

'What, love?'

'About ... Mrs McCaffrey.'

'They're very upset.'

'They're being ridiculous!'

'I know that, love, but ... '

'But what?'

'Well, I think they're coming down there to drag her home.'

'Not without a fight,' I snarled.

'Jude!'

'What?'

'What does Carmel feel about it?' That stopped me in my tracks.

'She's not even awake,' I admitted with a hard laugh. 'I took the mad woman's phone call myself.'

'Tread carefully, Jude,' Mum said. 'I tried to explain what it was all about, but they didn't want to know.' Then she chuckled in that lovely low way she has. The sound of it warmed me. I could picture her sitting at the kitchen table in her green dressing-gown, picking casually at the strands of grey that were beginning to spread through her hair.

'Mum ... ' I said. 'I ... '

'What, love?'

'Oh, nothing ... '

'They think you're the evil influence, Jude,' she said. 'So do be careful, won't you?'

'Sure,' I said. 'And thanks, Mum.'

'What for?'

'Well, for going out to the farm and trying to explain. I mean you didn't have to. It would have been difficult for you.'

'Oh, that's all right,' she sighed. 'I tried to tell them a bit, but I could see that they weren't listening, so I just left.'

'Did you see it yourself?'

'No. But the whole town is buzzing.'

'Do you mind?' I was suddenly anxious. 'Are people being antagonistic?' Mum and I had never exactly been popular in Manella. We'd kind of kept our heads down, never been part of any crowd. It was a small town. Some people were suspicious of us. It pained me to think that Mum might be ostracised for some stupid thing like this.

'Too soon to tell really, love,' she replied. 'Anyway, don't worry, Jude. You know I just want you to be happy.' I mumbled that I knew that and was about to say goodbye. I was glad afterwards that I didn't.

'Hey, Mum,' I said, 'you got any suggestions?'

'About what?'

'About how to save Carmel,' I said. Mum thought for a while.

'Well ... ' she said tentatively. 'Just a short-term thing. They won't be able to come and get her if she isn't there, will they?'

'You mean ... ?'

'Take her out for the day.'

'You mean not even *tell* her Mrs McCaffrey rang?' I said softly, a rush of hope hitting me as I realised that here could be my simple solution.

'Well ... perhaps you *should* tell Carmel,' Mum went on. 'But assuming she doesn't want to go home, then you could make sure neither of you are there when her father arrives.'

'Mum!' I began to laugh. 'I haven't seen this sneaky side of you for ages!'

'Well,' she replied heatedly. 'I think they *should* calm down! They were really over the top with me. She's eighteen after all.'

'Thanks, Mum.'

'Bye ... darling girl.'

'Hey, you two, thanks a lot for last night. I mean, I can't remember much, except that I was pretty far gone ... ' Katerina, a little pale, but looking more or less as perfect as ever, dumped a bulging soft purple leather satchel into the corner of the room, smiled briefly at Carmel and me as we sat at the table drinking tea, and headed over to fill the kettle. 'It was good of you to take the time ... ' she added, her eyes shifting away from us. I reached out and took another piece of toast from the plate in the middle of the table. I'd been building up to telling Carmel about the conversation I'd had with her mother and Katerina's casual appearance was annoying.

'That's okay,' I said, dry as sand. 'What were you on?'

'Excuse me?' She jerked around quickly to face me. That familiar glint of steel was back in her eyes, daring me to ask anything else. But I only shrugged carelessly. I was way past being intimidated by her.

'Well, you were on some kind of dope, right?' I said looking straight at her.

She pursed up her mouth and looked at the ceiling for a few moments. I could tell she was deciding whether to come clean, or whether to act outraged or noncommittal.

'Well, that's ... an interesting theory, Jude,' she said eventually, with an enigmatic laugh.

'Don't bullshit me, Katerina,' I said lightly. 'I'm a medical student. I know an overdose when I see one ...'

Actually we hadn't learnt much about drugs of addiction at this point in my course, but I thought I might as well try and bluff her.

'Oh dear!' she mocked. 'The moral squad is on to me again!'

'Not really,' I said. 'It's just that the next time we have to scrape you off the floor we'd like to have a better idea of what the problem might have been in the first place.'

Katerina's amused expression disappeared.

'I hardly think it was that bad,' she said defensively. She didn't like me talking like this one little bit. Too bad. There were a couple of uncomfortable moments during which no one spoke and no one looked at anyone else.

'Are you feeling okay now?' Carmel asked her.

'Fine thanks.'

'Well, I'm going to have to go now,' Carmel said, standing up and looking at her watch. 'We've got a long rehearsal this afternoon.'

'Oh,' I said, remembering the phone call. *Should I tell her now?*

'But you haven't had a shower!' I said, trying to stall her.

'I had one last night before I went to bed,' Carmel laughed, pretending to be offended. 'If it's anything to do with you! Which it isn't. Then again I suppose if you're trying to be a saint you have to go around minding other people's personal business ...' I threw a dishcloth at her.

'Aren't you even going to wash your face?'

'Nope!'

She had stopped in the doorway to smile at us. With the canvas bag over her shoulder and her hair pulled straight back from her face she looked so big and beautiful and in such good spirits I just couldn't ruin it for her.

'Okay, Carm,' I said. 'What time will you be back?'

'I probably won't be back at all,' she said. 'We've got our

first gig tonight. So we'll probably just get something to eat and then go on down to the bar.'

'Your first gig?' I spluttered in surprise. 'Really?'

'Yep,' she smiled shyly. 'It's coming together, you know. We're starting to sound okay ... '

'So how come you never told us?' I said, pretending to be outraged. In fact she had mentioned something, but I'd forgotten.

'Well, I thought it might be better for people to come when we've got a few gigs under our belts ... ' She grinned. 'I *am* going to ask you to come, Jude!' She turned to Katerina, not wanting to be rude. 'And you too, Katerina.'

Katerina nodded in an offhand way. It flashed through my head that she might have been just a tad jealous.

'It's at Virgona's,' Carmel said. 'Brunswick Street. You know it?' Katerina shook her head in a superior way. 'Well,' Carmel went on, 'apparently the club has lost appeal lately. The drinks are so expensive! Anyway, the guy is expecting us to draw a crowd for him over the next few weeks. If we don't, we're sacked!' She grinned happily. 'I don't care. It's all experience.'

'Okay, then,' I said, looking at the time and trying to calculate how long it would take her father to get down from Manella. 'You'd better go now or you'll be late.'

'Oh, thank you, St Jude, patron saint of the hopeless.' She made a sarcastic face. 'What would I do without you to organise me? See you both late tonight or tomorrow.'

'Yeah, bye,' I called. 'And good luck. Make sure you break a leg, okay?' Carmel waved and disappeared down the hallway.

Katerina and I were left looking at each other uncomfortably.

'I didn't know Carmel's band was *serious*,' she said, pulling the purple satchel onto her knees and opening the catch, frowning as she searched through her things. She spoke as if the thought really peeved her.

'Oh, they're very good!' I said enthusiastically. 'Very professional...' I was bullshitting. I actually had no idea what they were like.

Katerina began pulling things out of the satchel. A cardigan, an expensive-looking camera, a purse, two textbooks, and about half a dozen large square pieces of thick cardboard, which she placed on the table face down. I leant forward and peered over my cup of tea. Photos. The photograph on the front of each bit of cardboard was protected by a thick sheet of tracing paper. She put the cardigan on top of the pile, as though to hide them, and went on searching.

'There's this article I cut out for you,' she said. 'About dreams. I can't seem to find it ... thought you might be interested.'

'What've you got there?' I asked curiously, my hand outstretched to pick up the top photo.

'No.' Her hand darted out to stop me and our eyes locked. Hers looked very green in the pale wintry light coming through the kitchen window, very green and anxious. 'Look, I'd prefer you didn't,' she added in a soft voice.

'Okay,' I said, surprised.

'It's just that ...' She was clearly very embarrassed. 'Oh well, I suppose I don't really care.' She turned the pile the right way up and handed it to me.

'See what you think ...' she said stiffly. 'A few shots. Jordan wants to publish a calendar for next year, but ... I don't know.'

I lifted the protective paper and stared. The first was of Katerina lolling naked across a deck-chair. Her face and eyes were mostly covered by dark glasses and a huge hat, her feet were in stiletto shoes and her hands, which were holding a newspaper, were encased in long black gloves. She looked like a high-class whore. Her face leant forward, mouth parted as though she was about to kiss the camera. Only the position of the newspaper stopped us seeing her crotch.

'Jeeze!' I said. I moved on to the next one. This time she was kneeling naked, except for a tiny G-string, on the beach, patches of sand sticking to her golden skin, a giant wave rolling in behind her, and the huge blue sky above. The real focus was her round bum, which was jutting out provocatively. Once again the wide-brimmed hat and the open, painted mouth. I flipped quickly through the others. I suppose I was shocked. I'd never really taken any notice of this kind of stuff before. I mean, I'd passed by newsagents' stalls like everyone else, seen the front covers, all the bare breasts and cute bums, big mouths smiling coquettishly, but I'd never really thought about it. I'd never considered that the photos were of real girls. Real people.

'So,' I said, putting them down at last, 'you've decided to go through with it then?'

'Well, no ... actually, I haven't,' she sighed, staring at where the sun was making a quivering square of yellow light on the floor. 'I haven't decided anything yet.' I nodded and tried not to feel totally repulsed by the pictures. What was wrong with me? They were obviously very well done. Classy erotic photos. Was I some kind of prude that I found the idea of her posing like this totally ... well, embarrassing and tacky?

'What do you think?' she asked anxiously, looking at me. 'He says he's got an English publisher interested. There's about twenty-five thousand in it for me, plus royalties ...'

'Do you need the money?' I asked.

'No ... I guess I don't. Not really,' she replied slowly. 'But it's not just the money.'

'What else is it?'

'Well, I've always thought of getting into acting. Jordan thinks it would be a great way in ...'

'How?' I exclaimed. My reaction seemed to confuse her more.

'You ... don't think so?' she asked.

'No,' I said bluntly. 'I've only ever heard of things like this doing a serious actor's career harm.'

'Really?' She was looking at me seriously, her lovely green eyes troubled. 'So you wouldn't do it, Jude?'

'Well, it's up to you,' I grinned. 'No one is offering to pay *me* twenty-five grand to take my clothes off.'

I got up and set the pictures out across the kitchen table in a line, determined to work out what I really thought about it all.

'What was it like ... doing them?' I asked curiously. Katerina was on the other side of the table.

'In a way it was kind of fun,' she said. 'I mean it was a sexy situation ... and I found it hard to stay serious ... '

We were both so engrossed that we didn't hear Carmel coming back down the hallway. When she poked her head around the kitchen door we both jumped.

'You got anything on tonight, Jude?' Carmel asked sheepishly.

'Not a thing,' I said. Katerina had hurriedly begun to collect up the photos, but when Carmel stepped into the room there were still a couple left on the far edge of the table. Carmel looked at Katerina and then at me.

'What ... ?'

'Just a few pictures,' I said stupidly. I could see Katerina desperately trying to hide them and sensed her intense embarrassment.

'Well, I came back to ask if you want to come tonight,' Carmel said. 'In fact, I'd ... love you to.'

'Yeah?' I tried to grin carelessly. 'I thought you didn't want your friends to see how pathetic you are just yet!' We were both aware of Katerina putting the pictures back into her satchel.

'I've just decided that it would be better to play to you than to nobody,' Carmel went on.

'Thanks a lot!'

'Katerina, you too, if you like,' Carmel said a little shyly. 'Bring whoever you're with. It's quite a nice place. Drinks are expensive. But there's a good dance floor. Anton's coming.'

'Anton?' Katerina said accusingly, her back to us.

'Yes.'

'Where is it again?' Katerina was acting like she'd never heard of a club or a band before.

'Brunswick Street,' Carmel answered. 'Jude, what about Eduardo and Juan and Declan and Annie ... all those people? They might like to come.'

I nodded. 'I'll ask them.'

'Well, we might drop in,' Katerina gave a perfunctory half-smile. 'I'm having dinner with ... some people. We'll be looking for somewhere to go afterwards.'

'Good,' Carmel said. 'Jude will let you know exactly where it is.'

And with that she was gone once again without my having told her about her mother's conversation.

'I can't handle Carmel,' Katerina said suddenly. The front door had slammed shut and we were alone again.

'What do you mean?' I replied warily.

'Just that,' Katerina said huffily, throwing the strap of the satchel over her shoulder. 'I just can't handle her.'

'What particular thing about her ...' I tried to keep the defensive note out of my voice. I really sensed Katerina's loneliness at that point, her need for a friend, the way she'd let me see the pictures, asked for my advice. I knew she was confused. But there was no way I was going to put up with her slagging off Carmel. I would listen to anything, except that.

'She's probably my best friend,' I warned, eyeing her stubbornly. Katerina was at the doorway into the lounge room. She turned and flashed me one of her haughty looks.

'That's what I don't understand, Jude,' she said. 'You're special, really special. I don't know why you waste your time.'

'With Carmel?' I said coldly.

'She's fat, she's stupid, she's got no idea about ...'

'Shit, Katerina!' I cut in angrily. 'I can't believe I'm hearing this. I mean, in your ideal world everyone looks the same, do they? Listen to yourself, girl!' Katerina took an involuntary step backwards, rattled by my fury. 'Anyone who doesn't come up to scratch you cull out? Is that it?'

'It's just that you two seem so different,' Katerina returned heatedly. 'I can't imagine what you'd find in common ...'

'So?' I said. 'In some ways we *are* worlds apart! In other ways not. Why should that matter?'

Katerina shrugged and looked away.

'I really have to get going ...' she said.

'Yeah,' I grunted. 'Me too!' She walked out of the room, leaving me there, staring at the dirty dishes.

She's jealous. She's really jealous of Carmel and me and she doesn't even realise it.

But I couldn't dislike her for it. I understood then that those pictures were, as well as glamorous and sexy, a bit pathetic. I wondered what she was trying to prove. For the first time in months I was overcome with curiosity about her.

3

By the time I walked into the club with Declan, Annie and Patrick, it was ten o'clock and the place, although not yet really crowded, looked like it was starting to buzz.

Carmel needn't have worried about having no one to sing to. True, most of the crowd was packed around the bar, but some were beginning to move into the adjoining room to watch the band. There was a polished wooden dance floor directly in front of the band and around that stood tables to sit at. The music was incredibly loud, but it sounded all right. I stood on tiptoe to have a geek. Carmel was with the other back-up singer, just to the left of the lead singer, a dull-looking long-haired man in his mid-twenties with thin legs and a not very good voice. I recognised Alan too. He was playing keyboard and looked as though he'd rather be somewhere else. As I got nearer I noticed how terrific Carmel looked in her tight red skirt, high heels, and that dark top of Mum's she'd worn to Katerina's party. A pair of truly *gross* diamanté earrings hung from her ear lobes almost to her shoulders. Where the hell did she get those? They looked fantastic.

I smiled and waved as I led my friends through the thick air and groups of young students in black shirts and torn jeans hanging around the bar, but I don't think she saw me. There were a couple of people I recognised from uni as we slowly made our way towards the back of the room where there were some empty tables. José was sitting at one of them by himself, staring morosely into his glass of beer.

'Hey, José!' I called, putting a hand on his shoulder. 'You here by yourself?' I was actually wanting to know if Eduardo planned on showing, but I was too self-conscious to ask. José looked up, his face brightening.

'At last,' he said smiling. 'I've been here for about an hour.' We pushed a couple of tables together, pulled out the chairs and sat down next to him.

'How's it been?' Declan yelled into his ear. José made one of his wry faces.

'Okay. Okay.'

We all peered forward to where Carmel was standing on the low stage. Her eyes were half-closed as she concentrated on the song. She looked like she was having a really good time. It gave me a buzz to see her. I was glad that I hadn't told her about the phone call from her mother. You never knew, the old girl might have calmed down a bit after her bout with me. Maybe they'd talked it over and decided not to interfere. But even as I went over all the possible scenarios, I couldn't quite get rid of the uneasy feeling.

I'd met up with Annie, Declan and José at Juan's cafe earlier in the evening. We'd had something to eat and then walked the few blocks to the club. Juan and a few others had said they'd come down later.

'Want a drink?' Declan asked, getting up. Although he was probably the poorest of us, he was always the first to be generous.

'I'm in no hurry,' I smiled. 'Might have a dance first.'

'Yeah. Get us a white wine will you, Dec?' Annie held out some money, but he wouldn't take it.

'José?'

'Nah, mate, I'm right.'

I took a deep breath of the poisonous smoke-filled air and looked back over at the band and smiled. Carmel was doing well. She and the other back-up singer were moving in unison, back and forth, to the side, then together again, grinning at each other as they sang. Her fabulous voice was more or less lost under the loud amplifier. Still, the overall sound was all right, and she looked like she was having a good time. No one was dancing yet. I knew it wouldn't be long before I was up there, but I had to settle down a little first and get a feel for the place and the music. Maybe I would have a drink. I needed to relax. José was getting up, so I touched his arm and handed him some money.

'Get us a glass of something, will you?'

'Sure. Wine?'

'Yeah. Red. Thanks.' He disappeared into the crowd at the bar, and I noticed Declan's curly black head loping along above most of the others.

'Declan's a lovely guy,' I said to Annie. She smiled and nodded in agreement. I sighed enviously, and we both laughed. I wanted to ask her how they'd met. Had it been love at first sight? But the music was too loud to talk. Anyway, it just seemed they belonged together, Annie and Declan.

After my strange morning – dealing with Carmel's mother and then with Katerina and her photos – I'd gone off to the library to study for my mid-year exams. The medical library is a nice light place, full of quiet, swotting students. No one interrupts anyone much. There is just this dull murmur of purposeful activity that sort of seeps into me within minutes of entering those wide glass doors. I normally love it. But that day I'd found it hard to concentrate. It wasn't as if I didn't get any work done, just that I found myself drifting off every now and again. It didn't satisfy me the way it usually does. I love mastering new material; making the knowledge my own. But this day I had to keep forcing myself to do it. I was worried about Carmel's family; alternately wishing that I'd told her about the phone call and then going over all the reasons I hadn't. And underneath that layer of worry I was mulling over what Juan had told me the night before. A kind of sick fascination for the name Orlando built up in me that afternoon. I found myself writing the word on the top of each page of my notes. Hating to see it there, but not being able to stop myself from writing it again on the next page. By the end of the afternoon I was still battling to remember all the muscles of the soles of the feet, something I would normally have found a breeze.

> *The muscles in the plantar region of the foot may be divided into three groups, in a similar manner to those in the hand. Those of the internal plantar region are connected to the great toe and correspond with those of the thumb ...*
> *First layer. Abductor hallucis. Flexor brevis digitorum. Abductor minimi digiti.*

Orlando.

> *Dissection – Remove the fascia on the inner and outer sides of the foot, commencing in front over the tendons, and proceeding backwards. The central portion should be divided transversely in the middle of the foot, and the two flaps dissected forwards and backwards ...*

I had to learn all this because next Wednesday it was our group's turn to demonstrate our dissection skills. We'd been assigned this area of the body. I'd promised the rest of my group that I'd lead. I had to know it backwards.
Orlando.
The man who ordered Juan's and my father's torture sessions is alive and well. He has a nice family and a fine business and he is living in this city ... this city where I live. Melbourne. The city to which my mother had had to flee with her young child, to get away from him and those like him ...
Orlando.
'Here. You look like you need this.' José plonked a glass of red wine in front of me with a grin, then pulled up his chair.
'Thanks.' I took a sip and smiled at him. José and Eduardo had been playing music with a few other South Americans in

the city that afternoon. I'd heard it had gone well – they'd made enough for them all to have a slap-up meal at a hotel afterwards. I was dying to ask José if Eduardo would be coming later, but I bit my tongue. Maybe Eduardo had confided in him, told him I was a complete jerk.

'You seem uptight,' José said. 'Anything up?'

'Not really,' I said. He looked at me thoughtfully and then gave a grin.

'Well, nothing you're going to tell me, right?'

'Ah, it's nothing, José,' I said, touching his hand. 'Just a few things I've got to work out.'

'Eduardo said he was coming tonight,' José said. My face must have perked up a bit because he laughed.

'Yeah. Said he was coming straight down after he'd been to see his oldies.'

'José,' I said, hating myself. 'You ... you don't have to answer this, but ...'

'What?'

'Does he ... er, Eduardo, hate me for ... you know ... saying what I said?'

'Nah,' José said, then closed his mouth and looked away uncomfortably.

Jeeze, what was I meant to make of that? The little balloon inside me went *zip* ... flat as a pancake.

We were interrupted by Anton. He looked like a dream as usual, his olive skin glowing, his fair hair tied back in a ponytail, and his perfect white teeth straight out of a toothpaste ad. He was smiling.

'G'day, Jude!'

'Oh, hi, Anton. Pull up a chair, why don't you? This is José ... Anton.'

'Oh yeah,' José said. 'We've met, I think ...' Declan came back and plonked another glass in front of me and he and Anton shook hands. We all turned to the stage. Carmel was singing on her own and she sounded terrific. It was the old

Roy Orbison song, 'Crying'. The guys were backing her simply with lead guitar and keyboard, and the other girl was sitting it out on the sidelines. With the first few bars the noise from the crowd died. I looked around. People seemed to have stopped in mid-sentence, mid-cigarette, mid-sip; everyone was watching the large redhead with the sparkling ears. The one with the voice. At the end of the song the applause was loud and enthusiastic. The rest of the band looked a bit sulky as they picked up their instruments and got ready for the next number. It was as though they were put out by Carmel's appeal.

'She's great, eh?' I said to Anton.

'A knockout,' he agreed with a thoughtful frown. 'Want a drink?'

'I'm okay,' I said. He got up and went over to the bar.

It was at that point that Eduardo arrived with a couple of other people I didn't know. One was Rosa, the girl who sometimes played music with José and him. He gave me a tight little nod then greeted Declan and José with warm grins and pats on the back.

'This is Robert and Rosa, everyone! José, Declan, Jude ...' I felt a shard of anxiety slip in under my ribcage as I peered up at Rosa. Was she with him? I couldn't work it out. *Stop panicking, Jude!* Eduardo moved to the other end of the table, sat down and began talking and laughing loudly, including everyone but me in his warm invitation to come over and check out the new house he and Robert had just moved into.

'*Where does Rosa fit in?*' I wanted to ask. She was looking up at him as he talked, as if she thought he was the cutest thing she'd ever come across. Was I jealous? I don't know. But I didn't like her. She looked dumb and twitty and ... Yeah, I *was* jealous. It was a new sensation. I sat back mutely and tried not to care.

When the bracket ended, Carmel bounced down from the stage and came over to our table. Everyone congratulated her.

'Fantastic, Carmel!'

'Really good!'

Declan stood on one of the chairs and proceeded to 'interview' her amid much cheering and cat-calling from the rest of us.

'How do your see your career panning out, Miss McCaffrey?'

'When do you see yourself appearing at the Entertainment Centre?'

She grinned happily and when everyone had calmed down a bit she pushed her way onto half my chair because there weren't any spare ones.

'How are you going?' she whispered. 'You seem a bit ...'

'A bit what?' It was really starting to piss me off that I still hadn't told her about her mother's call. In fact it sat heavily on my conscience.

'Carm ...' I began. And then I decided that I couldn't do it here. What if she got really upset? I should at least wait until her singing was over for the night.

'What?' she said curiously. 'Come on, Jude. Spill the beans. We tell each other everything, right?'

'I'll tell you later.'

'Promise?'

I nodded. Carmel sighed and looked up at the other end of the table to where the others were talking animatedly.

'He's here,' she said pointedly.

'I know,' I said.

'He with that girl?'

'I don't know ...'

'Has he said anything to you?'

'Nope.'

'Ask him to dance when we start playing again.'

'Nah,' I said grimly. 'I don't think he likes forward women.' Carmel leant nearer and put one arm around me, squeezing my shoulders.

'Go on, Jude,' she said.

'What makes you think he'd say yes?' I laughed in spite of myself.

'Because there's no one like you ... he'd be mad, completely bonkers, to pass you up!'

'Sure,' I said, laughing. 'Go on. See, they want you.' I pushed her off the seat. One of the band members was motioning for her to get back on the stage. She stood up and collided with Anton coming back with drinks.

'Oops! I'm sorry.' He put the drinks on the table and kissed her warmly on the cheek.

'You're sounding terrific,' he said.

'It's all right?' she asked. 'Not too loud?' Anton turned to me in mock impatience.

'All right?' he joked. 'Girl, you're sensational!' He pulled Carmel onto his knee. She laughed and kissed him lightly on the forehead.

'I gotta go,' she said, getting up. But she stopped suddenly and gulped, staring at the entrance to the bar. We all turned to see what she was staring at.

A stunning vision, a woman in white, was standing in the doorway, flanked by a couple of very sharply dressed older men. Katerina. The two men were around thirty, and they stood protectively beside her as if she was a film star and they were the bodyguards. They actually had sunglasses on at that time of night! Then someone else pushed into the inner circle. It was Glen Simons, the handsome old creep I had been so horrible to earlier in the year, the one I hoped I'd never see again. So he *was* still on the scene! He took Katerina's hand authoritatively, as though he owned her, and the four of them just stood there staring around. Katerina was sort of smiling, but the men were very aloof in their snappy leather jackets and Italian linen pants, as if they suspected that someone had planted a bomb in the place. There was an immediate quickening in the atmosphere. Everybody in the room turned for a look. Perhaps they thought she was a film star. She could easily have passed for one.

Katerina, her head held high, began to glide slowly over to our table, a small ambiguous smile twisting her mouth. If she'd deliberately tried to make the most dramatic entrance possible, she could hardly have done better. Most of her hair was pinned high up on her head, with just a few soft curls falling down her back. The dress was made from some kind of clinging white velvet stuff. It was very tight with a low wide neckline and a slit that went up her thigh almost to her waist. She was way over-dressed for this kind of club, but I had to admit that she looked absolutely fantastic.

'Well, hello, you two!' She smiled breathlessly at Carmel and Anton and then turned to me.

'And Jude!' As though I was the last person she had been expecting to see.

'Hi, Katerina,' Carmel said quickly. I muttered hello sourly. I hated her so much for turning up like this.

'It's great you could come,' Carmel said generously. She was uncomfortable too, but I could tell she was trying not to be intimidated by the glamour. Katerina's men looked us all up and down silently as though we were all lesser beings.

'Well, sit down, guys,' I said with sarcastic brightness, deliberately ignoring the fact that I knew Glen. 'Have a drink, why don't you? Relax'. They gave no response to my tone. But I think it kind of startled Anton into action. He smiled at them apologetically.

'Yeah. Look, I'll see if I can find some more chairs.'

When they were all seated, the introductions began. I nudged Carmel. A couple of the guys from the band were urgently motioning for her to come back.

'Carm,' I said. 'Quick. Get back there. They want you.' But Carmel didn't seem to be able to move. She was locked in, watching Katerina as Anton began introducing everyone at the table. His manners were impeccable, as always. He remembered everyone's name and was able to say some nice little personal thing about each of them, which lightened the atmosphere a little. Katerina would fix each person briefly with her dazzling smile, then turn back to Anton with a kind of secret giggling, as though it was all a big joke and only she and Anton knew the punchline. It puzzled me. Something was going on, but I couldn't work out what. I don't think Anton could either.

'Carmel! Come on!' It was the other girl in the band. She was tapping Carmel on the shoulder and looked irate. 'We want to start!'

'Okay. I'm coming.' Carmel gave the newcomers at the table a tentative smile. I saw to my dismay that she'd suddenly become very nervous. Her hands were shaking and her mouth was trembling a little.

'Carmel,' I said sternly, standing up so the others wouldn't hear and grabbing her hand tightly. 'You're wonderful, you know that, don't you?' She gulped and nodded.

'I feel stupid suddenly,' she whispered. 'Oh, Jude, why did I ask her to come? I don't want her to see me singing. I'm not going to be able to do it with her watching ... '

Sometimes I can feel what's going on inside other people. I mean really *feel* it. I suddenly understood just how delicate and finely tuned was Carmel's sense of herself. How fragile she was. She'd had eighteen years of feeling like a complete dud, and just a few short months of feeling that there just might be some real possibilities in her life. It wrung me out seeing her like that. I searched my brain frantically for some way of getting her back on track.

'Okay,' I said sharply, 'so you stuff up. What's the big deal? Eh? We'll still love you. Me and Anton and ... all the others. And you'll still have that voice. What do you really care about her?' She smiled. My heart gave a leap. It was working! I went on a bit, congratulating myself at the same time.

'So, you mess everything up that you possibly can,' I went

on. 'Where is the big deal about that in the broad scheme of things ... eh?' Carmel smiled and shook her head, as though she couldn't believe how wise I was.

'Yeah. You're right, Jude.'

'Of course I'm right,' I went on, laying it on with a trowel. 'We *know* about the broad scheme of things, don't we? I mean, baby, we're *deep*, right?'

She giggled, let my hand go, and walked towards the stage.

'Oh, Carmel!' Katerina called from where she sat at the table. Her voice was clear, matter-of-fact, like a command.

'Yes?' Carmel said quietly, turning around.

'Your father,' Katerina began, and my insides began to heave. *Shit! Oh, shit. Why hadn't I remembered about Katerina being at home?* Your father has been waiting for you at the house all afternoon. He seemed to be in quite a state ... '

'What about?' Carmel's face had fallen. 'Is there ... something wrong? Did he say what he ... ?' A querulous mocking smile was playing around Katerina's mouth.

'Nothing *wrong* exactly,' she smiled. 'He just seemed very determined to take you home with him.' She looked at me. 'He saw your ... er, protest on TV last night. He said something about your going home having been arranged by phone between your mother ... and Jude ... ' Carmel turned to me incredulously. I gulped. The three of us, Katerina, Carmel and I, kept looking from one to the other. We were the inner circle. The rest of them were watching from the sidelines.

'Is that true?' Carmel asked me in a small voice.

'Yep,' I said, not looking at her. 'Your mother rang this morning.'

'Why didn't you tell me, Jude?' She was almost crying.

'I'm really sorry,' I said. 'I was going to tell you. Only ... '

'Only *what*, Jude?' Carmel said, her eyes ablaze with anger. Don't you think I can look after myself? Make my own decisions? I mean *really*!' She looked at Katerina. 'Is he still there or what?'

'I think so,' she said. 'When I left he was sitting on the step outside. I asked him in. Told him he could stay inside as long as he liked and that I was sure you'd be back soon ... but he insisted on staying outside.'

'Did you tell him where I was?' Carmel whispered. 'I mean the address of this place?'

'No,' Katerina shook her head. 'I'd lost the address, so I couldn't tell him. She smiled at one of the guys in glasses. 'Rod knew where it was though, didn't you, darling?' The guy gave a terse little nod. I wanted to smash her face in.

I didn't know whether to get up, go around to Carmel and beg her to forgive me, or simply walk out. I needed to get away. From Katerina, from Anton, from Eduardo and all of them. It was all too much. I felt I'd suffocate if I had to stay there any longer. But Carmel beat me to it. She picked up her bag and headed for the door. We all watched open-mouthed. The rest of the band had been waiting patiently for her to rejoin them, so their eyes followed her too. And probably because she'd sung so well, dozens of eyes around the room followed her big frame striding out. Necks craned, people whispered to each other. I felt sick. I'd ruined her band, her night, her relationship with her father ... what else?

Suddenly she was back. At the glass doors leading out onto the street she'd turned around, swung the bag up on to her shoulder and stormed back into the room. Everyone seemed to take a breath in at the same time as they watched her make straight for the stage, a blazing defiance boiling all over her face. She flicked the hair out of her eyes, pulled off the diamanté earrings and threw them angrily onto the floor behind her. Then she kicked off her high-heeled shoes.

'Sorry for the delay, everyone,' she snarled into the microphone. 'We're going to do a few more numbers for you now.'

There was a communal gasp and then all was still. It was as though she'd suddenly taken control, of the band, of the music, of everyone in the room. The skin on my arms prickled, went cold all over with excitement. She opened her mouth and the beautiful deep voice rolled out; it broke through really, through the whole two rooms like brooding distant thunder. The notes rose and fell, pulsed forward and back like an army moving in rhythm; threatening and retreating. 'Desperado'. The classic Eagles song. But she made it sound as though it had never been sung before.

By the time she got to the end of it everyone's nerves were tingling. The air was thick with melancholy and a queer elation too. Everyone's lost dreams had been laid out flat for those few minutes, like the cards on the table in that strange song. We'd somehow been brought together. We'd all become part of it. The last note died away and the room broke into thunderous applause, shrill whistles, and cries for more.

The next half hour was magic. Carmel ran through about six well-known songs. One after the other. Old classic blues and rock songs that most people knew, but her voice was giving them a new, raw edge. Even the rest of the band seemed to know that something quite special was happening. In the middle of the second song she took the microphone off its stand and roamed the stage, freeing herself. Seemingly only half aware of the crowd, she sang from the bottom of her soul. Within minutes everyone had risen, got as near to the stage as they could. They knew they were witnessing something they might never see again. With each new song I edged closer to the stage, until finally I was very near. I could see the beads of sweat along her forehead and nose, the damp hair sticking to her skin. I could see the pain in her face. I knew then why she was singing like that and it broke me up.

Already I was lonely, standing in the middle of all these hot, half-drunk people crowding around to listen to her. Through the haze of cigarette smoke and the basic sound system they were greedy for what she was giving them. But I was only aware of myself coming home from university every night, eating dinner alone. No one to laugh or sing with. No one to lie around the floor with and talk to. I knew Carmel was giving it all she had because this would be her last chance for a long while, perhaps forever, to sing like that. This was her finale. She was going home with her father. The pain on her face told me that.

I arrived home much later that night. It was the next morning, actually, because dawn was just starting to break as I put my key into the lock.

'See ya, Declan. Thanks.'

'You take care now, Jude.' He waved from where he stood just by the gate. Annie was watching from the car. She gave me a thumbs-up sign.

'Look after yourself, Jude!'

'I will. Don't worry.' I grinned wearily at them and pushed the door open. I had been dreading this moment for the last few hours. I'd pleaded with them to come and eat Thai soup, pizza, drink more coffee, play music ... pool, anything other than come back to find her gone. But now that I was here it wasn't so bad. Like most things, once I actually faced it, it wasn't as bad as I'd imagined.

As soon as she'd finished singing Carmel had left by herself without saying anything much to anyone. She just stepped down from the stage, unsmiling, tossed her bag over her shoulder, and waved goodbye to our two tables. It was as though we were the last thing she'd been thinking about. She was frowning and tense. Anton had stood up, ready to accompany her I think, but it was obvious she didn't want anyone with her. So he had simply watched her go, a puzzled frown clouding his face. Then Eduardo and Rosa had left together. I think I grunted 'see ya' to them, feeling as surly as an old goat. But by then I was past caring. José, Annie and Declan asked if I wanted to join them for coffee. 'Sure,' I'd said, as if in a bad dream, 'let's go and get coffee ... and then we could go to Mario's and play pool.'

The silence thundered at me as I made my way down the hallway, through the lounge, and into the kitchen. The house was creaking and groaning beneath my feet in a way I'd never noticed before. I found myself wondering if it somehow knew something was up. I walked into the bathroom, feeling as if I was the only person alive in the whole city.

I knew it wasn't just a question of getting someone else in either. Before that year I'd spent a lot of time alone. I was quite comfortable with my own company. No, there was something else eating away at me and I couldn't work out what it was. I walked back into the lounge room. Nothing seemed to have gone and nothing had been changed as far as I could see. The posters were still there. A mixture of Carmel's and my CDs was still spread out on the cabinet where we'd left them the previous evening. I tried to dampen the hope that had began to uncurl in my chest. Perhaps . . .

I tiptoed up the hallway to her room, very gently opened the door, and peered in. It was dark so I didn't see anything at first. As my eyes adjusted I made out a figure lying on the bed with an arm resting on the pillow behind the head. She was there! Lying on the bed looking straight at me. Carmel. I blinked and gulped.

'Hello,' I said softly. There was a pause.

'Come in, Jude,' she said eventually. I breathed out, stepped into the room, and closed the door behind me.

'So you didn't go?' I said, keeping quiet and subdued like her. She leant forward and patted the bed with one hand.

'Sit down,' she said. I did what I was told, then looked at her face. It was red and flushed, but she didn't seem to need sympathy. On the contrary, she seemed very remote and in control.

'I thought you'd be gone when I got back here,' I blurted out. 'I'm sorry about not telling you, but . . . Back to that town where you . . . don't belong! I couldn't stand the idea of it!' My voice had choked up, and not only couldn't I speak, I also couldn't stop the tears that were coursing down my cheeks. Carmel edged a little nearer to me. She put a hand on my knee and patted it a couple of times.

'See this,' she said gently. She handed me an envelope. I took it, pulled out the large slip of white paper, and began to read.

My dearest daughter Carmel,

I waited for you as long as I could. I really don't understand how you could do this to me. As I think you know, both your mother and I are anxious for you to come home. (I enclose $40 for the train fare.) Perhaps it was a mistake for me to come down to get you. But we know you don't attend your schooling any more, and so can't think of any good reason for you to be living in the city. Please come home as soon as you can, Carmel. We both love you very much and want the best for you. When you get here we can all sit down and decide together what course you might be able to get into at the local TAFE. (Do you remember Bert Monroe's daughter Monica? She's doing very well in her catering course. She told your mother that the teachers are all nice and friendly – and that there are all kinds of courses to pick from.) Best of all you could be living at home while you do the course. I don't want to harp on this, Carmel, but you're too young to be alone in the city. Mum and I were wrong to allow it in the first place. It's too easy to get in with the wrong crowd.

Come home, love, and we'll forget and forgive everything.

On a lighter note, did you know we had terrific rain (nearly two inches) last week? Thank God! This year looks like being a bumper season. If only the prices will hold till September when we sell the lambs.

Love from Dad

P.S. Had a short letter from Vince. He's been north working on a big cattle station east of Mt Isa. He lost one of his dogs from the back of a truck on the way into town one day and he sounds pretty cut up about it.

P.P.S. Mum heard somewhere that you were still seeing the boy from Yassfield. I hope this isn't the case and that you've both come to your senses by now. He's not our kind, Carmel. Sure it might be easy to be impressed with someone like him – all his money, etc. – but in the long run it's better to stick with your own kind of people.

See you soon, love. Just ring the night before you come, and we'll pick you up from the station.

I read it through again more carefully and then looked over at Carmel. But she was facing the wall. I couldn't work out what to say. It was such a nice, kind, fatherly, boring ... simply bloody *awful* letter. I put my hand tentatively on her leg.

'Carmel?' She gave a deep groan and sat up. She screwed both her fists up tightly and rubbed her eyes, gasping and sobbing. I put both arms around her and she leant into my shoulder, crying as if her heart would break.

'Come on, Carmel,' I said, almost afraid of the strength of her feeling. 'It won't be the end of the world.'

'Yes, it will be. It is. It damn well *is*!' she said, clutching me with both arms. I let her go on for a bit more.

'So you've decided,' I said softly. She nodded, my heart dived back into limbo land and I gave her what I hoped was an understanding squeeze. That father of hers knew how to push the right buttons. Parents were bloody master manipulators. It would be impossible to resist such an appeal to family love and loyalty.

'I'll help you pack everything up,' I said carefully. 'Maybe we can get someone to drive you so you don't have to go by train ... '

She looked up, a strange expression on her face.

'I'll help you,' I repeated.

She sat back, shaking her head.

'But ... I'm not going,' she whispered.

'What?' I didn't have a chance to feel happy. I was just shocked.

'I'm not going home,' she said again steadily.

'But ... you said ... ' I didn't quite believe her. I suppose I'd just seen her as someone who'd be easily swayed. All part of the *delicate* image of her I'd built up in my head. I hadn't imagined her being able to withstand this kind of thing.

'What are you going to say?' I said, still not allowing myself to feel glad. After all, she looked wrung out.

'I'm going to tell them tomorrow on the phone. Jude, I *can't* go back there!' I nodded, sensing that she didn't want any glee from me at this stage.

'But it will cut me off from them,' she wailed. 'I know it will. I'll be so alone after ... after I've defied them ... '

'I know,' I murmured. 'But it *is* your life ... '

'They might even tell me never to come back,' she went on, as though to herself. 'And then there's the twins and everyone ... I love my brothers! I don't want to be cut off from them! I was going to go home next week to see them all. Now they'll tell me I can't.'

There was nothing I could say. Perhaps she was right. I didn't think so, but then I didn't know them that well.

The next week went by in a subdued haze. Carmel rang her parents to tell them of her decision and they were, as she had expected, outraged. After the first phone call, they began to ring her at odd times of the day and night cajoling and threatening her with all kinds of things. I had to go to uni every day, of course, so I missed a lot of it.

At one stage her mother told her that she was never to come home again and that she would be cut out of the family will.

We had a laugh about that one, joking that the money was really what she had been interested in, of course! But it was devastating nevertheless. Her mother was shameless, a blatant dictator. Stalin had nothing on this woman. Once, when I'd made the mistake of picking up the phone before Carmel could get to it, she'd shrieked at me, *It's all your fault.* She went on to say that they had decided to pretend that Carmel had never existed.

'Never existed, Mrs McCaffrey?' I'd repeated.

'That's right! Don't you feel proud?'

'What are you talking about?'

Carmel was distraught for two days after that one. Then her father rang and seemed to know nothing of her mother's threats, because he ended the conversation on a sad, we-are-longing-to-see-you note. Letters arrived, too. A couple from aunts, one from a family friend, and two really heavy ones from her parents.

'We have done everything for you.'

'We are so ashamed to have raised such a selfish girl.'

'How could you have lied to us for all these months?'

'After all our years of hard work!'

Every time I saw Carmel during that first week she seemed to be either bawling or writing letters back to her family. She gave me one to read, anxiously asking if it was 'all right'. It was very short and to the point. She simply told them that she wanted to make her own life and that she loved them all dearly. By this stage I'd had enough. I told her to send the bloody thing, it was more than they deserved.

Carmel seemed to see the whole thing as a battle she had to fight on her own. She continued to work in the cafe and rehearse in the afternoon with the band. But after that first gig, when she had knocked the audience's socks off with her talent, the band's cohesion seemed to slide. Carmel came back each afternoon from the rehearsals with tales of intrigue and petty bickering. The lead singer seemed to think it was his role to boss everyone around and impose his ideas about what they should be playing. He'd begun to belittle the old blues/rock songs that suited Carmel's voice so well, and insisted on a harder, more aggressive style. Not the sort of thing she wanted to sing at all.

Alan seemed more or less oblivious of what was going on. When Carmel tried to talk to him he acted as if he was completely unaware of the lead singer's repressive edge. Carmel eventually realised that this was because he always had a few joints before rehearsal. Although Carmel liked Alan, she bemoaned the fact that he didn't stick up for her. The three men in the band only seemed to be close when they were rubbishing Carmel's ideas. Underneath they resented her superior knowledge of music: both Carmel and the other back-up singer could read music and knew, and could explain in theoretical terms, why something sounded wrong when it did. It had taken Carmel time to develop the confidence to speak up. When she did she had to contend with aspersions about her ability to 'move right' and 'look right'. Why didn't she lose weight? they wanted to know. The band could really go places if it had a couple of 'spunks' out the front. It was all said half-jokingly, but it undermined Carmel's confidence.

One afternoon during this time I came home early and found Carmel stuffing a hunk of iced bun into her mouth. She looked up guiltily. There was a big brown paper bag beside her with only one bun left in it. There had obviously been more.

'What are you doing?'

'I've just finished four of these,' she said miserably, 'and I feel sick.'

I didn't know what to say. Since the night of the protest, when Juan had told me about Orlando, I'd lost interest in food. A few bites of toast in the morning was enough, then maybe an apple or orange during the day. I didn't know why, I'd never gone off my food before. The idea of sitting down and eating four of these great big sticky buns made me feel like chucking up.

'I thought you were trying to lose weight,' I said. Carmel went on stubbornly munching on the bun.

'I haven't eaten anything for two days,' she mumbled defensively. 'Then I was walking home past the bakery and the smell ... I gave way and bought all these!'

'Oh God, Carmel!' I tried to laugh as I whipped the last bun away, wrapped it back up in the paper bag, and put it in the fridge. 'Don't eat any more or you *will* be sick. Have you been rehearsing?'

'Yeah.'

'Did dickhead bring you the dress he was talking about?' The lead singer was always showing off about his mother, who'd been a blues singer in Europe in her young days. He'd been promising for weeks to bring Carmel a spangle-encrusted blue silk dress she had worn when she sang in a German nightclub.

'It was too small,' she cried forlornly. 'It just looked revolting. I tried it on and they all laughed at me.' I sat down and stared across the table at her. I could tell she was really cut by all this. The week before she had said she was going on a diet to try and fit into the dress.

'So what,' I said, trying to cheer her up. 'You don't want to wear his dumb old mother's dress!'

'But I did,' she said. 'It was beautiful. A real torch-singer's dress. I would have been perfect, except for ... '

'What size was it?'

'That's the thing. It was big ... loose by reasonable standards. Size sixteen, at least. And I still couldn't fit into it!'

'So you thought you'd better come home and have a big guts-up?' I said.

She covered her face with her hands and started to laugh and groan at the same time. I joined in. I'm sure we sounded like a couple of sick cats.

'Oh, Jude, what am I going to do?' she spluttered. 'I'm starting to hate being in this band. The guys are awful. They don't work together ... I mean what am I doing? What future do I have ... ? Maybe I *should* go home!'

'Oh, shut up, Carmel!' I said, still laughing weakly. 'Or I'll ... '

'What?'

'I'll ... put you out of your misery,' I said, picking up a heavy saucepan and pretending to hit her over the head with it.

I sat down and put my own head onto the coolness of the laminex table, aware of the lightness in my stomach that had been making me feel slightly dizzy all day. Now, on top of the dizziness I felt quite drunk with the laughter. I knew I really should get myself something to eat right then, but even thinking of food made me even more queasy.

'I'll never be a singer,' Carmel blurted out, her eyes peering out from behind her long pale fingers.

'You already *are* a singer!' I said impatiently.

'Yeah, but you've got to look right,' she went on. 'That's part of it, and I'm too fat.'

'Cut the crap, Carmel!' I snapped. I could usually buoy her up into feeling all right again. But this time my heart wasn't in it. We sat there silently for a while, thinking our own thoughts.

Anyone with half a brain could see that those guys were belittling out of jealousy. She would outgrow that band soon anyway. I suppose I didn't really try to understand her problem with her weight. The truth was I thought she was beautiful and I couldn't understand that she didn't.

I suddenly felt profoundly uninterested. Who was I to try and fix up anyone else's life when I had my own ... my own obsessions to worry about?

A few weeks went by. Weeks during which I tried to avoid looking at myself in the mirror. I didn't want to watch my own face grow pale and pinched, nor see my arms and legs slowly become scrawny. I was becoming lighter all over. Bones were beginning to protrude in all different places: elbows, hips, knees. My collar-bone stuck out sharply like a strange bird's. I started wearing a scarf around my neck. People began to comment.

'Jude! You been sick?'
'You're getting too thin!'
'Gotta tapeworm?'

My jeans were now baggy. When I first noticed this I thought there was something wrong with the jeans. I was worried, but I had no idea what to do. I had an odd feeling of moving backwards. When I caught sight of myself in shop windows and street mirrors I had the oddest sensation, as though I was turning back into a child of twelve.

4

I sat on a seat as near as I could to the water, hunching down into my coat against the wind and looking out across the Yarra. It was that wonderful halfway time, neither day nor night, clear and cold; the pale blue sky was already beginning to slide away into the drama of night; the subtle landscape of watery gold and pink light washed across the sky above me. The river and me. Like music.

Like the dream I'd had the night before. We were on our way down from the mountains again, my father and I. Cutting our way through thick undergrowth, trying to get down to the river. We both knew what we were going to find when we got there, but still we were in a hurry. It was important to get there before the light faded. My feet hurt; stones were pushing through my light canvas shoes and my father's face and hands were cut and bruised. When, at last, we got there, we looked around and could see nothing except the beautiful setting sun dropping slowly behind the trees on the opposite bank, spreading its light like molten gold across the water, catching the trees and low bushes, making the tips and edges of them shine like stones.

I knew I was in Chile. In the high country behind the city, a long time ago. And I could feel danger all about me.

A tremendous dread built up in my chest as we began to search among the clumps of rushes in the banks of the river. I desperately wanted to run but because my father was there I couldn't. At last we found what we were looking for. The bodies were hidden between the clumps of tall reeds upstream. There were perhaps six men piled on top of each other, and three older women with grey hair and wrinkled faces. Although we looked closely into each face neither my father nor I recognised any of them. Each body was riddled with bullets. Strands of congealed blood waved like tiny flags in the water around some of the wounds. My father waded into the water and began carefully and very gently to push the bodies out into the current. I stood and watched them sliding off downstream. Then I turned away and found two young children near where the others had been. One boy of about eight and a little girl of around three. In spite of the bullet holes in their chests they looked peaceful, as if they were only asleep. My father stepped in front of me, as though he didn't want me to see the children and pushed them out into the current as well.

I was waiting beside the Yarra on the Southbank Promenade for a restaurant to open, thinking about my dream. I'd come down after my lectures were over and had been there for a couple of hours. There were lots of people about. Smiling, arm in arm. An occasional shout and burst of raucous laughter gave the place a warm, easygoing air, in spite of the cold. On the glass door of the restaurant it said six-thirty, so I only had ten minutes to wait. Streaky ribbons of yellow and red light fluttered below me in the water.

I stared over at the crowd waiting in lines to board the restaurant boat. It would be launched soon, gliding out into the bay, full of people who wanted only to eat, drink and be merry. I despised them at the same time as wishing I could be part of their easy, carefree fun. Some of them wore fur coats, with shiny high-heeled boots. Champagne corks were popping, and I could see the sparkle of glasses being raised in the distance under the dipping line of coloured lights. I got up and tap-danced a little, trying to warm my toes. Surely it would be open by now.

Orlando's. The name was spread proudly across both windows in elegant script. I shuddered before pushing open the door and walking in. There were about three other groups of patrons already seated. A woman of about fifty stood behind the small counter, by the partially concealed cash register. She was blonde and immaculately dressed in black silk. She smiled at me in a tight professional way.

'Good evening.' Her accent was thick and hard to place. 'A table for one?' I nodded numbly, followed her to a small table and sat down.

The place was large and nicely furnished. The slate floor contained various subtle shades of grey, the walls were white with bits of dark wood-panelling around the cornices and window edges. The tablecloths were crisp and white. Lovely round glasses sparkled on every table. Apart from the three small groups of people already eating and drinking, the only other person was a young girl of around eighteen who was waiting on the tables. She was moving quickly, serving bottles of wine and plates of food, and smiling secretly to herself. She came over to me, smiled, and stood waiting for my order. I realised I was hungry, that I hadn't eaten anything at all that day. Six weeks had gone by since the night Juan had told me. Six weeks of trying to forget, trying to keep away. My heart was hammering as I ordered a plate of pasta, some bread, and a glass of wine. Then I sat back and tried to calm myself. There were only the two women. And they might just be hired staff. How could I find out what I wanted to know? I stared around and tried to think of a way.

That morning I had risen knowing that I had to see him. That was all, I told myself. That would be enough. I needed to see this man, to look into his face if that were possible, to try to understand something about him.

It had been easy to find the restaurant. It was listed in the phone book. When I rang the number a girl had answered and she had told me that the restaurant had been relocated to the Southbank area.

The waitress brought my wine, a steaming bowl of pasta,

and a plate of warm bread. I thanked her and ate a couple of mouthfuls very quickly, without tasting it. Then it happened, the way it had been happening for weeks, every time I came in contact with food. I lost all appetite.

The place began to fill up. Most of the surrounding tables were now occupied and the noise level was high; at times it seemed to be verging on hysterical. A table of giggling office girls sat on my right and three serious young men in suits sat immediately in front of me. I listened alternately to their conversations as I played with my food. I made myself take a bite of bread, but it tasted like cardboard and was hard to swallow. I put some pasta on my fork, but couldn't distinguish the separate tastes. The bread was like the pasta, and the sauce was like the bread. The girls were talking about men and the men were talking about their work. As I eavesdropped I wondered if I would ask the waitress something when she next passed. Perhaps I could say I'd visited the restaurant when it had been in South Yarra, to try and get her talking about her boss. I tried to catch her attention, but the table of men beat me to it.

'May we order some more bread?'

'Of course, sir.'

'Where's Orlando tonight?' My head jerked up from my meal. I chewed and strained to hear her answer over the noise.

'Is something wrong?' The girl's face had dropped. The men laughed.

'Not at all, it's just that we're used to him being about.'

The girl began to smile again.

'There's a big party coming in later,' she said. 'He's in the kitchen preparing food.'

'So we'll just have to make do with Mrs Orlando?' one of the men joked loudly, glancing over at the lady in black behind the cash register. They caught her eye and she smiled over at them and waved. *Mrs Orlando.* I got up, feeling giddy. I picked up my coat and bag and walked quickly over to where she stood. She looked at me querulously because I hadn't been given a bill.

'I'm sorry,' I said, 'I've just realised the time. I couldn't wait. I had a small carbonara, bread, and a glass of wine.' But she wasn't listening. Her mouth had gone tight with displeasure. She moved out from behind the alcove and motioned briskly to the waitress to come over. I'd offended her sense of correctness. I should have waited for the waitress to bring my account. The girl rushed over, still smiling gamely, her hands full of plates and glasses. She was very busy, the only waitress attending to the whole room.

'Table three? Have you got the bill?' the woman said darkly. The girl indicated her pocket. Her hands were full so she was unable to get the order book out herself. Mrs Orlando reached down and took the book, sniffed, and began to flick through it.

'Just a carbonara, bread, and a glass of red wine, Mrs O.' The waitress repeated my words lightly before diving off towards the kitchen. They had both treated me as if I wasn't quite present. I felt humiliated, which I guess is what they wanted. More importantly, I felt I needed to have some fresh air soon. Her face a mask of displeasure, the woman began to ring through the items. *Six dollars fifty, four dollars.*

A man suddenly appeared in the small alcove with her. He was also dressed in black, but he had a white square linen apron tied around his middle. He was tall, grey and heavily built, with black hair all over his arms, and he seemed edgy, anxious to be off.

'My dear,' he said in Spanish. 'Did we order any more cream this morning?'

'Of course,' she anwered. Then to me, 'That will be fourteen dollars and sixty cents ... ' But although I heard her words they didn't register. I was staring at the man's face, side-on to me as he stood behind the woman waiting for her to tell him where the cream was. His features were strong and even. I think I was trying to see him in relation to Juan. He looked younger. Heavier but much healthier. Juan was ancient by comparison. This man was ageing, of course. There were wrinkles, and grey hairs, and a slight sagginess around his chin, but his chest and arms were muscular and he looked strong.

'Excuse me!' his wife snapped coldly. I shook my head, gave a stupid smile of apology, and dived into my bag for my purse.

'It's in the fridge!' she hissed out of the side of her mouth.

'No it's not!' he came back angrily.

'Are you Orlando?' I asked, handing over a twenty-dollar note. I watched him turn around. I could stare right into his face now. My words ricocheted back and forth, from him to me, echoing in my ears. After a few moments it didn't seem as if I'd spoken the words at all. I could see his brown eyes watching me. They crinkled up a little at the corners and his mouth opened briefly, showing a line of perfect yellowing teeth. It was a small flashing smile that disappeared almost as soon as it had arrived.

'That's me,' he said.

'The Orlando who owns this restaurant?' I went on stupidly. The woman handed me my change. They were both waiting for me to go.

'That's right,' he said.

I wanted to keep looking into his eyes. I hadn't found the first thing that I'd come here for, and I didn't want to have to go out into that cold night again without having found at least something.

'And you come from Chile?' I went on boldly. I felt quite powerful as I saw a sharp flash of suspicion cross his eyes. He blinked a couple of times and gave another brief smile.

'That's right,' he said again. 'And you? You're Chilean?'

'Half,' I said. 'My mother was ... *is* Australian.'

'You look ... very South American,' he said politely. But his body was tense with irritation. I nodded, unable to tear my eyes away from his face. The eyes, brown and gleaming in his olive-skinned face. He looked like an ordinary man. No, better than ordinary. His face could have been considered pleasant, handsome even. There were lines around the edges of his mouth. Were they cruel? Or were they just ... lines? His hands weren't particularly big or thick. One of them was half-covered in white flour. The hands of a cook. I could picture him out the back in the kitchen, up to his elbows in pastry, doing complicated things with syrupy peeled pears, tiny hot pies, and glacé fruit. Those hands had tied blindfolds around eyes, stuffed mouths with heavy stinking gags. They'd connected electrical clips to testicles, to nipples, to tongues. They had pressed the switch, made the current run down the wire into the delicate nerve-endings and flood the flesh with burning, shocking pain. Then more. And more after that. Until. Until the convulsed body spreadeagled on the bed in front of him was arching wildly, as involuntarily as a single leaf caught alone in a massive cyclone. Until the person didn't know who they were any more, or what they knew, or what they should or shouldn't tell. *My father*, sweating, bloodied, screaming silently through his gag before this man. Every nerve-ending fractured. Burning with pain. Those hands, the hands of his torturer, were right in front of me. One was plucking anxiously at the notebook on the counter.

'Yes ... my dark hair, and ... ' My voice dropped away. 'My skin.'

'So you speak the Spanish?' he asked. I could tell my fading voice had him baffled, slightly embarrassed.

'*Sí ... Sí, Señor, sí, un poquito.*'

'Good! Good!' he laughed. He wanted to get rid of me, but didn't know how. 'I have to get back to my work, *Señorita*. So if you'll forgive me ... ?' He raised both palms in front of him and shrugged, then he turned and walked back through the tables to the kitchen. I watched him, mesmerised. When he'd disappeared I turned to his wife. She was checking through some figures, her face still curled with displeasure.

'Goodbye, *Señora*,' I managed to say. But she didn't reply.

After that I couldn't forget him. The days passed. I went to my classes. I even learnt things. I had conversations, had meals with people, although I ate hardly anything. I couldn't eat and I couldn't forget him. He began to lurk around the edges of my dreams. Whatever I was dreaming was always suffused with this sense of threat: the tall solitary figure in the background, the good-looking man with the even yellow teeth who, although he was always smiling and I never knew quite who he was when I was dreaming, always filled me with terror. I had thought I would only need to see him once and all would be revealed. Not so.

I began to stalk him. Without telling them why, I cajoled some of my friends into coming back to the restaurant with me. It was out of their price range, but they complied a few times just to humour me. Even poor Declan, who lived on about fifty dollars a week, agreed to spend twenty of them for one meal at Orlando's, just to please me.

Then I began to sneak down to the river when I could, hanging around waiting for glimpses of him arriving and leaving. Once I even snuck through an open gate out the back, climbed the one small leafy tree in the concrete backyard, and had a good, although very uncomfortable, view into the kitchen. I watched through the large back window as he came in and out, organising the food and talking and laughing with the rest of the staff. Two or three times I waited out the back of the restaurant beyond midnight and watched him from a small lane opposite as he and his wife locked up. I was terrified of being discovered. My heart was racing as I listened to their clipped small-talk and watched them get into their car and glide away. Sometimes they spoke in Spanish, but not always.

My friends began to worry about me, the sudden weight loss and my new quietness. Especially Carmel. I would see her looking at me sometimes, frowning, trying to work out what had got into me. She was a good friend. I loved her. But I didn't want to talk about this to anyone. I knew it was useless, dangerous, knew it wouldn't get me anywhere. At least nowhere I wanted to go. Of course she'd ask me what was wrong every now and again and I'd mumble something about not feeling well. I stopped answering my mother's letters, even stopped reading them after a while. I would just see her writing on the envelope and drop it into the overflowing rubbish bin near my desk. She'd ring, but I wouldn't go to the phone.

'Tell her I'm asleep!' I'd hiss through the bedroom door at whoever had come to tell me. 'I'll ring her later.' But I didn't ring her. I had no intention of contacting her at all.

I'd find little notes from Carmel when I'd come home from uni. *Felt like making some lasagne. Please save me from myself and eat the rest that's in the fridge! Love, Carmel. P.S. See you when I get home from work.*

And when the gentle hints didn't work, she'd try a more forceful tone. *Jude! Anton and I bought some delicious Indian takeaway last night. Leftovers in the fridge, plus a container of your favourite bought specially for you. Please eat! You need to, Jude. I'm serious. Love, Carmel.*

Everything around me seemed to contract as my inner-life raged. Strange dreams intertwined with rehearsals for the showdown I imagined having with Orlando. *I'd say, you murdered my father, and he'd say, so? Or he'd say, prove it, and I'd say, sure, I'll do that. And he'd say, leave my premises, and then I'd say ...* There was always a different outcome in these inner dialogues. But they'd become more real to me than the people I was dealing with in my everyday life.

When I forced myself to think about confronting him I realised that I really had nothing to say at all. It was rather that I had developed an intense fascination with him. I needed to know what he wore, where he lived, how many children he had and how old they were. I was like a fan who had become obsessed with a rock star. I wanted to know everything about him.

My dreams became more vivid and convoluted. One that continually recurred was about me waking up knowing that I was inside his house. I would get up and begin to roam stealthily through the huge, semi-deserted rooms full of dust and sour smells, rats and cockroaches, broken furniture and mess. All the time I was afraid that I would come across him, that he would suddenly appear from behind a piano or creep up on me from behind a curtain. But I couldn't stop myself from looking. I wanted to find his clothes and all his personal stuff. In these dreams I was searching for a bathroom, a warm bed where he'd just slept. I wanted to *smell* him.

The worst dreams were those in which Orlando and my father merged into one. I couldn't tell one from the other. I would be following my father along a cramped hallway. We were going somewhere important; I knew I had to be there. Then he would turn around and I would see that the man I'd thought was my father was really Orlando. He would turn and smile with those yellow teeth. Terrible.

Every time I had this dream I woke up sweating, my heart pounding wildly and my hands and forehead damp and hot.

Eventually it happened. I knew as I felt myself get thinner, and as the bouts of dizziness came more and more frequently, that it was only a matter of time before I wouldn't be able to go to university at all. A big part of me baulked at this, fought against it with every ounce of energy I possessed. For so long I had been determined to stick to my blazing ambition of becoming a doctor and following in my father's footsteps. If I gave up university, what would become of me?

The crisis day came unexpectedly one beautiful morning in August. I got up and went to my window, saw the bright blue winter morning sky outside, lifted the sash and felt a gust of cold air against the skin of my face. Yes! I took a deep breath and for a few moments allowed myself to hope. Perhaps today would be the end of it, the beginning of my way back into my old life. To who I'd been. I could feel hunger nagging in my gut and that gave me added optimism. I would go down to the kitchen and make myself something to eat. I would sit at the table and spread the toast with thick butter and jam and make myself a comforting mug of hot milky coffee. I longed with a pang for the comfortable settled feeling of food in my belly; it would clear my head, give me a stronger idea of who I was and what I should do. That physical pang lit an emotional fire inside me. Today the dizziness would stop. I dressed quickly, afraid that my new optimism might blow away in the sharp breeze that had begun to invade my room. I went down to the kitchen and began to organise the toast and hot milk. I was hungry, hungry, hungry, I told myself. I would eat.

I put two slices of bread in the toaster. Then I got the butter and jam out of the fridge and determinedly placed them on the table. So far so good. The toast smelt wonderful, but very strong. Almost overpowering. I picked a small, sharp, black-handled knife from the drawer and an image came to me: a black crow descending towards a defenceless newborn lamb. I would kill Orlando. Yes. The idea hit hard. I could almost feel it take hold, the grip of its talons in the soft flesh of my shoulder, the scraping of one wing against my face. I sat down. Yellow light poured in through the kitchen window. Fat buttery yellow light. The crow disappeared and the idea grew, inflated out and floated upwards, tugging at my brain like a huge birthday balloon. A perfect shape, round and simple, a lovely red. *The best ideas are often the simple ones.* I remembered a favourite teacher saying this once, smiling. Surely it would be easy enough to do. It would only be a matter of planning it properly. The knife in my hand spread the butter around and around the toast and I watched the tiny pieces of bread-dust fly chaotically through the yellow light.

I'm sick of words. Sick of wild thoughts and mad dreams that go nowhere. No more words. Just act. Action is called for in extreme situations. This was an extreme situation, wasn't it?

I dumped a tablespoon of red jam on top and spread that out too, letting it run off the sides and onto the plate. Yes. As soon as Juan had told me I knew there would be nothing to say to this man. I must *do* something.

Katerina waltzed into the kitchen rubbing her hair dry with a towel. We were hardly speaking at all by this stage. After the night of Carmel's first gig – the night after I'd been told about Orlando – I had avoided her as much as I could. Not that I had consciously decided to. But I had a lot else on my mind.

'Jude, could I ask that we make sure the towels are hung up?' she said, all light and airy, as prissy as some bloody secretary in a lawyer's office. I'd tentatively begun to eat. I'd had two large bites and was trying to ignore the familiar feeling of nausea in my stomach.

'Yeah,' I snarled, 'you *could* ask that ... I suppose ... ' I hadn't intended to be so sour or offensive. I tried to go back to reading the print on the side of the bread packet as I chewed, but I could feel her eyes boring down at me. I had to make myself not look up. The strange thing was that after the night of the gig she seemed to be home a lot more. From my bedroom I'd hear her walking about the kitchen, playing music in the lounge. Men didn't seem to come around any more to pick her up and take her out. There was less fancy dressing up. She stayed in her room a lot. And when she did come out she was dressed in sloppy old jeans and sweatshirts. I hadn't seen her friend Kara in ages either. Maybe they were concentrating on their studies. I didn't know and I certainly didn't care, as long as I didn't have to look at her or talk to her.

'Jude, is there something wrong?' she said eventually, quite kindly. 'You seem so strange lately, so out of it ... ' I slammed my mug down onto the table and got up.

'No!'

'Well, I just thought I'd ask ... because ... ' She looked

determined to continue, but nervous too.

'The towels are wet,' I cut in sarcastically. 'And they're heaped up in the corners of the bathroom like dirty smelly old lumps of rotting fruit! Is that why you thought you'd ask?'

'Yes,' she said in a small voice. 'I just thought it would be better for everyone if we ... '

'Oh spare me!' I snapped, getting up from the table. 'Spare me from what you thought would be better for everyone ... ' I slammed out of the room without even looking at her.

You feel worse when you know that you've behaved badly. I smouldered all through my tram trip into university refusing to allow myself to see the truth: that I'd behaved like a moron, and that I owed Katerina an apology. After all she'd only asked me to do a simple thing, and quite nicely, too. I didn't like grotty bathrooms either and our whole house had got very grotty lately. No one seemed interested in cleaning up.

I walked up the steps of the Med building studying the timetable on the front of my folder. First biology, then chemistry, then an anatomy tutorial, then ... I stopped. Hordes of students were hurrying up the stairs around me, only a few coming down the other way. I stood and stared as if seeing the place for the first time. They were all young, some dressed in torn-off jeans with bright tights underneath, workmen's boots and suede op-shop jackets, others in jeans with old hand-knitted jumpers, baseball caps on their heads, carrying heavy bags of books. Long hair, short hair. Fat and thin. Some were alone, frowning and intent on where they were going, others laughed and called out, threw things to each other. The big glass doors opened and shut. Opened and shut slowly. Opened again.

I felt my legs gently slip from beneath me as I stared at the door, as though I had been plunged into a deep pool of water. The door swung open again. Exhausting. I didn't actually fall, just melted somehow to my knees and then shifted onto my bottom. Once down I didn't seem to be able to raise my head.

I stared at the moving shoes climbing the stairs. The grey concrete stairs.

'Are you okay?' Two sweet-faced girls had squatted next to me and were peering into my face. I looked up and vaguely recognised them. They were both in my year.

'I'm fine.'

'Are you sure?'

'Sure. Thanks. I'll just sit here for a few moments, then I'll come in.'

'Would you like us to wait with you?'

'No. Thanks.'

But I can't go in. I won't go into that place. It's all impossible now. I have no idea why I wanted to do Medicine in the first place ...

Eventually I got up and walked back down to the tramstop. We had an exam the next day. If I couldn't bear to go to lectures, then I knew I should go home and study for it. But I crossed the road and waited for the tram that would take me in the opposite direction. I bought a ticket to Southbank and thought about Katerina. I'd try to be pleasant next time I saw her. I'd say I was suffering from exam pressure or something. Make some excuse. There was no point in making an enemy of her.

Why am I going down there again? Do I even expect that he'll be there at this time of the morning? Get real, Jude! But I just need to ... What? I need to see him? But why?

I walked along the Yarra for a couple of hours, feeling cold and miserable and half crazy. Eventually I bought a bucket of hot chips and a coffee and managed to eat perhaps a dozen chips before I threw them to the gulls who were pecking and screeching around me, dipping and diving angrily against the cold gusty wind above the river.

The water was very dark that day. I sat and watched from a seat on the bank opposite Orlando's and imagined myself falling into its liquid blackness. Would it smell? Would I feel cold? I longed for the lack of all this bright glaring light and the sudden quiet that would envelop me. Would I hear anything apart from soft gurgling as I sucked the water into my lungs? The roaring sound of blood beating wildly through my legs and arms and chest? I could simply walk over to one of the two bridges, only a few metres from where I was sitting, and drop myself off. I would discard my coat beforehand and loosen my hair from the thick plait I'd made that morning. I'd leave on my jumper and jeans, my gold earrings and watch, the chain around my neck. I would let the strong black leather boots my mother had bought me take me down. Downwards. Through the black sludgy water, through the coldness, deeper and deeper until they reached the sandy floor of the river. My long wavy hair – the hair I'd inherited from my father – would fly out around my head. I would raise both my arms high, like a bright child in class, open the fingers wide, stretch out to meet whatever it was that had come for me. We would meet each other. Whoever or whatever it was, down there on the floor of the river. I would stand there, my hands spread, swaying slightly in the current. Not trying to swim.

I sat very still for a long while with that picture of myself. Then I shuddered all over. My teeth were chattering and my fingers were almost numb. I stood up, stuffed both hands into the pockets of my coat and began to walk.

By about three o'clock the day had become wet with drizzling rain. I had my long purple parka and my boots, but I hadn't watched for puddles or gutters and my feet were now wet. I bounced around on my toes trying to get the feeling back, wondering what it was that had kept me there all those hours? I didn't really know, only ... only that I just couldn't ... I didn't want to go home yet.

So here you are. Just a man. Orlando. Only a man. Will I tell you about the way you've become my own personal nightmare? How you have wormed your way into my brain? My sleep? How your eyes will widen when I take the gun from my coat pocket and point it straight at you. A gun or a knife? That was something I'd have to work out. Would I use a gun or a knife?

A rushing sound in my head made me feel momentarily as if I was falling. I was falling fast from a great height towards something terrible. I was falling into the heart of the volcano, towards the boiling red rock. But all around me was darkness. Everywhere about me cold, black, spongy dark. Falling. Falling through the black water, my hair fanning out like a drowning woman. But the figure at the bottom of the river has changed. The one sucking and gurgling on the murky black water has become my mother.

A slim woman in dark clothes, both arms raised high, swaying in the current on the bottom of the river. Her long red hair, with strands of grey, swirls and flutters gently out from around her head like exotic grass from a forgotten garden. Her heavy black skirt surges around in the water, back and forth, billowing out around her legs every now and again like a tent. Her face is very white and she too has heavy boots on. My mother. I can see her standing on the floor of the river, already gone, part of the undergrowth now, spots of moss and green algae already growing on her hands and skirt.

The rest is blackness. I can't remember even running. I think I shouted something and began to run, but I can't be sure.

The next thing I remember was fiddling in my pockets for my door key. Someone had helped me out of a car. Some stranger was gently leading me up to my front door. A police officer? I was outside our little house unable to believe that my key wasn't where it always was. Had I gone to sleep somewhere by the river? Enormous lumps of time must have passed, but I had no idea. It was now evening. My frozen fingers fumbled around stupidly inside the empty spaces in my jeans, coat and shirt before I finally gave up and banged on the door. Please let someone be home! But there was no answer, despite the shining hallway light. I almost turned away. Carmel would be at the cafe working. Behind me I heard a car engine start. Damn. Then the front door opened. My mother was standing there, dressed in a long black skirt and thick jumper, her hair fanning out around her face, exactly as I'd seen her that afternoon in the river. Even the boots. I wasn't surprised, but I thought I might have been dreaming.

She cried out and rushed towards me. 'Jude, Jude.' She was crushing me in her arms. 'Where have you been? I've been frantic with worry ... waiting for you all day. You're so thin! Carmel rang and told me you haven't been eating. Don't be angry, darling. What has happened to you?'

I let her hug me, but I couldn't speak. Inside I was chilly, with apprehension mainly. It felt as if the cold black river water was actually washing around inside me. So now at last I would learn everything. But would it be too late? I had no idea if I'd be strong enough to bear what she'd come to tell me. Part of me wanted to put my hands over my ears and tell her to go away.

My mother stayed for nearly a week. She fed me soup, washed my clothes, made her delicious herbal bread and coaxed me to eat it, and – I'm ashamed to say – cleaned our house. I saw the other two, Carmel and Katerina, fall in love with her. It only took about a day. Probably less for Carmel. Their relief was palpable when they came home and saw her calmly washing cups at the sink. Mum is an expert at not invading anyone's privacy. The first day I heard her asking them if they minded her washing all the towels in the bathroom, as if it would be a privilege for her to do it. Off she went smiling, the washing basket under her arm, to find the local laundromat. I'd hardly noticed until then how my slide into depression or obsession – whatever it was – had affected the others. But with Mum there, somehow everything lightened up between us. I stopped evading Carmel, stopped despising Katerina. And they stopped looking at me in that worried, puzzled way. I began to notice little things, too, like the nice smells around me, flowers in the vase on the table, freshly baked bread, and the soapy sweetness of our newly cleaned bathroom. I noticed the way Katerina and Carmel were sort of getting on with each other too. At least the awkward stand-off stage had eased, and they talked a bit. My mother spoke quietly, smiled a lot, and asked calm questions.

'Now, where do I hang this towel?'

'Do you have plans for after your degree, Katerina?'

'Do you both like curry? You do! Oh good. I'll cook tonight. That's if you haven't any other plans.'

No one had any other plans. Katerina actually came home and ate with us that first night, and every night from then on while my mother was with us.

But in the afternoons when we were alone my mother talked to me.

I tried to tell her about Orlando. About what I'd decided to do. My mother listened, but after all these weeks there was surprisingly little to tell her. Three or four minutes and those vague plans, weird dreams, longings to do something, were out and we were left looking at each other. She didn't say anything for a while. She lay there quietly on my bed, looking thoughtful, while I sat up in one corner, a mug of coffee in my hands, waiting for her reaction.

'So what do you think?' I said at last.

'To get rid of him would mean nothing,' my mother said softly. 'There are thousands more where he came from and ... everywhere else. You can't kill them all.'

So matter-of-fact, to the point. So sensible. Her reaction surprised me. And I felt deflated.

'It's you that I'm worrying about, Jude ... not him.' I turned away, not wanting to meet her eyes. I sipped my drink.

So she told me everything. Every afternoon for the four days she was with us she lay down next to me on the bed and talked about her life with my father. She told about when she had been taken into detention. How she'd left me with a good friend. She'd been beaten and tortured on and off for three days. Had felt quite sure that she would die there. But as long as I was safe, she had thought, she could endure it.

Then they brought me in. I was only two.

'You were such a beautiful, plump little girl, Jude. They told me they would kill you slowly if I didn't tell them where your father was. I didn't believe them. Days passed. You and I were alone together in this cell. Awful food and no proper milk for you. They gave you nothing to play with. You got cross and fretful. You cried a lot. All I could do was sing to you, say little poems, when all the time this terrible burden hung over me. What if they meant it? What should I do? Every time the door opened I had no idea if they were coming to kill us or just bringing food. They had already beaten me and I'd been raped by six or ten, so I knew what they were capable of. One day they took us into a special room. There were four of them. Men in uniforms. And a bed. They fitted two electrodes to your little head and said they'd torture you in front of me if I didn't tell them where your father was. They gave me a dose of it to make sure I understood.

'That was when I broke. I told them everything I knew. Not just where your father was, but everyone I'd ever known who'd even vaguely resisted.

'I even gave away my best friend, Maria Sanchez, without them even asking about her. The bravest, funniest, kindest woman alive. I'm sorry to have to tell you that I feel worse about giving her away than I do about your father. Because I knew how much he loved you. How he would have understood that I had to save you. But once I'd started I couldn't stop. They'd reduced me to ... nothing. I was just a block of fear. Just fear. I'd lost ... everything. Can you imagine what that is like, Jude? To lose everything?

'All pride and hope. All courage ...

'Maria was a teacher. She hid people in her school. People who were wanted. She organised false passports, worked with priests from the local church. They hid hundreds of people. Saved lives. She was really brave ... braver than anyone, and I told them all about her. Where she lived. I told them her plans, whom she'd helped ... I gave away the priests, nuns. Everyone I knew who'd worked with her ...

'The day we flew out here to Australia I heard that they'd got her. That she was being held in detention. I'd given her away. Six months later she was dead. But it's not the death that torments me, Jude. It's those six months. What brutalities she would have endured ... because her friend had given her away ...'

At the end of the week my mother left. She said she had to go back to the business or we'd be in trouble financially.

She left in the morning. Kissed me gravely on the cheek before getting into her little car parked out the front of our place. I could see that she didn't really want to go, that she hated leaving me in the state I was in, but I said nothing.

'I'm not asking you to forgive me, Jude,' she said. 'I don't forgive myself, so why should you ... ? Please just understand that this is what I live with ... what I have to live with for the rest of my life.'

I knew at this point I should move towards her, put my arms around her, bury my face in her shoulder, tell her I loved her and that I understood. Part of me wanted to do exactly that. But I couldn't move. I still had the black water in me. I could hardly even nod my head. I certainly didn't look at her.

The car drove off and I walked back into the house and fell into my bed with my clothes still on. I slept immediately, a heavy dreamless sleep, for about four hours. When I got up it was mid-afternoon. I showered, dressed, and went out into the street and headed back to the city. I had an important biology exam that day, but university didn't even enter my head. Virtually all I could do was walk. I had to think, try and sift through everything she'd told me.

In some crazy way I felt like I'd just arrived on the earth and I had to work out what it meant to be alive.

I headed up Victoria Street towards the market. The place was buzzing with activity. Men in leather aprons shouting out prices, rolled-up cigarettes smoking from the sides of their mouths. Men lifting heavy boxes of potatoes and cabbages, their fat leathery fingers counting money. The merchandise was set up in long wide rows: fruits and vegetables, rugs and clothes, elaborate displays of Australiana – koalas, leather purses in the shape of Tasmania, kangaroo-skin toys and lambskin coats. The smell of chips and toast and sausages filled the air. I bought a hot dog and an apple and ate them as I wandered along, stopping eventually by a trash stall. There were saucepans and irons, old radios and records in tatty covers, glass vases and grimy lamps that had little girls and dogs holding up the bulb. A young thin man sitting behind a stall eyed me up and down serenely then looked away, not expecting me to buy anything.

'How much is this?' I held up a brass, ruby-studded bauble hopefully. I'd noticed the hook in the back and decided that it would look terrific as an earring.

He shrugged. 'Two bucks?'

I nodded and reached into my bag for the money. He took the coin and gave me a strange look as I slipped the thing into my right ear lobe.

'What do ya reckon?' I asked him. He smiled slowly at me.

'Pretty gross,' he said.

'Yeah.' I gave a weak smile. 'That's what I reckon, too.'

I am alive today because the others are dead. My father. My mother's best friend ... Maria. Maria the brave one. Dead now and I am alive.

I was taking a short-cut home through some small North Melbourne streets when I found myself staring into the window of a tattooist's shop. Most of it was blacked out with some kind of dusty material and only a few designs were on display. They too looked dusty, curling at the edges. The place probably wasn't in business any more. Still I stood there, imagining what it would be like. There was 'Mum' curling around a dripping red heart in the middle of a thorn bush and 'Tiger Baby' across the chest of a naked girl. I laughed to myself. That kind of stuff was the pits. And yet... I spat on my hands and rubbed them warm in the chilly air. I thought about my skin, the clear olive skin I'd inherited from my father. My skin was beautiful. Everyone said so. My shoulders and arms, slim, smooth and virtually hairless. I tried the door thinking that no one would be there. But it swung back easily.

I looked into the gloomy interior. The walls were covered with pictures of all kinds of tatts. Great big complicated things mostly. Of men and their trucks, barbed wire, guns and blonde female fantasies. I walked in.

'Yeah?' came an aggressive voice. I squinted, trying to work out where it had come from. At last my eyes adjusted. There was a heavy-gutted man, about forty, in a blue singlet, sitting down behind a counter. He was drinking from a can and reading a magazine.

'What do ya want?' he snarled. I took a breath.

'I want a tattoo,' I said.

'Where?' he asked scornfully, as though he didn't believe me. I thought for a bit.

'On my arm.'

'What? On the top?'

'Yeah.'

'Do you know *what* you want?' he asked. I shrugged. This guy didn't realise. I was past intimidation. I was nineteen. Jude Torres. No one messed with me.

'Not really,' I snapped. 'You got anything I could look at?'

'Listen ... I've got little chicks ... girls ... like you, coming in here all the time, muckin' me around! Why don't you go home and think about it for a while.'

'No,' I said, hard as hell, quite sure now. 'I want to get it done now.'

'I bet ya you're a student, aren't ya?' he sneered. 'Trying to ...'

'And what's it to you if I am?' I cut him off darkly. 'Yeah, I'm a student! A medical student. Every week I cut up bodies. I know what I'm getting into ...'

'Ah shit!' he said. He sniffed, looked at his watch, chewed his gum a bit and then took another swig from his can. Burped. He picked up a plastic-covered book and chucked it down the counter at me.

'Have a look through that,' he growled. I stepped forward and picked up the book.

'Okay,' I said. 'Just give us a couple of minutes, will you?' He muttered something and turned up the volume on the tiny television set that was perched on a shelf on the wall. There was some kind of game show on with an audience that was applauding loudly.

'Take ya time,' he said.

'I will,' I replied.

'If it's big it'll cost ya. And if it's small, and *delicate* like, it'll cost ya too.'

'I know *that*.'

I walked out three hours later with the outline of an evil black snake coiled around a rather beautiful, slender rosebud on my shoulder. It felt tight and painful under my shirt, but I didn't mind. It felt good. I had to come back in three days to get the colour and finishing touches done. I had his card in my purse and his telephone number. If anything happened before then I was to give him a call. I'd nodded and said yeah, that I understood. But I couldn't imagine anything of any consequence ever happening to me again.

I walked quickly up past the fashionable end of Brunswick Street, into the old, seedy, working-class area where every second shop was boarded up or closed or being used for housing. There were a couple of milkbars still open, and a dry cleaner's, and on the other side a gaudy Chinese takeaway with bright-red dragons out the front. I was looking for the Lebanese barber I'd passed many times on my way back from uni.

'Men's Barber,' it said on the window. 'Haircuts for $9.' He'd never seemed to have any customers when I'd passed before. He was always sitting in the window reading some sleazy magazine. But we'd smiled at each other politely a couple of times as I'd passed. I was positive he wouldn't refuse to do me because I was the wrong sex.

I am alive and they are dead. Brave Maria, hiding people in her school. And my father, refusing to submit. Determined to continue his work. I am alive and they are dead. My mother chose me ... why?

'Just cut it all off.'

'What style you want?' he said with a curled lip. I could tell he wasn't happy about me being there, but he needed my nine bucks. He kept looking out the front window as if expecting to be 'caught' any moment with a girl in his old-fashioned chair.

'I don't want any style,' I said curtly.

'But ... you mean you just want it very short?'

'Just hack it off any old way,' I said.

'Young girl,' he said reprovingly in his thick accent, 'I don't just *hack* hair off ... ' He lifted up a clump of my hair with one hand, and we both stared at me in the mirror. I was small and dark and my eyes stared back, so fiercely that I was almost frightened.

'Beautiful hair,' he murmured, 'so thick and shiny. You don't want me to cut it all off. Why don't I try and ... ' But the grip of his hand at the back of my head had made me remember. I was appalled to feel my throat constrict and tears well in my eyes. We were both still looking into the mirror, but my vision had blurred. The barber watched as tears began to roll down my cheeks. He stood there rigidly for a few moments. Then his whole attitude changed.

'What is it?' he said kindly, letting my hair go and picking up one of my hands, rubbing it in his own like a kindly father. 'Come on. You have some trouble, yes? Maybe boyfriend no good, eh?' I shook my head miserably, mad that I couldn't control myself. His simple kindness was making my tears run faster.

'No,' I managed to sob at last. 'I just want my hair cut!'

'Then you shall have your hair cut, little girl,' he said, suddenly becoming very practical and business-like. He picked up his scissors and comb and placed them with great precision and professionalism on the shelf under the mirror. Then he began to spray my head with a fine mist of water from a plastic water-gun.

'Of course you shall have your hair cut,' he muttered again. 'Who wants stupid long hair anyway?' He gave me a warm smile, waited for me to smile back through my tears, then pulled an even strand of hair into the comb and clipped it off very short. 'Yes, short hair is much better,' he said. 'So much easier to manage! Who wants to be bothered with that stupid long stuff?' I smiled and closed my eyes and listened to his kind voice, knowing that when I opened them again I would be someone different.

The next thing I remember was that it had become dark. I'd been walking around for hours. Now up towards Carlton, where I knew there'd be a cafe open, somewhere to sit. If only I had my coat! It was freezing. I crossed my arms over my chest and hurried on up the hill trying to remember where I'd left it. In the tattoo shop? It was the coat Mum had bought me for the wet city days and nights. A sob rose in my throat, but I managed to swallow it. I would not think about anything. I would obliterate this last week from my memory. I would forget everything she'd told me, just go and have a good coffee, maybe a toasted sandwich, and then walk home. Go to bed. Wake up and talk to Carmel. The tight lump in my chest made me feel as if I was getting sick, a cold perhaps or the flu. I walked up Russell Street. Light, even rain began to fall, making the roads shiny and wet. Everywhere about me bright red and yellow lights flickered and shone. There was hardly anyone on the street. I felt like an ant, invisible, crawling along blind between the concrete and steel.

He was found in the coastal city of Concepción. Caught red-handed helping to collate a register of missing persons. People were frantic. Where have they taken my son? My brother? This work was always interrupted by the sick. Por favor, *Doctor . . . my child is sick . . . no money. He was easy to find once they knew the village . . .*

I placed my bag down carefully on the table nearest the window and went over to order coffee from the bar. The man washing the dishes merely grunted when I told him I'd like a toasted sandwhich too. The few men playing pool up the other end of the room turned momentarily and looked me over, but turned back to their game without any lewd comments or stares. I sat, exhausted, but immensely relieved, too. I was inside at last. No one was going to bother me. And the place was warm. I cupped my chin in my hands and stared out into the night.

My mother came to me then. It wasn't a matter of being able to will any of the images or thoughts to come or go. They just happened. Vivid flashes would *hit* me, and it was as if she was with me, sitting at the table, talking to me in that nice low way she had, and I'd sit there, ramrod straight, straining and wondering why I couldn't reach out and touch her, touch the memory. Then the intensity of it would drain away until it was just like any other kind of dull purposeless thought on its way to nowhere.

I saw her waiting for me after a day at primary school. Her face bright with the expectation of seeing me, and myself, in thick tights and school shoes, running straight past her, pushing away her gentle enquiries about what I'd done that day. I'd arranged a game with one of my classmates and was determined to get it in before I had to head off home to our evening together. Our quiet productive evenings together, they were what I remembered best. Reading and drawing and listening to the radio. Gardening. It was the happiest childhood for me. She provided everything I needed. No visitors except classmates of mine sometimes. Her full attention whenever I wanted it. Now sitting in that cafe it chilled me to realise that it may not have been the happiest time for her. What awful memories she had kept from me.

'Jude, I just want some kind of peace . . . ' She had said that often enough. 'I just want you to be happy.' Her brow wrinkling up, the weight of the world on her shoulders. That troubled intense face she had when she thought I wasn't watching, sitting at the kitchen table, one hand cupping her face, the other doodling with her pencil.

'What are you thinking of, Mum?'

She would look up with a start.

'Oh, nothing, darling . . . '

I began to cry as I sat there, tears running down my face, into my coffee. I let them roll. No one could see. I was just thinking of her, picturing the red and grey hair, tied back in knots with elastic bands or pins. The way she used to lie next to me on the bed when I was little, reading me to sleep, singing songs in Spanish. The best of mothers. What kind of daughter had I been?

I must have nodded off curled up in the corner near the window. When I woke the morning had broken. The grey sky above the shops opposite was streaked with golden light. A van nearby was off-loading flowers: great buckets of roses and white calla lilies. There were even a few people in the steet hurrying about with takeaway coffees and white bags of croissants. I got up stiffly and paid for my coffee.

'You tired, eh?' the grumpy man asked, giving me my change.

'Yes,' I shrugged. 'What's the time?' He held out his watch for me to see.

'Nearly seven.'

'Thanks.'

I walked home, suddenly dying to see Carmel, to tell her everything that had been happening to me, and to show her my haircut. I knew she wouldn't like it much, she was always saying how much she loved my inky-black locks, but I wanted to extol the virtues of ultra-short hair. *It's so short I'll hardly even have to wash it!* I practised saying that a few times on my way through the front gate and then again as I put the key into the front door. But she wasn't home. The house was empty. Rehearsal, I supposed grimly, with that bunch of misogynist deadheads. I walked down to the kitchen. With a bit of luck she'd have a night off from the cafe and we'd be able to talk then.

I made toast and some cocoa with three spoonfuls of sugar. Curled up in bed, under the rug I'd brought from home, I picked up my book and began to read, sipping my cocoa and munching the hot buttery toast. It was all right. My mother's visit had at least got me eating again. The food was delicious and my mind was floating easily from one thing to another. I could feel myself slipping off. And it didn't take long. I'd been hungry, but I didn't even manage to finish one piece of toast. Within a few minutes I had fallen into a heavy sleep.

When I woke I was completely disoriented. The blind was up, but all I could see was blackness outside and the vague half-light from a streetlamp. Night. But which night? Then I heard the key turning slowly in the lock of the front door, and footsteps pounding swiftly down the hallway. A couple of doors slammed. Someone was down in the lounge room, roughing it up. I became rigid with fear. *Get up. Grab something to protect yourself!* Katerina and Carmel didn't move around the house like that. I picked up the heavy lamp on my dressing-table, tiptoed to my door, and gingerly opened it. *I'll throw the thing at his head.* Then I realised how stupid I was being. What match would I be for someone within the confined space of this little house? Far better to escape out the front door. I peeped out and tried to judge the distance. The door was shut. Would I be able to make it up the hallway and open it before he'd heard me?

It was then, while I was standing there holding the heavy lamp, shaking and trying to decide what to do, that Carmel appeared in the hallway. She walked in from the lounge room, wearing a big duffle-coat and heavy men's boots I hadn't seen before. She stopped suddenly, her hand flying up to her mouth.

'Jude! My God!' she gasped. I stared back at her gulping. My legs weak with relief, I had completely forgotten about my shorn-off hair.

'Carmel,' I said, trying to smile. 'Was that ... was that you out there, making that noise? I thought ... I thought ... ' But I didn't bother to finish the sentence. I simply sank down where I stood, staring at the floor. Everything seemed unreal, out of sync. Carmel looked strange. I felt very weird ...

'I didn't know you were home, Jude,' she said, staring at me in wonder. 'I wouldn't have made such a racket ... and you've cut your hair.' I hadn't expected her to be thrilled, but the flatness was unexpected. 'And what are you holding that lamp for?' I put the lamp down carefully and tried to smile.

'What time is it?' I whispered.

'Just after one,' she said.

'At night?' I said wonderingly. It was hard to believe I'd slept that long, 'God, Carm, I'm so glad to see you. You wouldn't believe ... have you been at Juan's working?' She nodded.

'But you're normally home before this,' I said. She shrugged noncommittally.

'Where were *you* last night, Jude? You didn't come home.'

'I was ...' I was about to begin my long convoluted story, but when I turned to look at her I saw that her face was very pale, she was trembling and she was staring at the wall in front of her as if in shock. I put out my hand and rubbed her cold one. She didn't seem to notice. Something terrible must have happened. Some new instalment in Carmel's family soap opera perhaps.

'Carmel,' I said softly. 'What's up? Tell me what's happened.' She slumped a little. I put an arm around her shoulders. I could see her trying to hold her face together.

'I went over to Anton's place after work,' she said evenly. 'It's his birthday tomorrow ... I thought I'd surprise him and arrive unannounced. I saw his bedroom light on and thought he was studying. They always leave the back gate open.' Her voice petered out. I leant in closer and squeezed her shoulder encouragingly.

'And?' I said quietly. I'd only been to Anton's house once. It was a really nice big white terrace in Carlton, owned by his family and shared with a couple of older lawyers. The place was beautifully furnished, with polished floors and stained-glass windows.

'So I slipped around the back,' Carmel went on, 'into the back of the house. Then I crept up the passage to his room ...'

'And?'

'And I found him in bed with Kara,' she said dully.

'No!' I gasped. I shook my head. For once in my life I was stumped. Shocked. I didn't know what to say.

'Yeah,' she said.

'But ... did you just ... barge in on them?'

'Yeah,' she sighed.

'Did you do anything ... I mean did you *say* anything?' I felt my sense of outrage growing.

'No ... I was so stunned,' she said slowly. 'I said nothing! I wish I had said *something*!'

'But they must have seen you.'

'No, they didn't. You see, I'd tiptoed up the hallway and poked my head around the door to give him a surprise. The lamp on the desk was on, so I saw them lying on their backs ... asleep! Heads propped up on his pillows. She was snuggled into his shoulder, his arm around her ... ' Carmel gave a low sob. 'Can you believe it, Jude? They were cuddled up together like the perfect couple!'

'Jeeze!' I whispered, tightening my grip around her shoulder.

'They looked so ... *right* together, Jude. And I felt so stupid that I'd ever thought that he and I ... that ... fat, ugly me could have belonged with *him*,' she whispered through tears. It was hard to believe what she was telling me.

'So did you just come back here?' I asked. Carmel nodded and gave a weak smile.

'Yeah, I just came back here and smashed a few things around, thinking I was alone ... I just wish ... ' She stopped and I looked up at her face. It had grown hard and tense with anger.

'What do you wish?' I said.

'Well, I just wish I'd *said* something! Woken them up and shouted. Done *something*! I mean I just tiptoed back out like a good little girl who makes no trouble! Why should he get away without knowing how much he's hurt me?' Her voice broke and she began to sob again. I didn't say anything, just let her cry.

'I mean, it is rotten behaviour, isn't it, Jude?' she gasped through her tears.

'Of course it is,' I answered.

'By anyone's terms, it's shitty!' she spat out. 'The bloody two-faced bastard! He told me so often that he *loved* me! All the time. Only yesterday. He said I was the most ... interesting, most lovable person he'd ever met. He said he was so glad he was with me, that he was proud of my singing ... '

She was crying and moaning. Her eyes were screwed tight, her head thrown back against the wall, both fists clenched. She began to beat the floor rhythmically with them where she sat.

'Jude. I'm an idiot, I know. But I *believed* him! And now I don't think I can bear it!'

'I know,' I said softly. But I knew that I didn't really.

Carmel had dived into being in love with Anton in a way that was foreign to me. You could see it in her face, the way she moved. Her whole being had been lit up. I knew I would probably never experience that kind of emotional connection with another person. In that way we were different. Sure, I'd loved David. And I'd felt pain when we'd parted. But my world hadn't turned upside down or inside out. I still knew who I was and what I wanted to do with my life. But Carmel was different. I reckon she was a natural, a naive romantic. She had adored Anton. Her fledgeling inner-self had come alive because of him. I searched for something to say to her.

'It hurts me here and here,' she gasped, pointing to her throat and chest. 'Really, I'm not kidding! It's hurting me physically.'

'I believe you!'

She sat up suddenly, pushed her hair away from her face, and looked at me seriously.

'I want revenge, Jude,' she said.

'Jeeze, Carm ... I don't know,' I said a little shakily. 'What do you mean?'

'I've got to do something. Now. Or I'll go mad!' she said, standing up.

'What? You want to go and have it out with him?' I asked tentatively, standing up too. 'With both of them?'

'Well, I can't just go on! Can't just go to bed and get up and ... ' I looked at her, thinking about my own obsession with revenge – if that's what it had been – over the previous few weeks. The idea of Carmel getting into that same kind of mess was mind-boggling.

'It's too late for confronting them,' she said thoughtfully. 'I want to hurt him, *hurt them*, in some way.'

I said nothing, hoping she'd calm down. After all, Carmel normally wouldn't hurt a fly. She was a very gentle person. Much more so than me.

'I have to do something,' she said again. I took a deep breath.

'Carm,' I began, 'as much as you hate him for this ... hate both of them ... the thing is, he probably *does* love you.' She shook her head furiously.

'No! He would never have done this if he'd loved me.' I sighed and wondered how I should talk to someone whose ideas about love were straight out of a nineteenth-century novel!

'I mean, sometimes crappy things happen, Carm,' I blundered on. 'They don't have to mean the world ...'

'I will never, ever speak to him again!' She was shaking her head and frowning, wanting me to understand what she was saying.

'But why should it be ... it's not *necessarily* over between you and Anton. I think you should talk to him.'

'Jude, I will never speak to him ...'

'But it might have only happened once,' I said. 'Find out what his real feelings are! You know Katerina. She probably set it up. Just to spite you ...'

'Katerina?' Carmel repeated disbelievingly. 'To spite me?'

'Yeah. She's jealous of you,' I said. Carmel gave a harsh laugh.

'That's a joke!'

'I saw her face when you were singing that night,' I said vehemently. 'You were so good and she was sick with jealousy! In spite of all her fancy clothes and those guys. You're the one with the talent.' I grabbed Carmel by both arms and squeezed her hard. 'Come on, let's go get something to eat. Why don't we get a bit drunk or something?'

I wasn't sure that I was getting through, but she looked thoughtful as I led her through the lounge room into the kitchen. I pushed her into a chair.

'And you know that whole money thing with her family and his. The country aristocracy bit!' I grinned at her. 'She probably couldn't bear the idea of someone like you nailing him!'

'I still want to *do* something, Jude. I need to ... ' she said softly. I sighed and waited. But she was looking at the wall opposite, frowning. Her eyes were very red and her face was puffed up with tiredness.

'What have you got in mind?' I said, not really wanting to hear the answer.

'Well, I guess I could ... I dunno, throw a brick through his front window.'

'What, now?' I said cautiously. 'It's nearly two. I mean ... '

'Yeah, now!' she said quickly. 'That's what I want to do. I want to heave a big heavy brick. I want it to come sailing through that bloody stained-glass window he loves so much. I want the glass to smash all over them as they lie there in bed. Give them both a fright. And if we get away in time they'll never know who did it.'

We? Oh Jeeze.

'Carmel!'

'What?'

'Are you serious?'

'Absolutely!'

'But what if ... '

'I'm deadly serious, Jude.'

'Okay.'

On the way out of the house I picked up half a bottle of whisky that had been left by Juan on the night of the protest, and slipped it into the pocket of my old coat. Neither of us normally drank, just a glass or two of wine every now and again. But this night was different; it was cold out there. I'd filled Carmel in with what had been happening to me, and by the end of that we were both shot through with this unreal feeling that we were actors in someone's TV soap opera. It was then that we started laughing. I'm not sure how or why, but it was around that point that a sense of absolute craziness descended on us.

I took a quick gulp of whisky at the front door and handed the bottle to Carmel.

'Here. Have some.'

'Thanks,' she said, and took a mouthful, then shuddered. 'God, do people *drink* this stuff?' I pretended to read the writing on the bottle seriously.

'Shit no!' I said. 'You're meant to inject it! Sorry, my mistake.'

We laughed again as the terrible hard taste disappeared and the burning sense of wellbeing began.

'It's not that bad, you know.'

'Here's to it.'

'Yeah. To the success of our mission.'

'The next mouthful tastes even better,' she said, after taking another gulp. That made me snort. We slammed the door behind us and took off into the night. We'd both rugged up well and planned to walk the whole way, about two kilometres, to Carlton. But we'd only gone about half a block when a small car pulled up alongside us and tooted.

'Just keep walking,' I said. 'Don't turn around.' We quickened our stride and stuck our noses in the air, trying to suppress the giggles that were threatening to explode. The last thing that was going to intimidate us was some creepy guy wanting to pick up a girl. The car tooted again. I half looked around. Someone was getting out. Then the car door slammed.

'Hey, is that you, Jude? Carmel?' My heart gave a leap. I recognised that voice. A tall figure was moving over towards us, curly hair sticking out from under one of those stupid bright knitted beanies. Eduardo. Jesus! I gulped and suddenly felt very shy.

'Er ... hello,' I said uncertainly.

'Hello. Hello!' he said warmly. 'I thought it was you two. I was passing, saw your light on, and then noticed you walking off.' He started to grin. 'Where are you off to at this time of night?'

'Where are *you* off to at this time of night?' Carmel threw back at him.

'I was looking for you two, of course,' he joked, and then gave me a warm smile that made my knees melt. 'Can I give you a lift anywhere?' he asked.

I looked at Carmel and she looked at me. Then she nodded warily.

'Well, yeah. If you're going down Carlton way,' I said.

'I'm going exactly the opposite way,' he said. 'But hop in anyway and I'll drive you.'

'But you see, Eduardo,' I said, feeling stupid, but determined that he should understand that our mission was a secret. 'We have to ... er, *do* something. So you'll have to let us out before we get there because we don't want anyone to ... er, know what we're going to do.' He was quite near us now and staring down at me, laughing. God. I'd never felt so dumb in my whole life. Carmel didn't help at all. She burst into loud, semi-hysterical giggles; then, when she wouldn't stop, I started.

'Hell, this is getting really interesting,' Eduardo said, opening the door for us. 'Are you sure I can't stay to see what you've got planned?'

'Positive!' Carmel spluttered.

'Absolutely!' I snorted.

'But I'm the epitome of discretion,' he protested. 'I swear, I won't tell a soul.'

'No!'

All the way he kept throwing guesses to us in the back seat. We'd promised earlier to tell him if he was in any way warm, although behind his back Carmel and I had agreed that we were not going to give anything away, even if he guessed exactly.

'You going to dig up the pavement?'

'No.'

'Shoot a cop?'

'No.'

'Pinch something?'

'No.'

'Chuck a bomb through someone's front window?'

'No. No. No!'

We made him stop in a nearby street. It was a pitch-black night, and there hardly seemed to be any traffic around. Just all that gloomy, hard electric light glaring down onto bleak concrete.

'We'll be right now!'

'Thanks for the lift, Eduardo!' we chorused. The door was impossible to open, so he ran around to open it for us. Carmel got out first. As I was following her, Eduardo grabbed my hand, helping to pull me out. When I was upright he didn't let go. I stood silent, not looking at him, my heart pounding, not knowing what to say. Excitement swept through me like fire. He was still holding my hand. I turned, our faces were only centimetres apart. We looked at each other through the darkness. Then he leant forward and ran one of his hands over my spiky short hair, pulled me to him, and kissed my mouth, quick and hard. I gasped in shock, it was as if he'd stung me. I was filled with a surge of fierce, hard joy. I wanted to shout and jump up on the roof of the car and dance around, hold my arms out to the dark sky and draw it into me. Embrace everything. But I couldn't move, I couldn't say a thing. Eduardo went back quickly to the driver's side.

'See you both then,' he shouted jovially, as though nothing had happened, 'and good luck!'

'Thanks!'

'Guess I'll read about it in the papers tomorrow if anything goes wrong, eh?' he laughed.

Then the car spluttered to life and with a sudden roar he was gone.

By the time we got to Anton's street we were half drunk and so giddy with laughing that we could hardly stand up. Carmel had found a suitably large brick in a nearby neighbour's front yard and insisted that she be the one to throw it.

'Carmel.' I grabbed her arm and pulled her back to me. 'Why don't we just go home now, eh? I mean ... let's not do it.' She pulled away, stared down at the brick in her hands, then lifted her face to me. There was a resoluteness about the way she stood there, her big body filled with a kind of furious pride.

'You can go if you like,' she said. 'But I'm going to do this.'

I hid behind a nearby tree opposite the house and watched. She stole quietly towards the wrought-iron front gate and crept into the yard. Everything was quiet. The big white house was in a wide dark street, well populated with trees, and there were other big terrace houses on either side. I saw her raise her arm and then tilt it towards the window. The brick flew out of her hand. I hid my eyes just before the smashing sound. There was a muffled male yelp and then a short, high-pitched scream. Then silence. Carmel ran back to me, panting heavily.

'Come on!' she said. 'Let's cut!' We took off, running as hard as we could and taking cover near buildings and under trees.

It's amazing how your body takes over when you're really scared. After all our giggling and joking, I think we were both suddenly aware that we'd just done something serious, not to mention very nasty. No laughing now as we flew down the small, cobbled side streets and up and around corners. Dreading the moment when the headlights of a car would come cruising out of the darkness behind us. Or hearing someone's feet pounding along the footpath, steadily catching up.

After running for about a kilometre, we ducked up a dark

lane and stood puffing under an overhanging branch, listening for any sound. There was a creak, then muffled voices, a man shouting something about the next day, a slammed door, and a yell from a kid. We hardly breathed as we waited. Was that eerie thumping noise feet? Or was it someone banging something? After about half a minute it faded away altogether. Nothing. Off we went again, not speaking, through another laneway and into Rathdowne Street.

On this wide, well-lit street, with lots of traffic, we at last felt safe. We stopped running, and our breathing gradually slowed as we walked through to Brunswick Street and up to the Edinburgh Gardens. Their gloominess was enticing at that time of the morning. We walked through the iron gate and on to the narrow path that encircled the gardens; other tracks spread out like tiny webs across the lawn. The enormous trees stood silent and shining wet in the light, an army of liquidambars and cypresses, poplars and beeches, clustered in groups across the lawn, their branches drooping low and wide and welcoming. Still we didn't talk. We linked arms and walked slowly through the different pathways. When we got back to the main gate, we set off again along another track in a different direction. There was only the scraping sound of our boots as we trudged along, and the far-off noises from the surrounding streets that had nothing to do with us. Vast circles of yellow light from the tall Victorian lamp-posts spilt out around us like fine dust. Every few metres there was another one, and behind each the murky darkness of bushes with shiny leaves and old-fashioned garden beds surrounded by spiky wrought-iron fences.

'Do you feel better?' I asked at last.

'I'm all right,' she said.

By then it must have been about three in the morning. We headed across the grass towards the small rotunda in the middle of the gardens. I remembered the bottle in my pocket, but when I pulled it out I saw there was nothing left.

'Damn it.' I threw it with a clatter into a nearby bin.

After climbing the dozen or so steps we walked around the small interior of the solid stone structure a few times, dragging our fingers along the blistered paint of the balcony edge and looking out over the gardens. *I could be anywhere in this world, anywhere in the world.* I watched the sky as a huge mass of cloud slowly rolled away, revealing a bright, almost-full moon.

Very quietly Carmel started to sing a Spanish song we both loved: '*Canción de cuna para un niño vago*' (Lullaby for a Homeless Child). It was one of the first sad songs I'd sung to Carmel in Spanish, and I remembered how I'd felt sort of exposed, as though she might think I was being maudlin or overly sentimental. But she'd listened as though the words in this language that she didn't know somehow made sense to her. And then she'd asked me questions. What did this word mean? And that one? And why did the song talk about a river when it was about a homeless child? I'd explained how most of the year the Mapocho River, which runs through Santiago, has a flat stony bed, strewn with litter and rubbish, and that this is where a lot of dogs and homeless children hang out. Heaps of children, some as young as six and eight, huddle together and sleep under the bridges at night, surviving by begging or stealing. Carmel had asked me to write out the words in English and in Spanish. Then, after we'd sung it a few times together, she'd gone to her room and had set about learning it. I'd listened to her practising the Spanish phrases over and over, every now and again coming in to my room to ask how something went or how it was pronounced. Tonight she sang it so simply, her rich voice trembling over the deep notes, making light play of others. She was looking at the moon, but I knew she was singing it for me.

The moon in the river flows through the city. Underneath the bridge a child dreams of flying.

The city shuts him in, a cage of metal. The child grows old without
*   knowing how to play.*
How many like you will leave their homes? With money it is easy for
*   love to exist. Bitter are the days when there is none.*

Sleep quietly, my child, nobody will cry out. Life is so hard, you must
*   have your rest.*
Another four children will keep you warm. The moon in the river
*   flows through the city ...*

From that song we went on to others. Some lighter. Some just as sad. In Spanish and in English. We hardly spoke at all. I don't know whether it was the still night, or the way we felt, but I couldn't remember us ever sounding better. Of course it was mainly Carmel's voice, but I was finding the harmony in each song easily. Because there was no one else around, and we had no accompaniment, we were able to invent, be totally at ease as we made our voices sob and shout; both of us were flattened out in a way. It was the saddest time and the happiest. By five o'clock our throats were dry and our voices were exhausted. We got up from the cold stone of the rotunda and, rubbing our numb behinds, set off for home, still singing.

We rounded the corner into our street and saw that the front light was on. I looked at Carmel. Her mouth had clenched into a tight, grim line.

I knew she was thinking what I was thinking.

'If she's in there ... ' Carmel said under her breath.

'Listen. Do you want me to go in first and check it out?' I said.

'But you'll go crazy.'

'No, I won't,' I said, meaning it. 'I won't say anything if you don't want me to.'

Carmel stopped when we got to the front gate and made me look at her.

'Jude, I don't *ever* want to talk to Katerina about it,' she said. 'I really mean that. I never want to talk to her, Anton, or that ... that Kara again. Ever.'

'That's okay by me.'

We let ourselves in and walked tentatively down the hallway. I went in first. I pushed open the door into the lounge room and saw a handsome young guy, whom I didn't recognise, sitting half asleep in an armchair. He blinked a couple of times, smiled a little apologetically, and rose to his feet.

'Hello,' I said. 'Er, who are ... ' Carmel, who'd stopped in her room to put her bag away, came in behind me.

'Vince!' she exclaimed, rushing past me and throwing her arms around him. 'Vince! How did you get in? Where have you come from? It's great to see you!' He was dressed in worn jeans and a heavy woollen jumper. As they were hugging each other I saw that he was so much like her and I wanted to laugh. The same eyes and colouring, the same shape of face. Carmel was radiant when she turned to me.

'Jude, you remember my brother Vince?'

'I sure do!' I smiled at him. 'How are you?'

'Good! Good thanks, Jude!' His smile was warm, but he looked very tired. 'Listen, I hope I didn't give youse a fright or nothin', coming in like this. But the door was open ... ' He looked from one to the other of us, smiling. 'You always leave your bloody door open, or what?' Carmel and I looked at each other.

'I thought leaving my truck right outside the house might have told you it was me.' Carmel and I giggled with embarrassment. We hadn't noticed any truck. We'd been too busy singing.

'Oh God, Vince,' Carmel groaned. 'We've been having the most ... terrible time. Both of us. Oh my God!' She looked at me and laughed. 'Where do we start?' She ran over and hugged him again. 'What a great surprise to see you, though!'

'It's good to see you too, sis,' he said warmly, rubbing her back with one of his rough hands. But I could tell that his mind was on something else. Carmel was so excited that she hadn't picked it up yet.

'I bet you're hungry,' she said. 'Come on, let's make a big feast. Eggs and toast and stuff ... '

'Yeah, I could do with something ... ' Vince smiled. Carmel bounded off towards the kitchen, but stopped at the door and turned around.

'Vince,' she said. 'It's five a.m.! What the hell are you doing here?'

'Carm ... I'd better ... ' His eyes shifted uncomfortably to the poster on the wall. 'I gotta tell you something.'

'What?' The animation drained from her face.

'I've been home ... ' he said.

'And they've sent you here to talk me into coming back,' Carmel snapped. 'Oh, don't start, Vince, please! I just can't! Do you understand?' She walked back into the room and stood in front of him. 'All that money I owe you. Well, I've saved half of it. You can have that. I've been working, Vince. And I'll get the rest! I promise you ... '

'Nah, sis. It's not that,' he cut in. She stopped. He was looking away again, at the poster of Allende on the wall, frowning.

'Well, what is it?' she asked. He sighed deeply.

'Mum's real crook ... ' he said, looking at her.

'How do you mean?' Carmel said.

'Well, she's got cancer,' he said slowly. 'Breast cancer ... She's fucked, Carm. Completely. She's gunna die ... maybe only ... weeks to live ... '

Carmel was absolutely still for a couple of seconds, then she sort of shuddered, as if she was trying to push something terrible off her back.

'So they asked you to come and tell me that so I'd go home?' she flew back at him.

'Nah . . . ' her brother said softly. 'It wasn't like that. It was my idea to come and tell you.' Carmel sniffed. I'd never have believed she'd be like this, so cold and furiously unsympathetic. It must have been the shock.

'Is she in hospital?' I asked. Vince turned to me, relieved to deal with a practical question.

'No. Not now. She went in for a lot of tests two weeks back. But there's no point. She's way beyond any treatment. Wasn't picked up early enough. They've got a nurse coming . . . every day. Mum doesn't want to be in hospital.'

'But that's stupid,' Carmel said loudly. 'Why didn't she come to Melbourne? They can do all kinds of things now . . . there's all kinds of treatments . . . '

'It's too far gone, Carm,' Vince said again, 'and the specialist she saw was from Melbourne. He goes up to Manella every fortnight to see patients.' He looked at me and I could tell he was very upset. 'She didn't tell anyone. Didn't want anyone to know. He told her that they can't do anything. It's gone into her bones. She'll be dead in a couple of months. That's what he told the old man . . . maybe less, maybe just weeks.'

We cooked breakfast and ate it more or less silently. Then Vince and I helped Carmel pack up her things. She left me with a few numbers to call. Juan for starters, and then the guys in the band. They'd have to do the gigs without her.

We clasped hands before she got into the truck with her brother.

'I'll get up there as soon as I can,' I said.

'Yeah, thanks, Jude,' she replied. 'Come as soon as you can.'

Vince started the engine and they were off.

I went back inside and had a shower. I'd missed nearly two weeks of university already, and one very important test. I'd had no sleep. I was tempted to take another day off. After all, by mid-afternoon I'd be ratshit with tiredness. But something stopped me from deciding to do that. It would be so easy to get behind. Too bad about feeling tired! Too bad about lectures being the last thing I felt like. Too bad about feeling devastated about Carmel leaving, worried for her, and anxious about what was going to happen to her mother.

I turned off the hot tap and gasped as the water quickly turned icy. I made myself stand under it for a good minute, until my blood had cooled right down. I would go to university that day. Get hold of the notes I'd missed. Ask the lecturer if I could sit the test late. Make up some excuse.

I will sit in class, I will participate and I will learn!

After all, I was Carlos's daughter.

And Cynthia's, too.

A sob broke away inside me, surging up my throat like an enormous angry green wave. White-tipped with fury. And love. Cynthia. My mother. My mother, who'd saved my life. At that moment I felt I knew nothing, except that I was going to be a doctor.

Katerina

1

I know everyone has a clear idea of me already. I'm the bitch, right? The one who is so easy to categorise, so easy to hate. Because of how I look and the fact that I have a brain in my head, people think they can pigeon-hole me. They think: *life has to be so easy for her; she's beautiful, clever, wealthy* ... Someone like me would *have* to have it all together or there'd be no hope for anyone else, right?

My first year at university and I've waded in far above my head; I'm so deep in shit it doesn't matter.

I got caught up in all this *stuff*, struggling for breath, for *air*, while people around me went on laughing, stroking me and telling me they wanted me to star in their next jeans commercial! I mean that literally. There I was, off my face on pills and feeling like I'd snuff it any minute – hallucinating on someone's fancy marble toilet seat in Toorak – and a group of *friends* came in and went right on talking about when they'd do the filming!

The front cover of *Vogue*, jeans commercials, pin-up calendars. Wow!

But who won the prize? Was it me? I don't feel as if I've won anything.

It's hard to work out when things happened exactly. It's only afterwards that you realise that events held great meaning for you, that they changed you in some important way. But it's almost impossible to disconnect one thing from another. All these important moments have become jumbled, toppling over and squashing together in my mind.

But one afternoon does stand out. I came home after having

spent the morning at Jordan's place. Jude's mother Cynthia opened the door. That was a surprise. I'd only ever seen her in the distance in Manella before. She was an interesting-looking woman, with her long red-grey hair, and she smiled at me and asked if I minded her staying for a few days, that Jude had been a bit sick. *Sick? Was that what had been wrong with her?* I suppose I smiled back as I passed her and said that it was fine by me. But I really can't remember, I was *completely* freaked out, shaking inside after what I'd just been through. No. Not shaking. More like, *screaming* inside. Like the way a car screeches around a tight corner; black smoke, a terrible high-pitched vibration careered up and down my spine, then around my head in a criss-cross of live wires. I'd been up till five that morning. There'd been a lot of dancing, quite a few pills – just uppers: ecstasy and speed – drinking, laughing and then . . . this photographic session.

Why the hell am I feeling like the lowest form of life on earth? Had I encouraged it? What should I have done? I remember hearing Cynthia's and Jude's low voices as I made my way down to the empty kitchen. I tried not to feel paranoid as I stood shivering and waiting for the kettle to boil. As usual those pigs hadn't washed up after themselves. Piles of dirty dishes and half-full cups of cold coffee were spread out over the sink, the butter was going soft on its glass plate. Anger suffused me. *Louise will be back from Europe soon. I'll get them both kicked out. Tell my parents that they're quite unsatisfactory as housemates.* I threw the dishes into the sink and poured the boiling water into the coffee plunger. My arms and fingertips tingled and the screaming in my head changed into a dull, foggy buzz.

How it irked me that that Carmel – *that fat nobody* – had pulled Anton. I thought back to the beginning of the year, when she broke the chair. Then I hadn't thought her worth a second glance. She was a hick from nowhere who knew nothing. Coming from the kind of family she did, I had imagined she might be *useful*, that she might, without anyone asking, do the housework. She was so apologetic and awkward. Just like most of the country girls I'd been to school with, so eager to please.

But surprise, surprise! It turned out the girl could sing like an angel. I'm not usually competitive. But seeing her blossom over those first few months drove me crazy. And then she and Jude shut me out when I really needed friendship. That's the truth of it. Their closeness shut me out and *that* got me doing things I was sorry about later.

It was while I was spooning the sugar into my coffee that I realised I would have to step off for a while, cut right out of this fast scene. Things were getting ... well, too much. I shivered as I felt a high-pitched scream start up again at the base of my neck. It had all suddenly got beyond me. Me! Who'd always been in control. I plonked myself down and decided there and then that I would stop hanging out in all those smart clubs and fast places. I would cut out the dope and the rich guys, ease up on it all. The thing with Jordan that morning had been a sort of culmination. A warning.

I brought the hot strong coffee to my mouth and decided that I would throw myself back into my studies. Maybe go for honours. Why not? I was smart enough. I took a few gulps and felt my head clear. The screaming stopped. I became overwhelmed with ambition. I wanted to see my name on that board outside the Law faculty in five years' time: Katerina Armstrong, top of the Law school, graduating in Arts/Law (Hons). That would show Louise.

Coffee was what I needed, but it wasn't enough. Not by a long shot. I got up quickly and went into the bathroom. A long hot bath. That was sure to make me feel better. Put me right back on track.

Looking up into the steam-filled atmosphere of the bathroom I thought about the circle of people I'd gravitated towards as soon as I'd hit the city. They had so much money and such inflated ideas about themselves and their importance in the world. We all did. I was flattered by their attention. And so much of it, especially early on, *was* fun. Great nights in classy clubs, stunning clothes, expensive restaurants, and ... all kinds of things.

Every house I'd been invited into was full of beautiful things. Glassware. I have this thing about nice glassware. Swedish fluted champagne glasses and Waterford crystal. Anyway, compared to being with boring students of my own age, whose idea of a good time was hanging out in the uni cafe drinking cheap wine from polystyrene cups, I *was* having fun. Advertising executives and film producers, rich lawyers and the heads of city accountancy firms. The fast set, who owned boats and fancy holiday houses, who lived in fabulous city apartments and flew around the world for business meetings. And they wanted me, that was the flattering, exciting, bizarre part! They wanted to wine, dine and parade me around. There was an exchange, of course. *No such thing as a free lunch and all that.* I didn't want to know about it. I thought I belonged.

But I'd misread the signs. Those people *ate* girls like me for breakfast! It took me a while to realise.

At last I'd had enough. My body was as pink as a cooked lobster's. I stood up slowly and leaned out of the bath to grab my towel from a nearby chair. Damp. Someone else had used it before me. My teeth were on edge as I rubbed myself dry. When I opened the door, one towel around my head and another around my body, I stopped in surprise. Jude's mother was washing the floor. All the dishes had been done and the benches were clean. A pretty tablecloth had been placed over the table and a small vase of flowers sat in the middle. She caught my look of surprise and smiled.

'I hope you don't mind, Katerina?'

'Well, no ... ' I said. 'Thank you, but ... er, you shouldn't.'

'Oh, it's a pleasure. Really!'

I smiled uneasily when I noticed a huge pot bubbling on the stove. A delicious fresh smell of stock and vegetables had seeped out into the air. It made me feel very hungry.

'It's soup,' she said simply. 'It'll be ready soon, if you want some. Lamb shanks, barley and vegetables.'

'I'd love some.'

'Good.' She seemed pleased and went back to cleaning the floor. As I walked through she looked up.

'Is there a shop around that you go to for good bread?'

'Yes,' I smiled, thinking of the Greek lady only a few doors down. 'I'll go and get some as soon as I'm dressed.'

'Oh, would you?'

'Sure. A pleasure.'

'Thanks, Katerina!'

So I began a comeback. I managed to put the episode with Jordan behind me and get stuck into my studies. It certainly helped having Jude's mother there for the week. I think we all really loved it. The cleanliness. The nice food smells. Within a day, without anything much being said, the household suddenly seemed to mesh. Carmel and I started to get on. Nothing deep and meaningful, but we could talk about where we'd last seen a vase or if there was any milk left in the fridge or if it was going to rain or not, without getting on each other's nerves.

Jude was still quiet, but she was friendly enough and her mother's calm presence over the week more than made up for any taciturn behaviour on her part. But I was edgy underneath. Although for the most part I succeeded in concentrating on my studies, every time the doorbell rang, or the phone went, or someone spoke loudly, I jumped. Sometimes my hands would tremble so violently that I'd have to sit on them. I'm not sure what I was afraid of exactly, but I found it hard to be still for any length of time. I'd be sitting at my desk working and it would all come crashing back, clear as day. This deep shudder would wash right through me. I'd stay frozen for a few moments, absolutely terrified, then gradually the fear would subside and things would return to normal.

I did my best to push it all aside. What would be the point of dwelling on all that rubbish? I was determined to get on with my life.

Cynthia left after about a week and the house fell back into its former griminess. Dirty dishes were left on the sink, no one bothered to wipe down the stove or sweep the floor. I tried not to care as I ploughed on with my work. I was getting good marks and that pleased me. With Cynthia gone, Carmel, Jude and I reverted to our separate lives. At odd times I found myself ruefully wishing it wasn't so, that we could give each other another chance, somehow begin the year again. Everything would work out better the second time around, I was sure of it. I suppose I was lonely.

I walked into the kitchen a few days after Cynthia had left and saw Jude coming out of the bathroom with a towel over her shoulder. I gasped. Her hair had been chopped off really short. And there was this ugly raw-looking thing on her right arm. A tattoo. A real one. It looked sore. She stopped as if shocked to see me.

'Hello,' I said brightly. 'How are things?' She nodded coldly, didn't look at me, and walked straight past without so much as a word. Things had cooled a bit between us all after Cynthia had left, but never before had either of them been so blatant about it. Their exclusiveness was always so maddeningly polite. They would simply stop what they were doing, put on these fake smiles, and then wait until I'd left the room so they could resume whatever it was they had been up to. Their smug little world of singing and playing guitar, all those tatty South American friends and the crazy political stuff were beginning to irk me seriously. The 'Save Timor' poster on the fridge annoyed me every day, and every day I vowed to myself that I'd rip it off, but I never quite dared. I followed Jude up the hallway, anger rising in me.

'Excuse *me*, Jude,' I said icily. 'Is there anything wrong?'

'Nothing,' she said.

'Well, then, why ...?' I faltered. She was glowering at me. She seemed even more fierce with no hair. All the confusion I'd felt over that last month, the lies I'd been told, the let-downs, the crappy flattering rubbish I'd been dished up by men I should have known better about. I shrugged.

'I don't know,' I said lamely. 'I thought something was up ...'

She shut the door in my face.

I walked back to the kitchen overcome with rage, inexplicably in tears. *How dare that little rag treat me like that! I'll ring my parents, get them both kicked out!* Two sharp taps on the front door stopped me in my tracks. I walked back up the passage, thinking. It would probably be one of *their* friends. One of those dark Chilean boys with bright teeth and sloppy clothes. But I opened the door to this attractive blonde woman with bright green eyes who was smiling at me. It took a couple of moments for me to register that it was my own sister, Louise.

'Hello, sis,' she laughed, and held out her arms. 'I'm two weeks early!'

She was dressed in a pale-blue cotton jumper, jeans, and long black leather boots. Her neck and face were lightly tanned and she'd lost at least a stone in weight.

'Lou! You look ... terrific!' I stammered, caught off guard. She laughed. We kissed and hugged, then I helped her carry her case down the hallway.

'You going to move back in?' I said, hoping suddenly that she was planning to. *It'll be a way of getting rid of one of them, at least.* 'So where's all your stuff?' Louise wrinkled up her nose at the mess in the kitchen and shrugged.

'I don't think so ...' she said, turning to me and then smiling broadly, quite unable to contain herself any longer. She grabbed both my hands in her own. 'I've met someone. The *most* wonderful man!'

'Really!' I said, trying to look pleased. So that was it. She'd lost weight and her skin was glowing. She'd also lost that dull, homely look that I was so used to associating with her. For as long as I could remember my older sister, although quite good-looking, had always managed to seem dowdy. She'd become a new person during her eight months away. I tried to be glad for her, but underneath I was uneasy. Louise had never been one for boyfriends.

'And ... we're going to get married,' she burst out.

'God, really? But ... '

'But what?' Her face clouded momentarily as she registered my shock.

'Aren't you ... too young?'

'I'm twenty-three! And we're not going to get married for another year.'

'So why ... ?' I began. 'Oh, that's great, Lou.' I leaned over and kissed her. 'I can't wait to meet him!'

'You will soon,' she said happily. 'He'll be arriving on Thursday. We're going straight from the airport up to Mum and Dad's ... you'll come home this weekend, won't you?'

'Well, sure,' I said, hesitating for only a moment. 'I guess so.'

'Great!' She got up and hugged me. 'You'll love him!'

'What does he do?' I asked.

'He's a surgeon,' she said, flopping down again in the chair opposite me, unable to hide her pride and happiness. 'Ten years older than me. I met him in Paris.'

'Is he French?'

She nodded.

'What's his name?

'Jean-Paul,' she giggled. 'Isn't it lovely? And get this! He's been to Australia twice before and he *loves* it! Very happy to move here. Sick of Europe and all the pollution. We're probably going to settle somewhere on the New South Wales coast. He adores our beaches!'

'Well, that's great, Lou.' It was hard getting those words out. I felt as if I'd swallowed a lemon. Of course Louise would marry a surgeon. And Mum and Dad would be *so* pleased. They'd have the 2.2 kids before anyone could blink. And everything else besides. Everything was sure to work out perfectly for her. It always did.

She only stayed for the afternoon. We went and did some shopping, then came home, had lunch, and drank a lot of coffee. She told me all about being overseas. The places she'd seen and the people she'd met. She couldn't wait to finish her course so that she and Jean-Paul would be able to work in the same hospital or at least nearby. The plan was still to go home to Manella eventually and take over Dad's practice. I couldn't believe it. She had it all worked out. At about five in the afternoon she called a taxi.

'It'll be much easier for everyone if I stay with Elaine,' she said airily. 'She's got a spare room and everything. I don't want to upset your housemates at this time of the academic year. I'll see you on the weekend. Okay?'

'Sure, Lou. See you then.' I was browned off. She was off to stay with her best friend and she'd hardly asked me a single question about *my* life. She slammed the car door and wound down the window.

'You'll love him!'

'Sure,' I said quietly as she drove off.

I walked back into the house and lay on my bed for a while. No one else was home. I hadn't seen Carmel for a few days, and I assumed Jude was off at the library studying. I'd seen her leaving the house a couple of hours before, a pile of books sticking out of her bag.

I began thinking about all of the people I'd been mixing with over the past few months. It was sobering to realise that only two had remained real friends: Kara, my old buddy from school, and Julian, the young gay guy I'd met at the beginning of the year at one of the clubs I used to frequent. Jules was lightly built, had long curly fair hair, and was about twenty-five. He dressed always in white or cream; wide shapeless pants and long embroidered shirts. He'd started off as our crowd's dope supplier; he would deliver anything that anyone wanted, quickly and without fuss. Speed, coke, LSD, even heroin, although not many went for that. Needles and syringes were somehow serious, whereas pills were just ... well, just fun.

Jules hung around the edges of this fast rich crowd, in spite of the fact that he was very slow-talking, slow-moving, and, as far as I could gather, didn't have much, apart from a lovely old-fashioned flat he was buying in Parkville. He didn't even own a car. I guess he was tolerated because he was pretty and humorous – and because of his access to drugs, of course. For the first couple of months I never took any notice of him, apart from when I needed something. But gradually we became closer; after a time he felt like my only friend in the world. He'd come by with the stuff and we'd sit in my room, sometimes with Kara as well; we'd maybe have a smoke or pop something and then talk for a few hours. I think he enjoyed our company because we didn't pry. From the snippets he gave away, he seemed to live a wild, semi-dangerous existence in that half-lit world of drugs and torrid promiscuity. There was a new guy on the scene almost every week for Jules. But we took care never to ask him much.

I liked his dry summing-up of people and the droll humour that turned against himself as often as it made fun of others. I never really thought of him as a drug-dealer. It was just the way he lived. I had the feeling that he would have preferred doing something else, but had never really summoned up the energy to try. I suppose he was addicted himself, but again it wasn't something I thought about much. So many of my friends took stuff. Jules never acted as if he was doing anything particularly risky, although he sometimes hinted that things could get heavy for him if there was any problem with payment. I enjoyed his gentleness, the fact that he didn't seem to want anything from me but to talk.

Jordan hadn't contacted me after that last terrible morning, but other people occasionally called. I'd been seeing a young lawyer from a merchant bank on a more-or-less regular basis since the time I decided to bail out. Conner Neil was nice; in his mid-twenties, an American from Boston, handsome and very rich. He rang a few times, asking me out, but I made excuses. He gave up almost straight away, which really hurt my pride. When we'd been together he'd acted like he was crazy for me. It was very hard to admit that no one missed me much, when I'd been under the impression that they all adored me.

I was still lying on the bed when the phone rang. It was Jules. Did I want to go to a gay rave at a city warehouse that night? It would be huge and loud and raucous, and the last time we'd spoken had made him think that I needed cheering up. Everyone would be in drag and off their faces.

'You know, Kats, you just might find it *interesting*,' he said slyly. I smiled. He often called me Kats or Queenie – very tongue in cheek – but I liked it. Jules was always teasing me. It amused and puzzled him, for example, that I read books that weren't on my course.

'Why do you do it, Queenie?' he'd say, real wonder in his voice as he picked up whatever it was I was reading, fingering it as if it was something from another planet. 'When you don't have to? Why would you tax your gorgeous head with all these ... *words?*' It always made me laugh. Endeared him to me, really. But I couldn't explain it; Jules had a kind of aversion to anything he didn't immediately understand.

I hadn't seen him for a couple of weeks, but he'd described these warehouse parties to Kara and me before. I have to admit that nothing he'd told us made either of us even vaguely interested. *Men dressed up as women. Men getting off with other men. Give us a break, Jules!* Kara and I thrived on male attention. The gay scene didn't interest us at all.

'What would I wear to something like this?' I asked cagily.

'Something tight,' he said matter-of-factly. 'Definitely something revealing, sexy. You'll have a lot of stiff competition, Kats, I promise you . . . '

'Who from?' I said warily. 'I thought there were mainly guys at these things?'

'These boys really go to town when they get out at night.' He sighed. 'And I want you to look sensational.'

'Why?'

'Oh, Kats! Because you're with me. Just come, will you!'

I suddenly felt insecure. I hadn't dressed up in ages.

'What about my white crushed-velvet? You know, with the low neck and the split up the side.'

'Oh God, *no*!' He groaned. 'That's far too *nice*.'

'Well, what?'

'Haven't you got any tight little hot pants?'

'*Hot pants*?'

'Yeah,' he went on quickly, 'with an iridescent pink see-through chiffon blouse and one of those hot silver-spangled bras underneath?'

'Oh Jules!' I laughed. 'You mean like Madonna.'

He tsked loudly.

'Madonna is *out*, Kats. You should know that! Look, I have to go. I'll leave it to you, okay? We'll pick you up at about eleven.'

'We?'

'I'm getting us a ride in a 1969 powder-blue Bentley.'

'Okay,' I said. 'See you then.'

2

I entered the huge barn-like space of the Port Melbourne warehouse in a tight, very short red dress that only just covered my bum, silver lamé stockings, and high-heeled red suede shoes. That afternoon I'd divided my hair down the middle and dyed one half silver and the other half bright-red with some non-permanent hair colour, thinking of Louise the whole time I was doing it. *A surgeon. God, how unimaginative!* Then I called Kara. She came around and plaited my hair into about a hundred tiny tails. On the red side we wound silver baubles onto the end of each plait and on the silver side, red baubles. Kara painted half my mouth with silver lipstick and the other half with red, to match my hair. I looked very weird, but *classy weird*, if you get my drift, and anyway I didn't care. After Louise's announcement I was in the mood for weirdness. While Kara was working on me she told me about the brick that had come sailing through Anton's window at midnight two nights before.

'And what were *you* doing in Anton's room at midnight?' I asked surprised. She gave a sly smile as she fitted the last bauble to the last plait.

'What do you think?' she said, pushing me towards the mirror above the couch. 'You look fantastic!' We could both hear the kettle boiling in the kitchen. Kara skipped out to make coffee.

'Kara,' I yelled after her. 'Tell me please!'
'What?' she called back.
'About Anton! What do you think?'
'Oh, nothing much,' she said airily, carrying in the cups.

'He's very cute ... but *unfortunately* he seems to be very taken with that ... fat girl.'

'Carmel?' I said. 'So they're still ... ?'

'Oh, for sure,' she said, making a face. *'Carmel this and Carmel that.* God, it makes you wonder, doesn't it?'

'What do you mean?'

'Oh, you know!' she said. 'I mean, he's really cute! And she's ... '

The conversation petered out after that. When Kara doesn't want to talk she doesn't. That afternoon she was being very cagey.

'Who do you think threw the brick?' I asked when she was leaving.

'Some lout,' she shrugged. 'Probably drunk. It wouldn't be personal. Just bad luck for Anton that they chose his house ... and that lovely window.'

Jules was very pleased with my efforts.

'Sensational,' he had said softly as I stepped into the hallway. That had been enough. I knew I looked right. We climbed into the luxurious old car and sped off.

The warehouse was a mass of fractured colour. And sound, so hard and loud that I felt as if it was invading my body. I stood still, partly in shock, next to Jules and watched the laser lights bouncing and spinning in all directions: fluorescent green tunnels one second and iridescent pink spiky shapes the next, picking out for just an instant a painted, grimacing face, a bizarrely clothed arm, or a tangle of legs, before disintegrating and moving off again into a million slivers of multi-coloured light. I edged closer to Jules, terrified that he'd slip off without me, leave me stranded in all this noise and craziness.

'Isn't it brilliant?' he shouted into my ear. His teeth were bright-green in the glaring light.

'Yeah,' I yelled back gamely. 'Brilliant!'

'You want...' His hand opened to reveal about fifteen tiny pills. All different colours; heart-shaped, oval and round. 'Do you want a lolly?'

'No...' I laughed. 'I don't need anything!'

'My shout tonight,' he said. 'You don't have to pay.'

'No. I'm right. Honestly.'

He shrugged and smiled, slipped a small pink one into his mouth, and poured the rest into a small white bag that he'd pulled out of another pocket.

'Can you hold them for me in your purse?'

'Sure.'

I slipped the tiny package into the small metal evening purse I had slung across my chest and promptly forgot it.

Jules took my elbow and pushed me into the mass of wildly dressed, panting dancers. They were like swarms of creatures from another world – some spun out on their own, others gaudily bunched together like exotic insects, shouting, cat-calling and laughing manically – magnified thousands of times by the sheer thumping energy of the place. Five thin, wiry-faced guys up on the stage played their instruments with the usual haughty disdain; all dressed in tight leather shorts, with red braces, bare chests and red silk ties around their necks. Heavy black boots and long white socks. They reminded me of Hansel from the fairytale. Hansel gone badly wrong. The music was loud, too loud, but I suddenly didn't care.

Jules and I began to dance. The big crowd had intimidated me at first. A bit like being adrift in a rough sea; I was used to discretion, lightness, subtlety. But now these rolling waves of bodies, gaudily clad and glistening with sweat, were pulling and pushing me to be something else. It wasn't long before I was right into it. Jules liked to have fun dancing and so did I. He held my hand, spun me around, pulled me close. We began to laugh and shout to each other above the thumping racket. It was a rougher, wilder, more bizarre crowd than I'd ever experienced before, mainly men, some dressed as women, but many others simply dressed up for fun, with kohl around their eyes, strange hats, garters and fake jewellery.

Men approached Jules at regular intervals, but he only laughed and called that he was 'taken' and kept dancing with me. They'd run their eyes over me as if I was some strange, highly amusing specimen. But they were friendly in their own way and I found myself giving back as good as I got; a wise-crack here and a smart quip there. As the minutes wore on I forgot about the stuffiness, the strong smell of sweat, the cigarette smoke, the sheer size of the crowd, and threw myself into the music. After an hour or two the whole place was pulsing of its own accord. In and out, around and under. Heaving and roaring like a huge animal. I loved the feeling of being flung around, like a doll on the end of a piece of elastic, a tiny, bouncing, sweating doll in the middle of this great amorphous mass.

'I'm parched!' I shouted across at Jules.

'You're a piker, Kats!'

'No, Jules, I need water!'

Sweaty and puffing, we went to get a drink. I saw that not everyone was dancing. There were dark corners: bodies on couches, people entwined on mattresses on the floor, groups on the sidelines sharing joints. I went into the toilets and had to step over four people injecting into their ankles. Their eyes were glazed and they looked desperate and hopeless in a way that frightened me a little. I'd never really come face to face with that before. I sat on the toilet and decided that everything was too loose, too desperate, but I was enjoying myself anyway. I came back and stood next to Jules by the wall, both of us sipping soft drink from plastic cups and staring around. I wondered what all these people did during the day, and giggled to think that some of them probably had to turn up for work in a bank at nine o'clock the next morning.

The last thing I remember before it happened was the onset of a headache. It was around three in the morning and I knew that I'd probably had enough. We'd been there for over three hours. I turned to Jules, about to say that I'd catch a cab home. But Jules wasn't where he'd been only a minute before; there was just a space. I twisted right around, trying to catch sight of him in the crowd. That was when the lights went on.

Blinding fluorescent lights. Harsh and merciless. A loud gasp went up. I looked around in shock. Everyone was now stripped of all their magic. We were just a crowd of people – some handsome, some sleazy and plain, a few quite old and others very young – but ordinary. Very ordinary. No one was exotic in this light. The music crashed into silence.

For some brief seconds there was the sound of men outside; someone was yelling orders, then the big doors at the end of the room opened and a stream of uniformed police poured in.

'A bust!' someone breathed. But that word had no meaning for me. I must have been in shock, because it didn't register. I gaped as the police – all strangely alike, strong and young with shut-off, determined faces and wielding batons – strode in. The crowd moved back instinctively, creating a small space in the middle of the room. At the same time I saw people around me diving into their pockets and pulling out small packets and throwing them into the air. I was too stupid and too surprised to have any idea what was going on. An older policeman with a moustache and a heavy stomach stood in the centre of the crowd and spoke into a small microphone.

'We have a warrant to search these premises for illegal substances,' he barked out. 'No one is to move from where they are standing. All the doors are manned, so there is no way any of you will leave without authority.' I looked around wildly. What was going on?

At last the penny dropped. I dived for the zip of my purse. *I must get rid of it. Where the hell is Jules? Why did he give them to me? Where is he?* But I was too late. A young policeman was standing right in front of me, looking first at my fumbling hands and then into my face.

'Your bag, Miss?' he said, quite politely. I gulped and slowly pulled the chain over my shoulder, frantically thinking of something to say. Only the most absurd sentences came to mind. *I was just leaving. Sorry, but I can't really stay, you see my grandmother is sick ... I've already called a taxi.* He was rifling through the tiny purse with strong, business-like fingers. And then the pathetic coward came out in me. *I don't really belong with this crowd, Constable,* I wanted to say. *This isn't my scene at all. I'm a nice girl ...* I would have said it, too, if I had thought it might work. Out came the white lolly bag. I gulped as he emptied the pills into his other hand. He frowned, looking down at them for a moment then up at me, eyes impenetrable, mouth twitching slightly into a sneer that disappeared as soon as it arrived. This was my moment. He wanted an explanation. I took a frightened breath and summoned up my most provocative smile.

'They're not mine, actually ... ' I said in my best private-school accent, surprised that my voice managed to sound reasonable in spite of the fact that my knees were knocking. 'You see, a friend asked me to ... '

'*Actually,*' he cut in loudly, brutally mimicking my toffiness, 'you're in deep shit, girl! Hey, Brian, over here!' I watched as another policeman came over to us. All around me people were being searched and questioned. Many of them I could tell were doing exactly as I'd done, making up elaborate excuses. Behind me someone yelped and began to cry. Others were arguing and someone else was getting abusive.

'You haven't got any right to go through my pockets ... '

'We'll go up your arse if we have to!'

'I want to call a lawyer.'

'You can call someone at the police station.'

'I want a lawyer now!'

'Shut up!'

There was a highly organised system at work. Individuals were slowly being weeded out from the rest of the crowd. I was led over to a small group standing in the alcove near the toilets. There were about twenty-five of us collected together like a flock of sheep. More kept coming. Two policemen stood in front of me. The one asking the questions was the same one who'd rifled my bag. His offsider was older with an ugly, ruddy face, fat lips, and greasy hair.

'Full name, please?' The young one said. I hesitated for a couple of minutes.

'Full name, please,' he snapped. 'Don't muck us around. You try giving a false name and you'll be in bigger shit than you're already in!'

'Katerina Anne Armstrong,' I said in a small voice, feeling a sob rise in my throat. No one had ever spoken to me like that before.

'You got any ID?'

I fumbled in my purse, trying to work out the most sensible course of action.

'No, I don't think I have ... ' I said.

'Have a look!' he said, refusing to see the plaintive look in my eyes.

Please, I don't do anyone any harm. I'm not a drug addict ...

I pulled out my driver's licence and handed it to him. I was still under the absurd impression that if I played the game right, then these two men would let me go. After all, the whole thing didn't make sense. They weren't my drugs, and I hadn't taken any that night.

'Address?'

'Canning Street, Carlton.'

'Number?'

'What did you get here?' a senior officer broke in, not looking at me. The young one counted out Jules's pills into his hand.

'Seven ecstasy, four speed, four hearts.' The older one was noting it down carefully. 'Fifteen pills.' Then they dumped the pills into a white plastic bag.

'Okay, you can take her in car four,' the senior officer said gruffly, writing something down on his clipboard, and still not looking at me. 'She'll go for trafficking.'

Trafficking?

On my way out I saw groups of young men standing up against a wall in their underpants. Some policemen were going through their clothes, feeling the pockets and patting them down. Others were shining torches into their armpits. One guy was being led over to a sectioned-off alcove; a policeman was fitting on a plastic glove. I shivered, thankful that I'd at least been spared that indignity.

'Where are you taking me?' I asked. I was being hustled towards a police car with a blue light blazing on top.

'Russell Street,' the young one said shortly.

'What for?' I asked stupidly.

'What do you think?' he snapped sarcastically, pushing me into the front seat. I was sitting beween him and the driver, conscious of my silver legs on display. Within a few moments the back seat was occupied by two other policemen. They sat on both sides of a young, tangled-haired, very doped-out guy who was swearing and struggling, in spite of being handcuffed.

'Why ya fuckin' pickin' on me, ya pigs? I could show you fifty guys in there that had more on 'em than me!'

'Okay. Okay. Calm down.'

'Try and charge me, ya morons, and I'll have ya for assault! I want your number, pig! I'm gunna report you!'

I cringed and hoped that the police wouldn't associate me with him.

'Why don't youse go and get the real criminals, huh?' he raved. 'You got nothin' better to do than ... '

The four policemen in the car remained silent. The one on my left even looked bored as he stared out into the night picking his teeth with his fingernail. The driver leant over to the glovebox and got a cigarette.

'Why don't you answer me, pig? Huh?' The guy in the back seat continued to taunt, but the police remained nonchalant, as if they weren't even hearing him.

'Right. We ready?' said the driver quietly, taking a deep drag on his smoke.

'Yep. Let's go,' the other man answered. The car sped off, the siren blaring, the flashing blue light spinning around on top. Like a toy. I felt like one of those little plastic figures that kids collect. I'd been popped into this toy car and some hero would come by any moment and save me. The car roared up the sombre dark back street towards the glow of the city lights. At an intersection, waiting for the lights to change, I was filled with an incredible sense of all this not being quite real. Life had been put through a grinder and was coming out the other end completely skew-whiff.

As we neared the city the young guy in the back quietened down. The car headed up Flinders Street past the railway station and I heard him clear his throat a couple of times. It was a cold night and not many people were on the streets. Even so, I lowered my head. People in nearby cars were all trying to peer at us. Or at least it felt like it.

Then he spat at me. I felt the slimy globule hit my bare arm and cried out in alarm before I could even think. The policeman behind the wheel gave a furious snort and braked. The car screeched to a halt. The fact that we were in an outside lane in the middle of the city obviously didn't matter. I flew forward, nearly hitting my head on the dashboard. Cars banked up behind us. No one tooted. The siren and the blue light had a power of their own.

'Listen, you *little poofter shit*!' the driver snarled, turning around to the back seat, his face contorted with anger. He grabbed the guy's thin shirt, ripping it with his fingers. 'You do one more thing like that and you'll be very sorry. I promise you! *You understand me?*' The policeman next to me had pulled a hanky from his pocket and was wiping the spit from my arm.

'Sorry about that,' he said.

'Thanks. It's okay,' I managed to say, almost melting with gratitude for the kindness in his voice.

'No, it's not okay!' The driver was still holding the guy by the shirt.

'*Did you hear me?*'

'Yeah,' came a subdued mumble.

'Good!' The driver shoved him backwards and turned around to the wheel again.

The longest night of my life had begun.

I was hustled quickly from the car into a small, badly lit interview-room with just a couple of chairs, a desk, and a bare lino-covered floor. I was questioned for over an hour by two plain-clothes detectives – a man and a woman – before I was allowed to make a phone call. Neither of them believed my story and they made it very plain.

'When can I make a phone call?' I asked politely for the third time.

'Soon,' came the peevish reply. The woman interviewing me was cold and unimpressed with my refusal to admit the drugs were mine. Dressed as I was, it was hard to summon up my usual cool confidence. I think I was still in shock. Underneath I still believed it would only be a matter of time before they would realise their mistake. After all, I *was* speaking the truth. Everything would click back to normal soon, and then I'd be able to go home. No harm done. I was expecting them to apologise any minute for keeping me, and to offer to ring a taxi for me to get home. I was cold and tired and hungry. My bed in Canning Street was starting to seem unbelievably attractive.

It has to finish soon. It just has to!

But the questions continued. I alternated between blind panic, a terrible weariness, and boredom. I looked for reasons why they didn't believe me. My clothes! If I was just allowed to change out of this ridiculous gear and get rid of the hair colouring I was sure they'd believe me. The uniformed officer sitting next to the two detectives was much nicer than the other two. He even brought me a coffee when I said my throat was parched.

'Now, you say you had no drugs tonight?'

'That's right.'

'And this ... this *friend* asked you to mind them for him?'

'That's right.'

'And what's this friend's name?' I think this was the fifth time she'd asked the question.

'I don't want to tell you, because I don't want to get him into trouble,' I said.

'Do you realise that to be carrying such material, especially in this quantity, is a very serious offence?'

'Well ... I guess I've never really thought about it,' I said, knowing it sounded weak, but it was the truth.

'You've never thought about the fact that these substances are illegal?' she sneered.

'Well, I guess I knew ... I just never thought about it much.'

'You never thought about it?'

'No.'

'And you say you're a student at Melbourne University?'

'Yes.'

'Studying what?'

'Arts/Law.'

Her lip curled. And she began again.

'At what stage did you get to the rave tonight?'

'Who invited you?'

'How did you get there?'

'Whose car was it?'

'Are you part of the gay scene?'

'Why did you go then?'

We were all exhausted. She raised her eyebrows at the uniformed guy taking the notes and yawned.

'I've had it,' she said and left the room without so much as looking at me. 'Let her make a phone call now.'

They brought in a phone. I breathed a sigh of relief. I would call Anton. He was a lawyer. Sort of anyway. He would know what to do, who to contact. The biggest dread at this stage was my parents finding out about any of it.

'Anton. It's me, Katerina.'

I knew he had a phone by his bed and I knew it would take him a little time to register who I was.

'Katerina!' he said sleepily. 'It's 4.30 a.m. What's wrong?'

'I'm at Russell Street police station,' I whispered. The uniformed officer was still in the room and I didn't want him to overhear. 'I think I'm in trouble.'

'You're *where*?'

Anton arrived within about half an hour, dishevelled and still sleepy. I hugged him, half crying. I don't think I'd ever been as pleased to see anyone. I was in the middle of filling him in with the details of the whole business when another older man strode into the room.

'I'm Senior Detective Bowen,' he said in this soft, clipped, strangely ominous voice. He sat down opposite us behind the table. He looked about fifty, was thin, and wore a well-cut, baggy suit. He had a moustache and very hard, glassy-blue eyes. He'd been holding a folder of notes. He stared across at us for a few unnerving moments before throwing the manila folder onto the desk.

'Miss Armstrong, is it?'

'Yes,' I said, pushing my shoulders back.

'I've read through this ... crap.' He slapped his hand onto the folder. 'And I thought I'd better make a few things clear to you.' I stared back into the cold eyes and began to shake. He was the first man I'd ever come across who was looking right at me but didn't *see* me. Didn't, even for a moment, take in the fact that I was young and beautiful. *And innocent.* I was just a cardboard cut-out. He wasn't interested in me at all. Anton put his arm around my shoulders.

'You *have* been feeding us a lot of bullshit, haven't you?' he went on coldly, very softly, still staring straight at me, refusing to acknowledge my shaking hands.

'No, I ...'

'As things stand, we will be charging you with drug trafficking,' he said, raising his voice a little. Anton had been sitting quietly, but now he looked up, about to protest. But the detective held up his hand, indicating that he wanted to continue. 'I hope you understand that it's a very serious charge. You have admitted that you have taken such drugs as we found in your possession in the past and that you have on occasion sold them on to your friends. Tonight we found you at an illegal venue with fifteen tablets in your bag. This doesn't look good for you at all, Miss Armstrong.'

'But that's ... not. I don't *sell* them!' Anton nudged me to be quiet. The man opened the folder and read down the page.

'You said you sometimes have sold a tab on to friends if they needed some?'

'Yes, but that's not ... ' My voice petered out. 'Only in the way I might sell a pen or a lipstick or something if I'd paid for it and didn't want it any more ... more often I've given them away.' *Oh shit! I'm getting in deeper by the minute.* He dismissed me with a shrug.

'Should you be found guilty of this charge — and the case against you is very strong — then a conviction will be recorded against your name.' He leant forward and continued very gravely. 'I want you to understand, Miss Armstrong, that *when* this happens, apart from a possible gaol term, you will never be allowed to practise law in this country.' My mouth fell open in outrage.

'But how could I ... I didn't know that ... I ... '

'I'll just make that clear again, Miss Armstrong,' he continued relentlessly. 'Apart from a hefty fine, this may also get you some months in gaol. *And* you will have completely ruined your future career!'

The bastard! He sat back smug and cold to let it sink in, tapping his slim fingers on the desk.

I stared at him, feeling that same sense of warped reality that I'd experienced earlier in the police car. Instead of things becoming clearer, I was getting deeper and deeper into this morass. Anton was frowning.

'Would there be any circumstances in which the charge could be changed to one of possession, Detective?' he asked. Anton always managed the right tone, intelligent and respectful, but not cloying. The man moved his eyes from me over to Anton.

'Miss Armstrong has no prior convictions,' the detective began carefully, still tapping his fingers on the table, 'and this number of pills *could*, just possibly, be seen as possession. However, she has not cooperated with us at all over the last few hours. So unless things change we will submit a very formal case against her. By that I mean that we will charge her with trafficking ... Fifteen pills after all are a lot for one person. It is certainly enough to warrant a trafficking charge.'

'What do you mean?' I broke in. 'I've cooperated! I've told the truth.'

'Miss Armstrong.' His eyes were boring into me. 'You say you were supplied these drugs by a friend. We need to know his name. We need to know who supplies him. We need to know everything you know about this source.'

It took a few seconds to register.

'But he's my friend,' I burst out. 'I can't give him away!'

3

But that's exactly what I did do. To save my own future I gave Jules away. The one guy who'd been a real friend to me all year. Of course it took a while. I had to be talked into it. First by the detective, and then, more subtly, by Anton.

After the detective sussed out that Anton was basically sympathetic to the idea, we were left alone to talk. I know Anton had my future at heart. He had no real concern with Jules. Nor any idea of the closeness of our friendship.

'Katerina, this guy disappeared when he smelt the raid,' Anton argued. 'Are you going to put your future on the line for someone who did that?'

'I don't know for sure that he did that, Anton. He was there one minute and then he just sort of disappeared. I don't know where he is.'

'He disappeared,' Anton repeated quietly. 'Knowing you were carrying his stuff!'

I nodded. But I was way beyond working out whether I agreed with this scenario or not. All I knew was that I didn't want to give Jules's name to the detective.

'If I give his name, they'll arrest him,' I said slowly. 'And he wouldn't cope with gaol ... ' I shuddered, thinking of Jules in any kind of rough environment. Anton shrugged.

'I'm interested in what's going to happen to *you*,' he said. 'Trafficking is a very serious offence. You probably won't go to gaol because it's your first offence, but it will certainly ruin your future in the law ... *And they weren't your drugs*. You mustn't wreck your own future because of some misguided sense of loyalty.'

'They weren't my drugs, that's true.' I was desperate to see it his way. At the same time I hated myself for being so eager.

'That's right,' Anton said firmly.

'But they could have been,' I said in a small voice. 'Easily could have been mine. I've often bought that amount and sold them on to Kara or whoever.' Anton winced and frowned. I wondered briefly if he was wincing about the drugs or at the mention of Kara.

'But they weren't yours this time,' he insisted again.

'That's right.'

Anton explained the deal that the detective was offering. In exchange for Jules, my trafficking charge would be changed to the less serious one of possession. I would have to face court, but if I pleaded guilty I would only have to pay a fine. And with a bit of luck and work on the police's part a conviction need not be recorded against me.

I protested and cried. Then I did it. I told the detective everything I knew about Jules. About the three Romanians who made the stuff in a little makeshift factory out the back of a suburban house in Glenroy. About their fourth member who bashed anyone who didn't pay up. I even remembered the name of the street. Jules hadn't told me, but I'd seen it on a bit of paper in one of his pockets. It was surprising how much I did know once I got down to it.

At six o'clock the Bail Justice was called in. An immaculately groomed woman in her mid-thirties set up a tiny courtroom in the interview-room. If I hadn't been at the centre of the drama, I would have found it funny. She stood formally behind a small table that had been brought in specially, and in front of the two detectives, a couple of policemen, Anton and me, she ran a short, formal court case.

'With the power that has been vested in me by the state ... I hereby call on Constable Nick Barkley.'

'Present, madam.' The policeman who had found the pills on me stood up.

'And Detective Bowen.'

'Present, madam.'

'And Katerina Anne Armstrong.' Anton gave me a nudge and I stood up too.

'May we hear the facts concerning this case, Constable?'

'Certainly, madam.'

'From the beginning then ... '

Within an hour I was free to go. Bail had been set at five thousand dollars. Anton organised the money. I was to appear in court in two months on a charge of possession of drugs, to be changed at police discretion to one of trafficking, should more evidence come to light. I guessed this was their way of maintaining their hold over me. If I went back on the evidence I'd supplied about Jules, or had merely fabricated it, then they'd be able to get back at me.

When Anton and I finally walked out the front door of the station, the sun was rising, a glorious pink glow settling over the city streets. It felt like the first morning that had ever broken. Inside I was lost, bereft. For the first time in my life I hated who I was. But the air against my skin was invigorating. The weariness left me for a few moments and I felt as if I could have run a mile. I wanted to run, to get away from everything. Myself most of all. Anton took my hand, led me back to his car and drove me back to his place in silence. I had a quick shower and then settled into the big bed in his front room. A piece of heavy cardboard was taped over the broken window. Anton brought in a warm cup of cocoa and sat on the bed while I drank it.

'We'll talk about all this when you've had a sleep,' he smiled.

'What about you,' I protested weakly. 'Don't you need to sleep?'

'I'm going around to your place,' he said grimly, 'to find Carmel. I haven't seen her in two days. How come no one ever answers the phone around there?'

I shrugged. I hadn't seen her either.

'You think everything will turn out okay, Anton?'

'Yeah,' he said, without a moment's hesitation. 'Of course it will.'

'I feel bad about Jules,' I said.

'Don't,' Anton said. 'He's not worth it. Just go to sleep. I'll be out in the kitchen when you wake up.'

I got up about midday and showered again, this time washing all the colouring out of my hair. Feeling much better and more like my old self I walked down to the kitchen in Anton's dressing-gown. Anton was where he said he'd be, at the table reading the paper. He looked up at me and smiled uneasily.

'I'm afraid the press have got hold of it,' he said. I stared at the two pages he was holding up. The headlines 'Police Raid Gay Dance' and 'Police Chief says Gay Youth Scene Rife with Drugs' blazed out at me over a series of pictures. Snapshots from the night before: a dozen young men facing the wall dressed only in their underpants; a tall, thin guy, his face obscured, being led off in handcuffs. There were pictures of police wielding batons outside one of the entrances, and groups of startled-looking patrons staring blindly at the camera. Anton pointed at one of the smaller group photos and I bent and looked closer. There I was in my stupid little skirt and divided hair in the middle of a crowd on the footpath waiting to get into the police car. I flopped into a chair next to Anton and sank my face onto my arms.

'Listen,' he said. 'You're not recognisable.' I nodded, but somehow it didn't make much difference. In the photo my face was half blacked out and the bizarre costume and make-up would have made it hard for anyone to recognise me.

'Really, Katerina,' he went on encouragingly. 'You'd have to look very hard to tell that it was you.'

'I can't remember anyone taking photographs,' I whispered. Anton sighed.

'They were obviously alerted.'

'Who?'

'The press. They must have been tipped off.'

'Oh God!'

We scanned the columns of print for any further identifying information. But the article itself was mainly focused on spokespeople from the gay community who were describing the search as brutal harassment and suggesting an independent inquiry. And that view, of course, was countered by the police response, which was that all rules had been strictly observed. At the end of the article it said that various charges had been laid against a number of young people and that police had not yet released names.

'Does that mean they *will* release names?' I asked.

'I don't know,' Anton said. 'But I can find out. Maybe we could convince that detective not to give yours out.'

'Oh, Anton!' I grasped his arm and briefly buried my face in his shoulder. 'It's just Mum and Dad and Louise and ... oh God, Gran, and ... ' He patted my shoulder and laughed quietly.

'You don't have to explain to me. I come from Manella. I know what you mean.'

Anton dropped me off at Canning Street at about five that evening. I walked in to find Jude washing the dishes. She turned around, smiled and said hello. I nodded coldly, not meeting her eye, and after putting on the kettle left the kitchen for the lounge. I would wait there, then make my drink and take it up to my room. It was dark and cold in the lounge room, and untidy. Piles of newspapers and CD covers cluttered the floor and a few grimy cups half-filled with coffee sat on the table. I recognised them as the ones Kara and I had used the day before. Or was it the day before that? Kara's stale cigarette smoke was still in the atmosphere. I pushed the curtains aside and raised the window to let in some fresh air. Then I turned on the heater and stood in front of it, warming my hands. An ache hit my chest as I remembered Jules. Would he be sitting in that lovely old-fashioned flat of his overlooking Royal Parade? Perhaps innocently drinking or eating something? No idea of the trouble about to hit him. Or would they have him already? A guilty lump formed in my throat as I imagined him being arrested.

'A friend of yours came around.' Jude poked her head around the door. I'd forgotten about her even being there, I was so wrapped up in my own thoughts.

'Who?' I said stupidly, not looking at her. *I don't have any friends.*

'A guy called Jordan,' she said. I shuddered. The sound of his name was enough. Jude must have noticed. 'Is he your boyfriend?' she asked curiously. I gave a dry laugh.

'Not exactly,' I said shortly, trying to ward off the image of him in the cream linen shirt, a gold chain around his neck, and those shiny slip-on shoes. 'He's just someone I know.'

'That's good,' she said lightly. 'Because I didn't like him much.' She paused. 'I thought you said he was a photographer?' I looked up, startled. 'Ages ago,' she smiled, as though reading my thoughts. 'Remember, you showed them to me. The photographs.' I nodded coldly.

'Did you decide to go ahead with it?' she asked.

'No, I've decided not to . . . ' I said.

'Oh, why?' she asked. I shrugged and looked away. I wasn't about to spill the beans to her. We hadn't been friendly for weeks. She sat on one end of the couch, then let herself slide down on her bottom, her legs sticking up over the arm of the chair like a little kid's. Both hands were clasped over her stomach.

'Ah, well,' she said softly. 'He acted as if he was your

boyfriend. He seemed put out about something. A photograph of you in the paper today or something?'

'*What?*'

'I couldn't work out what he was talking about,' she said.

I stared back at her, a rush of rage hammering through my head.

That would be right. Jordan would see that! He wouldn't know if I'd had a fatal accident or died of a broken heart, but he'd be sure to see me in the paper making a fool of myself.

'He said he saw me in the paper?' I asked.

'Yeah. Something like that,' Jude said. 'Hey, Katerina, what's up?'

It was the way she said it. Kindly, just one person to another. The solid wall of defiance I'd built up began to crumble in my chest. I felt this incredible need to tell, to confess, to ask advice.

'I'm in trouble,' I said.

'What for?'

I shut my eyes. Where did I begin?

'Different stuff,' I said, turning to watch her reaction. 'Drugs ... possession of drugs that weren't mine. And with Jordan. I don't know where to begin about him.' Her face didn't change at all except to frown.

'How do you mean?'

I suppose it took me less than five minutes to tell her everything. She was quiet as I spoke, and for a while afterwards, and then she whistled, a low, deep, melodious whistle. And that made me smile.

'Katerina,' she said. 'You *are* in trouble.'

'I know,' I whispered. 'I keep thinking of my parents ... and then of Jules. My career ... I mean, I don't think I want to end up a suburban lawyer, but I want to have a choice, you know ...'

'You don't seem like someone who would ever be involved with drugs,' she said. 'You seem so ... intelligent.'

'Don't be so superior!'

'I'm not. It's just that it's hard to imagine you mixed up with drugs ...'

'Yes, you are!' I snapped. 'Carmel once said *I* was superior. Do you remember? But that's wrong. It's you two. You've both got everything sewn up, haven't you?'

'What do you mean?' She looked bewildered.

'Yesterday, for example,' I fumed. 'I said good morning to you and you closed the door in my face!' Jude frowned.

'So why did you arrange for that friend of yours to get on with Anton,' she snapped back. 'I mean *why*? When you know what Carmel's like. How much she loves him!'

'Oh God!' I shook my head. 'I didn't. I didn't arrange it! I had nothing to do with it.'

'Bloody bad luck the brick didn't hit 'em both,' she said angrily. I gasped and stared at her. But she didn't have to say anything else.

'God!' I exclaimed. 'I mean ... what did Carmel think she was doing!' Jude gave a quick laugh.

'She knew exactly what she was doing!'

I shut my mouth and looked away. I think I was impressed in spite of myself. Throwing that brick would have taken a bit of inner fire. I remembered hearing her sing. How deep and strong she had sounded.

It's called 'clearing the air', I suppose. Jude explained how angry she'd been when she'd seen Carmel so hurt by Anton and Kara, and I got a lot off my chest too. About her and Carmel. I admitted being jealous at the same time as being wildly annoyed with both of them. I came clean about the way I felt about all their dirty dishes and the fact that they didn't even try to keep the bathroom tidy. And the way they'd stop talking when I came into the room. It felt good to bring it all out in the open. Just sitting there in the red glow from the heater, talking, as the darkness grew around us.

'But how did you first get involved with them? Jules and

Jordan?' Jude was lying flat on her stomach on the floor, her face turned away from me, her voice muffled.

I sighed, closed my eyes, and threw my head back.

'How did you meet them?' she asked quietly. I shrugged and tried to remember.

Glen Simons. He'd been the first I'd met in that crowd, I suppose. And he'd introduced me to Jordan, and Jules had been hanging around the same scene. The first time I'd ever seen Glen was when I'd gone out with Kara. She'd been invited out to Stacey's nightclub and wanted me to come along too. It was about the third week of university. We were the youngest there and were both immediately impressed; everyone was cool and hard in the way we both liked. All the men were eyeing us off. I loved that too. I was holding my own in this ultra-hip crowd. Kara and I both danced and drank a fair bit that night. Some guy invited me to the races the following Saturday, then offered me a hit of speed, which I declined. Everyone assumed they'd see us again soon. It was three in the morning by the time I left, and by that time Kara had disappeared. An older man approached me. Would I like a lift home? I liked his baggy, well-cut suit, his sophistication, the lines around his eyes. I liked his shiny Jag, too, and the way he opened the door for me. Outside my house he'd asked for my number and told me in a rather offhand way that I was the most beautiful girl he'd seen in a long time. I smiled. He seemed refined, good-looking ... and sincere. *I liked it that he was older.* At the door he put a hand under my chin and swivelled my face around. I thought he was going to kiss me. But he was just looking at me.

'My name's Glen,' he said softly.

'I know,' I said.

'You could go a long way with a face like that,' he said.

'I know,' I answered. That made him laugh. He cupped my face in his hard hands and kissed me briefly on the mouth. Then he smiled and walked back to his car. I remember thinking, *He's right. And I will too. I'll get whatever I want.*

'At a nightclub ... earlier this year.' I said, looking at Jude.

'But I thought ... Carmel and I thought ... ' She sat up properly and laughed. 'You seemed to move in such a *classy* crowd!'

'Yeah ... '

'But, I mean, are they all into ... *porno calendars* or what?' she exclaimed.

'It's not porn,' I said hotly. 'It's just ... I thought I could handle it. I liked the attention. And I was ... ' I stopped. I had never had such a frank conversation before. It was alarming. I was admitting everything to someone I had no reason to trust. What if I had nothing left when this conversation was over?

'What?' she said.

'I was off my head a lot of the time,' I said in a small voice.

'What, on pills?'

'Yeah.'

The phone began to ring. Neither of us got up to answer it. The room had got very dark. I could hardly see Jude's face. A branch on the birch tree began to scrape the side window. Only the low hiss and red glow from the heater warmed the strange atmosphere. I covered my burning face with both hands and wished I could cry.

Moments passed. Then there was a hand on my shoulder. Just one hand, warm and firm.

'I'm sorry,' Jude said softly. 'You're right. I ... Well, both Carmel and I. We didn't give you a chance.'

The phone began to ring again. This time I got up and answered it.

'Is that you, Katerina?' It was my mother, sounding peeved.

'Yes. Hi, Mum.' I tried to come across as bright and in control. She was very good at picking up if anything was wrong.

'Darling, where *have* you been?'

'I've just come in,' I lied.

'Louise said you didn't look well,' she said accusingly. I sighed.

'Well, I'm fine, Mum, honestly,' I said. Trust Louise, I thought. Home for four days and already running the show again.

'Well ...' she went on. 'Isn't it simply wonderful news about Lou? Daddy and I are thrilled.'

'Yeah,' I lied. 'It's terrific. What's he like?'

'Oh, he's lovely! Very handsome, very *French*. I think he's good for Louise. He likes to laugh and you know how serious she can get.' There was a pause while we each waited for the other to speak. 'And you're coming up to meet him at the weekend,' she said, more as a statement than a question.

'Oh, I don't know, Mum.' I suddenly didn't want to comply with their neat little plans. I was overcome with a contrary need to be the fly in their ointment. Louise had always called the shots, and I was sick of it. 'I will if I can. I've got a lot of work to catch up on and ...'

'Katerina, we'll be devastated if you can't come!' she cut in.

'Well, I'll try,' I said.

'And I've got some bad news too, darling,' she said. I closed my eyes and began to tap two fingers on the wall. If I had to listen to a whole lot of stuff about people I hardly knew, I'd scream. My mother was always ringing up about someone. *Would you go and see old Mrs Herbert in hospital? I know it's an effort, but ... Auntie Jean has broken her arm. Would you call in on her?*'

'What?' I snapped.

'Katerina, what *is* the matter with you?' she asked. I took a deep breath and contemplated telling her.

Oh nothing much, Mummy. I've just been charged with possession of drugs. I may have wrecked my future career. Then again, I may have saved it by lagging on a good friend who has been nothing but kind to me.

And this photographer guy who more or less raped me has got these soft-core porn shots of me. He's putting the pressure on to publish them. I know if I say no he'll try and use them against me in some way. So all I can do is pray my name won't hit the papers, Mum. For all our sakes, eh?

'Are you keeping up?' she said.

'What?'

'With your work. I hope you're not wasting time.'

'Yes. I'm keeping up.'

'You're going to pass your exams?'

'Of course.'

'Oh, good girl. And you're eating properly?'

'Yes!'

'Now, look, that little girl you share your house with?' I turned around to where Jude was still lying on the couch.

'Which one?' I said lowering my voice.

'The McCaffrey girl.'

'Carmel,' I said. 'What about her?'

'Her mother is very ill.'

'Really?' This was unexpected. I hadn't seen Carmel for days. I looked around as though she might suddenly appear and tell me my mother was exaggerating.

'Has she said anything?'

'No,' I answered. 'But I haven't seen her much lately. I mean, *how* sick is she?'

'Well ... she's dying, darling,' my mother said slowly. 'Of cancer. So do be careful, won't you?'

'How do you mean?' I said stupidly. 'I mean what can I do?' My mother gave an impatient sigh.

'Nothing, of course. Just be kind. That's why I'm ringing.'

'Okay. Thanks, Mum.'

'Now, we expect you on Friday?'

'If I can, Mum.'

'See you then.'

'Did you know Carmel's mother is sick?' I asked Jude.

'Yeah. She went home yesterday morning,' she replied. 'With her brother.'

'God, that's terrible!' I said. 'How many kids are there?'

'Seven,' Jude answered. 'One brother older than Carmel, three a bit younger, fourteen, sixteen and seventeen, and then there's the twins . . . '

'How old are they?' I asked.

'Eight, I think,' Jude said. Her voice had gone husky. I didn't look at her, but I was suddenly shocked and very moved. I think Jude was too.

After a while Jude sat up.

'Listen. If you're going home, why don't you come with us?' she asked.

'You're going back for the weekend?'

'Yeah. A friend of mine, Declan, has a car. He's going to drive the three of us. Declan, Annie and me. We all want to see Carmel,' she said. 'We can drop you off at your parents' place if you like.'

'Okay,' I said slowly. 'Thanks. I'll do that.'

So it was back to Manella. Apart from a few weekends here and there I'd hardly been home all year, much to my parents' disappointment. I rang my mother back that night.

'I'll be coming home *definitely* on Friday night,' I said apologetically.

She was so pleased that a fresh wave of guilt flooded me.

'That's wonderful, darling! Daddy and I will be thrilled to see you! Jean-Paul is anxious to meet you, too. It will be lovely to have the whole family home together again.'

'Okay then. See you Friday.'

'Anything wrong?'

'Of course not,' I said.

I put the phone down and knew I'd have my work cut out keeping my state of mind from her.

4

In spite of the fact that Jude and her friends were quite friendly to me, the four-hour trip to Manella with them was very strange. I met the others and got into the car determined to use the time to think through my own problems. But it was impossible. After a while their conversation invaded my thoughts, and I had to listen. Political detainees, government policy, human rights! They were so involved with all this stuff I'd never even thought about. So deeply interested. Anyone could be forgiven for thinking they were organising World War Three! All the plans and strategies. There would be some demonstration against the Indonesian military in the city square in a few months' time, and a campaign against some milk company operating in Africa next year. The talk was so intense, full of teasing and loud laughter. It made me feel that we'd been living on different planets all year.

After a while they got on to Jude's predicament. I was sitting in the back seat looking out the window and trying to work out what they were talking about. Annie turned around to me at one stage.

'Katerina, did you know that Jude is going to get advice about whether she can prosecute Orlando?' she said.

'Who is Orlando?' I asked. Declan and Annie looked at Jude. Jude looked at me.

'He's one of the men who ordered my father's execution in Chile,' she said curtly. 'He owns a restaurant in Melbourne.'

'Oh,' was all I could manage. Once again I had the distinct impression that they were living in a different world from me. Their talk, the casual laughter, and the warmth they felt for each other seemed to circulate around the car like a current. And it made me feel more alone than ever.

We eventually arrived in the town. I felt strangely bereft, knowing that I'd soon be leaving the closeness and security of the car and its occupants. It would all go on without me. I gave directions to Declan, who was driving. Everyone slowly quietened as the little car began to wind its way up the hill towards our house, which was ablaze with yellow lights. Declan was about to stop out the front, but I pointed out the track leading up and around to the back. The house itself was hardly visible in the darkness, just the light blasting out from behind the tall trees and hedges. It looked like a castle from a kids' picture book. Dark and gloomy, big and wonderful.

'It's a lovely place,' Annie said quietly.

'Yes,' I said, knowing that I would normally have been pleased with her comment. But this night I wished my family had a more ordinary home. I wished for a house that they might all have felt easy about coming into for a quick cup of something before they went on their way.

'Would you like to come in?' I said, knowing they wouldn't.

'Nah, thanks,' Jude said quickly. 'Thanks, but Mum's expecting us.' She got out and helped me get my bag out of the boot.

'Have a nice ... ' She smiled at me. ' ... relaxing time, eh? And don't think about all that stuff.'

'Okay,' I smiled back and picked up the bag. 'And tell Carmel I'm sorry about her mother ... and that I'm ... er, thinking of her,' I added, feeling very self-conscious.

'I will,' Jude said. She got back into the car and they took off.

Once inside I was immediately warmed by my parents' gladness to see me. They took me straight into the formal sitting-room at the front of the house.

'We've heated your room, darling,' Mum said, taking my coat. She was dressed in a pleated navy checked skirt and a cream cashmere jumper, a lovely gold brooch at her throat. Dad poured a glass of champagne and handed it to me with a smile.

'Here's to our girl!' he said. 'The others will be back soon.' He was dressed like a country gentleman. A silk cravat around his neck, comfortable woollen jumper, and slacks. I raised the glass to my mouth, thinking that I much preferred the look of him in his work clothes; those old army pants and big hand-knitted jumpers he wore out on the farm.

'So, where are they?' I asked, taking another sip. 'The happy couple?' Now that I was home I was curious about my future brother-in-law.

'They'll be here any minute. Asked in for a drink next door,' Dad said heartily. 'You know what a favourite Lou is with old Edward and Barbara.'

'Yes,' I said. I must have looked sour because Mum burst into a peal of laughter.

'Oh, get that look off your face, Katerina,' she chortled, squeezing my arm. 'They love you, too! You're *both* favourites!'

'You know I'm not,' I said. 'You know they love Lou best.'

'Rubbish!' exclaimed Dad.

'Absolute rot!' from my mother.

I sat down, embarrassed to think that my self-esteem could have reached such a low ebb.

'To our clever, *beautiful* daughter,' my mother added, 'who is doing so well.' I took another deep gulp, which almost finished the glass. *Be careful. Be careful.* Everything in the room, the open fire, the lovely music, the deep carpets, was soothing. There was no need to panic.

'Dinner will be soon, darling. You must be starving,' Mum said, fussing around with table napkins. 'We thought we'd have it in here. The dining-room is too big and cold at this time of the year for just the five of us. And we certainly didn't want to put you in the kitchen!'

'Lovely,' I said, pushing my hands towards the fire. 'Thanks, everything is lovely.'

'I've asked Jim to get Tessy ready for you,' my father beamed. 'He'll come in and take you out around seven tomorrow morning. That's if you don't want to sleep in.' Tessy was my horse, kept out on one of our properties about six kilometres from town. And Jim was a workman who'd been with us for years. Dad trusted him absolutely with the running of the place, but the old man's real love was horses.

'Oh Dad! I'd love that. I don't want to sleep in. Thanks!' They were both pleased at my enthusiasm. Then the front door opened and Louise and her fiancé walked in.

'This is my sister, Katerina!' Lou said loudly, face glowing, fair hair pinned back in a loose top-knot. She was dressed in a long green silk blouse, tight stretch trousers, and the most wonderful soft green leather lace-up boots I'd ever seen.

'Jean-Paul!' she said proudly, taking my arm and pulling me towards him. I shook the tall stranger's large slim hand and looked into the bright brown eyes that dominated his otherwise ordinary face, and liked him immediately. His curly dark hair was cut short around his head and the smile that lit up his face seemed absolutely genuine.

'Well, congratulations!' I said. 'I've never had a brother-in-law before, but you look as though you'll do the job splendidly!' Everyone laughed.

'Katerina. Thank you,' he replied in *the* most charming accent. 'And I guess you must be the *second* most beautiful girl in the world!' We all laughed again and I felt as if I'd never left my place in this house. This was my kind and gracious family, everything was how it should be. Even Louise seemed wonderful. *How could I ever have got involved in anything else?*

Mum went to tell Gina that we were ready for dinner, and Dad got up and pretended to check that the table was set properly. We talked about riding and horses and the best kinds of saddles and bridles. Jean-Paul had grown up in the countryside in France, but had never ridden a horse. Lou and I teased him about how his bum would feel after only a ten-minute ride on our oldest nag. But he remained determined at least to have a try. They were sitting opposite each other in front of the fire, smiling, joking, and bringing me in to the conversation every now and again. The warmth of their feeling had quickly permeated the darkest, coldest crevices of my heart. Anxiety melted away inside me.

'This is wonderful.' I sank my teeth into the roast beef and pushed some fresh minted peas and a slice of baby potato onto my fork, wondering what the others would be doing. I'd never been to Jude's place, but her mother intrigued me. I tossed up whether to ask my parents if they knew her, but I didn't want to risk stopping the flow of conversation around me. I remembered how once last year, when we'd gone into her shop to get something, my mother had come out frowning. 'What do you think that woman was thinking about?' she'd said. And we'd both laughed. 'She's off with the fairies.'

'What's her name?'

'Cynthia Torres,' my mother had said, her eyes narrowing slightly. 'Married to some ... fellow ... somewhere in South America.'

'Oh? Where is he?'

'Dead, they say, but ... '

They might be all eating fish and chips or some of that weird-smelling, spicy South American food that Jude cooked a lot. They would be talking over each other, laughing loudly with their mouths half full. Tibet. China. East Timor ...

Our table had been set with the best polished silver; lovely tall-stemmed glasses that had originally belonged to my grandmother sparkled stiffly by each plate. Pink and white rosebuds in a small round silver vase sat squarely in the middle of the white linen tablecloth. Before the beef had come, while we were having our soup, I had just been able to smell their fragrance, wafting towards me, ever so faintly. And I'd realised, probably for the first time in my life, *God, I'm lucky. These people, my parents, my sister, love me, and for no good reason at all.*

'How is Gran?' I asked.

'She's staying with Jock at the moment,' my father said. Jock was his brother. 'But she'll be back on Sunday night. What time are you leaving? You might get to see her before you go.'

I mumbled something about having to fit in with when the others wanted to go back.

'Of course, of course.' They were both at pains to show that they understood. Usually I'd have been impatient with everything about a quiet dinner at home with my parents and sister. Bored senseless with their gentle questioning, the snippets of local news. But this night I was taking it all in carefully. Wondering about it. And feeling very thankful.

Louise and Jean-Paul were left to sleep in, but I got up early the next morning to ride. After a quick shower I donned the riding outfit I'd had since I was fifteen. Riding jodhpurs, warm jacket, long flat boots and brown riding helmet. I waited outside the back gate for Jim to arrive. On the dot of seven the old ute lumbered up, mud spots all over the lower doors and mudguards.

'Someone's keen!' he shouted, pulling open the door. 'Ya get sick of the bright lights, eh?' I smiled and hopped in next to him, loving the familiarity of his teasing and the worn, good-natured smile on his deeply lined face.

'Yep. They couldn't keep me away, Jim.'

'Good for you, girl!'

The last grim weeks rolled away as I cantered along the narrow dirt track, across a fern-embedded creek, and up through the hills. The property was two thousand hectares of mainly rich and fertile flats bordering the wide river, where crops of barley, rye and oats were grown in season. But my track, the one my gran had shown me when I was only six and when she'd been well enough to ride, was cut into the less fertile rocky hills behind. Tessy had recognised me as soon as I'd got out of the truck. 'G'day, girlie,' I whispered into her soft nose. 'How've you been without me?' Then Jim and I had laughed as she'd whinnied and stamped her back hooves in greeting. Within minutes we were off, flying along together – she knew exactly where I wanted to go – across the green grass, over the bridge towards the mountains. I thought of Glen and Jordan, and of Jules, but out there in that country they were as unimportant as the few small drifts of grey cloud that were scattered across the horizon on an otherwise perfect sky. A spill of unimportant rubbish that would fade away when the wind blew. They meant nothing.

The mountains in front of me stood like jagged blue cut-outs in a child's painting. I loved being out alone in that crisp morning air. I loved the feeling of Tessy's warm body beneath me, the sound of her breathing as she made her way through the rocky edges of the hills. After half an hour we were climbing steadily and slowly towards the peak of our property. I was longing to get off the horse, stand there in the bright winter sunshine, and spin slowly around on my own two feet, taking in the panorama of hills and mountains, rivers and houses, all around. I wanted to look down on the town below, as I'd done as a child, and pick out the main street, the disused mill on the left, and our house, with the tiny rectangle of blue water in the backyard, sitting lonely, squarely on top of the one hill in town. This peak was the most perfect of places. When at last Tessy and I got there I wondered how I could have gone without it for so long.

I got back around midday. My mother was in the kitchen packing bright-coloured tins and plastic ice-cream containers into a couple of cardboard boxes.

'How was your ride?'

'Wonderful!' I said, and walked to the sink for a glass of water. She smiled and waved towards the table where some freshly made sandwiches awaited me.

'Where's Lou and Jean-Paul?' I asked looking out the back window. The sun was still shining. I had thought they might have been sitting on the sun deck and I'd planned to join them.

'Daddy's taken them out to the farm in the truck to show Jean-Paul around,' she replied, frowning as she counted through the containers in her boxes. 'Now, darling, would you do me a favour?'

'Of course, Mum,' I said, making my way over to the table.

'Take this box out to that family for me, darling? I have a church meeting this afternoon in town and anyway I think it would be nicer coming from you.'

'Who?' I said, picking out a fresh tomato sandwich and taking a bite.

'The McCaffreys,' Mum said, as if I should have known. I stopped munching, immediately wary.

'That poor sick woman,' my mother said as she settled the last tin into the box, 'with all those children.'

'But Mum,' I said, trying to keep the anxious note out of my voice. 'I don't know that they'd really want it ... from us.' I was appalled with the idea. Something like that would go down like a ton of bricks with Carmel. I saw in a flash the brick that had come flying through Anton's front window and shuddered. *That brick had been meant for me.*

'Nonsense, darling,' Mum said, 'everyone's helping. The Red Cross have been taking bits and pieces out. Gwen Harris has been supplying them with casseroles and cakes. It's a very difficult time for that poor man with those children. They don't want to have to be worrying about getting meals.'

Country kindness, caring for your neighbours. All my life my mother had been doing this kind of thing!

'I don't even know where they live!' I protested.

'It's not very far. Your father's been there. Goodness, Katerina, it's nothing. The round trip will take you an hour!'

I finished my lunch and went to change. Instinctively I found my oldest trousers, a man's shirt, and a moth-eaten jumper of Dad's over the top. I pulled my hair straight back from my face, pinned it into a tight little bun and pulled out my gold earrings. I'm not quite sure why. Mum frowned when she saw me, but said nothing. Her BMW had been packed with the goodies, and she'd drawn a little map for me, so there was nothing for it but to oblige.

Even so it took me ages to find the place. I was feeling so tense and self-conscious by the time I pulled up in our smart European car outside that funny, lopsided shack of a place that I was actually sweating. It was all too complicated. I got out of the car and went around to open the back door. I would drag in all this stuff and then clear off as quickly as I could. With a bit of luck no one would be there. *Fat chance with a dying woman in the house!* Still, I might be able to get away with leaving it all on the verandah.

I took the two boxes and made my way through the rusty back gate and down the path to the house. I almost groaned when I saw four people sitting in the shadow of the back verandah, watching my entrance. Jude, Annie, Declan and a boy of about seventeen, who I guessed was one of Carmel's brothers.

'Hi,' Jude called cheerily, pretending she wasn't surprised. 'What have you got there?' Then the back door opened and Carmel and her father walked out. I saw Carmel's mouth drop open as she registered who I was, then her whole face tightened as if some kind of internal clamp had been screwed into position. I turned to her father, who was squinting at me, trying to work out who I was.

'Well, hello there,' he said. 'Who have we got here?'

'Good afternoon,' I said. 'Katerina Armstrong ... er, these are from my mother ... she thought it might help ... just a few things. So sorry about your wife.' My voice died away. I caught sight of Carmel's face, that awful red flush rising quickly up her neck to her cheeks.

'We don't need anything,' she cut in hotly. 'Really! We've got tons of ... everything.' Her eyes were blazing, and she was standing near the door as though trying to block my path. But her father was walking towards me, past his outraged daughter, quite oblivious.

'That's very good of your mother, love. People are very good,' he said as he took the boxes from me. 'Come in now. Come in and see Nance. She likes to see whoever comes ... '

'Oh no!' I said drawing back, panicking at the very idea. 'No, really, I won't worry her. I just came to bring the things ... for my mother.'

But he was insisting, motioning for me to go in, holding the door open. I couldn't refuse. I walked past the others, past Carmel, who was glowering at her feet, and into the house. There was a small, dark, rather smelly lobby filled with boots and bags and other assorted stuff, and then through another door the kitchen. I looked around in amazement. What a mess! Everything seemed to be strewn about. Newspapers and boxes, tennis racquets, an overflowing basket of washing, used dishes, pots and pans. The place stank of food and boys. I'd never seen such a chaotic room. I couldn't imagine how a whole family, how anyone, might live there.

'This is Joe and Shane,' Carmel's father said, carefully settling the boxes on the one space he could find on a side bench. I turned around and saw two young boys playing cards on the floor under the window. More brothers. They looked up at me and then went back to their game. I smiled. They were lovely-looking kids. Huck Finns with grubby clothes, bare, scraped knees, and roughly cut hair. One of them had freckles along the bridge of his nose and the other had a couple of teeth missing.

'You must be the twins,' I said. 'Which is which?' They smiled and had another look at me.

'I'm Joe,' said the freckled one, peering up at me curiously. 'Who are you?'

'Katerina,' I said.

'And I'm Shane,' said the other. Then they grinned again, a little self-consciously this time, and went back to their game.

'Up this way.' Their father was signalling for me to come. I followed his slow-moving figure into a long dark hallway, a creeping feeling of dread stealing over me. *I've never been even close to a really sick person before.* I felt slightly ill. The knowledge that Carmel was out there wanting to stick a dagger through my ribs probably didn't help. He opened the door and beckoned me in.

The bedroom was small, but to my relief quite light. The soft winter sun was coming in though a large front window between the bare branches of a big deciduous tree outside. The first thing I saw was the mournful face of Jesus in a big square picture on the far wall opposite the bed – his eyes sombrely seeking my own as I moved into the room. Then I noticed the smell, not unpleasant, but sweet and musty, like the piles of rotting autumn leaves my father burnt every April. The woman, Carmel's mother, was lying up against a whole lot of multi-coloured pillows. She was dressed in a long-sleeved flannelette nightie and was very thin and yellow, with lank grey hair. But her eyes, when she looked up at me, were wonderful, sunken in their sockets, but gleaming a heavy navy blue, bordered with thick lashes that fanned out over her skin when she blinked, like small brushes.

'This is the Armstrong girl, Nance,' her husband explained gently. 'Her mother sent her over with a lot of stuff for us.' The woman's thin face broke into a smile.

'Well, that's good of you, love.' She patted the bed. 'Sit down and tell me your name.' I sat down tentatively on the pink satin cover.

'Katerina,' I said.

'Oh, of course!' She looked impatiently over at her husband. 'Neville! You know she lives with Carmel in town!'

'Oh yeah.' He shrugged, a little embarrassed. 'I forgot that. The other one's here and I get a bit confused.' The sick woman's face clouded momentarily.

'She's a little *Miss*, that one,' she grumbled tersely.

'You mean Jude?' I asked surprised. Mrs McCaffrey nodded sourly.

'She thinks she knows everything!'

'Oh, she's all right,' I found myself saying lightly. 'She's really quite nice underneath.'

'Is she now?' They were both looking at me with keen interest, as though I'd said something of great significance. I had no idea why they should have it in for Jude and be so willing to hear what I had to say.

'Oh yes, she'd do anything for you,' I went on, thinking how odd it was, me sticking up for one of them! 'She's got a heart of gold.'

'Well, is that so?' Mr McCaffrey asked thoughtfully. 'We thought she might be having a bad influence on our Carmel, didn't we, Nance?'

I opened my mouth, about to say something else, then thought better of it. What a funny pair! I watched them mulling over what I'd said.

'Well, I'll leave you two to have a yap,' Carmel's father said at last. His wife nodded and he walked out.

'So how do you feel?' I said, wanting to break the silence. I was immediately embarrassed. But she didn't seem to find my question ironic or to take offence.

'Oh, not too bad, love,' she said. 'The nurse comes out every day ... soon it will be twice a day. It's very good of your mother to think of me, send out those things ... it means a lot, you know.'

'Yes.' I felt a sudden rush of emotion. *How awful it must be to know you're going to die!* I turned my face away from her. *This poor woman, as if she'd want my tears!* Her thin dry hand reached out and patted my leg.

'Don't worry, love,' she said. 'I've been wanting to see you.' I looked at her in surprise as I pulled a hanky from my pocket and blew my nose.

'Really?'

'Yes,' she went on. 'Everyone said you were so pretty, much prettier than your sister. But I haven't seen you since you were about six or seven, so I couldn't pass judgement.'

'Really?' I laughed, pleased.

'And you are pretty, too,' she said firmly, patting my knee again. 'You're as pretty as everyone says.'

'Well, thank you.' It's hard to explain, but coming from this odd sick woman it was a real compliment.

'I wish Carmel would lose weight,' she said suddenly. 'She's a terror for eating the wrong things, isn't she?' I looked at her in surprise, cleared my throat and looked away. This was turning into a strange conversation. Did she want me to answer that? I honestly didn't know what to say. For a start, I had no idea of Carmel's eating habits.

'I don't mind dying,' she said, as though this was a natural follow-on from what we'd been talking about. 'There's no tragedy in dying. It's just the kids, you know, leaving them before they've grown up properly.' I nodded. Once again my eyes brimmed with tears. My gran had told me that her mother had died early, leaving her and her two sisters alone in the world.

'Yes. That must be the terrible part,' I said. 'They're lovely, those two young boys ... I, er ... haven't met the rest of them.'

'Oh yes. Joey and Shane.' She smiled and sighed. 'What about Carmel, though? How is she? Do you think she's happy down there?'

'Well ...' I said. 'I think so.'

'The city is so big ...'

'Well, I think she's doing okay ...'

'That's good,' she replied. 'I trust you, Katerina. I wouldn't know about that other girl. You live with Carmel. You should know ...'

I nodded stupidly and almost laughed. *Oh God, if only she knew how far off the mark she was!*

She began to move around uncomfortably in the bed, rearranging the pillows, sighing and closing her eyes a little as if she was exhausted.

'Is there something I can do for you?' I asked softly. She fell back against the pillows as though frustrated, and looked at the clock on her bedside table.

'No, love. It's time for my pills again, that's all.'

'Can I get them for you?'

'No, Nev will bring them in.' She leant across and picked up a small bell and shook it sharply a couple of times. 'Well, I'm so glad to have seen you at last, Katerina. I remember the day your Mum and Dad were married.'

'Really?' I said, intrigued.

'Oh yes.' Her face was alight with the memory, even as she began to twist her body about in distress. 'We all went down the church for a squiz. Your mother looked a picture! Princess Grace to a T. Everyone said so.' There was quick knock at the door and Mr McCaffrey came in with the pills and a glass of water on a green plastic tray.

'Here you are, love,' he said, settling the tray down and unscrewing the lid of a brown bottle of pills.

'Are the young people still out there?' she asked, as her scrawny hand took the pills and brought them clumsily to her mouth.

'Yes, love,' he answered, holding the glass of water to her lips. 'They're all still sitting out on the back verandah.'

'Nice for Carmel to have the company, isn't it?' she said, swallowing, and then relaxing back into the pillows. I got up to go.

'You thank your mother for me, won't you?' she whispered, grasping my hand in her thin cold one. 'Tell her I remember her wedding day like it was yesterday.'

'I will.' I squeezed her hand. 'I'll tell her.'

When I got out to the kitchen, two older boys were telling off the twins for not cleaning up after themselves. Their voices were loud, rough and good-natured.

'You're bloody hopeless, Joe.'

'Yeah, we're not your friggin' servants!' When they saw me they stopped and eyed me curiously.

'This is Anthony,' their father said, pointing to the older of the two boys. 'And Bernie.'

'Hello, Anthony. Hello, Bernie,' I said. The younger boy seemed less forbidding. The resemblance to Carmel wasn't as marked in these two. They were both tall and very dark. The older one was obviously very conscious of his bad acne, because he kept putting his hand up to his face in an attempt to hide it.

'Boys, this is your sister's friend, Katerina Armstrong,' their father said formally.

'We know who she is,' the younger one said sullenly. 'We live in this town.'

There was a short silence.

'How would you two like to come back to my house with me?' I asked the twins suddenly. 'I've got a swimming pool.' Their father smiled and shrugged to say he didn't mind.

'In this weather?' Anthony mocked.

'It's solar-heated,' I said cheerfully.

'Wow! The younger boys' eyes were dancing. 'Yeah! I want to!'

'It'll give them a break,' I said, looking at the older boys, 'and my guess is you all need a break from them, too?' They had the good grace to smile. 'And they can stay for dinner,' I went on, very pleased with myself.

'That'll be real nice,' their father said quietly. 'I haven't been able to do much for the kids, what with Mum being sick ... '

'Okay, guys, collect your things,' I said, turning to their father. 'I'll bring them back out after.'

'No need,' said a new male voice. I turned to find yet another brother! This must be the oldest one. Vince. He'd come in from outside and he had dirt and oil all over his hands and jeans. The only other garment he had on was an old V-necked jumper, also grimy with oil stains. No shirt or shoes. His face was tough and tanned and unsmiling. A lock of coppery curly hair, same as Carmel's, but with flecks of white dust in it, was falling over his forehead. He stood there, tall and straight, stern as a Roman centurion, muscles in his legs and arms pronounced beneath the rough clothing.

'I've got to go into town later,' he said. 'So I'll pick them up.'

'Okay,' I said.

'What? About six or seven?' he said walking through the room to the fridge. He took out the water container, opened it, took a swig, and then slammed the fridge door shut.

'Any time after seven,' I said. 'We'll have an early dinner. Do you know our house? It's up the ...'

'I know your house.' He wiped his mouth with the back of his hand and grinned, looking at me directly for the first time. 'It's that little cheapo number on the hill, isn't it? Tell your parents from me that they oughta get that joint fixed up. It's bringing down the general tone of the town ...'

I laughed, and felt a pleasurable heat rise to my cheeks.

Around me all the boys and their father were laughing too.

'I'll do that,' I said.

'Good on ya.'

Carmel walked me stiffly to the gate. Jude and the others had said goodbye and were watching us from the verandah. I had no idea if Carmel approved of my taking her two younger brothers off for the afternoon, but I figured that our relationship could hardly get any worse.

'Well, thank you,' she muttered, not looking at me.

'You're welcome,' I said demurely, and walked out to the car.

I look back on the afternoon that I spent with the two boys as another kind of start for me. Something simple and wonderful. First we turned on the solar heating. Then I made them milkshakes while we waited for the pool to heat up. They were so excited by everything, so pleased about getting away.

At the beginning I was a bit concerned because they seemed

to want to check out the whole house by themselves. I waited in the kitchen, listening as they walked from room to room, making awe-struck comments and noises.

'Oh wow! Get a load of this!'

'It's a stairway, Joe. See!'

'Her parents must be so rich.'

'How would you know which room to go to?'

But to my relief, after about the first five minutes they lost their sense of awe. We went into the garden and the conversation started to bubble up naturally again. Mum arrived back from her meeting, and not long after that Dad came home with Lou and Jean-Paul. Everyone was delighted that I'd invited the boys back.

'Very thoughtful of you, darling,' Mum whispered to me in the kitchen. 'They probably need cheering up.' *Of course, no one had any idea of what they were doing for me.*

Lou and Jean-Paul went to change and Dad asked the boys questions about school. What grade are you in? Do you have spelling tests? What's the capital of India? Silly stuff like that. But the boys answered very politely, and shared sneaky grins when his back eventually turned and he said he was going to read the paper.

Mum's answer is always to feed people up.

'How about another slice of cake, dear?'

'More biscuits, Shane?'

'Mum!' I said laughing. 'We're going to have a swim. Stop it or they'll sink!'

After about an hour they decided they couldn't wait any longer – the pool was barely warmer than frozen and my parents grumbled about them catching their death – but the boys simply pulled off their clothes and jumped in. They played like seals: squealing, panting, sliding about. They called out to each other, dive-bombed, let out wild yelps and whistles.

I could see my parents enjoyed the whole thing from behind the glass in the downstairs sunroom window.

'Come in, ya chicken!' Joe called to me through his missing front teeth. 'It's fantastic!' So I did. Me! Who would never have dreamed of swimming in cold water. I borrowed an old pair of Mum's bathers and dived in. They were rapt, swimming under water, pulling my legs from under me, dunking me and challenging me to races. I'd been a good diver at school and they were very impressed when I showed them my style and demonstrated a few points about the different dives.

'So keep your toes pointed and try to flip at the end ...'
'Grouse!'
'I can do that.'
'Watch me, Katerina!'
'Is this right?'
'Watch me!'
I hadn't had as much fun in ages.

Afterwards we all sat around outside on the patio and ate potatoes, sausages and slightly burnt chops. We were all rugged up against the cold. My mother had pulled out these old jumpers and coats from somewhere and insisted we wear them. We ate grinning at each other, and burst into raucous laughter when the sauce container Dad had been shaking and squeezing suddenly farted a heap of sauce over his whole plate.

'Oh my goodness me!' he exclaimed. The boys spluttered with glee, ate heartily and drank gallons of soft drink. Most of all, I think they reminded us — my parents and me, and Lou and Jean-Paul — what fun life could be at eight.

The talk ranged happily around their school, their family and the local football. I was surprised at how much my parents knew.

Their big brother was obviously the boys' prime source of information about most things.

'Vince says that Conroy can't play, 'cause ...'
'Vince knows ...'
'Vince had a job in the Kimberley. He reckons ...'

When he arrived to pick them up it was around seven and quite dark. I was sitting with the two boys up in my old treehouse explaining the games my sister and I had played up there with our old dog. I saw Vince and Dad walking slowly down the garden towards us, talking quietly. He was dressed in exactly the same way as he had been earlier, except for a pair of work boots on his feet. And for some reason I felt shy, a brand-new experience for me.

'How's it goin'?' He grinned up at us, stopping a couple of metres away.

'Good,' I said.

'Look at this, Vince!' Joe said, as he slithered down the old rope quick as a monkey, and landed at his brother's feet.

'And this!' Shane was down just as fast.

'Hmm ... not bad.' Vince patted him on the head and then looked up again at me. 'Your turn now.' I laughed. It was quite a long way down. I hadn't slithered down that rope since I was ten. I contemplated showing off, but I didn't risk it. Instead I edged back into the tree-house and came down gradually via the branches.

'Piker.' Joe teased me as I joined their small group. I tousled his hair and we began to walk back towards the house.

'Well, listen, thanks a lot.' Vince turned from my parents to me.

'That's fine. They were great,' I replied, unable to meet his shrewd look. *It's as though he's looking inside me, wanting to see what makes me tick.*

'No, it was good,' he insisted quietly. 'The kids needed a break.' I nodded to show I understood. Mum, Dad and I stood in a line and watched the three of them clamber into the beat-up old ute and slam the doors shut. Vince wound the window down.

'Give our warm regards to your mother, Vince,' my father called formally.

'I'll do that.'

'And your father, of course,' Mum added.

'Right. Well be seein' ya then,' he said, and started the engine. I ran around to his door. He looked surprised.

'Whenever I'm home next I'd like to take the boys out again ...'

'Okay,' he said, and grinned. 'But you don't come home often, do ya?' I shrugged, feeling an idiot.

'Well, whenever I am anyway ...' I said.

'That's great,' he said. 'Thanks again.' Then they were gone.

The phone was ringing when I went back inside the house. Thankfully the rest of the family were in the kitchen, so I was alone in the front room. It was Kara. She'd been searching for me all day. Had I gone into hiding? I knew something was up. I knew without her telling me. I just needed to know how bad it was. She'd seen my name in the *Herald Sun* that morning. Had I seen it? I couldn't speak. She wanted to know if I was all right. *Was I all right?* Yes, I guessed so. The article was very small, she assured me. No photos or anything. I wasn't to worry too much. My name was just there among a dozen others. Charged with possession of illegal drugs. They'd listed me as a first-year Melbourne University Law student who was to appear in court in two months. Kara wanted to know about Jules. No one had seen him for days. Had he been caught, too? Oh God! She wanted to know if my parents had heard anything. How was I going to keep it from them? What was I going to say when they did find out?

5

When Jude and I were dropped off at the house in Carlton on Sunday night it was after eight. We made ourselves some cheese on toast and settled down to eat it at the kitchen table. The weekend at home had given me more than fresh air. I felt renewed and more buoyant than I'd felt in months.

The doorbell rang and I guessed it would be one of Jude's friends because she winked at me and eagerly disappeared down the hallway. I hoped it would be Eduardo. She'd admitted in the car on the way back that she was mad about him, but couldn't tell if he really liked her.

I began to eat, feeling tired, going over the weekend and what I had in front of me. Somehow I'd have to try to steer my way through it all. Why should my parents ever have to hear about it? They never mixed with people who read the tabloids, they hardly ever watched television. Some in Manella would gossip, but I couldn't imagine those people ever getting near my parents.

Jude returned, her face tense with apology.

'I'm sorry,' she whispered. 'It's that guy ... Jordan. I didn't know if you wanted me to show him in or not.'

'That's okay.' I got up, my heart switching down into a lower gear.

He was waiting for me in the lounge room, sitting on the arm of a chair near the heater looking studiously morose. As soon as I saw him I simply wanted to run straight past him and out the front door. But Jude was banging things around in the kitchen behind me and it gave me a bit of confidence. I could tell she was reminding me that she was there and ready to support me.

'Hello, pet.' He stood up. *Pet? How dare you call me pet?* I stalled him by staying very still, not smiling and staring at him, trying to contain myself. He was dressed in linen as usual; black wide pants and a cream shirt, his full-length leather coat lying across the back of the lounge. My mind went hazy. Images and emotions dipped and swung about my head. Where had I met him? Who'd introduced me to him? How could I have been so naive?

I suddenly saw him from Jude's point of view. The gold ring in his ear, the soft pampered fleshiness of his bland handsome face, the chain around his throat. I shuddered as I noticed one of his hands tapping the back of the chair. More gold there. The ring and the heavy bracelet. My throat contracted into an awful dry retch. Our eyes met. Yes, he was a seriously handsome man. About thirty. He wasn't the sort to be dismissed by a schoolgirl.

'*Listen! I'm not going to put up with this schoolgirl bullshit!*' he'd yelled that day when I'd baulked at posing the way he wanted me to. When the session had finished at last – we'd reached a compromise on a shot that pleased neither of us – and I was pulling my jeans back on in his bathroom, deciding that I'd had enough, that I wouldn't get involved with anything like this again, the door had slowly opened. Without knocking.

'*Jordan please. You know I'm going with Conner . . .* '

'*He won't know,*' the voice slurred into my neck, '*we don't have to tell him.*'

'*But I don't want to.*'

'*Sure you do, honey.*'

'*No, I . . . please. I don't want to.*'

'*But what do you think we've been up to all morning?*'

Awful words. *What do you think we've been up to all morning?* We'd been taking photographs. At least that's what I'd thought was happening. Nothing else had been going on. Had it? But they were sexy photographs; he'd encouraged me to pout and loll about in the sexiest way I knew. And I'd enjoyed it. Had fun showing myself off. Felt the power of my own attractiveness. Had I had any right to say no when I'd been posing more or less naked for this man all morning?

Then the escalating panic as I felt him push me down onto the floor.

'No!' I said again quite loudly. 'Jordan. I'm saying no. *No!*' One heavy hand across my mouth to shut me up. Should I scream? Bite him? Fight? But it was a big apartment and there was no one else around.

The hard surfaces of the bathroom kept me quiet. I sobbed and swore, but basically shut up. I knew it would be easy to crack someone's head open against all that beautiful marble. I imagined the back of my skull splitting open and a pool of deep-red blood spreading out around my head, flowing across the shining floor.

'Hello,' I said. Jordan, slowly smiling, took a couple of loping strides towards me, like some awful predator. I turned my face away as he bent to kiss me. I could tell he smelt my fear.

'What are you here for?' I asked. He shrugged, pretending to be casual, easygoing.

'I've come to talk about you and . . . about the calendar,' he said.

'I've already told you I don't want it published,' I snapped. I could almost taste the bitterness in my mouth. The knowledge that I'd allowed myself to be taken in by this creep, to be tricked, cajoled, and used, sickened me to the core. The humiliation of knowing what a vain *sucker* I had been was the worst part of it all.

'Why don't you just go!' Jude said loudly from the doorway, her mouth half full of the apple she was eating. Jordan spun around in surprise. Jude was simply standing there, one foot resting against the wall, eating her apple and casually watching us. Jordan looked her up and down, took in the cropped hair and cheap, unfashionable clothes. She was so small, dark and defiant. A flood of love for her washed through me before I'd had a chance to think about it.

'I see,' he sneered, turning to me. 'So your little dyke mate knows all about it, does she?'

'I said, piss off!' Jude snarled aggressively. I gasped. I was so physically afraid of him myself that the idea of someone else not feeling the same seemed incredibly foolish. Also astonishing. I was about to tell her that he was dangerous, that she should be careful, when I saw that her brazenness had affected him too, put him off balance.

'All in good time,' he said. He pulled a form from his pocket and held it out to me, a silver pen in his other hand.

'I was hoping we'd be able to have a nice talk and sort a few personal things out,' he said, eyes lowered. There was a heavy moment before I heard my own voice.

'Like the rape?' I said calmly as I took the paper and made as if to read it. 'You've come to talk about that, have you?'

'And what proof do ...?'

'None,' I cut in coldly. 'None at all, because there was no one else there and I didn't get my head smashed in ...'

'Oh c'mon, girl, don't tell me you didn't want it.'

I looked up from the paper and stared at him. I swayed a little as I imagined plunging the silver pen straight into his heart like a sword. He looked away and I knew that he didn't believe what he'd just said. The weak bastard! It is one thing to do something terrible, quite another to lie to yourself about it.

'Okay, okay,' he said brusquely, crossing his arms over his chest as though he'd somehow understood what had been going through my mind. 'Let's get on to the formalities straight away. If you just put your name down there everything will be taken care of. You'll be paid and you won't have to worry about a thing. And, of course, your real name won't be used.'

But there'd been a shift of power in the room. I could see he'd felt it too. He was desperate for me to sign so he could get out. Rape is such an uncool word to say aloud.

'No,' I said firmly, handing back the form. 'I won't.'

'Katerina,' he pleaded, his eyes flickering sideways uncomfortably, 'I don't know what you're on about. They're very good photos. The boss is very pleased with them.'

'I've changed my mind,' I said.

'Those photos represent nearly two weeks of my time, baby,' he said, the menace returning to his voice. 'And I don't make a habit of working for nothing. You see,' he smiled at me as if I was a little girl who'd misunderstood something important, 'if this calendar doesn't go ahead, I don't get paid.'

'I don't care.' I was still staring into his face, holding my ground.

'Well, I do care,' he hissed.

'Consider it payment for what you took,' I said. 'What you took against my will.' His face reddened. A flicker of pure fury pulsed through his eyes and around his mouth. I was humiliating him. He was like a horrible spider pinned to a backboard, all eight legs floundering and protesting.

He folded the contract slowly and placed it in his coat pocket.

'So that's your last word is it?' he said softly.

'That's my last word.'

'Well, I don't think we can let such good pictures go to waste.' He smiled again, rancour and hatred all over his face, and waited for me to register. My heart pounded like mad, but I said nothing.

'I think I'll manage to find someone who'll be interested in them, now that your name is so well known.' He reached over and flicked my hair with one finger, laughing when I flinched. 'I take it you *have* seen your name in the paper today?'

'Yes,' I said feeling the blood rush to my face.

He laughed again before backing slowly out of the room. 'And it will be there again, baby, when your court case comes up. I'm sure there will be a lot of interest. Little Miss Law

School without her clothes on.' There was nothing I could say.

'We all have to live with our mistakes, sweetie,' he called. 'It's a shame you're not even going to be paid for yours!'

Jude and I stood together, listening to him open the front door, and then slam it as he left. I was shaking. His visit had transported me backwards into a nightmare, a tangled sticky nightmare. Would I ever escape?

'He's all bullshit, that guy,' Jude said gruffly.

'You think?' I said, my heart lifting.

'For sure.' She smiled at me. I was still standing in exactly the same spot as when he'd left. 'He's a nobody going nowhere. Don't even think about him.'

'Jude,' I said. 'What do you honestly think I should do?'

'Let's eat first,' she said. 'And then try and forget about him and everything else. Just concentrate on your work. All this stuff will blow over.'

'You really think so?'

'I'm sure of it.'

6

Jude was right in a way. There wasn't much I could do except try to forget everything and hope Jordan wouldn't follow through with his threats. Exams were in less than a month and if I was going to do well, I had a lot of work to do. Every time the phone rang that week my heart would race. I would hold my breath, expecting it to be my outraged family – Mum or Dad or Louise – livid and cold with anger, having heard of my misdeeds. But although it *was* often, the conversations were always pleasant and loving. Louise and Jean-Paul had decided to marry the following autumn. Only six months away. She asked me to be a bridesmaid alongside Elaine. Louise wanted the bridesmaids to wear deep russet red, but Mum thought that it was an appalling idea. She was adamant that something subtle – peach, pale apricot, or even lemon – would be far more suitable.

'After all, Lousie,' she called when Lou was on the phone trying to convince me, 'we don't want your sister to look like a *shop girl*!'

The invitations were to be sent out over Christmas. Would I come home soon and help them finalise the list? Already there was some bad feeling and a couple of noses out of joint because Auntie Jean had been told about the engagement before Gran. And when Uncle Jock heard that his Rolls wouldn't be needed on the day – Lou had decided that a fleet of new Mercedes would look better – he walked away from a family get-together in a huff.

If Jude was home after one of these phone conversations I'd run out and tell her the latest and we'd both fall about the room laughing. With just the two of us in the house together, we had begun to get along. We were both intent on our studies, so I suppose that helped. But every day it got a little easier. We had started to find out a bit more about each other. I'd let down my guard, stopped being so cool and aloof. And she had stopped dismissing me as a rich bimbo.

My name had not appeared in the paper again, so my family seemed even less likely to find out about everything. My court case was listed for early December, after the exams. I began to relax.

Of course I had to prepare for my court case, so the week after we returned from Manella, Anton and I went to meet the barrister who had been briefed on the case. It was embarrassing having to explain all the sordid details to her – she was so prim and proper – but Anton insisted that she should know everything, so I just took a deep breath and answered all her questions. We'd had to wait for about an hour before being shown into this incredibly plush office, about twenty storeys up and overlooking the city. The barrister, a woman in her fifties, was sitting behind an enormous polished desk in a silk shirt and square jacket. She stood up to greet us, but her stern, rather handsome face didn't move a centimetre towards a smile.

'So you admitted to the police that you had sometimes sold drugs to your friends?' she asked, incredulity practically dripping from her thin painted mouth as she read through the notes in front of her. I found myself wishing Anton had engaged someone else. Wasn't she meant to be on my side? Her manner made me feel like I was back in the police station.

'That's right.'

'Do you know exactly what you said?'

'Well ... just that sometimes my friends and I bought pills and sold them on to each other,' I replied in a small voice.

She sighed heavily and covered her eyes briefly with one hand.

'Oh, dear,' she muttered to herself in that flat voice again.

'If I could have a dollar for all the people whose lives have been ruined by this kind of business.' Her words chilled me. *Surely she doesn't think I've ruined my life!* I stared at her bowed head, waiting for her to look up and smile and tell me that luckily I wasn't one of them. But she remained engrossed in the notes in front of her, oblivious of me. I was not used to feeling so young and stupid.

'You must have had some idea that these drugs were illegal?' she went on tiredly.

'Well, yes, but, no ... I'd never really thought about it.'

'And you're studying Law?' she went on. I suddenly wanted to scream that it was all very well for her to be so superior. *Hadn't she ever been conned by anyone? Been enticed into a world that seemed really attractive?*

'Do you know what has happened to the supplier? Er ... your friend?'

'No,' I sighed. 'I haven't seen him. I went to his house once, but he wasn't in.'

'I'd advise you not to go to his house again,' she said quickly and severely. 'It would be far better for you to cut off all connection with him.'

'Really?'

'You're not out of the hot water yet, Katerina,' she said. 'Should the unthinkable happen and those ... er, photographs you mentioned be published, the press might smell a rat. Deals like this are not exactly above board, as you know. Your charge could just as easily change back to one of trafficking ... ' A shiver of fear passed through me. 'Which, as you know, could have very serious consequences indeed ... ' I nodded. 'Now I don't think that will happen,' she said. 'But I do have to let you know the possibilities. These things sometimes get ... well, out of hand. And it often depends on something as arbitrary as whether the newspapers have got enough interesting stories for that day or not.'

'I see.' I looked over to Anton, who was frowning and

listening intently. When he saw my face he smiled reassuringly.

'Let us assume that the charge will go ahead as possession of illegal drugs,' she said crisply. 'And that is the most likely scenario. Then ... '

She went on, asking more questions, taking notes then looked at her watch before putting her pen down carefully. I thought she was going to give me a final ticking off before telling us our time was up, but it was really just a summing up. 'Assuming everything remains as is,' she said, 'if we put in a guilty plea, I don't think we'll have too much trouble convincing a magistrate to put you on a good-behaviour bond. But ... ' I stared at her unsmiling face and wondered why I'd ever thought I'd like a career in the law. 'I hope it's obvious to you that you must keep your nose very clean until this court case is over.' I nodded, an unexpected wave of relief flowing through me.

'Of course,' I said meekly.

'Don't even speak to your drug-dealing friend,' she said. 'And you realise that you'll probably be asked to give evidence against him at some stage.'

'How do you mean?' The idea of having to give evidence against Jules was repugnant. There would surely be some way I could get out of doing that.

'Well, when they charge him,' she snapped.

'Oh yes. Of course.'

I must have looked worried because she suddenly smiled at me. It lit up her face and took about ten years off her age.

'I simply want you to understand the seriousness of your position, Katerina. Fifteen tablets could quite easily be converted into a charge of trafficking ... '

'I understand that,' I said. 'So what happens now?'

'Anton will brief me properly,' she said, 'and we should be in a position to make a strong plea for clemency by December.'

'Thank you.'

7

Jude had been in constant phone contact with Carmel. I had overheard bits and pieces of their conversations and occasionally asked Jude how things were going up there. Carmel's mother was steadily getting worse, although not as rapidly as had been first suggested by the doctors. The cancer had been diagnosed eight weeks ago, so she'd already outlived the worst scenario presented to her. All the kids were helping, but Carmel was doing most of the work; all the cooking and cleaning, as well as looking after her mother. She sometimes got frustrated and bored, and sometimes her mother drove her mad, but she knew she didn't want to be doing anything else, things being as they were. She was looking forward to Jude visiting after the exams, and wanted news about the band, the cafe and all the friends they shared.

'Do Carmel and her mother get on?' I asked.

'They're very different.' Jude shrugged. 'Carmel's mother is smart in that sharp way. She's practical and she knows everything. She doesn't recognise Carmel's talents ...'

'What are Carmel's talents?' I asked without thinking. 'Er ... I mean, apart from her music?' Jude just looked at me. I turned away, embarrassed.

'She's a fantastic person,' she said quietly.

'I guess so ...' I blundered. 'I guess I don't really know her.' I went to bed thinking about it. And wishing that there was someone in the world who would say that about me. *She's a fantastic person.*

A couple of times I tried to sound Jude out about Carmel's attitude towards me. Did she hate me? Did she really think that I'd organised Kara and Anton? But Jude obviously felt uncomfortable about relaying this kind of information, so she didn't say much. She just implied that Carmel had been deeply hurt by Anton and that she didn't want to speak to either of them about it. Ever.

I'd begun to lead a fairly lonely existence. I wasn't seeing any of my old crowd except Kara. Swot-vac had come around and I had decided it would be easier to stay near the university library to study than to go home to Manella. Perhaps it was more that I didn't want to go home to help organise my sister's wedding. The constant phone calls about it were enough. I thought I'd probably go crazy if I had to try to study in that kind of atmosphere.

It was Kara who found out that Jules had been arrested. Until then I'd become adept at putting him out of my mind. After heading around to his flat that day and not finding him home, I'd decided that he must have done a flit. He had friends in Sydney, so I told myself he'd gone up there after the bust to lie low for a while. I'd also persuaded myself to be annoyed that he hadn't contacted me. In my head I was trying to even up my betrayal of him with his lack of concern for me. To live with myself I had to find excuses. He had known I had had those pills on me. He'd given them to me! Why hadn't he called to see if I was all right?

It was a shock when Kara told me. Jules had been caught with a lot of drugs in his possession and had been charged with trafficking. He had been unable to supply the bail set by the court, so he was waiting in the remand centre for his trial. Kara said she'd heard that they'd been watching him for days and had closed in on him when he was dealing the stuff to teenage kids outside a community centre in Flemington.

I ached for him, knowing he must have taken a very fast social nose-dive over the past few weeks to be driven to that. He'd always had such a casual disdain for 'pushers'. *Oh, Jules.*

I couldn't forget him after that. Day and night he was there underneath all my thoughts. I needed to talk to him, find out what he was thinking. Perhaps I needed to confess. I don't know. I also felt terrible thinking that he was stuck down in the remand centre because he didn't have enough money for bail. Surely arranging that was the least I could do for him. I gingerly broached the subject with Anton. It would be five or ten thousand. Couldn't we organise it somehow? But Anton, so supportive of me, wasn't at all interested in Jules. And I didn't feel I could push it if he didn't want to.

So I swallowed my pride and rang up a couple of old boyfriends. Conner first. The conversation only lasted about two minutes. Two long, humiliating minutes. He hardly even remembered me, much less Jules. Who else could I call on? Glen. I knew he had plenty of money.

'Oh, sweetie, it's nice to hear from you. What have you been up to? Who? Oh really? No, I don't remember him. My spare cash is tied up at the moment. It's too bad, isn't it? Listen, pet, last time I saw Jordan he seemed a little *miffed* with you. What's going on?' I put the phone down and took a few deep breaths to calm myself.

Stuff the lawyer's advice. I decided to go and see Jules for myself. I applied to the authorities, went through all the necessary red tape, and received permission. I went down to the remand centre one cold Wednesday afternoon.

He smiled when he was shown through to the visitors' area and saw me waiting for him, pecked my cheek, and generally acted pleased that I'd come. We were shown out into the central recreation yard where there were some other groups of inmates and visitors and told we had three-quarters of an hour. He seemed a little thinner and paler, and his hair had been cut short, but otherwise he looked well.

I was dreading telling him. But I wanted to get it over with.
'Jules, I told them those drugs were yours . . . '
'Well, I thought you might have.' He shrugged and smiled.
'I tried not to. I didn't want to give you away, but they

threatened me. Said I wouldn't ever be able to be a lawyer if I didn't tell where they'd come from ... ' It all came bursting out in a flood.

'Don't worry, Queenie,' was all he said.

'You mean that?' I reached for his hand. He gave me a brief squeeze and then pulled away, folded both arms across his chest, and looked at his feet.

'Of course,' he said, 'I would have done the same.'

I felt more depressed than ever when he said that.

'Is it terrible here?'

'No ... well. You know. I get by ... '

We chatted about different things. He liked his lawyer. He was young and nice-looking and brought him cigarettes. He'd suggested that if Jules pleaded guilty he could reduce his sentence to only a few years. And Jules had agreed.

When there was a lull in the conversation he asked me about a few people, but when I said I'd dropped out from the scene he looked disappointed and didn't ask any more questions. In desperation I told him that I was trying to raise bail for him, but wasn't having much luck.

'Don't worry, honey. This time will be taken into account when I'm sentenced.'

'Oh, I see ... So do you want me to keep trying?'

'Not really.'

'What are the other ... guys ... in here like?' I whispered, wanting to reach him in some way before our time was up.

'It was a bit rough for a start,' he said, lighting a cigarette. 'But now ... I've met someone nice.' He flashed me a grin straight from the past – wild and carefree, the old Jules – but it disappeared before I had time to respond. 'So I'm basically left alone.'

I sensed that an important part of him wasn't even there. He answered my questions, smiled and even joked, but in a distant way, as if he'd already left the world – the world I knew anyway.

'Can I bring you anything?' I asked. 'Next time I come?'

Jules bent his face to my ear and put both arms around me in a tight embrace.

'Bring in some lollies, Queenie,' he whispered. 'Anything. Pack it into some book or the bottom of your shoe or bra or somewhere safe, eh? You're too classy to get pinched.' I nodded, thinking that my looks hadn't stopped me being pinched last time.

'I'll do my best, Jules,' I said, trying not to let his fake hug offend me.

'Good.' He smiled and left with the warder who was waiting for him. As I watched him go I tried to summon up a memory. Just one clear memory from all the good times we'd had. A smoke, a laugh, an admiring look. Where had they gone? Where did all our minutes, our hours, and our days go? He didn't turn at the door, didn't even hesitate, certainly didn't wave. He just disappeared inside and I was left feeling that I could have been anybody. Or nobody.

I walked out onto the city street and stood for a minute feeling as if I'd come across some new and strangely ominous landscape. Cars and semi-trailers and rattling trams lumbered past. So much noise and stink. People rushed out of office blocks towards the railway station, hopping off trams, across intersections, down subways. There for a minute and then gone. Yet there was a stillness all around me. A dead stillness. The lead-grey sky was suffocatingly close to my head. I felt as though it was closing in around me. And the concrete pushed up beneath my feet like bulging rock. There was something live and menacing in the gritty afternoon air. Jules *had* been my friend, hadn't he? Or had I just imagined it?

I felt I was moving back and forth on the brink of understanding something important, but each time I got close it eluded me at the last moment. The signs all around me, advertising beer and holidays and good times, cajoled and beckoned: come and laugh, throw off your shoes, gulp it down and widen your smile. *Life's a bitch and then you die.* I began to hurry, clutching my coat across my chest against the bitter wind, knowing that I would never go back to see Jules. Ever. Our friendship was over. It had been tried and found wanting. Like me.

See you in court, baby. They might as well have been my last words to him.

I walked for a long way. Probably for more than an hour. Then I caught a bus for the last few blocks, let myself in to the house, and threw off my damp coat. No one else was home and the house was dark and cold. I turned on all the lights and both heaters, trying to ward off my disappointment and loneliness.

All the way home I'd hoped like crazy that Jude would be there, that maybe we'd eat together and listen to music or whatever. I didn't want to be alone. But she'd left a note on the table saying she was down at the cafe, and to come down if I wanted to join her. I was grateful for the note – it showed how things had changed between us – but I had no desire to go out again. It was too cold. Besides, I had lots of work to do. I'd wasted the afternoon.

I tried to hit the books, but I couldn't settle so I gave up. I mooched around the house, trying to find something to distract me.

All the time I kept thinking of him: the wide trousers, the thin hands, the angel face. I wondered what he dreamed about inside that place. I wondered where he'd come from. Was he an only child? Where had he grown up? He'd mentioned his mother once, but the memory of what he'd said was vague. Something about her working in the post office in a country town. What was the name of the town? I couldn't remember. It was somewhere small, somewhere hours away. There'd been a soft pride in his face when he'd spoken about her. Edi. That was her name. Edi, short for Edith. I wondered if Edi knew where her son was.

Loneliness on a Saturday night is much worse than on any other night. At about ten I finally lay down on my bed. There were no messages on the machine or notes from anyone under the door. I'd had no invitations anywhere for about two weeks. I shut my eyes and thought of the small white block of coke wrapped in silver foil at the back of my drawer. It had been there on the periphery of my mind for the last couple of hours, waiting for its moment. The day before, when I'd been rummaging around for something, I had picked it up and felt completely uninterested; even thought about throwing it out. But I hadn't.

I jumped from the bed and fumbled through the debris in my drawer to find it.

The small mirror and the razor blade. The thin glass tube Glen had given me months ago sitting innocuously in a jar with my pens on my desk. I pulled them all together and with dull, precise movements began to chop the stuff up into a fine line of powder. My mind was on hold. I was thinking of nothing at all. When everything was ready I picked up the glass tube and began to snort.

I heard a key in the door, then muffled voices: Jude's and a man's. She poked her head around my door with a big smile. 'Hi, there. Still working?' I'd snorted up one half and was in the middle of the other.

Jude's face contracted. She walked in and sat down on the bed, looking at me. I was so used to seeing people snorting and smoking, even injecting stuff, that I'd forgotten about how serious it would look to someone who didn't have anything to do with it.

'What is that?' she asked.

'Oh, it's just coke,' I said sheepishly. I was high already.

'Why are you ... doing it?' she asked softly.

'Oh, Jude,' I said, flopping back into the easy chair in the corner. How could I organise my thoughts to answer that? I began to giggle. The room in front of me was becoming soft and blurry. My muscles relaxed. I was flying, dipping and soaring around the room.

'I'm not *addicted*,' this small, on-the-ground part of me said, looking at her seriously. 'Believe me. And don't worry, I can handle it. I just ... like it every now and again.' Her face was swaying in front of my eyes like a puppet's; behind her the door seemed to be swinging open and shut of its own accord. 'Honestly, Jude. You should try it some time. Very relaxing!' With that I broke into a fresh gust of laughter.

She nodded and walked out.

I woke, cold, lying on my bed, about four hours later. My jaw was chattering, my mouth was dry, and I had a headache. I sat up shivering, and tried to pull a blanket around me. I'd fallen asleep without even a jumper on. The chilly night air had numbed my limbs. I heard again what had probably woken me. Noisy love-making from the next room. Panting and laughing and bouncing bedsprings. I slipped off my shoes and lay back on the bed, listening. I wanted to be glad for her. Truly. She'd talked a little about Eduardo. I hoped it was him in her bed now.

But deep down I wasn't glad. I felt sick, and those lively sexy noises made me feel more than desperate. I put both hands over my ears, screwed myself into a foetal position under the covers, and groaned.

Later, when all was silent, I wandered down to the bathroom and got into the shower. My face in the mirror was pale and strained, a faint tinge of violet under my eyes. *I've become ugly, horrible. No one wants to know me. Be careful. No, no. It's just the coke. Everyone becomes paranoid on their way out.*

But I vowed to remember that image of myself, next time I felt like doing it.

8

The next morning Jude was alone in the kitchen eating toast when I surfaced.

'So did you have a good time last night?' I asked casually.

'Yep.' Jude took a sip of tea and sighed theatrically.

'You don't sound too sure,' I said, pouring myself a cup of tea.

'He's still involved with Rosa,' she said moodily, 'so I told him to beat it until he can decide.'

'Oh,' I said.

'I'm the jealous type,' she said grimacing. 'I can't stand the idea of him with anyone else.' I was about to say he'd sounded pretty decided last night, but there was a knock at the front door. We looked at each other warily.

'Are you expecting anyone?' Jude asked, getting up. I shook my head. I hadn't thought of Jordan for days now. But Sunday morning was a strange time for someone to call.

'Look through the keyhole, if it's Jordan, don't open it . . . ' I said.

'Of course not.'

Jude ran up the hallway, calling out for me to look after the toast.

She came back with Anton, who looked like death warmed up. He was dressed in jeans and an old jumper, a three-day beard on his face and his hair hanging in dishevelled blond knots around his face.

'Oh, hi,' I said brightly, coming forward to kiss him on the cheek. 'Have you been up all night or something?' He brushed my cheek with his own, slumped into a chair at the table and groaned darkly.

'So you had a great night last night, I take it?' Jude joked. 'You want a cup of something?'

'Got any coffee?'

'Sure.'

Anton swivelled around to face me. My mood did a quick nose-dive. I had a feeling he was going to say something awful. Perhaps he'd heard about me going to see Jules in the remand centre. Oh God! A lecture was the last thing I needed.

'Have you spoken to Carmel?' he asked grimly.

'No,' I said, then looked at Jude, who had her back to us. 'Ask Jude, she talks to her all the time.' The high-pitched grinding noise suddenly erupted. Nobody said anything until Jude was pouring water over the ground coffee in the pot.

'She won't talk to me!' Anton blurted out. He stared at Jude and then at me, a picture of pained confusion. 'She won't even say *why*,' he went on, thumping the table with both palms. 'I've just been up there and she wouldn't even let me in the house.'

'To Manella?' I asked in surprise. He nodded.

'Went all the way up there and she told me to go! Doesn't want to see me any more. What can I do . . . ?'

'Do you know why?' Jude said. Anton slumped down a further few notches in his chair and shook his head.

'No, I don't,' he said mournfully. 'That's just it. I have no . . . idea.'

Jude gave me a swift, sharp look and began to pour out the coffee.

'She saw you and Kara sleeping together,' Jude said bluntly.

'*What?*' Anton sprang up in his chair like a jack-in-the-box.

'She *saw* you,' Jude continued, 'the night before your birthday. She went around with a present. Snuck up the passage to surprise you and found you with Kara.'

'Oh, jeeze!' he groaned.

'She wanted to kill you,' Jude went on ruthlessly. 'So I went with her and we threw that brick through your window.' Anton was looking at Jude aghast.

'You're joking!' he whispered, turning from Jude to me and then back to Jude again.

'You're joking,' he said again.

Jude and I looked at each other and then at Anton. Jude shrugged.

'Sorry, but ... it's true.'

I don't know quite why or how, but we all started to laugh at exactly the same time. It was one of those magical moments. Anton got up from his chair and slumped against the bathroom door, pointing at Jude every now and again and shaking with silent laughter. Jude and I sat at the table spluttering into our cups, unable to stop. Then Anton began to walk around the kitchen, picking things up and putting them down randomly, sighing and saying 'I see ... I see ... now I understand ...' and then breaking out into fresh snorts of laughter.

'Shut up!' Jude yelled and threw an old wet dishcloth at his head. He rushed over, grabbed her by the shoulders, and shook her, still roaring with laughter.

'You're a pest, Jude! A bloody ... pest. There should be a law against you!' he yelled.

'It wasn't my idea,' Jude protested. 'Ask Carmel! Anyway, what would you know? You bloody wanker!'

It was great to have a laugh. When we eventually stopped we were lying around on the lounge-room floor, the heater blazing, throwing insults at each other.

'You've got the morals of a diseased rat!'

'Bloody cockroach politician!'

'You should talk.'

'You both stink!'

'Shut up, Katerina, or we'll cover you in tar and cut all your hair off!'

'I'll cut your dick off!'

After a while all of that petered out and we were silent for some time.

'I really love Carmel, you know,' Anton said softly. He was lying on his back, arms crossed over his chest, eyes closed.

I could see he was genuinely cut up at the idea of losing her.

'I mean *really* . . .' he said, half sitting up to look at us both, making sure we both understood he was serious. 'Sleeping with Kara meant *nothing*.' He turned towards me apologetically. 'No offence, Katerina. I mean she's your friend and everything, but . . . *it was nothing.*'

'Well, tell Carmel that,' Jude said impatiently. 'It's no use telling us.'

He sighed and lay down on the floor again.

'She doesn't want to know me, so what do I do?'

Jude got up and went to the CD player.

'Do something *big*,' she said, looking down at us. 'Something wild and grand to prove it.' A fast South American dance tune suddenly blasted through the room.

'Like what?' Anton shouted above the music, looking over at her hopefully.

'I don't know,' Jude shrugged. 'But something big. Hire a plane. Write her a message in the sky. I don't know. The right thing will just occur to you.'

Anton and I looked at each other and rolled our eyes. Jude was being . . . *Jude*. As crazy as usual.

'I mean, I want to be there,' Anton said miserably. 'I want to help with her mother and everything.'

'Then you have to prove it,' Jude insisted. She turned to me. 'Both of you,' she said. 'You've both got to prove it.'

I nodded. Bloody Jude. *How come she knows everything?*

9

Jude and I had both almost finished our exams when the phone call came from Carmel, about seven one morning. We were both up, showered, and drinking cups of tea. Jude answered and I could tell from her face that it was serious. She spoke quietly into the phone, told Carmel she'd be there as soon as she could, then said goodbye.

Jude put the receiver down slowly and turned to me.

'Her mother's dying now. She's losing consciousness ...' she said quietly.

'Are you going up there?' I asked.

'Yeah,' Jude nodded and then sighed in exasperation. 'But the train leaves at four and my exam doesn't finish until a quarter to ... so I'll have to wait till tomorrow ... If only I could bloody drive!'

'But you haven't got a car,' I said.

'I know Eduardo would lend me his.'

'If you can get it, I'll drive you,' I said quickly. 'My last exam is this morning.' Jude's face broke into a warm smile.

'Would you?'

'Sure. I'd like to go anyway ...' I hesitated. 'Maybe I could help, take the younger boys out for a while. Maybe I could do something ... I don't know.' Jude's hands both suddenly darted towards mine. She held them momentarily and then squeezed them.

'You're all right, Katerina,' she said. 'You know that?' I smiled and looked away, pleased by her impulsive gesture.

'So what time shall we leave?' I asked.

'Say about five. I'll just go and ring Eduardo and ask him

about the car. I'd better call Mum and everyone too.'

'Don't be too long, because I'll have to ring my parents, too, and tell them I'll be home.'

But when it was my turn, I couldn't get through. The answering machine was on, so I left a message.

'*Mum, Dad. It's Katerina. I'm coming home tonight. Don't worry if you're going out. Just leave the side door open. You've probably heard, Mrs McCaffrey's got very bad. Anyway, see you tonight . . . Bye till then.*' I thought warmly of my last visit, and about riding Tessy again and maybe taking the twins out. I picked up my bags and shouted goodbye and good luck to Jude, who was sitting a physiology exam that afternoon.

'I hope you do well, too,' she yelled up the street after me. 'What is it?'

'Common law,' I said and made a face. It was my least favourite subject, but I'd studied hard and expected to do okay.

We were both tired by the time we set out in Eduardo's beat-up little car. Jude's exam had gone well, but she still had one more to do the following week. All mine were over, so although I felt apprehensive about what we were driving towards, I also felt relieved. I knew I'd passed, possibly even done quite well. And that was satisfying. Actually I couldn't help feeling really good. *In spite of all the rubbish I got involved with, I'm not a porn star or a drug addict . . . instead I'm on my way to becoming a qualified lawyer!* We didn't talk that much on the four-hour trip, but we were easy enough together. We played some music and then Jude fell asleep for a while. I didn't mind. I quite liked the silence of the country road. I knew my way around those hills and gullies well.

When we reached the last part of the journey, the funny little winding track leading up to the McCaffreys' house, Jude woke up.

'What if the family doesn't want us?' she said nervously. 'They might want to keep this very private.' I nodded, suddenly worried. I'd been thinking along those lines myself while Jude had been sleeping.

'But Carmel wanted you to come, didn't she?' I said in a small voice.

'Yeah, but ... there's all her brothers and her father. They mightn't want me here at this time. I should have checked.' I'd never heard Jude sound so unsure before.

'Well, you'll just have to come back to my parents' house then,' I said with false heartiness. 'We'll call in and say hello, and if it's not okay for you to stay, we'll leave quickly.'

'Okay,' she said.

I wondered if it might be better for me not even to show my face at the McCaffreys'. I was probably the last person Carmel wanted to see.

'Do you think I should just drop you and head off without even coming in?' I asked Jude, hoping she'd say yes.

'Then how would I get back into town if I need to?' she replied impatiently. 'If they don't want me there?'

'Oh, yeah.' I pulled the car up and turned off the engine.

'Here we go,' Jude groaned, opening the door.

Neither of us was prepared for the atmosphere of the McCaffrey household. It wasn't as if the boys and their father didn't greet us warmly. They all seemed glad to see us and that made us both feel better. They told us that Carmel was sitting up with her mother in the bedroom, but she'd heard our car and would be out soon. The twins each gave me a grin, as though challenging me to remember the fun we'd had last time. Mr McCaffrey sat us down at the table and brought in fresh tea and some cake.

'Come on now, girls. Eat up. You've had a long trip,' he said, trying to sound hearty.

But they all very quickly slipped back into a quiet sadness, which seemed to pervade the house. Everyone was waiting.

So different from the last time I'd been there. Each boy seemed to be sitting alone with his thoughts. Yet the conversation kept going in a slow, desultory way, which was probably a kind of comfort to them all.

'Did you get the washing in, Vince?'

'Yep,' he said, with a smile, 'before the rain, too.' He looked across at me. 'How long did it take you?'

'About four hours.'

'The last five kilometres is hard if you don't know the road, isn't it?'

Every now and again, when the conversation dipped away from Mr McCaffrey, I saw him sort of get lost in the room, his light-blue eyes looking into space, occasionally glistening with tears. His face worn with the waiting.

When Carmel came into the room she looked strained and tired. But her face broke into a wide smile when she caught sight of Jude. They hugged each other and stood in the middle of the room, half crying and half laughing, all the boys looking on, curious and a little embarrassed.

'It's so good to see you!'

'And you, Carmeloo.'

'The exams. How did you go?

'Fine, fine.'

As I stood waiting to greet Carmel, I felt all over again that it was wrong for me to be there. That I shouldn't have come. But Carmel greeted me warmly, too.

'And Katerina,' she whispered shyly, taking my hand for a moment. 'Thanks for bringing Jude, and for coming yourself ... ' I gulped and looked away, overwhelmed by her generosity.

'That's fine,' I managed to say stiffly. 'I was glad to.'

Carmel asked if we'd like to go and see her mother, explaining that the doctor would be coming soon and also the priest to give her the last rites. Neither of us knew what to say or what to expect, but we both nodded and followed Carmel up to the bedroom. The others, who'd been spending time with their mother in shifts all day, stayed with their father in the kitchen.

'She's been drifting in and out of consciousness for over twelve hours now,' Carmel explained as she ushered us into the room. 'The doctor was out this afternoon and he doesn't think she'll make it through tonight.'

The same musty smell I'd noticed last time was now even stronger, overriding the smell of perfume and soup. I stared down at the tiny figure in the bed and was overcome with how cruel it was. In six weeks she'd become as tiny and fragile as a sparrow, the narrow bones in her chest showing through her cotton nightie, virtually no hint of a breast now. Her yellow skin was drawn taut across her face. She was lying almost flat, except for a thin pillow under her head, her eyes closed, breathing heavily and unevenly. Carmel picked up her hand.

'Mum,' she said quite loudly, leaning down into her face. 'Jude and Katerina have arrived to see you. Isn't that good?' Mrs McCaffrey seemed to stir and frown a little, almost as though she understood. The other hand lifted about twenty centimetres from the bed, fluttered slightly and then subsided. Her eyes, with the wonderful thick lashes, remained closed. The sound of her laboured breathing was terrible. The spaces between each breath seemed to grow. I felt myself beginning to panic, waiting for each breath. Would this one be her last? Or this next one? Such an effort just to breathe!

The twins tiptoed their way in behind us.

'Will you blokes stay here and look after Mummy?' Carmel said to them. 'I'll just go out to the kitchen with Jude and Katerina. They want to finish their tea.'

The boys jumped onto the bed, either side of their mother, and lay, heads propped up on their elbows, looking at each other over their mother's unconscious body, as though they were about to watch a movie on TV.

I was washing up the cups at the sink when Carmel came up behind me with a few more dishes.

'Do you mind doing these?'

'Of course not.' I took them, glad to be of help. The doctor had just left after giving Mrs McCaffrey another shot of morphine, and the priest had just arrived. The whole family was going to be present for the last rites. I'd said my goodbyes, having decided to leave before the ceremony began.

'Do you want to come in, Katerina?' Carmel said.

'No ... it's getting late. I'd better go now,' I said, wiping the cups.

'Well, thanks so much for coming and bringing Jude ... ' I looked at her and, without warning, began to cry. She put an arm around me.

'Carmel, I'm so sorry,' I said through bitter tears. 'For everything!'

'It's okay,' she said. 'It doesn't matter. None of it matters.' We stood apart looking at each other, me trying to smile through my tears. A mischievous twitch began around the corners of Carmel's mouth.

'So you've got Eduardo's car?' she suddenly said. I nodded.

'Does that mean he and Jude are on together?' she asked.

'I can't work that out,' I smiled. 'And I don't think Jude can either!'

Someone was calling her from another room. She looked at me and patted my arm.

'Well, tell us all about it next time,' she said. 'I want juicy details! Jude is being super-evasive!'

'Okay, I will,' I said. 'Bye now, Carmel. I hope ... your mother ... ' *What could I possibly hope for her mother?*

'Oh, I know. I know,' she said gently. 'See you soon, eh?'

Mr McCaffrey and Vince came out and insisted on seeing me to the car, both their faces knotted up gravely.

'Well, I hope you both get a bit of rest tonight,' I said, shaking their hands quickly and getting into the car.

'I don't think she'll make it through the night, love,' Mr McCaffrey said quietly. 'Thanks for coming.'

'That's fine, really,' I stammered. I'd done nothing, but people kept thanking me.

'Say hello to your Mum and Dad, too,' he called, lifting his arm to wave.

'I will. I will.'

10

As soon as I walked into the room and saw them standing around waiting for me I just knew. My father was standing by the fire, his face ashen, his mouth a straight line. My mother stood behind the velvet fireside chair to the right of him, her hands fiddling nervously with the tassels along the back. I stood still, locked in their gaze, not knowing what to say. I was shocked to see how old and careworn my mother had become. Her face looked like any other smartly made-up older woman's face, lined and wrinkled, not beautiful at all. I was so used to seeing my mother as special, beautiful.

They both looked exhausted.

My father turned around and picked up a thick tabloid newspaper from the mantelpiece. He opened it and flipped through a few pages.

'We received this yesterday,' he said coldly, holding it out for me to take with trembling hands, 'but apparently it came out last weekend.' I took the paper from him, outwardly calm. But inside I was a fridge. There it was, a half-page picture of me frolicking at the beach, naked except for a G-string. It was a shot that Jordan had particularly liked because my body was twisted in such a way that practically all my bum was exposed and one whole breast. I looked very sultry and provocative, the sea visible through my spread legs. The headline was 'Uni Student Caught in Gay Bust'. I didn't raise my eyes until I'd read the whole article. It took ages because my blood felt frozen and everything around me had slowed down. The article actually wasn't all that incriminating. It described me as a law student and 'part-time model' who'd been charged with possession of drugs, and said that if readers wanted to 'see more of sexy Katerina' they should look out for a hot calendar that would be coming out the following summer. Jordan had done a job on me all right. A nasty, vindictive job. But it could so easily have been worse. There was nothing about how many drugs I'd been found with, or what I *could* have been charged with. Nothing about Jules. It was one of those stupid articles that would be forgotten the next day.

After what seemed like years, I got to the end of it.

I looked up at my parents. I wasn't crying. I hardly felt anything at all.

'Who sent you this?' I said at last.

'It's a newspaper!' he snapped. 'Published for everyone to see. Don't tell me you don't understand that!'

'I know that,' I said, 'but neither of you buy this kind of paper. Who gave it to you?'

'What does it matter?'

'I'd like to know.'

I was shaking. I was sure that Jordan didn't know where my parents lived. I'd told him nothing about them. I closed my eyes and prayed silently that they'd tell me it was some nosyparker from Manella. That some workman with a grudge against Dad had dropped it outside their door to humiliate him. I could live with that. My father handed me a yellow envelope. There were five more copies inside and a note from Jules, scrawled on a piece of blue prison paper. *Thought you wouldn't want to miss your daughter in this!* I stared at the note and tried to understand. I hadn't been back to see him in weeks. He must have decided to punish me in the only way he knew how. The only way open to him. Shit! I felt as if I'd been stabbed.

'What have we done to deserve this?' My father spoke softly.

I wanted to say something. Not really to justify myself, just to say something.

'You've broken your father's heart, Katerina,' my mother

said, 'and Louise's. She's absolutely devastated. She came up today, but left because she couldn't face you. She doesn't want to go ahead with the wedding. You've humiliated her so badly.'

'I've humiliated *her*!' I said. 'Funny, I wouldn't have thought ...'

'Of course you have!' my father shouted.

'How? What's she got to do with this?' I shouted back. 'Or is it that she's got everything to do with most things ... for you! I'm sick of Louise. Sick of her!'

They just looked at me. Of course it was just tactics on my part. They didn't have to explain. Of course I'd humiliated Louise. Because in a family like mine so much goes *unsaid*. So much is just assumed. They just *assumed* I wouldn't get into something as crude as the drug scene. They just *assumed* I wouldn't think of flashing my body all over a pathetic newspaper like that. After all, they'd spent all that money on my education. I'd had the best of everything. Why would I?

I sighed, not knowing what I could possibly say.

'Your sister had all the invitations written,' my mother said accusingly, a sob threatening to spill out into her voice. 'The caterers had been booked. She'd even ordered the material for your dresses ... and now. She can't go through with it now!'

What colour? I wanted to ask. *Did you decide on the russet pink or the pale apricot? Oh God! I'm sorry, Mum.*

'And what about you, Mum?' I said. 'Have I ... broken your heart, too?'

I didn't mean to sound like that. Not at all. I was shocked, I suppose, and sorry to have caused them such pain. But I was also filled with irritation at the way she stood there, *behind* my father, as if she had no thoughts of her own. I don't ever want to be like that. And I don't want to have to live behind Louise all my life. She winced and stared back at me in shock.

'Of course you've hurt your mother,' my father said furiously. 'You've hurt and humiliated us all.'

'Please,' I said in a small voice. 'I want to explain ...'

'Explain!' he yelled. 'I don't really want to hear why my daughter has behaved like a common little tramp!'

'Then I'll go.' I moved towards my bag on the couch.

My mother gave a small cry of protest and took a couple of steps towards me.

'Oh no, Katerina,' she said. 'Don't go. I want to hear ...'

'Well, I *don't* want to hear,' my father cut her off.

'Albert ...' she whispered, putting a hand on his elbow. 'I don't think we can ...' He brushed her aside.

'Leave!' he shouted at me. 'Go back to those degenerates ...! Those people you obviously like mixing with ... I want no more to do with you.'

'Katerina is my daughter. I want to talk to her ...' my mother said. She didn't often speak up, so we both looked over at her in surprise.

'*Talk!*' my father shouted, throwing both hands up and walking to the far end of the room. 'Talk!' He pushed the piano lid down savagely, making a loud discordant sound. His face had turned a very unhealthy shade of purple. 'What is there to *talk* about?'

Mum and I stared at each other. *What is going on inside her? Why doesn't she walk across the room and grab me? Even hit me? I wouldn't mind. Don't just stand there, Mum. Please.*

I picked up the bag I'd thrown onto the couch and walked out. They both stayed rooted to their spots in the lounge room.

I went out the front, towards the steps that led down to Eduardo's little car. At the top of the steps I turned. The curtains hadn't been drawn, and I could see through the window into the lounge room. They were both standing in exactly the same poses as when I'd left. Rigid as a couple of store dummies. My father with one hand on the shiny piano, my mother next to the chair, each looking in the opposite direction.

I began to cry as I drove the car down the hill. By the time I had it on the main road back to Melbourne, about four kilometres from Manella, I was sobbing. There wasn't much traffic, but every now and again I would be dazzled by the oncoming lights of a car travelling fast in the opposite direction. I honestly didn't care what happened to me, but Jude had told me that the little car was Eduardo's pride and joy. *It wouldn't be fair to wreck it.* So I pulled over to the side of the road and sat crying for about ten minutes. Then I pulled fresh tissues out of my bag, dried my eyes, turned the car around, and drove back into Manella.

It was an odd feeling passing the turn-off to our house, wondering when, if ever, I would turn the steering wheel right and head up that road again. Would I ever be welcomed back into the house I'd always assumed was mine?

My father never spoke lightly. He prided himself on being a reasonable man. That lovely place on the hill, all its lights blazing. I felt sliced through, as though my body had been physically damaged. I was floundering around in the cold now. Alone. I felt like a newborn baby. Out in the cold air, torn away from the warmth, the ease, of the perfect bath. *Would my parents still be standing where I'd left them?*

I went on, out to the McCaffrey farm. There didn't seem to be anywhere else I could go.

11

Nance McCaffrey lasted through the night. Everyone took turns to sit with her. Even me. Sometimes there were ten of us in that little room, all these bodies draped around the floor, on chairs and the bed: her sons, her husband, Carmel, Jude, me. All in various stages of exhaustion, talking quietly to each other, and listening to her rasping breath fill the room. It was amazing to see that dying was actually this very practical, down-to-earth business.

Carmel and Vince did most of the nursing, positioning pillows, lifting up the frail body for sips of water, wiping her brow. The doctor had left at midnight and said he'd be back again at seven in the morning. The boys had pulled a fold-up bed and a little couch into the bedroom, and we all arranged ourselves wherever we could. At various times during the night, Carmel and her brothers went out to sleep for a while in the lounge room. But no one stayed out there long.

Mrs McCaffrey was unconscious most of the time, her breathing heavy and uneven. But a couple of times during the night she woke, whispered the names of her children, and held out her hands for her boys. The older ones would come forward and hold her hands tenderly, whispering.

'It's me, Mum. Anthony.'

'It's Vince, Mum. Your troublemaker.' The fleeting smile on her mouth told us she'd heard him.

Their gentleness was painfully moving. I hardly spoke at all because my throat seemed to be permanently constricted. I think I was in a state of shock, shot through with a sense of unreality. But then I don't think anyone else there was operating on a normal plane either. That night was somehow quite outside ordinary experience.

'Here I am, Mum. Bernie ...'

'Mum. Mum, it's Gavan ...'

'And where are the twins?' she would ask fretfully, 'You've got to look after them ...'

'They're here.'

The twins crawled onto the bed on either side of her, which seemed to comfort her. She muttered a few incoherent things to them and then fell back into sleep or unconsciousness, her tiny, claw-like hands resting on their heads.

When they weren't lying next to their mother, the younger boys seemed drawn to me. They would sneak up to me, and I would casually throw an arm around each of them, as though it was the most natural thing in the world. They would edge in nearer and eventually slump asleep against my shoulder.

'You're good with them,' Carmel said softly. 'They like you a lot.' I nodded, pleased, but unable to utter a word.

I saw the morning come in through the window. A pink sky at first, and then pale light streaming into the room like gold dust. I was surrounded by people breathing evenly, the only one awake in the room. The life force of the woman on the bed seemed to be beating about the room like a huge, injured bird. During the night I had almost felt the shadow of her wings over me at times, awkward and troubled, looking for release. I watched the light get stronger, and when I saw that it was shining straight into her face I gently loosened my hold on the twins and got up to pull the curtain across.

'Have I told you that you look like your mother?' came a clear whisper behind me. I turned, startled, clasped her cold hands, so pleased that she knew who I was. With me gone the twins had moved back in beside her, half asleep. I covered them with a blanket; their fresh, troubled little faces pressed into their mother's side. I was filled with outrage. *She couldn't die. It wasn't fair!*

'Where's my Carmel?' she suddenly said quite loudly, her eyes wide open and darting about, looking at me in distress. 'Get me Carmel and Vince ... and the other boys!' She had begun to gasp and twist around where she lay, half sobbing, her hands clawing and punching at the air in front of her as though she wanted to sit up.

'My Carmel ... and my little ones! Get them. I need to ...'

'The twins are right here, Nance,' I said, distressed myself. 'Please don't worry, the twins are right here.'

I hurried out to the kitchen where Carmel, Jude, Vince and a couple of the other boys were lying around, half asleep.

'She wants you,' I said. They woke quickly and followed me back down to the bedroom. Carmel went to her mother. Jude and I held back near the door, unsure if we should be there. Somehow, because it was now morning, it seemed more appropriate just for the family to be around her. But Mr McCaffrey, who'd been sitting in the same spot all night, sleeping most of the time, was adamant.

'Come in, girls.' He waved from the other side of his wife's bed. 'Come on in, now. You're welcome.'

Jude and I moved tentatively back into the room.

'I'm here, Mum,' Carmel said. 'It's me. I'm here.'

Her mother settled a little.

'Are you in pain?' Carmel asked, looking up at Vince for some clue as to what was the matter. He glanced at his watch.

'The doctor will be here soon,' he whispered. 'Give her another shot.' Mrs McCaffrey began to heave around the bed again, her eyes jerking from one person to another, only half focused.

'Sing for me, Carmel,' she said in a loud, hoarse voice. 'Sing.'

Jude and I saw Carmel gulp in surprise.

'What would you like me to sing?' she asked. But her mother had resumed her slow breathing, her eyes closed again.

Carmel began to sing an old hymn. It had a nice melody, but the words were sad. Full of longing. She sang softly, sitting on her mother's bed, holding her hand. But she had only got through the first couple of lines when her mother became agitated again.

'Not that!' Mrs McCaffrey managed to say. 'Not all that old stuff!'

Carmel stopped singing in surprise, then looked up at Jude and me.

'Sing one of your new songs, Carmel,' her mother cried in a pained whisper. 'Like when you were on telly ... '

'A Spanish song?'

'Yes. The one you sang on telly.'

Everyone began to quietly laugh.

Jude disappeared and came back with the guitar. Carmel patted her mother's bed, but Jude was reluctant.

'No!' she whispered, trying to make Carmel take the guitar. 'She wants you.'

'*Play*, Jude,' Carmel ordered. 'Come on! And I'll sing.' Jude nodded, and with eyes downcast she began to pick out some notes.

'This one is about poor people in Chile,' Carmel explained. 'They have no houses, so they squat on disused land. Once the police came to clear them away and shot a little girl ... by mistake.' Carmel looked at Jude anxiously. 'That's right, isn't it?'

'Yep,' Jude said, without looking up.

'Sing it, Carmel,' her mother said crossly, beginning to toss her head again from side to side, 'I want to hear you sing.'

Carmel opened her mouth and began the song. Of course the rest of us didn't understand a word, but it sounded good anyway. Very plaintive and sad. When it was over, Mrs McCaffrey turned to her husband with a faint smile. 'We were lucky, Nev,' she said. 'We had the land, didn't we? Not much else, but we had the land, didn't we?' He leant over and touched her face with his hand.

'That's right, love, we've been lucky,' he said softly.

Carmel and Jude went on singing more songs in Spanish for

about an hour, until it was clearly morning outside. Mrs McCaffrey seemed to love one of these, because she opened her eyes when they'd sung it through once, asked Jude what the words meant, and then demanded that they sing it again.

Sigamos cantando juntos
atoda las humanidad
que el canto es una paloma
que vuela para alcanzar lejos
estalla y abre sus alas
para volar y volar ...

Let us continue to sing together
To all of humanity
For a song is a dove
Which flies to reach afar
Exploding and spreading its wings
To fly and fly ...

Jude translated the words of the first verse and then they both sang that part through together. Between each verse Jude continued to play guitar, stopping to translate the next few lines to come. I suppose, because we knew what this one was about, it was very moving.

My song is a free song
Which wants to give itself
To anyone who wants to hold out a hand
For anyone who wants to soar ...

At the end of the song, Mrs McCaffrey reached for Carmel's hand.

'I like that song, Carmel. Will you sing it again for me?'

'Of course, Mum,' Carmel said gently. She looked at Jude and they smiled and played it a third time.

For most of the time Carmel's mother lay quiet, listening

and peaceful, a faint smile of enjoyment on her face. But after an hour she became distressed again, so they stopped singing and put the guitar away. Very soon after that she slipped back into unconsciousness, resuming the deep, erratic breathing of before.

A car pulled up out the front of the house and we all looked up when we heard the door slam and footsteps coming towards the house.

'That will be the doctor,' Carmel's father said dully. 'What about a few of you getting some breakfast going?' Jude and I immediately volunteered. But Bernie and Gavan got up, too.

'I'll come and show you where everything is,' Bernie said. 'Need to stretch me legs.' We followed them out to the kitchen, passing the grave-faced doctor on his way in.

The little boys were still lying next to their mother on the bed, and Carmel, Vince, Anthony and their father stayed in the room to speak with the doctor.

I spent the next couple of hours cooking and cleaning. The doctor left, and the priest came again, and then the nurse. Jude and I managed to produce enough toast and eggs for everyone. When breakfast was over, the whole family went back in to be with their mother, and I stayed in the kitchen, determined to get the place into some kind of order.

I washed and dried all the dishes, then I cleaned out the cupboards under the sink and reorganised them. I snuck around with a little spray bottle of cleaning fluid I'd found and zapped grime, on the stove, on the walls, on the windowsills and skirting boards. I'd never done this kind of thing before, but I found it so satisfying I wondered wryly if I'd missed my real calling in life. I also wondered whether I was going mad, because in the middle of all this drama, I was concentrating on the splodgy run of sauce stains on the cupboard under the sink. I found a bucket in the laundry, filled it with soapy water, and began to clean the kitchen floor. Occasionally some of the family members surfaced from their mother's room. They smiled at me and excused themselves as they passed through on their way to the fridge or the toilet. No one seemed surprised that I was cleaning their house; no one said anything much at all.

I think it was about ten o'clock. The twins had come out to see where I was. I'd settled them at the sparklingly clean kitchen table, and had just finished feeding them some chocolate milk and biscuits. They were both very quiet and watchful, but I could see that neither of them quite believed that their mother was going to die. Jude was out the back collecting washing from the line. Then a strange stillness descended on the house. The twins stopped their chatter and I stopped what I was doing, standing in the middle of the kitchen, listening. But there was no sound. At least nothing specific. And yet every background noise seemed somehow magnified. The minute details of that kitchen, the worn design on the lino, the bright light coming in through the window, the crack in the table, the sound of the dogs barking outside – seemed to converge in one almighty rush. And then everything slowly drained away.

I knew what had happened without being told. I stood still in the middle of the room and waited. Vince and Carmel walked in as I waited for the last bits of the million tiny particles that were flying around in my head to subside.

'She's gone,' Vince said simply, his face soft with pain. He shook his head a couple of times as if he couldn't quite believe he'd spoken the words, then went to stand next to the twins at the table. He put a hand on each of their shoulders. 'Mum's gone.'

'Oh,' I said, feeling weak. 'When?'

'Just before. A few minutes ago,' Carmel replied. 'She just . . . stopped breathing.'

I moved towards Carmel then, holding out my arms. As I

hugged her I felt that enormous rift between us slide away like a piece of very complicated machinery on a conveyor belt. Effortlessly.

Jude came in from outside, as though she, too, had somehow sensed what had happened without being told. The other boys filed down the hallway, one after another, then their father. His face was ashen, filled with the enormity of what had happened. There was a lot of hugging and quiet crying. Jude and I stayed out of it. I took my cue from her. As I watched her busy herself by putting on the kettle and moving chairs back around the kitchen table so that everyone could sit down, I decided that my role would be with the twins. They were staring around, wide-eyed with apprehension as they watched everyone, not fully understanding what had happened. I took each of them by the hand and walked across to Vince.

'Do you think they should go and see your mum?' I said to him softly.

'Yeah.' He gave me a small, strained smile. 'Come on, guys. Let's go and say goodbye to Mum.' I watched them disappear into the hallway and I thought I would faint when I looked at the backs of their two heads, the littleness of them, the ears and the small necks. Joe's feet were in old wrecked sandshoes and he didn't have socks on. Shane's legs were skinny and white in shorts that would have been more suitable for summer-time.

Who will look after them? Make sure they clean their teeth and have clean clothes and ... ?

When they came back out both of them were crying. Their father, who had been sitting silently at the table, held out his arms when he saw them. The boys fell into them, burying their faces in his shoulder. The rest of us stood around and tried not to watch as he soothed them and began telling them things.

'Mum's suffering has ended now, boys ... she's with God, you know. Be brave now. You know how proud she was of you.' All in this quiet, gentle voice, rubbing their backs with his rough hands.

Vince and Carmel began to make a list of all the people they'd have to call. I walked outside for a breather.

It was an unbelievably beautiful day, crisp and bright with a clear, pale-blue sky and a small tug of wind that made the trees rustle every now and again. The fresh smells, of trees and grass and animals, filled me with a sense of wellbeing. In spite of the chaotic, messy atmosphere of the McCaffreys' backyard, I was conscious that so much about me was alive and growing. Even the intermittent barking from the dogs in their makeshift kennels up near the shed seemed wonderful, so full of push and shove. Half a dozen hens picked around the dirt near the rusty old back gate, their combs bobbing up among the high grass like blobs of blood. And there were cows, too, on the hill near the house, feeding peacefully. *Why her? The mother of a big family? Why not that chook out there scratching around for worms? Or the tree? Why not me?*

I sat down on the back step of the verandah and looked around. There were lots of things piled about haphazardly, the grass on the lawn was worn away in patches, and there were boots and brooms and bags all about me, but instead of thinking what a dump it was, as I had the first time, this time I liked it. I liked the ordinariness of it. The lack of concern people had for how any of it appeared. *How that woman would have hated leaving all this: her house, her chooks, all those children, her life ...*

I must have stayed out there for about twenty minutes, but after a while my baggy pants and man's long shirt weren't enough. I felt chilled through, in spite of the sun.

The back door slammed. I looked around. Vince smiled as he headed towards me proffering a cup of tea.

'You want this?'

'Oh, thanks,' I said, and took the cup. He then pulled an old sweater from over his arm.

'I brought this out for you ... Carmel thought you might be cold.' It was a tatty old work sweater, oil stains and holes in each elbow. Even smelt a bit, but I put it on gratefully.

'Thanks ... I was starting to feel really cold,' I said shyly. I could feel his awkwardness, too.

'Why don't you sit down?' I suggested.

'Okay.' He sat down, leaving some space between us.

'They tell me you've been kicked out of home.' He grinned at me. Quick and easy, as if we were conspirators in something funny.

I nodded nervously and glanced at his profile. Jude must have told them. *My God, I hope she hasn't told them why.* Vince's directness was disconcerting. I felt exposed. When I turned to face him his eyes were so blue and shrewd and ... it was impossible to look at anything else in his face, so I turned away.

'Er ... yes,' I muttered. 'It's not too good.'

'Don't worry,' he laughed. 'Happens to the best of us. They'll get over it.'

'Did you ever get kicked out?' I asked, surprised.

'More or less,' he laughed. 'I was away for about twelve months after the last fight!'

'Did you just ... turn up? After being away?' I was curious about him, but I didn't really want to get into this kind of conversation. He might start asking me questions. For some reason I wanted Vince to think well of me.

'Yep.' He nodded and grinned. 'Just turned up like nothing had happened. They welcomed me with open arms.'

'But I bet you didn't do anything ... too bad,' I said quickly, looking straight ahead. I could sense him turning to me, smiling again, and the heat rose to my face. A shiver of shame ran down my legs as I remembered Jules's note.

'Well, I certainly didn't take my clothes off and get my picture taken,' Vince said lightly. 'That's for sure! Or get caught with pills.'

'Oh my God!' I gasped, and put my face into my hands. 'How did you ...? Who told you that?'

'That little mate of yours, Jude.' Vince laughed. 'She's got the biggest mouth!'

Desperation, like a flood of stale black water, rose in my chest. I turned away from him, my face hidden in my hands, wishing that I could cry, but knowing I was too miserable for that, too churned up, too boiling with misery.

'Hey, come on,' he said gently, putting a hand on my shoulder. 'It's nothing.'

I gasped a couple of times and then dived into my pocket for a hanky.

'Oh, yeah, nothing,' I said grimly and blew my nose. 'According to my father, I've wrecked the family. My sister doesn't want to go ahead with her wedding because she's so ashamed ...'

'Well, that's her bad luck, isn't it?' he said, looking straight at me. 'They'll come around! She'll have the wedding. What's a few pills ... a few friggin' stupid pictures in the whole scheme of things? Hey?' I couldn't help laughing a little through my humiliation.

'And it's over now,' he went on. 'The worst has happened ...'

'But no,' I whispered. 'It might not be ...'

'How do you mean?'

'The guy who sent that photo off has still got the negatives ... he might try and use them again.'

'What? Has he threatened you?'

'Oh yeah.'

Vince was quiet for a bit, frowning. I put my hanky away and rubbed my eyes with the back of my hand. I turned to him after a while.

'But what does your lawyer say?' he asked.

'All she can do is threaten to take him to court,' I said in a low voice. 'But I don't want it publicised. I mean, what if one of those papers gets hold of the other pictures ... while the case is on? My charge might change. It might never end.' My voice trailed off miserably.

Vince stood up. I thought he was going to go back inside, but he was thinking. He pushed his hands deeply into his pockets, and walked around on the grass in front of me, kicking out every now and again with the toe of his boot.

'Well, that's not on,' he said after a while.

'What?' I said.

'Can't let him do that,' he said stiffly. 'Shit, that's ... '

'Yeah, but how can I ... ' I shrugged. 'How can I stop him?'

He bent down and picked up a twig that was lying in the grass, stared down at it intently for a few moments, and then methodically began to break it into tiny pieces.

'I got mates,' he said. 'We'll go and see him.'

'See him?' I repeated stupidly. Vince grinned at me.

'Yeah,' he said. 'We'll pay him a visit ... after ... ' His face clouded over and he looked back at the house. 'After the funeral.' I nodded. 'Give the bastard a hard time, take the stuff ... ' He sat down next to me again. 'Don't worry,' he said. 'We'll fix it. I got a mate in Melbourne. He knows how to fix up those kinds of mongrels.'

'Really?' I wanted to ask him more. *Who exactly was this mate? What exactly were they going to do?*

'Yeah,' he said emphatically, beginning to scrape the bark off a bit of twig with his fingernail.

'God ... I don't know, Vince ... ' I mumbled.

'You don't have to.' He flicked the last of the pieces of twig away and then stood up again, 'Just don't worry about it. I better get in again,' he said. 'See how the kids are doing.'

But just at that moment we heard the crush of rubber on gravel and around the corner of the house purred a shiny grey undertaker's car and the local ambulance.

I saw the shock on Vince's face as he remembered his mother lying dead in the front room. The awful cold shock.

His face screwed up in intense pain, his wide shoulders heaved and there was one terrible sob, then he slumped forward, head against the verandah post, both tight fists banging on it angrily. I got up and put my arm around his waist.

'I can't believe it.' He groaned. 'I can't believe she's gone ... forever ... and ever and ever ... ' Tears were splashing down his cheeks.

The car door slammed and a middle-aged man in grey walked sombrely towards us. I kept holding Vince, glad to be there, to be of use to someone.

Manella – October

Huge showers of sparks flew up into the black sky, illuminating for a few brief seconds all the dark shapes of the trees and hills all around. The firelight danced over faces, hands and the clinking glasses. So much laughter and talking; perhaps fifteen people trying to make themselves heard above the roar of the enormous burning logs, the spitting and crackling. Above it all, the great silent dome of bright stars.

They were in luck. The end of October and it was a clear night with hardly any wind.

'Here's to everything, Vince! To your mother!'

'Yep. Here's to Nance!'

'Nance!' The glasses rose as one.

'And Carmel. You gunna sing?'

'Later!' she laughed. 'I'll sing later.'

What a crazy, wonderful idea to light the bonfire that night. After the funeral in the morning, and the wake that went on forever, the rosary the night before and the endless stream of visitors, all those relatives and neighbours and the countless cups of tea. The handshakes and kisses. The mound of clods covered in flowers, the priest in his lace and gold sprinkling incense, and everyone finally walking away. Away. Leaving her there in the ground.

The funeral had been at eleven, and at around three in the afternoon, when the huge turn at the hall next to the church was finishing up, Vince had begun to sound people out about when they were going back to town.

'You want to stay another night?' he asked Eduardo. 'We're having a bonfire down by the creek. We've been clearing some scrub over the last few weeks with the old man. It'd be a good time to get rid of it.'

'Yeah.' Faces livened up at the idea. 'That'd be good.'

'Juan, Declan and Annie. How about it? It'll be fuckin' freezing though!'

'We'll have to ask around for old blankets, sleeping-bags.'

'Sounds good.'

'Stay out all night, eh?'

'That's right, all night.'

'Right.'

'We'll get a barbecue set up and ... have a bit of a party.'

'Can I ask Mum?' Jude said.

'You do that.'

'I will. She'll love it.'

'And Katerina? You gunna stay?' Katerina turned around and saw Vince smiling at her in his shrewd way, the unfashionable, badly fitted suit he'd donned for the funeral somehow making him look more handsome, more himself than ever. She was standing by the sink drying up dishes for an old lady who was talking as though she knew everything about her and her family.

'Sure,' Katerina said. 'I'll be there.'

'Good,' he nodded curtly and turned to ask someone else.

So that's what they did. Everyone seemed to want to let loose for a while. Katerina went with Vince and the twins to buy beer and wine. Jude, Eduardo and Carmel organised the meat. Everyone sat in the McCaffrey kitchen covering potatoes in silver foil and making salads. Then it was all heaped into a couple of boxes and thrown into the back of Vince's ute. It was getting on for evening, so they all climbed in and burned down to the creek, where the boys had piled up all the dead trees and stumps.

'Where's your father, Vince?' Juan asked.

'He's back up at the house. Tired out. His sister is with him.'

'That's all right, then.'

'Yeah, he'll be all right.'

The twins were running around the bonfire like maniacs, throwing on more logs, laughing, challenging anyone who'd take them on for a duel. They'd found some long dry sticks and had burnt the tips to a fiery red coal so they would look more dangerous. Vince told them to stop a couple of times, but they couldn't help themselves. They loved the look of the luminous coal at the end of the stick, and ran around the circle of the fire, their sticks glowing behind them like comets. Through the dark they ran, coming back to the heat of the fire every now and again for a recharge.

'Space Invaders!' Shane yelled.

'Power Rangers.'

'Ya dork!' Joe tripped over something in the dark and got up laughing, brandishing his magical sword at his brother.

The food was cooked and eaten. Everyone was talking and laughing and stopping every now and again in the middle of it all to stare into the bright hot coals.

Anton arrived after most of the food had been eaten. Everyone turned at the sound of his car, wondering who it was. He pulled up some distance away then got out and walked over to the fire, hesitating in the shadows of a tree before moving towards Katerina and Jude, who were sitting with Vince and the twins on the sidelines a little way from the others.

'Hello,' he said quietly. 'Good fire. You can see it for miles.'

He stood for only a moment, then slipped uneasily onto the edge of the bigger group lying about on the other side of the fire. Carmel's back was turned to him. Whether she'd seen him arrive or not was anyone's guess.

'So,' Jude whispered to Katerina. 'He's come.' They'd both noticed him being ignored at the funeral. Not ignored exactly, just offered the polite smile that Carmel would give any stranger, before she turned away.

'Have a beer, Anton.' It was Juan calling out from where he was sitting with Eduardo and Cynthia.

'Thanks.' He moved over to take the can that was being handed to him. Carmel turned around sharply at the sound of his voice, but it was too dark for anyone to see her expression. One of the twins ran over to offer him a sausage in bread. Anton smiled and held up his hand to take it.

'Okay, what'll we sing?' Declan shouted.

'Someone sing something before Annie starts!'

Everyone laughed as Annie swung around in mock outrage. 'What are you all talking about?' she barked back.

'Pack up all your cares and woes!' she began to wail, singing flat to annoy everyone. 'Here I go, singing low, Bye, Bye, Blackbird!

'Ah shit! Shut her up!'

'Give us a break!'

'Put a cork in it, Annie.'

By about eleven the singing had begun in earnest. Jude had brought her guitar. Vince had his tin whistle and Eduardo had his three bamboo flutes. It went on and on. Everyone wanted to sing. It was past midnight as they stood by the wonderful roaring flames in little groups, singing as loudly as they could.

Only once was there a call for Carmel to sing on her own. She was sitting next to Katerina and Vince, holding one of the twins, who'd fallen asleep in her arms. Katerina was holding the other one. 'Okay,' she said, smiling, and she sang a German folksong with no accompaniment.

All' mein' Gedanken die ich hab',
die sind bei Dir.

The magic in her rich voice stopped everyone for a few minutes, had them all listening, thinking of someone they'd loved. Perhaps of someone they'd lost. Anton didn't look at her while she sang, he'd squatted down to help Vince lift in a heavy log. They threw it on together and then Anton parked himself at the edge of the group, elbows on his knees, his face lowered into his cupped hands, looking into the fire and listening.

The hours flew by as their voices soared up into the darkness with the sparks and ash and smoke. The twins were piled into sleeping-bags and laid on the huge tarp. Bernie and his friend Simon tried to catch two horses who'd crept up quietly on the group to have a look at the fire. Someone went down to the creek and filled a billy with water for tea.

Who would ever know what Carmel and Anton spoke about when they eventually ended up together, standing apart from everyone else, throwing bits and pieces of escaped twigs into the fire. But Katerina and Jude watched. They watched as their bodies moved towards each other in the glow of the red light, almost touching, but not quite, and wondered what was being said. How intensely they were talking! Carmel throwing her hands around wildly to make her points. Anton, serious, but smiling every now and again, jumping back from her as if pretending to be stung, then moving forward, closer in again. He seemed to be deeply interested in something she was saying.

Jude and Eduardo were the last two left standing at about four in the morning. Two dark silhouettes sharing a bottle of something. From one to the other it passed, the low murmur of talking punctuated by high quick jabs of laughter. The rest were under blankets or sleeping-bags, still talking quietly. Katerina, lying on a tarp between the sleeping twins, was talking to Vince, who was a few metres away in his sleeping-bag.

'So you're going back up there again soon?' Katerina asked.

'Not for a while,' Vince replied. 'Want to hang around a bit for the old man and the boys ...'

A burst of raucous laughter came from the fire. Vince and Katerina sat up. Jude and Eduardo had their arms wrapped around each other, kissing. What did that mean? They stopped to laugh every now and again as if they were only play-acting.

'She's a wacker, that Jude,' Vince said. Katerina smiled, slightly embarrassed for some reason she didn't understand.
'Yeah. She is.'

Carmel thought she was the only one awake to see the dawn. She sat up, still in her sleeping-bag, and watched the beginning of a tinge of crimson light seep along the top of mountains in the distance. The air had become soft and close and a heavy cloud had almost completely blocked out the stars. She smelt the ash and the smoke on her clothes and took a couple of deep gulps of the morning air. Patches of dew shone like small pearls along the outside of her sleeping-bag. She'd only had perhaps an hour of real sleep, but it had renewed her, made her feel quite awake. Around her lay the sleeping bodies of the others. Jude's mother Cynthia was next to her, a thick strand of hair half covering her lined white cheek. On the other side Juan was lying on his back, the grey ash in his thinning hair and eyebrows making him look like some ancient statue on a tomb. On the other side of the fire was Anton, lying somewhere near where they'd talked. Her brother Bernie was curled up like a wombat at her feet in his old brown blanket.

Carmel looked around and felt a rush of deliverance descend, like soft light rain.

There was a low whistle. Carmel turned. She could just make out Jude sitting up smiling at her on the other side of the still smouldering fire. Carmel grinned, waved back, and watched Jude get up and slowly pick her way towards her.

'Let's go for a walk,' Jude whispered, pointing to the hill at the back of them.

'What, now?' Carmel asked, not really wanting to leave the warmth of her sleeping-bag. 'But it might rain. Look at the clouds.'

'But by the time we get to the top the sun will have risen properly. Even if it is raining, it'll be fantastic.'

'Okay. Let me get my shoes on. That hill is rocky.'

They donned coats and boots and tiptoed past the other sleepers. As they headed down towards the creek, they saw Katerina coming back up with a kettle of water in her hand.

'I couldn't sleep,' she said. 'So I thought I'd get the fire going again and make some tea.'

'Want to come with us?'

'Where?'

'Up the hill.'

'Oh, yes!' Katerina's eyes brightened and she put the kettle down.

They had to follow the creek for a way before they found a spot that was narrow enough for them to cross. Laughing, Carmel and Katerina took a running leap, both of them managing to jump across. Jude was grim-faced at having been left on the other side.

'What if I don't make it?' she called.

'Come on, Jude. You suggested this.'

'Courage, Jude!'

'I never knew I was going to have to jump a river,' Jude grumbled.

The next minute she was flying towards them, her face contorted with the effort. A big jump but not big enough. She reached the opposite bank with one foot, but the other fell into the sloshy muddy water. The others let out a cry, caught her hands, and helped her scramble across.

'Oh, shit.' Jude made a face as she hopped around in her muddy boot. 'Why the hell didn't either of you bring a helicopter?'

The other two dissolved into laughter. Katerina collapsed onto her back and Carmel held her stomach as if she was in pain. Jude, grinning ruefully, sat down on the grass and fumbled with her laces.

'Look!' Carmel shrieked. Jude had taken off her boot, and it was full of mud. A fresh burst of hilarity erupted.

Not one of them knew what they were laughing about. Jude wrung out her sock and put it on again. Then she cleaned out the muddy boot with a stick as best she could and put it on as well.

'How does it feel, Jude?'

'Oh, just fantastic,' Jude said grimly, 'What do you think?'

They passed through a couple of barbed-wire fences, heading away from a herd of curious cattle, before they were finally free to begin their climb up the hill.

It didn't take long. It was mostly easy climbing over the wet grass. But the final hike to the top was steep and slippery. Little was said as they manoeuvred their way around thistles and boulders. Just a cry or a curse every now and again when someone's footing slipped.

'Are you right?'

'Yep.'

'Watch out for that bit of moss there.'

'Okay.'

Once there, it was just as Jude had said it would be. Each of them roamed around by herself for a while, then they stood together by a large rock to watch the deep-red sun break through the clouds. Jude gave a sharp clap as it finally emerged, free and whole and round as a balloon.

'Well done,' she whispered. The others smiled. Streams of gold and pink light had spread out across the sky like bolts of precious silk.

'It's great, eh?' she breathed, looking around at the other two.

'Yeah.'

They stared ahead into the wind and were quiet for some time. Katerina, Carmel and Jude. It was wonderful being up there, feeling their hair blowing back and the sharp cold raindrops starting to spit into their faces.

'It's gonna pour,' said Carmel. 'We'd better go.'

The others murmured agreement, but no one moved. They

looked down through the drizzle and saw the blurred outline of the campsite below. A few figures were moving about.

'That will be Vince for sure,' said Carmel, pointing at a figure crouched at the fire. 'He's getting it going again.'

'No, I think it's Juan. That green coat.'

'I don't think it's *anyone* we know,' Jude said mischievously. 'It's a colony of aliens. We are the only humans left after the Third World War.'

They shivered and laughed, all suddenly aware of themselves standing on that hill in the odd, grey, luminous light under a glorious shining sky. Everything had converged, become somehow precious. Carmel linked her arms through the others'.

'We should go now,' she said again softly. 'I don't want to get soaked.'

'Yep,' Jude said. But still no one moved.

It was that feeling that they were all hanging on to. The feeling that only happens in the dead of night, or, like now, in the very early morning, in the drizzling rain, when the clouds part for a moment and a fat pink sun stares across the world like the benevolent eye of God. The wonderful, fleeting sense that they were the only three people still alive in a beautiful, beautiful world.

PENGUIN – THE BEST AUSTRALIAN READING

ALSO BY MAUREEN McCARTHY

Cross My Heart

A vibrant, passionate, sprawling novel, set in outback Australia. The story of Mick and Michelle, chasing a dream, crossing their hearts for the future.

Shortlisted for the 1993 NSW Premier's Literary Award (children's books). A Children's Book Council of Australia Notable Book, 1994.

Flash Jack   Maureen McCarthy

Thirteen-year-old Jack's family is having some problems, and being robbed over the summer holidays hasn't helped things. In fact, nothing seems to be going right. But then Jack meets Diana – and she's like no one he's ever met before . . .

Chain of Hearts

When troubled seventeen-year-old Sophie is sent to live with her aunt Fran in the country, family secrets and emotions that have been buried for years rise up to be counted. Unputdownable in true McCarthy fashion, this is a novel full of insight, compassion and courage.

When You Wake and Find Me Gone   Maureen McCarthy

Kit feels her life is finally on track: friends, university and independence from her big Catholic family in the country – it's all coming together. But when Kit's sister becomes critically ill, she makes a startling discovery about her sister's identity. This leads Kit on a journey of self-discovery and takes her to the political minefield of Northern Ireland. It's in this world of violence and political extremism that Kit discovers her father . . .